Uncertain Harvest

Charles Simpson

Fomite
Burlington, Vermont

Fomite
58 Peru Street
Burlington, VT 05401
www.fomitepress.com

To my friends and fellow students of Southern Mexico,
I extend my deepest appreciation for what you have taught us.

MIRANDA:

"Oh, wonder!
How many goodly creatures are there here!
How beauteous mankind is! O brave new world,
That has such people in't!"

The Tempest, Act 5, Scene 1

PART ONE: AUSTRIA

Chapter One

ED STOOD ON THE summit — or near enough for a good story when he got back to New York. His open mouth chewed thin air, which hit his throat like liquid nitrogen. Each breath ended in a shroud, dissolving before his eyes. Or maybe it was his vision that was blurred. Just north of forty, his legs ached but he'd reached the edge of the glacier. Okay, not all the way up. No one does that on skis. The Piburg crest still loomed above him, massive, indifferent.

He was way above the tree line. As his triphammer heart slowed, he saw that one more step toward the edge could send him flying into the valley. Tiny flecks of color he knew to be houses were scattered over a white field below—red, yellow, blue. At a point they clustered to form Oetz and he could make out the iron bridge over the Achrainweg, a charcoal slash. Those blocks to the right would be hotels. They boxed in the central square, dwarfing its 18th-century church. Albrecht Dürer might have sketched those half-timbered houses and tiny-windowed shops where development had yet to arrive. Or perhaps it was all post-war, a clever fake. Further up the valley, his eye traced columns of smoke to low-pitched farm houses. Mixed among them, he knew from his walk yesterday, were new chalets, high-end Audi Quattros and Beemers in the driveways. Holiday houses or rentals, due to this economic summit, were now full. How much of this was real? The stone and stucco were tangible. Somewhere in the square he could imagine a toymaker with square-rimmed glasses sitting in the window of an old shop. But the actual shop fronts he'd seen were full of Piaget and Schaffaus watches. Still, the church advertised two masses each Sunday and the barns seemed authentic. Did an EU subsidy keep an old generation of dairymen lugging their milk to the railhead? Or were they phantoms among the tourists? In this setting, money determined what was real.

Other than the mountains. It was the same palisade of rock and ice that had confronted the first humans trudging out of Italy, and Africa before that, timeless and indifferent. He adjusted a ski pole in the snow, leaning forward. Were those paleo-humans foolish enough to climb the Sölden glacier? No, that was a modern folly.

Taking compact binoculars from his rucksack, he focused on his hotel. With its gingerbread balconies and low-pitched roof, it was a rustic inn magnified ten times over. Last night the dining room had featured a Tyrolean festival of sorts, dancers in three-layered skirts and velvet dirndls sashaying with hands on hips to an accordion band. Their outfits were out of a Bruegel picture. Young and once-young, thin or buxom, they spun and jiggled. What to think of this ancient folk gaiety played for an audience remaking the modern world?

Ed's mind drifted. As the sun slid across the sky, one distant window after another flashed with reflected gold.

His pause had turned the sweat on his hair to ice where his knit cap touched his collar. Half a life ago he'd climbed Tuckerman's Ravine in the White Mountains, the high point of college braggadocio, and tumbled more than skied down the vertical drop. One time was enough to let him write up a story for the Tufts student paper. He loved giving himself assignments, creating his own news. He'd passed wine bottles with the street people in Porter Square and slipped into meetings of Boston's subway workers as their union prepared for a strike. Journalism had proved more visceral than chemistry or biology, though these courses had turned out to be useful. Reporting the news let him open doors from one world to the next, showing him wordplay and behavior he'd never have imagined. Now at midlife, the stakes were high enough to give him vertigo. There was a predatory gang down at the conference center and it was his job to take something away from between their teeth. He'd once interviewed the patrons of an Italian social club in Dorchester, adding color to the story with a description of their huge espresso machine, the pictures of Naples on their wall, the fact that everyone but him carried a gun. It was a piece on the waste-carting business. But even that world wasn't as cold as this. And not just the weather. The trash truck moguls had tolerated him, enough at least for a cup of coffee and a biscotti.

What was it about mountain culture? Somewhere he'd read that when members of a party climbing Everest succumbed to oxygen deprivation and died, they were left as stone monuments, cautionary tales about inadequate preparation. Here the real refrigerant was money. He expected lots of dangerous drops and turns before he reached the bottom of things.

His breathing settled as he lingered over the visual treat. The village far below, the cliffs exploding upward, the sinking sun. This was Bierstadt's Yosemite, magnified and without the warmth. Conifers clawed at the slopes, a green-black smudge that gave up just a quarter of the way from the valley floor. He tried to imagine summer in the hill pastures, settled farm life or even a steam locomotive crossing the valley. Not easy. As the valley rose, there was little counterpoint to the implacable stone.

Climbing was a lesson in anticipation. He'd cheated a little, taking the gondola for the first 2000 feet, but earned back the view over the next three hours, trudging upward on wide, telemark skis. At one point the snow became bottomless, nothing to pole against, so he'd switched for a while to compact aluminum snow shoes. They were now tied to his pack.

Above him rock moraines thrust from glacial cover. Below were faint traces of his own tracks, the ribs of a long snake leading from a line of shriveled trees. The afternoon wind was already noticeable and the marks of his passing were oh-so temporary. He hoped they'd still be useful guiding him back. Though his lungs felt seared, the slow climb had helped him adjust to the thinning air. Perhaps not. A spinning sensation passed through his head and he shook his vision clear. It was definitely colder. Even boosted by the gondola ride, his climb had taking longer than he'd planned. The sun was falling toward the far peaks. Definitely time to leave.

His bindings squeaked as he shuffled in-place, flexing his legs. He anticipated the plunges and turns of the decent, a broken line across blank paper. The elite got up here by helicopter, but that wasn't in his budget. And climbing was a mapping exercise, a dress rehearsal for what he'd see again in reverse, much faster. He rubbed his thighs. It would be important to avoid going airborne.

Climbers in summer would see mossed-over boulders, snowmelt flushing toward the valley floor. Now there was just the big picture: grey cliffs, blue snow, a black wall of trees. In the weakening light, his sense of distance was slipping. And what had been gentle powder was now knife-edged crust. Alpine hotels aside, this place had not really made peace with civilization.

Today was sweet because he'd stolen it from the round of meetings and interviews to come. As science and economics writer for New York's *Business Chronicle*, he was posted to the Global Sustainability Conference, but that wouldn't start until tomorrow. Sure, the politicians and bankers would bury the press pool in "schlag", but the spectacle still had to be recorded. "I'm not expecting you to read their minds," his editor had said, "but you're our street dog. Set your teeth in their fat ankles. But nicely." There'd be standard pronouncements about the stability of the euro and the security of the world's future due to a falling rate of carbon emissions. Make that a falling rate of increase. And more of the world's population were earning at least two dollars a day, even if they were a falling percentage. Hurrah! He could expect a retread of last year's Davos press releases. But a gig was a gig, and this one came with expenses paid.

And fireworks were always possible. That aging "populist" government in Greece might still kick back against austerity and the IMF.

At last night's Tyrolean restaurant show—soaking up atmosphere was a job requirement, he reminded himself—a juggler in a waistcoat had made magic with a winsome partner who tossed him brightly colored balls. As the ark of color became a blur, the performer sneezed and it all fell to pieces. Everyone laughed. Not a bad image of things going wrong. A little Brexit sneeze could bring down the whole EU. Ed thought about that old Gershwin number, something to hum on the breadlines back in the '30s. *"In 1929 I sold short, in England I'm presented at court. But you've got me downhearted, cause I can't get started with you."*

If the world economy was fragile, there was little evidence of that here. Which doubtless was why Oetz was chosen for the summit. Seemingly impervious to depression or war, it was like the gold in a Swiss vault.

He looked from side to side and frozen sweat rattled in his hair. What was he waiting for?

The *Chronicle* was a family-owned paper nearly as old as the *New York Times* but with a more select circulation — executives and government officials, "the deciders", as George Bush would have called them. Was his employer in trouble? No more than the *Times*. But outside the boardroom, who knew? Not even his mother's vegetables, god rest her soul, were as throughly cooked as newspaper subscription data. And the paper's piece of the news, early market trends, was a smart focus. And part-timer though he was, hopping over the abyss between assignments, he had no complaints today. He'd deliver a respectful analysis as the shakers and movers pontificated. The crowd was heavily European with a scattering from the BRICs—Brazil, Russia, India, and China. Among the "emerging economies", only those that embraced IMF and EU economic austerity were welcome, with debt speculators eyeing them the way crocodiles watch ducks. Judging from the early arrivals, this was shaping up to be a meeting of Europe's *hochadel* or "upper nobility," whether Teutonic or not.

With celebrity CEOs needing the cloak of stewardship as they pulled the stops and pressed the peddles on the global economy, the business press was a required audience, expected to respect the invisible status distinctions among the financial nobility and to applaud on cue. The *Chronicle,* on the skeptical end of the spectrum, still had to avoid being thrown out of the game. As a first-timer, Ed had been briefed on the subtleties of deference. Straighten your tie but deliver the scoop.

Ed knew he was an odd choice for the assignment. He was principally a science writer with a bent toward environmental exposés. The feature editor thought he'd bring an unusual perspective, perhaps discover how the smart money was preparing for when the East Coast would be underwater. He'd a history covering the fallout from NAFTA, not just business failures in Detroit but how Oaxacan farmers had been pushed into the slums of Mexico City. In that work, he'd delivered market forecasts but also how Iowa corn made lousy tortillas, what he thought of as human granularity. In a piece on hydraulic fracking, he'd included the description of a kitchen sink in Oklahoma catching fire while the wells next door were "flared off" like a scene from "Blade Runner". His reporting was a mix—the charts and grafts of standard economic journalism hitting the friction of consequences for human lives. That combination had proved slippery, and his career had slid from staff writer to stringer as the *Chronicle* tightened its belt. But he'd never given up the frisson, and hoped he never would.

Not that he was a crusader, not when veteran reporters at the *Washington Post* and the *New York Times* were applying to teach in public schools or to drive cabs. Hell, he'd report on a roller derby if it paid the rent.

Ed had bounced from one paper to another in the New York metro area—the *Long Island Examiner,* the *Newark Republican*—finally ending up at the *Chronicle.* After some "restructuring" in the newsroom, what had been his salaried job was now "contingent", an ironic commentary on the larger gig economy. New assignments depending on how the editors received his last story. But the upside, such as it was, lay in the freedom to shop around, to try to sell himself to other publications. Not that he was having much luck at that lately. But no worries today. He was skiing in Austria.

This year's conference theme was 'Responding to Climate Instability.' He took that to mean the insiders were scoping out the profit potential of storm barriers for Boston and Lower Manhattan. Miami? Well, as they say about bad mortgages, the future of that place was looking underwater. And hadn't Hurricane Sandy put Wall Street into galoshes, so the challenges were real enough. For fifty years, the response of the elite had been the Davos meetings. But they'd descended into celebrity spectacle so the global movers had set up this new venue. The idea was that without the theatrics, serious business could be done. Without Bill Gates or Bono on the stage, Oetz would be the real board room for the new century. But those rolling the dice still needed press attention. Not live TV, certainly, but the economic pundits. As for the *Chronicle,* Ed had learned from the grapevine that no one on the paper's regular staff wanted the assignment. Either they'd seen it as another Davos, glitter without substance, or they couldn't take the chance. A week away might mean they'd return to find a cheaper replacement sitting in their cubicle. So the coin toss fell to Ed. He had to turn in daily summaries and at least one analytic long-form commentary for the weekend edition. Piece of cake. Or in this case Linzer torte. As for the commentary, he already had a title: "Why Economic Predictions are Usually Wrong."

Ed rocked on his skis. As the bumper sticker says, 'Ski today, work tomorrow.' Along with private guards who walked the streets and hotel corridors, a cordon of Federal police at the end of the valley kept out the unwashed or the merely curious. Hence the absence of paparazzi. Awash in luxury, the village had become a private club. He hoped this atmosphere would lull his interviewees into indiscretion.

Ten minutes had passed since he'd reached the end of his climb. He was seriously chilled. In Scandinavia, the Sami people would call the glacial field before him 'North Farm', home of perpetual winter. The sun was easing down among the far peaks and his thousand-Euro-a-night room and a hot meal seemed very far away. Still, it wasn't just the wind that had him shivering. There had been that weird confidentiality agreement he'd signed. Just to sort out potential conflicts of interest, his editor had said. And the conference required it. He was bound to make no contact with his broker for six months following the meetings. What a laugh! Then the *Chronicle* had added its own rules. It claimed ownership of everything he might write about the meetings for one calendar year, including the right to kill a story. Ah, the management of perception!

Not what J-School had led him to expect. In Teddy Roosevelt's time, Lincoln Steffens had a year to write his newspaper stories. As late as the 1990s, before advertising dollars fled and print found itself at the bottom of bird cages, reporters still had pensions. Or was that another urban myth? Now the lucky graduates of journalism programs were writing sidebars for *People* magazine.

Dragging a hand from his glove, he felt for the holographic ID on the lanyard around his neck. If he lost that they wouldn't even let him back into his room. From his pack, he took out a steel bottle and unscrewed the top. The dregs of tea, cold but not yet frozen.

Now the sun was deep in the ridge line and pursued by purple ink that moved across the valley like a shroud. A gust lifted a swirl of ice crystals above a rocky outcrop. The understory of cloud cover caught fire. A snowfield that had been Caribbean turquoise became suddenly inflamed, then bruised. The fir trees below where he needed to head were stooped, a line of old men in overcoats. Darkness pooled on the valley floor.

Ed rummaged among his supplies and found a blood orange. He peeled it with freezing fingers, coloring the snow at his feet. The kitchen at Schnalstal Lodge had made him a lunch: salmon and brie sandwiches, tea. He'd rationed them out as he climbed, as if he were crossing the

Antarctic with Robert Falcon Scott. Now there was only the orange. His worn utility knife rattled in his backpack along with nylon cord from somewhere, a cell phone without a single bar of reception, and a hunk of grey and petrified chocolate. Bart, his younger brother, would have laughed at this pathetic kit. Having rotated through more than one Afghan winter with his army unit, Bart would have packed supplies for a week.

The gondola Ed had taken terminated at a restaurant. He'd been tempted by the food he'd smelled on disembarking, but feeling self-sufficient, he'd gone on by to attempt the assent. Now the facility would be closed, no hot bowl of soup to cradle in his hands. No coffee.

Okay. Time to stop screwing around. He slipped his fingers back into stiffening gloves, rolled his shoulders, and set his hands in the pole straps. He was about to push off when a corner of the boulder to his left exploded. Seconds later the sound of a giant hand clap rolled across the valley, a solitary note of applause. It came from everywhere. Was some trail crew shooting ordinance to bring down a potential avalanche? But using a rifle? Then snow exploded ten feet to his right.

Chapter Two

CROUCHING, ED LEAPED FROM the knoll where he'd stood, leaving bits of orange in the snow. Bending low, he polled for the tree line. Invisible hummocks shocked his knees, then dropped away under his feet like an elevator in free fall. At six feet two and with a red tasseled hat, he knew he wasn't blending in, but at least he was a moving target. He tightly crisscrossed the fall-line, maximizing speed. He was the rabbit in that Winslow Homer painting, with the fox close behind.

The trees, their limbs weighted and bent, came into focus. Hardly stately, they were sinewy survivors but they'd hide him. To his left was a near-vertical pitch, maybe an old rock slide. He leaned forward and projected himself down the chute. Nothing looked familiar. If he'd made any tracks here, the wind had swept them away and he was flying blind.

He heard another handclap over his gasps and the wind screaming in his ears. What was going on? Avalanche teams used howitzers to generate shockwaves, never rifles. Was there a maniac out hunting?

Carving around the first clump of gnarled trees—eye-high dwarfs—he searched for the fastest vertical drop. Gravity was his pal. What seemed smooth meringue on the way up was now all gullies and ridges. His stomach floated. Lean, carve, pump, pitch. His thighs were on fire. Where was everybody else? Even so late in the day, there should be someone out. Was he too far above the trails? And how close was he to that upper landing of the gondola? Should he head right, left? If he were back in New Hampshire the ski patrol would be herding stragglers down about now. Maybe in Austria they just let you die. Bushwhacking may not have been such a great idea.

Each rock and mogul was like text flying past on microfilm, moving too fast to read. His mind wandered. No one hunted in conditions like this, and not near a five-star resort.

Maybe he was the butt of a bad joke, someone trying to throw a scare into him. He pictured a survivor of the Wehrmacht mountain division, laughing through decayed teeth. Hadn't a few Japanese soldiers clung to their Pacific island tunnels for fifty years? Why not some Germans? But they'd have to be ninety now. More likely someone just didn't like the press and was putting shots at his feet like in a Western movie. Dance, cowboy! And he was dancing. If some homicidal mountain man wanted to protect his turf, Ed had no argument with that. Most happy to leave. Had something he'd written pissed off the wrong people? Enough to follow him up here when they could more easily beat him up in a hotel bathroom? It made no sense. And pushing him in front of a Manhattan subway train would be easier still.

Now he was a thousand feet closer to the valley floor. The trees, more numerous, stretched over his head. He relaxed slightly. If he cut through that break to the right, it should put him close to the lift. There had to be trails turning up soon, maybe even the ski patrol.

Without warning, his right ski shattered. The slope fell away in front of him and he was air-borne, weightless. Then he hit bottom, flipped, and slammed down. Sliding, he instinctively drew in knees and elbows, tucked his chin. His aluminum snow shoes ripped away from his pack, lost somewhere in the underbrush. His broken ski clattered at his ankle. I'm not going to make this in one piece, he thought, closing his eyes tightly. Then he hit a snag and pinwheeled. The leg with the intact ski was wrenched away and the rest of his body hurtled into deep powder, then iced-over tree roots. He flipped like clothes in a tumble dryer. When the cycle stopped, he was buried. Deliberately, he tried shallow breaths, first of snow and then air. Blackness gave way to grey. Then, like a second collision, pain blew the fuses of his mind.

Agony brought him back to reality. One knee was twisted under him, an arm buried to the shoulder. And he was blind.

How long had he been lying here? Had he blacked out? Carefully, he rocked back and forth, loosening the arm. He tried to dig the snow away from his face but he was head-down at a fifty degree angle. His hat was gone but he had his gloves. Good. Still, his fingers felt like wood. Wasn't it Jack London who said, lose your gloves in the Yukon and shake hands with death. No difference here.

Turning, he looked up at the trees and saw a red smear on a limb a few feet away. His hat had followed him down. Out of reach, but if he had his pole, he could get it. Lots of heat gets lost from the head. Things were sliding back into focus.

What could he move? His bad leg was buried, the agony centered below the knee. He turned his body to ease the pressure. Methodically, he inventoried each extremity, then rotated his head. It was just the leg that refused to work.

The word 'RICE' came to mind—rest, ice, compression, elevation— the mantra from his high school days on the slopes, and something Bart quoted to him. The kid had been the family athlete and what he'd learned, he'd tried to pass on to Ed. That included taking his older brother to the top of Mt. Sunapee and setting him loose. By his second descent, Ed could stay upright. Then, on leave after basic training, Bart had demon- strated what a whiz he'd become with an Ace bandage. Too bad he wasn't around now. And hadn't been for two decades.

If being immobile counted as rest, Ed had that covered. And ice. Finding a strap still attached to his wrist, Ed swung out his pole and fished in his hat. Compression? Not yet, but at least his leg was elevated. A hoarse sound made him realize he was laughing. The shooter was the least of his problems.

Jack London, of course, would gather pine twigs and start a fire, doubtless with his last match. Robert Falcon Scott on the other hand, freezing to death in the Antarctic, didn't have twigs. Ed had a world of trees but no matches. He rotated his arms to circulate the blood.

The snow that had cushioned his fall now acted like quicksand. Add the pitch of the slope and he couldn't even sit up. He had to get to his feet, one working leg or not. Moving his remaining ski, he crossed it with the pole to make a platform under his butt. He wriggled until he was able to sit. Nothing protruding from the leg, no blood-covered bone, nothing hot and wet. But by God, the leg hurt. Either a fracture or the world's worse sprain. No matter, if he could just stand. Robert Falcon Scott— gotta love the name—died just a few miles short of his supply camp. But too weak to move from a windblown tent, he'd still kept the journal that made him famous. Stupid and arrogant they may have been, those Brits, but they were plucky. Now, how to get off this mountain?

A whistle would have been convenient to have. But at least he had a cell phone. He'd been tempted to leave it in his room to completely set his work routine aside but at the last minute he'd succumbed to habit and zipped it in his pack. And miracle of miracles, that pack was still on his back. Stripping off a glove, he fumbled out the phone and hit 112, the European emergency number. Then he saw there were no bars, no reception. Oh, fuck. Then he remembered he'd tried it on the glacial crest and gotten nothing.

Time to regroup. What did he have? A folding knife, a length of line left from whatever, and the chocolate. A better man would ration that brown chunk but not Ed. In a moment he was licking the last of it from the tinfoil. Didn't he need energy? And heat?

Darkness was the absence of light, and that was certainly the case under the trees. Overhead, clouds coalesced, tinged with silver but revealing centers of lead. Winter days in the mountains were short. If he could reach those tree boughs there, he might be able to line a snow tunnel with branches and wait for help. What help? And in these clothes? They were fine as long as he was in motion but nothing that would let him survive the night. All right, that option was out.

He still had his voice, at least till it gave out. There was the shooter, but hell, he was way up above. What if he could he roll himself downhill. Yeah, right.

He needed a plan, even a bad one. He'd give his knee a few more minutes to stiffen up. If it was sprained, that's what would happen. Using the one pole and the unbroken ski, maybe he could slip and slide?

Waiting wasn't easy. The temperature seemed to be falling like mist on his face. How did convicts in solitary confinement keep their sanity? He pictured the Count of Monte Cristo, locked in a stone cellar. The Count had used memories to build a better place in his mind, object by object. Ed imagined his own apartment in Manhattan, an old tenement building the developer had gutted out as if it were a mackerel, knocking down walls to create fewer but pricier lofts. What did he have there?

One wall was shelving. His sound system, CDs, books. There was a photo of his parents and their two boys at the beach in Hyannis. Bart wore swim trunks down to his knees—the surfer look—and far from the six-four he would become. The books were a blur, too many, too chaotic to capture titles and he'd never organized them the way a college professor might have. But the CDs offered possibilities. They were in categories: Baroque, jazz, Latin. He pictured cassette labels: Bach, Telemann, Grappelli. He was surprised to see more than a foot of baroque.

This wasn't helping. He needed to make noise. Sing, even. His mind moved to another shelf, this one with folk and protest songs left over from his college days: Dylan, Baez, Willie Nelson. There was Leonard Cohen, and Tom Paxton. He needed something simple, easy to sing. Not the complexity of Dylan. But Paxton's "Ramblin' Boy" might do. He hummed the chorus, mouthed the words. Shit, a song about death? That wasn't what he needed.

He'd never been a sing-along guy but there were times driving at night, coffee cup in one hand and a Sicilian 'Guinea stinker' between his lips, he'd belt out whatever was playing on the radio. He remembered something by Ewan McCall, but better done by the Pogues, "Dirty Old Town". That really painted a picture.

He could see the view from the train running between Newark and Baltimore, the abundance of industrial decay. The image fit, along with the lead singer's broken-toothed grin. There was only the one verse he was sure of so he kept repeating it, playing with the volume. "I kissed my girl by the factory wall."

"Who's over there? You all right?" The voice was female, late twenties maybe, husky. She was shouting. English with a surprising echo of Boston.

"Where are you?"

The ski patrol? Not with that accent. His friendly assassin? Not likely. Beggars can't be choosers, and there were worse ways to end it. He surrendered to the voice.

"Over here!" he croaked, his voice raspy. "I had a fall. I can't move!"

He heard branches breaking, skis slapping hard on the slope to gain traction. Then he saw a flash of orange through the trees. It took a while but finally a woman came into view, gasping from exertion and wiping away the snow that cascaded onto her face from above. Now she was looking down at him, the zip on her silver parka open. Her frame was slight, even in goose down, average height. But someone's height is hard to tell when you're flat on your back. Her cheekbones were sharp, nose narrow, cheeks flushed and freckled. Wreathed in her own breath, she was an angel in bib overalls and a flapping jacket. Snowmelt fell from her nose as she looked down at him. Her goggles hung loose at her neck and her blue eyes squinted. She had very light eyebrows, almost invisible.

Wiry hair escaped from the edges of her knit cap, catching the last fragments of sun. Raggedy-Ann. She took out a huge handkerchief and wiped her face. Ed raised a hand.

"I've been tracking your voice for ten minutes," she said, looking around. "Jesus, you picked a great place to face-plant."

There was more exasperation than sympathy in her tone. They'd just met and she was already disappointed in him.

"What happened, you break your fool leg?" He must have interrupted her last run of the day, knocked her out of her groove.

She looked him over from head to foot, almost professionally. Was she the ski patrol? Her stiff curls bounced around her face and her shoulders were spattered with pine needles. She seemed strong for her size. He hoped so.

"Yeah, well, I did take a fall. Then again, the slope could use a little grooming."

"Grooming? Right. But I don't see you on any trail. Got lost?" She looked around at the trees, the rock ledges, then down at him. "What's broken?"

"I can't tell but I don't think my leg can hold weight, my weight at least. Then there's my ski." He gestured to the bit of jagged board attached to one boot. "I must have hit a rock."

"Not just skiing off the trails but out of control. What are we going to do with you?"

Was that a touch of sympathy?

"Your bindings should have released." She was poking his foot with her pole. "You're in a fix. We're miles from the top of the lift and a lot more from the base lodge." She bent and released his twisted foot from what remained of his ski. She rotated his ankle, then his knee. But not gently. "Anything crunch?"

Ed lit up with pain. "I can't tell if that's the bone or a ligament. Do you know what you're doing?"

"I'm all you've got so let's pretend."

"You going to write me a ticket? If you arrest me, you'll have to take me into custody, get me off this mountain." Did she look like she had the strength?

"Well, this is a first. No one's ever taken me for a cop before. You must have hit your head."

Why wasn't she taking out her cell and calling for help? Oh, right. There was no reception. Or was she just disinterested, a driver slowing at the scene of a traffic accident before pulling away?

"I won't ask to see your badge but I really hope you're part of the patrol. Am I right?"

"Wrong. Just a happy vacationer. No official responsibilities at all."

"Wait, wait, wait. Can you call for help, get someone up here?" Would she simply disappear?

The trees and the sky slipped further toward dark. Another hour and he doubted anyone would find him.

"Do I look like the ski patrol?" she said, turning to show him her back. No red cross.

"No, just another civilian, but one with more common sense than some."

He could do contrite. Let her scold. It went with that Irish face. And those eyes. Cerulean, cut with Arctic ice. Like a Siberian husky.

"At least you did this at the end of the day so you got your money's worth." She had regained normal breathing. "And me, I suppose you did me a favor. If I'd stumbled on you earlier, I'd have wasted even more of my own day here."

"My sentiments entirely," he said. She wasn't cutting him much slack but was softening. "Of course, statistically, most skiing accidents do happen on the last run of the day."

She turned up her mouth in distaste. "Quite the joker, you are. You're lucky I came along. The slopes are deserted. It was only by chance I heard you bellowing. Thought it was a dog caught in a trap."

"Disappointed?" They were bonding. She wouldn't walk away, would she? "I want to assure you that vocalizing isn't me strongest suit."

Why had he slipped into stage-Irish? In response to her Kennedy patois, clipped and a little nasal? The last time he'd chatted up an Irish girl he'd been tending bar in Brooklyn trying to bridge the gap between stringer assignments. Vaudeville brogue had become part of his persona, an affectation to engage the few female customers and keep his professional identity at a distance.

"But I find singin' gets me mind off an imminent demise, don't ya know?"

"Cut it out. How long have you been here?" Her voice flattened out.

"Half hour, hour. Hard to say. I haven't been entirely lucid. And did I say the name's Ed Dekker. Of the *Business Chronicle*. At your service." He reached up to shake a hand she hesitated to accept. "I'm here covering the conference."

"Hard at work, I see." She finally took his hand. "Well met, Mr. Dekker. A financial scribe, eh? I guessed you weren't head of the European Central Bank." A grin played briefly across her lips. "I'm on the schedule here, teaching the bankers a little about ecology."

"The environmental minister from the Isle of Skye, perhaps? So tell me, are the selkies still on the endangered list?"

She snorted. They were both stalling, putting off the moment when he would have to get to his feet.

"Jaysus, there you are, flat on your arse but still doing the journalism," she said. "To you in the business press, I'm a biologist. But to disappoint you, I don't study mythological beasts, only insects. They turn out to be more interesting." She poked him with her ski pole. "What should matter is that my degree isn't the one you need. And this meeting isn't a chat-up in the local." She was taking charge. Someone had better, he thought.

"I can try to get you off this hill or I can go for help." She looked up at the sky. "What I can't do is call for help. My phone is dead. The mountain at this height must be out of cell tower range."

"Not that it matters," he said, trying to sound worldly, "but sometimes when a high-level group meets, they shut down public electronic communication for security reasons."

"Oh, come on." She wasn't having that. "And cut off contact for a lot of important people? No, it's some glitch. The point is, I can't call from here. Maybe there's reception lower down, but it might be dark before I or anyone could get back here."

"And find me." He completed her thought.

"So, what's it to be?" She folded her arms. "It's not getting any lighter." Her voice shifted into uninflected English. With the western sky behind her, her face was hidden from the last of the sun, her hair an auburn corona.

He couldn't decide.

"Much as I hate to say it, there's a good chance the ski patrol will miss you in the dark. This area is immense and with the wind, I doubt if I'll be leaving much of a trail." She had decided for him. "We have to get you down. Can you get to your feet?"

This was still the question. She leaned down and pressed her fingers into the tendons behind his knee. He shrieked, unsuccessfully covering it with a cough. Undeterred, she finished her inspection.

"Nothing obviously broken, in my amateur opinion. But I've only read the book, and that was years ago."

"What book was that?" He was stalling.

"*Where There Is No Doctor*. It goes along with me when I work in the field.

"I won't be asking you to do brain surgery."

"We'll need rope."

"There's cord in my backpack." He rooted it out. It was a piece maybe 10 feet long. "Going to make a splint?" He didn't want her to think he was a compete imbecile.

"So to speak." She was braking off pine branches. "I hesitate to use the word 'snowboard' with a gentleman of your maturity but I propose to tie the bad leg behind the good and see if you can manage on one ski. If you lean on my shoulder and use the pole you have, we might pull it off. What do you say?"

He liked that she had a plan. And was saying 'we'.

She tied branches on either side of his knee and bound his legs together. Standing up, she assessed the situation like a tow truck driver looking at a wreck.

"Gentleman of maturity?" he muttered.

She moved to his injured side. "We'll snowplow. Or I will. Now, up and easy." Grasping his elbow, she pulled and he pushed with the pole. To his surprise, he found himself upright. The slope veered away before him and he was dizzy. Beneath her parka, now zipped, her body felt slight.

Checking the knots again, she looped a few turns of cord under his ski. "This will act as a brake." She did all this with her gloves on, including the knots. Then she tightened the brace on his leg, putting fire and ice into competition.

"Let your endorphins kick in. They'll dull the pain. The swelling will lock your knee and keep you upright. The body has this marvelous short-term survival power, though you'll pay for it later. It's all in the book."

They pressed together, side-by-side. "Are we ready? We'll head down on a diagonal to reduce the angle of incline. Aim for that tree. Turning will be the challenge. If it gets bad, hold your breath. You'll make it." He was a six-year-old on the bunny hill, but one designed by a witch.

"Grip my shoulder. Harder, I won't break. And use your pole."

They were in motion. She regulated their speed with the edge of her outside ski and they swayed from side to side. To his surprise, they made it to the tree and turned. Then they did a second diagonal.

Crisscrossing, they worked their way down. Eventually the slope opened into a field and the forest thinned out to scattered trees. As they cut one slanted path after another, Ed gave in to a feeling of dependence. She did the footwork and he followed along. It was sort of a dance. Her knees flexed and her shoulders rolled, absorbing the gullies and moguls. She was stronger than he'd expected, thank God, but sweat coated her forehead. This wasn't easy and it went on and on. Her hair tickled his nose.

In the next instant they were both down. Sprawled on his back, Ed was encased in pain that raced up his leg and sank its teeth into his knee. He was being devoured by wolves. Getting up was out of the question. But after a moment, she hauled him upright and they set off again. By the fourth fall they'd worked out a system for propping him back up. He was a scarecrow, and poorly-made at that. "A coat upon a stick," as Yeats had it. But the bindings on his legs held. And he was deeply in love with her shoulder.

They'd stopped speaking. The slope demanded all their attention, rolling like a blue-grey ocean toward infinite darkness.

After forty-five minutes of slashing back and forth, forcing their way through snow-laden branches and detouring around boulders, they were again in dense forest. Then came a proper trail. By now she was gasping. Trembling, even. They found a fallen tree and she helped him to a sitting position, his legs outstretched, twisted by the single ski.

"Wait here," she said, controlling her breathing. "I'll get help." She stood beside him, head down and leaned on her poles. It was hard to know who was shaking more. Then, before he could argue, she was gone.

He settled into waiting as if the forest was an empty room. Was it Jack London again, urging the trapper not to lose focus? Cold slowed the heart and deprived the brain of oxygen. Then painless sleep would follow. Not a bad way to go, considering. He gave some feeble twists to his upper body, trying to send blood to his head. His legs were simply boards. Was the rope too tight for his circulation? He couldn't reach the knots.

Time passed. Now he could barely move his arms and he was very drowsy. Only the pain in his knee, a banked fire, kept him awake.

With darkness dissolving the trees into indistinguishable black, he suddenly saw a light. Coming from below, it bounced, flickered, and disappeared. Then it came back more brightly. Minutes passed. Finally, a snowmobile ground to a halt in front of him pulling a stretcher set on a sled. Two hooded figures dismounted, then a third got up from a prone position on the sled. His red-headed angel. The crew maneuvered him like a mannequin, cutting him loose from the ski, checking him over, and lifting him onto the low gurney. Standing to one side, the redhead reattached skis she'd brought along with her. Ed was strapped down and could see her only from the waist up. With a hand signal, the driver fired up the machine and they set out. All he could see, and dimly at that, was the second EMT seated backward on the machine, watching him. Above the muffled rumble of the sled, he heard the driver speaking German into a radio. The woman—she'd never said her name—would be following behind, keeping close to the snowmobile and its halogen light.

As warmth generated under the blanket by chemical heat packs returned to his core, Ed begun to shiver uncontrollably. He was coming alive.

When their procession reached the top of the aerial lift, an empty gondola was standing by. The patrollers carried his stretcher aboard and set it on the floor of the empty cabin. They checked his vital signs once more, then tucked new chemical heat packs around his chest as the lift swung into motion. The woman stood silently at his side gripping her skis.

It was too dark to see out the cabin windows and, he figured, for the woman to venture down the slope. Or more likely, she was too exhausted. He thought of her as next of kin, riding along with him in the back of an ambulance. A brisk wind rocked the cabin and the wheels above clicked and jolted over each tower support. It was hard to keep his eyes open. He caught the smell of tobacco and came awake, seeing the patrollers off to one side, smoking. Gradually the heat in the compartment—these Europeans had all the comforts, he thought—sent him back toward sleep. He fought it.

"Let me introduce myself again," he stuttered. "I'm Ed, Ed Dekker. You saved my life." The woman was kneeling down now, tucking a flap of blanket under the strap across his chest. Aware he was conscious, she withdrew her hand. It was not as if they hadn't touched, he thought. He tried to lift his own hand but his arms were bound down.

"Aisling," she said reluctantly. "First syllable pronounced like yesterday's fire, "ash". You get your choice of 'ling' or 'leen', but I prefer the second. It's a bit stronger." She flashed a smile and got to her feet.

"While we're on the topic of lives saved—and don't count yours yet—what the hell were you doing up on a glacier? And so late in the day? That area is closed to the public. There are signs all over at the top of the lift. With the conference on, they pulled back the patrols to better cover the marked trails. And like I asked before, why were you skiing alone?"

What could he say?

"It was only by luck I heard your voice," she continued, wiping her nose on a gloved hand and half unzipping her jacket. The gondola was warming up. "Sometimes bushwhackers like you aren't found until the spring melt when they're a bit of bone among the edelweiss." Her eyes narrowed. "You know about the wolves?"

He shook his head.

"They're making a comeback around here, or so I'm told. Species restoration, and all. That's why they tell you to sew your name in your clothes."

"Thanks. Climbing up seems stupid now but it made sense at the time. I had one day to relax before I got swallowed up in smoky rooms. And I've never seen mountains like these. You're a skier; you understand." Or not. She must think he was a buffoon.

The cables clicked again above the cabin. "How can I thank you? And you guys over there?" He raised his voice to the patrollers on the other side.

"It was our pleasure, Herr Dekker," said the shorter and broader of the two. They switched from German to English without pause. At some point they'd checked his ID and knew his name. "It is our normal level of service here at Oetz." The EMT displayed perfect teeth.

The slighter of the two lifted his hand holding an imaginary glass; a toast. "Rescue from the slopes in the day, hot chocolate in your room at night." He slapped the shoulder of his comrade and they broke into laughter. They were younger than he'd first thought. "You'll be pleased to know you're on the way to the hotel clinic. We have an X-ray machine and a doctor is standing by. We are used to your kind of injury. From what I can see, it is a bad sprain only. If not, it's off to the real hospital." He made a sweeping gesture with his hand, maybe the sign of a helicopter evacuation.

"Jesus, I hope you're right about the sprain," Ed said softly. He couldn't afford to miss the meetings.

Just then the gondola lurched and thudded to a stop at the lower station. Crew members wearing red coveralls opened the door from outside and grabbed the stretcher. The resort must have mobilized the emergency squad, he thought. With the patrollers following along, he was carried down a path flanked by fifteen-foot snow piles to the hotel's side door. Then he found himself on a steel examination table where a physician in an alpine sweater and loose lab coat waited. The doctor conferred briefly with the patrol, signed their clipboard, and began to cut away Ed's pant leg. When he reached the knee, Ed prepared for the worst.

"First, vee take a picture," he said, without obvious concern. He slid an X-ray plate under Ed's knee and swung a scanner into place overhead. As he stepped behind a lead screen, Aisling moved to join him. The doctor, using his hands as if he were shooing away flies, waved her toward the door. As she was about to disappear, Ed yelled out.

"Wait! I have to thank you. How can I reach you?"

She hesitated, hand on the latch. "Raus mit deiner jungen Frau!" The doctor shouted, impatient to complete the X-ray.

Seeing a Sharpie on the desk by the door, she picked it up and walked to where Ed lay. "This may be a mistake but here's my name. Ask at the desk for my number. Turning his hand over, she wrote "O'Keefe" on his palm. "I'm here for the week."

He smiled. "O'Keefe", like the Canadian ale?"

"He's in good hands," interrupted the doctor. "Not to worry. A little discomfort, then he'll be fine." The X-ray machine was buzzing as she disappeared.

Sled to gondola to clinic. Package delivery. Ed closed his hand around the name.

Chapter Three

AISLING LEFT HER SKIS in the warming hut outside the hotel lobby, then crossed in front of a huge stone fireplace and hit the elevator button. Once in her room, she shed her clothes, ran a bath as hot as she could tolerate, and slipped into the water with a mini-bottle of Weissburgunder Pinot Blanc from the room bar. In hotels like this, there was no price list posted.

"My god, that was a workout," she muttered to herself. "And this clown, Ed Dekker!" For a minute she had toyed with the idea of leaving him and simply going to find the ski patrol. The steam rose around her and she settled down, her shoulders underwater. The tub was long enough to let her actually stretch her legs. She sighed, moving a loofah sponge across her chest. Like the plush bathrobe, it came with the room. Mouthy he was, that's for sure, but he hadn't been a whiner. If the trip down was bad for her, it had to have been worse for him.

Well, they say you run into interesting people in these places—she'd never been to Europe, let alone to a first-class resort—and this encounter was certainly interesting. Now she knew at least one person not in her field with whom she wouldn't have to be on her guard. Assuming he was the innocent he claimed to be. As luck had it, she was scheduled to present in two days so she'd have tomorrow to recover. Too bad this Ed guy might never be able to stand upright. She rubbed the long muscles in her thighs. Maybe she wouldn't be able to walk either.

How old was he? she wondered. His immature joking had thrown her off. And the one crooked tooth, that was a pleasing defect. She'd never trusted a Hollywood smile. Despite his pain, he'd been quick on the repartee. She'd have to watch it with this guy. She was here to work.

Too tired to go to the restaurant or even wait for room service, she dried off, crossed to her bed, and slipped naked beneath the down comforter. She still had the sense of his arm on her shoulder as she fell asleep.

By 7 that evening, the hotel staff rolled Ed back to his room, leaving the wheelchair for his use. The doc had proved efficient if not empathetic. An experienced resort physician, he must have pegged Ed as a light-weight, a one-time visitor. Fortunately, there had been no fracture. He'd injected Ed with cortisone to bring down the swelling and a pain killer to help him sleep. Now Ed sat with a bag of blue synthetic ice on his knee. He'd removed the leg brace to bring the ice closer to the pain. The contraption, a web of Velcro straps, lay on the floor beside him.

"Use the wheel chair," Krobber had cautioned, "but don't get dependent. Walk the corridors. And no beer or wine. No alcohol of any kind." Krobber said the last as if it were the biggest disappointment. "You're a lucky man."

He had been lucky. Not even ripped tendons. Just a severe sprain, made worse on the trip down the mountain. With a few day's rest, he was assured, he'd be on his feet with only the brace and cane. His wheelchair attendant had adjusted the length of his new walking stick before he'd left. It was an aluminum tube with an ergonomic handle and lay on the coffee table in front of him. Ed didn't want to think about his increasing bill. The wheelchair, at least, could be returned. With luck he'd be back in New York before his editor could harass him about the charges. One thing to be thankful for — the cane lacked a geriatric claw. Frailty wasn't the look he needed as he mingled with the serious players. Then again, maybe a cane would make him look rakish. Like an eye patch. He unclenched his hand to look at the word she'd written, blurred but still legible. Perhaps she'd think of him as a war correspondent, someone fresh from a conflict zone? Right.

He was told to stay with the ice, move when he could, and check back with the clinic in 48 hours. A back-up ice pack was in his mini-fridge, dangerously close to the out-of-bounds booze.

To take his mind off a stiff drink, he put in a call to his brother. If the prolonged sorrow from his mother's cancer and death hadn't been enough to send the boys in separate directions after high school—Ed to hide out in college and Bart to find refuge in the military—the passing of their father the following year had marked paid to their childhood. So much for the permanence of human ties. But in the years since, Ed had tried to repair the damage. Not that he and Bart were Christmas-visit close—their travel schedules made that impossible—but they'd been managing to meet up once or twice a year lately, even if it was at airports for drinks or dinner. That connection had grown a bit and included occasional late-night e-mails. But never a call for help.

Ed worked out of New York and Bart, once his stint in Special Forces was over, had settled in the Washington area. Then, to Ed's surprise, his brother had announced his impending marriage, and would Ed be best man? It had been awkward. He was meeting the bride, Elizabeth, for the first time and felt he was drafted just to be evidence that Bart had a family, a childhood even. Had he bonded with Bart's new in-laws? No. Liz, as she insisted he call her, seemed a brittle blond from the Maryland Catholic prep school world. But rather than being content to "finish" at Sweetbriar or some such place, Liz had taken the bit in her teeth and run -- eventually to Georgetown Law. He'd give her that. Still, when the ceremony was done, Ed sensed she and her family were glad to see the last of him.

He leaned over and switched the limp ice pack for a fresh one from his room refrigerator. After Bart's deployment in two war zones, he'd certainly know about rifle fire. And snipers. Bart had set up a security firm with a war buddy. The partner, who'd left his legs back in Afghanistan, collated the search for intruders inside corporate servers and management iPhones while Bart was the ground force. While he never asked,

Ed figured that Elizabeth's family money had bought Bart's piece of the business. And the firm had prospered, even if the transition to a peace-time world wasn't without challenges for his brother, Not that he wanted to play shrink, but Ed was sure Bart still carried his deployments with him—hyper-awareness, explosions of anger. But more than a decade of marriage had mellowed him. The catalyst, Ed figured, was Molly, Bart and Liz's eleven year old daughter. With Liz up for a law partnership and working long hours, Bart had to take up the slack at home, at least as the fallback. He'd become the one to count on for dinner or a Saturday trip to the park. Not that Bart cooked. With two incomes, they'd taken on Claudia, their housekeeper, who usually left a meal warming in the oven. But Bart tried to make it an occasion—maybe Telemann on the stereo, Molly's phone off so there could be conversation. Ed knew that his brother was making an effort.

Bart didn't pick up right away and Ed left a message. "So, my man, I have a hypothetical. Say I'm on a mountain with an unobstructed view for a five hundred meters on all sides. The valley's miles away below me and I'm feeling like God's younger brother. Then someone takes a shot at me. From where I have no idea, but I'm thinking they're in Alpine white or something, including the rifle wrap. The first shot hits rock a meter from my head, the second nearly kisses my ski tips. So—again hypothetically—would you say I was down range from a sloppy assassin or was someone trying to intimidate me? And being successful, I might add." That should pique his interest. Only when he ended the call did Ed remember the six-hour time difference between Oetz and Washington, where it was now after 1 am.

Ed had just swapped ice packs again and settled back with a glass of mineral water when his cell phone rang.

"Yo, bro." Bart seemed wide awake. "The most likely answer is "B". You kicked a tar baby and now you're stuck. Or is that expression a vio-lation of journalistic norms of political correctness? I'm never sure. But seriously, what happened? I know you have a knack for shoving that pencil of yours where people would otherwise sit down."

"Did I get you up? Sorry about that. I wasn't thinking."

"No problem. Last night I was staking out a restaurant in Virginia, babysitting a corporate exec out for a late dinner with his side squeeze. When I got back, I noticed your message. It's always hard to wind down, so entertain me."

"You on the lookout for assassins or a raging husband?"

"From the height of this doll's heels and her cut of her jib, otherwise known as a dress, I'd say the second."

In Bart's firm, Executive Action, he did the necessary—sweeping offices for listening devices, vetting prospective corporate and some-times even government employees. A late-night stakeout was a pleasant variation, provided he'd gotten Molly settled. Executive's two other employees, operators, also veterans, filled in the gaps while Bart's partner, Jamie Buckworth, steered the ship.

"So, come clean. Who you messing with?"

"I'm in Austria covering a financial conference. Before it starts, which is tomorrow, I wanted to get out on the slopes. How often does a guy get a paid trip to European ski country? So earlier today I'm out there alone, up on this mother of a glacier. The view would take your breath away. Anyway, I'm entirely alone, haven't seen anyone else for hours, and some miscreant starts plugging away at me."

"Miscreant? I like that. Real Damon Runyon. But apparently you survived."

"After a fashion. I blew out a knee during my get-away. At this moment I'm sitting in a plush hotel room making love to a bag of ice. But, sadly, not in my glass. I'm looking at a walking splint and a cane. Oh, and let's not forget the wheelchair. I need to move around tomor-row or the paper will make me pay the bill."

"Blew out, as in you're blotto with pain?"

"Not enough to stop me from feeling sorry for myself. But here's the upside. I was pulled out of a snowy grave by this very fetching redhead. Then she dragged me down half the mountain until we could connect with the ski patrol and ultimately the hotel doctor." He looked at his hand. "We're going to meet up again, I'm sure."

"The doctor?"

"Right. He was cute. No, the redhead."

"So, you still landed on your feet. Or foot. I always thought you had the knack."

"She's my additional incentive to recover."

"Can't argue with you there, kid. But keep a clear head. You know those meds can lead to confusion."

"More elation than confusion. But if someone did shoot at me, what can I expect now?"

"That is the bottom line. You're at a hotel?"

"A really fancy resort. The big mucky mucks are here and the venue is saturated with security. So I'm giving you an intellectual puzzle, not an SOS."

"Still, lock your door. And you remember that trick with the chair under the knob?" The line was silent for a half minute. "The shooter had to have followed you for a long way meaning he, or she, was highly motivated. But not to kill you. Otherwise we wouldn't be having this conversation. Best guess? They were forcing you into an accident. At which, I have to say, they were successful. What's your angle at this conference? Going to interview political dissidents or something?

"There are no dissidents here. From what I can tell, the participants are Europe's version of Wall Street, the financial elite. Think a mob confab with access to the world's treasury."

"Anyone spilling secrets to you?"

"I hope. But I don't expect intentionally. I'll need a few breaks if I'm going to crack open any oysters."

"Someone thinks you might, enough at least to show their cards. But I know you. Just because you have a personal incentive to dig, don't become reckless. Maybe this girl you met on the mountain is the shooter."

"Oh, come on!"

"Just sayin'. You're lost in the boonies and she just happens along?"

"She found me well after the shots were fired and two miles away. She's a biologist of some kind, part of the program here. The only coincidence is that we both ski and were skipping out before the business end of things gets going. I've been known to interest women other than as a victim, you know. But speaking of women, how's Elizabeth?"

"Good. But let me move to the other room." A moment later Bart continued. "Thank God she's earning more than I am. You can't believe what living around D.C. costs. But lately she's at the office or on the road so much I'm starting to feel single."

"You've got Molly to boss around. From what you tell me, she's great company. If I wasn't the lone wolf I am, I'd be jealous of your domesticity."

"She is a colt. You ought to see her move on the soccer field. Or 'pitch', as she keeps reminding me." Bart paused. "You ever think of settling down?"

"Yeah. Someday." Ed shifted his ice pack. "But I've got to find a girl who wants to live on skid row."

"Skid row? More like SoHo these days," said Bart. "All that creeping gentrification." Bart had once visited him in New York and demonstrating an eye for real estate, he'd encouraged Ed to buy space in a tenement building undergoing conversion. Once the old-law flats were stripped out, the price magically increased five-fold as floor-through lofts. But it was still cheap at the time and a bargain at today's prices. With his brother's encouragement and his own share from their parents' small estate, Ed had sprung for it.

"Your problem is you're too self-deprecating," Bart continued. "You lack inner conviction."

"Whoa, brother. Where's this psychobabble coming from? Oh, I get it. You've been in counseling. Send a guy to an analyst and he becomes a shrink himself."

"Close, but no cigar. Not a psychoanalyst. Just a counselor. You know how people use the word 'work' these days? They say 'I'm working out'; 'I'm a work-in-progress.' Well, Liz are I are working on our relationship. When we have time, that is. But I won't go into details. 'Issues' is the other over-used word. In our case, anyway. But you have a more pressing problem. Or are one, at least to someone."

"That's the thing," said Ed. "I haven't done shit here yet. The copy I've sent was simply to describe the place, talk up the agenda, build a little reader expectation. So far at least, I've just been a travel writer, for God's sake."

"Then it's what you will write that matters."

"Must be. Think of this place as a G-20 confab with snowmen, or Davos without the Hollywood stars. But while the players here pretend to be plotting the future of mankind, what I'm seeing is just a lot of wining and dining. And the setting? It's a fantasy. It's Santa's Village with every elf in blond braids."

"You poor suffering bastard. But Heidi can be dangerous, as you're finding out."

"Things get underway tomorrow so I've still got lots of time to step on people's toes."

"I can remember back when you exuded obnoxiousness. Did you fart in a crowded elevator? Seriously though, watch yourself. You need to be mobile, not a stationary target. You mentioned a wheelchair? For real?"

"It's here, but I can hobble. They cart you around in those things to limit their liability. I'll be fully operational in a few days. But goodbye skiing."

"I could get over, give you a hand."

"Don't think about it. I'm fine. That's not why I called. Besides, with all the bigwigs, this place is totally buttoned up and they wouldn't let you in."

"Your call. I'm thinking that popping you would have been easy so the game must be to discourage you, send you home early. So play nice with others."

"I'll try. Problem is, I'm like the Dixie Chicks. I don't know how to make nice. Seriously, while I'd love to get my hands on something big here, there's nothing so far."

"So far."

"Your respect for the fourth estate is much appreciated. But there's half a dozen other reporters here. Why not them?"

"At Executive Action we do threat scenarios. And I've seen many in the last few years. I'm speculating, but I assume the conference participants want flattering press coverage. Then you turn up, someone with a history of sticking it to people. So management decides to blunt your edge or send you home."

"I guess." Ed was feeling groggy from the pain killers.

"I don't want to polish your bowling trophy, but maybe you're more of a threat than the other reporters, assuming they haven't been intimidated as well. I know you think I drag my knuckles on the ground, but I read your scribbles. You're an ankle biter."

"You're over-rating me, but thanks. The other journalists are from much bigger outfits—*The Financial Times, Der Spiegel, The Economist.* They're worker bees, if not the queens. And looking around yesterday, I got the impression the organizers are keeping the press pool small. Oh, and back in New York, I had to sign this nondisclosure thing. It gives the *Chronicle* control over anything I write. It was the price of admission."

"Their backup system. Say you live to write about bankers fleecing widows and orphans, they can still squelch your stories through pressure on New York." Bart lapsed into thought. "How are you transmitting?"

"I send text to editorial re-write. The paper gave me an encrypted laptop, state of the art. Said to be uber-secure."

"Hate to disabuse you, brother, but there ain't no such thing." He paused. "What kind of a phone are you using right now?"

"My cell, and calling from my room. If it were daylight, I could describe a lovely view of the Alps. Should I try?"

"Don't be smart. If you're a person of interest, they would have bugged your room. As for phones, you may as well shout your business in the hall. But what's done is done. Sure you don't want a visitor?"

"I do want a visitor, but not you."

"So I gathered. Look, keep in touch. If they're listening in, the damage is already done. So keep that door locked."

"Unless it's her knocking. By the way, did I mention copper-colored hair?"

"Goodnight. But I want to hear from you tomorrow." Bart cut the connection.

Swinging his leg off the coffee table, Ed hobbled to the door, his shredded pantleg flapping. He rechecked the dead bolt and attached the security chain.

Chapter Four

ED SKIMMED THROUGH THE packet of conference information and found tomorrow's schedule. The opening plenary was at two in the ballroom, a leisurely pace which suited him just fine. If he could spend the morning in bed, he might be on his feet by noon. Then there were his interviews. The media office had set him up with several, including with a biotech scientist. Maybe he'd get something interesting there.

He hadn't eaten since the sandwiches he'd taken up to the glacier more than eight hours ago and he must have burned 5,000 calories since. Next to the phone was a leather-encased room service menu. Decisions, decisions. Not about the food but the company. He might not be up to dancing but why eat alone? Just the thought made the pain recede.

Though the letters on his hand were smeared and unreadable, he remembered the name, O'Keefe. "Like the ale," he repeated. The desk put him through to her room. On the fifth or sixth ring, just as he was deciding this was wishful thinking, she picked up. Now she had an office voice. Was she with someone and over-correcting?

"Hello, Aisling," he said, careful to say it correctly. "It's Ed Dekker, the guy you brought back from the dead?" She didn't respond immediately so he plunged ahead. "If this were Athens in 500 B.C. we'd now have a life-long bond." Where the hell had that come from? "But let's translate this debt into something manageable; I'm thinking dinner. Have you eaten?"

"Tonight?" He could tell she was surprised. But she hadn't hung up. "I do remember a 'Dekker' but assumed he'd still be comatose. You're more resilient than you seemed. Fortunately for you, I checked into your bio on the *Chronicle's* web page and concluded you're not a known serial killer."

"Disappointed? Or have you had your fill of excitement for one day?"

"It's just that I'm methodical. It also appears that you are employed so I gather we won't be splitting the check."

"I was going to pay my half but if you insist?"

"It's a good thing for you I distrust charm. Then again, being charm-less could be your come-on."

"I was thinking we could order from the kitchen and eat in my room, if you dare. There'll be the night nurse here, of course, changing my IV drip and spooning me mashed vegetables. Or you could. I'm just trying to assure you that you'll be safe."

"Sounds delightful. How's the full-body cast?"

"I asked for one but my insurance plan won't cover it, given that I just have a bad sprain. But don't hold back with the sympathy. I find it very soothing. But seriously, I'm back in my room juggling ice packs and chewing the pillow from hunger."

She was silent.

"Let's see what they have." He flipped a few pages and found the entrées. "Fortunately, they have this in English as well as Italian and German. I see here pork loin, chicken Kiev, porterhouse steak, some sort of Tyrolean pot roast. Those too heavy? There's also a quiche."

She was waiting him out.

"Either I provide dinner or you'll have to put up with chemically-enhanced roses from a greenhouse in Columbia or somewhere, grown with child labor."

"If you put it that way, I don't have much choice," she said, breaking her silence. "When I got back to my room, I collapsed. I may be as sore as you are. And no, I haven't eaten. You actually woke me up."

He was making headway.

"And I'm curious about what became of you," she continued. "As I was drifting off, I heard what I thought might be a medevac helicopter."

"You're not getting rid of me that easily. It was most likely dignitaries arriving with a bit of panache. I'm still just an elevator ride away."

"That food talk has me wide awake. Let's speed this up. Order me what you're having. You can think of it as a test."

Hot dogs it is, he was about to say, but capped it. "Done. I'm in room 403, in what they call the Südflügel. Shall we say 15 minutes?"

"South Wing. Got it. But twenty. I need to dress. Can't go through the hall in pajamas." She hung up.

He thought of the sweat on her neck, shivering as he called in the order—Angus steaks, baked potatoes, winter squash, salad, coffee,. Plus a goodish merlot. Which meant in the forty-euro range. Ouch! Too bad he wasn't going to share it. He was told to expect the waiter in thirty-five minutes. Like Nazi trains, he assumed the food trolleys ran on time. Grabbing his cane, he lurched to the bathroom to shave and shower. Getting out onto wet tile, he barely escaped another catastrophe. Pulling on trousers was the real challenge. With the knee brace strapped to the outside of his pant leg, he hoped he could forget the cane. As he was looking around, wondering where they'd sit, he heard a knock on the door. It had been eighteen minutes, too soon for the food. He had to lean on the wall as well as use his cane to get to the door.

She was dressed in a black skirt and beige wool sweater over a white blouse, her hair swept back and tied with a ribbon. No jewelry, no make-up he could see. She grinned and looked hungry.

"I ask myself, is it wise visitin' a stranger in his hotel room at nine-thirty in the night?" She peered over his shoulder. "What would me sainted ma think? But thanks be for your impairment. It's reassuring." She had to maneuver around him. "Nice cane, by the way." Her lilt surrounded him like perfume.

"And may the Pope bless ya for yur pastoral visit," he replied.

Limping, he followed her to the sitting area. She chose the couch and smiled when she saw the wheelchair. He sank into an armchair. "A pleasant room. It says a lot about you, especially the art. I have the same pictures in my room." They gazed together at generic scenes of cows on Alpine meadows.

"Can't have too much of a good thing," he replied. He was a beat or three behind her.

"Do they really put sod on their roofs?" A couple of houses had grass growing on top. "I thought you'd know, with the name 'Dekker' I mean. The internet says it's High German for the lad who lays shingles. Or straw."

"You did check me out."

"Only what a girl must do in this day and age, lad." She smiled. "No time to get into your articles but the titles were intriguing. 'Beer Capital to Barrel Dregs: the Collapse of Newark, N.J.'; I liked that one. Nothing wishy-washy."

She saw his confusion. "I'm doing you a favor, you know, breaking the conversational ice."

"It's the term 'lad'. Is that a sly reference to my seniority?"

"No. Chronology is only loosely related to maturity. And I did discover your age. It's a decade more than mine. More or less." She gave him an exaggerated shrug. She held the high cards.

"Did I say you look wonderful out of your ski duds?" he offered.

"'Duds' isn't even '80s. Maybe '50s? I suppose I could treat it as retro. And you're looking, well, alive."

"That's kind. But enough about me, as they say in old movies. Tell me about the name 'Aisling'. Is it like an old family brooch, lost for a thousand years ago and rediscovered? I can hear someone at Stonehenge calling, 'Aisling, mind the geese now!'"

She burst into laughter. "You're getting your footwork back, for a gimp. 'Gimp' by the way, is definitely '40s, from a Humphrey Bogart movie. But in that one, the gimp was a young girl." She smoothed her skirt. "But you're close. Aisling is an old Gaelic name associated with dreams and visions. Completely inappropriate for a natural scientist, but what can a body do?"

"But you own it, I see that. You must have been your mother's dream."

"That may well have been, for good or bad. As long as I'm coming clean, the 'O'Keefe' part is from 'O'Keeffe', the clan who own County Cork to this day, or so they tell me. Before that, it was 'Ó Caoimh'."

"Ah, medieval royalty. Likely the ancestors had their own harpist."

"Didn't we all? That and the rampant lion on our family crest." Her mouth turned up.

"I believe it," said Ed.

"But facts and dreams, like past and present, belong in separate pockets, don't you agree?"

She surveyed the room again—a laptop, a cluttered pile of papers, books. A report lay open on the desk titled "Global Energy Demands", dated this year. Another on climate change was visible along with a third about the global seed vault on a Norwegian island in the Arctic.

"Nothing on skiing, I see. That accounts for something."

"Now wait a minute," he protested. "I'm considered an excellent skier, given the right conditions. I was first string on my grammar school team in Caribou, Maine. But back then, of course, skis were wood and the newest thing was the rope tow." He measured her shoulders; a tennis player, he thought. Or maybe a swimmer. He figured she could really ski when she wasn't lugging around dead weight.

"You never lived in Caribou, Maine. But setting that aside, how did you come to be sitting on your ass in the middle of nowhere?"

"Ass, is correct. You'll find this difficult to believe, but here goes." He was the reluctant witness. "Picture this. I'm on the Sölden glacier taking in the view, thinking about the run back to the hotel. I can almost smell the hot chocolate I'll have when I make it down."

"A wholesome image. Never an impure thought."

"The picture of innocence. It's taken me the day to climb up and now the light is fading. Not surprisingly, there's no one else around. Suddenly, bullets start kicking up the snow, very close to me. This proved highly motivating, as you'd appreciate. So I beat it out of there. It turned out I was moving faster than I could manage. And then, there you were."

She looked him over, not as shocked as he'd expected. Maybe just dismissive.

"That's original. I hope you didn't tell that to the hotel doctor. He'd have sent you for a concussion scan." Her eyes narrowed. "You say someone tried to kill you? How does that make sense? Unless you're not the mild-mannered reporter you seem. Maybe your bio is all fake and I'm looking at a terrorist on the run from Interpol."

"Want to see my passport?"

"Wouldn't prove anything. You'd have a fake. There is another test, though. Repeat after me, 'Bond, James Bond.' I'm good a reading voices for honesty."

"If I were Bond, I'd have had a parasail rig in my backpack and made a soaring escape."

"I'm still suspicious. Why am I here in your room, putting my virtue at risk? You know what Bond does to women?"

"Seriously. You found out for yourself that I'm a mere journalist. Yeah, I've covered some dicey stories, but nothing that would motivate someone to hunt me down. In 2008 I was posted to Baghdad by Gannett for a month—they'd become the new corporate owners of the *Newark Republican* where I worked at the time. Their bureau guy had caught shrapnel and had to be evacuated so they sent me over. I know what gunfire sounds like: rifles, pistols, mortar rounds. First, I thought I was hearing an avalanche crew. But these were high velocity bullets, not the thunderclap of big ordinance. So I ran for the hills. Or in this case, down the hills."

"That's weird," she said. Her voice had fallen back to the smoky register he'd heard when they first met. "What do you think happened? You must have some idea."

"I've wrestled with that. First possibility, the shooter mistook me for someone else. But that's weak because he would have had to track me up from the lodge. Another possibility? Someone wants me out of the conference. Not necessarily dead. I imagine a bullet-riddled corpse spoiling opening day for the conference might be awkward. But if I'm hunkered down in my room or on the next plane out?" He opened his hands. "Problem solved."

"Makes sense. Someone wants you out of here. Did you get a look at this individual?"

"Not a chance. But it's whetted my interest in the conference, you might say."

"Got your attention?"

"Yeah. Has to be related to what's going on here. I'm thinking, news of petroleum deposits in the Amazon, IMF officials tanking the peso? It's got to be something. Course I'm running on less than eight cylinders just now. Did you didn't notice anyone from the Bilderberg group in the lobby?"

"Bilderberg?"

"A figure of speech. Conspiracy folks think a Bilderberg cabal secretly runs the world. But no one can be sure since they never let the press into their meetings. And as these include doddering European royals, I seriously doubt the group is more than a social club. Now if this were the 13th century...?"

"You'd be hiding from the king's assassins. Or the Knights Templar. I've read Dan Brown, too." She'd cut him off.

"Hey, don't be dismissive. There are interest groups trying to control the globalization process, shaping the world community."

"Sounds cozy. Do they meet for lemonade on the front porch?"

"More in paneled rooms with overstuffed chairs, single malt on a side table. And far from the inconvenience of electoral politics."

"You're saying these unknown characters call the shots?" She arched her eyebrows.

"I have no idea. Frustrating for a reporter, no?"

She shook her head. Bits of late 20th century history ran through her mind like a newsreel. "We know one thing, if I can believe you. Somebody thinks you're trouble." She gave him a sideways look. "Scheduled any iffy interviews here?"

"Still making those arrangements. But I have to assume that information isn't entirely private."

"Still, it's best to be discrete." She looked around. "And how do we know this room isn't bugged? In which case, don't repeat my name as I leave." But she didn't.

Funny about room surveillance, he thought. That was what Bart had mentioned.

At that moment there was a rap at the door and a muffled voice said, *"Zimmerservice"*. Aisling glanced at Ed's extended leg and stood up. Before turning the lever, she squinted through the peep hole. Standing aside, she made room for a young man in a waiter's jacket pushing a linen-draped cart across the threshold. With a flourish, he snapped out the cloth and covered the small table near the window, laying down napkins and setting out plates as if he were dealing cards. After holding a chair for Aisling, he removed the domed lids, releasing the smell of charred steak. Ed lurched up to join her and the server opened the merlot. Ed gestured for Aisihng to play expert and she paused for a moment, then nodded. As a final touch, the young man set down a bud vase holding a single rose. Ed slipped him a folded bill and he withdrew.

"That was generous," said Aisling.

"With pizza, you give the delivery guy three or four bucks. Here, I'm just guessing."

A leather folder lay on the table's edge and Aisling opened it, her eyes widening. "This had better be good. Can you afford to eat like this on a reporter's salary?"

"Listen, if I'd settled for burgers I'd have been grumpy company. Besides, I doubt this place supplies those little ketchup packets that I like. But maybe we can get together in Newark some time where I can take you to an authentic greasy spoon. For now, we'll have to pretend we're used to this level of luxury."

"Would you wear a battered fedora?"

"With race track slips in the hatband. Now let's eat."

They dug into their meal. "You need help with that?" She waved her fork very close to his sirloin."

"Maybe just to cut it up."

She grinned. "You made a big mistake there. But I'll give you a pass. You need to replace all those lost calories."

"Ah, the simple economics of the Pleistocene." He raised his knife, fending off her fork. "Running from T-rex and all."

"You mean the Cretaceous. No dinosaurs by the Pleistocene."

"All right then. Let's say the Neanderthal spring, when real men battled wolves. You did say there are wolves in these mountains, didn't you?"

"An open question. I guess we'll never know."

He gave a silent-movie shiver.

In a short time, the beef, fingerling potatoes, and grilled broccoli were smears on empty plates. Like the Italians he knew back home, Aisling left her salad for last, the vinegar cleansing the palate. Drawing down her wine glass hadn't slowed her progress.

"Think a sip would hurt me?" he said, about to empty the bottle into her glass.

"Who knows what they injected you with. Add alcohol, you might sleep for a week." She sipped and gave him an innocent look. He wondered if she'd grown up in competition with brothers, racing to the table to get her share. He watched as she demolished her strudel.

"You going to eat that?" She pointed her fork at his desert.

He pulled it closer, raising his fists.

"Any more thoughts on why you're a wanted man?"

"No. You?"

"It shouldn't be difficult to figure. Forget about the chances of getting dirt from the sessions. Most, at least, are open. So it boils down to your interviews with key people—bankers, CEOs, scientists."

"You mention scientists. I've set something up with this one researcher, a guy working for a seed/chemical outfit. They have their lab people here to impress the investors. They're mostly window dressing, I'm sure, but this one guy is the real deal. I'm hoping to get a line on the direction of his work."

"Is this common in these conferences? I mean, the emphasis on science?"

"Well, someone invited you, and you're a biologist."

"I was thinking I'm comic relief, given all these finance people. Or maybe I'm the gravitas, something to make the audience feel high-minded."

"Actually, I've studied the agenda. There's quite a bit of science, starting with big pharma here to pitch their new vaccines. I'm sure we'll be hearing about plagues rising out of the Congo to strike us down unless hedge fund investments save us. But proprietary information? Not likely. Loose lips and all that."

"Why would a business paper like yours be interested in diseases? I'd have thought you'd be more interested in, say, Cypriot bank failures."

"That too, now that you mention it. The near-collapse of the Cypriot economy a few years ago led the European Central Bank to confiscate a number of big off-shore accounts using the claim of reporting irregularities. Which just happened to be owned by Russian oligarchs. But it's not just money that moves markets."

"Every disease means the rush to a new antiviral drug. I can see that.

So who's anticipating the next ecological catastrophe?" she asked " Be interesting to find out, wouldn't it?"

"Does any of this tie in with your own work? All those creepy crawlies?"

"Now you're over the line. I do study insects, but give them the respect they deserve. They support the entire food chain so yeah, that would include the financial system as well."

"Nicely put. Actually, with Naturtek pitching drought-resistant grains, among other things, the money tie to biology is very strong. If the company's wheat and soy turn out to have a commercial advantage under adverse climate conditions, the company could make a bundle when the Sahel in Africa dries up."

"You're talking about climate collapse?"

"Right. Drought creates opportunity. Emerson Foley, head of the Seed Preservation Trust, is here to make an address, so I expect crop economics will get a lot of attention."

"You're saying catastrophe is just a chance to cash in? Isn't that more than a little cynical?"

He shrugged and watched her run the last piece of bread around the edge of her plate. Now it really was dishwasher-clean.

"The problem with a room service meal is the distance from the kitchen." She patted her stomach. "But enough is enough. This was delicious and I need to thank you." She raised her arms and stretched. "That is, unless you intend to split the check."

"No. What's a year's salary among friends? I'll tell the accountant at the *Chronicle* I had to eat in my room, cripple that I am."

"You're on an expense account? And still a cynic?"

"I have a per diem, adjusted for location. While the paper would love to put me in a youth hostel, there just ain't none around." He looked at the window, now a black mirror. "If they sock me with the overage, you're worth it."

She reached across the table and touched his lips with her finger.

Chapter Five

THEY SAT IN SILENCE for a while, the window capturing their ghosts. She seemed reluctant to leave and Ed shifted his gaze to her reflection. Beyond, lights were barely visible, a necklace of street lamps from the hotel to the village. A black SUV circled the oval in front of the resort, moving at a measured pace. Security, he thought. But he didn't feel secure.

"There's another possibility, you know."

She tilted her head and squinted at him. "What's that?"

"Before I came, I checked this place out. My little adventure today wasn't the first crime to take place here. In fact, we may be on the scene of the oldest documented murder in Europe. Older even than the killing of Tutankhamen down in Egypt."

"He was killed? I hadn't heard."

"So they say. And there are similarities. In each case, the evidence comes from mummies. But here, the investigators also have the crime scene."

"Do tell. Is this a tale from your days as a police reporter?"

"I only covered that beat when the regular guy was too drunk to drive. That's when I started wearing the fedora. Seriously though, you might be interested. It's all about forensic anthropology."

"Close enough, but I'm game." She settled back in her seat. "Maybe it will take your mind off your own troubles. You're not saying the perp was the same guy who came after you?"

"Probably not. The murder here took place 5300 years ago. But the body only turned up recently, 1991 to be exact. A gift of glacial melting."

"The upside of global warming."

"You take what you can get."

"Preserved?"

"I think the term is freeze-dried, stable enough to become the most thoroughly examined corpse in ancient history. Scientists named him Otzi because he was found near here in the Otztal Alps. Actually, quite close to where we are now. High-altitude cold and low humidity kept everything intact—blood, hair, stomach contents. And it all went to the lab."

"So we know the condemned man's last meal." She wondered where this was leading.

"We do. Based on food remains and pollen on his clothes, he came from the Italian side of the mountains in early summer. He appeared headed to a pass at about 1500 meters, half the height of the surrounding mountains. But he never made it. At first, it looked like he'd fallen to his death, fully clothed and carrying all sorts of weapons—a knife, a copper-headed axe, a longbow with a quiver of arrows. Then scanning X-rays revealed an arrowhead embedded in his shoulder. It had severed an artery. As the criminologists say, he bled out and fell forward."

"Meaning?"

"He was in flight."

"Oh." She paused. "Like you."

"You could say that. Here was a guy dressed by the L.L. Bean of his day. His state-of-the-art survival gear included leather shoes, three layers of clothing, a bear skin hat, a fire-lighting kit, and containers that likely held food. The odd thing was that many of his arrows were unfinished, as was his six-foot bow."

"So he was on the run but took off before he was quite ready." She rested her chin on her palm, drawn into the story. "Then someone from the lowlands tracked him down."

"That's the likely narrative. Maybe he'd broken an older bow and was regrouping."

"But above the tree line?" Her eyes wandered toward the mountainous mass outside the window. "So we're talking tribal warfare? Humans have always been bloody-minded."

"I lean toward a personal vendetta." His eyes caressed her copper-colored hair. "Probably over a woman."

She arched her eyebrows. "Isn't it always? But his pursuers overtook him."

"He let his guard down. Or grew tired. They figure he was in his fifties; old for the time. Think of him as an experienced hiker but no sprinter." Ed was almost Otzi's age. "But note that the assassins didn't strip the body. You'd think they'd want the weapons. A copper-headed axe would have been a find back then. And at least some of his arrows were fletched and ready to fire."

"Fletched?"

"Feathers glued to the shaft for balance and stability. If he wasn't sleeping with someone's wife or daughter—which I lean toward—he was in the Special Ops of his day." Ed was thinking of his brother, Bart.

"But all that preparation didn't save him." Her voice grew melancholy. "He's hurt. He crawls away into some crevasse, and dies alone. And we repeated the same thing a thousand times over the next millennia." She sighed. "But at least in this case, he gave his body to science."

"Noble, if inadvertent," said Ed.

"And your point in telling me this?" She studied his face. "You think there's a curse on these mountains, maybe because someone dug old Otzi up?" She arched her eyebrows. "And like Tutankhamen's grave robbers, everyone involved in the dig ended up cursed."

"Odd you should say that. A number of the group that found Otzi did meet violent deaths."

"Except that you, I have to assume, didn't dig him up. A second flaw in your reasoning is that in any three decades, a percent of every cohort will die naturally. I'm afraid you failed your dissertation defense."

"You're right. I'm just reflecting the atmosphere of this place."

"Well, whatever. I suggest you forget the curse thing, but still watch your back." Her lips were drawn thin.

"You're serious?"

"Just saying. I get a little of that creepy vibe myself." Her eyes tracked to the window and she drew her sweater tight across her chest and did up a button. Throughout the evening Ed's eyes had skipped over her linen blouse. Had she just caught him at it? No, she was looking away.

They sat in silence for a while. Finally Ed said, "You've done your research on me. Now tell me something about yourself." He wished he'd ordered a second bottle of merlot. "You're a biologist?"

"Lepidopterist, actually." Animation returned to her face. "I study moths and butterflies." She gave him a wide-eyed, ethereal look. She was a garden fairy. "And insects, more generally. My doctoral research was on butterfly migration. If you've got monarchs traveling 3,000 miles from Canada to Mexico, they've got to follow a nectar and pollen trail. My interest has been in mapping habitat along the way. And its preservation."

"Keeping the flowers growing?"

"Milkweed, mainly. The monarch diet is very specific. A useful adaptation once, but no longer. In each seasonal migration, a billion individuals have to find food. Adults eat a variety of things but the cater-pillar stage can only live on milkweed. This lets them store natural toxins which don't affect them but make the adults distasteful to predators. The butterflies advertise this characteristic with their coloring."

"The more beautiful you are, the more deadly, right?"

"Toxic, at least. But I'll take that as an oblique complement." She wrinkled her lips.

"Oops!"

"An evolutionary biologist asks how such a complicated life cycle develops—egg to insatiable caterpillar in one place, weeks in the prison of a chrysalis, finally emerging as the greatest of all insect travelers. The first generation heads north from Mexico to the Texas coast. The next reaches the Midwest; a third makes it to New England and Canada. Each generation must time their activity to the milkweed season." She was in lecture mode. "Then, remarkably, the final generation—what we call the Methuselah—returns to pine groves in the mountains of Mexico in one continuous flight, three thousand miles in a matter of months."

"Talk about a non-stop trip," Ed said.

"They largely float and soar, exploiting the wind for assistance like tiny, technicolor hawks. Something in their DNA points them to a precise destination where they gather, mate, and lay eggs. It's an improbable narrative, but it works. Or it did. Over the last twenty years, fifty percent of them have failed to make the loop."

Her voice dropped. "You may well ask, what's the problem? In a word, agriculture." She banged the table. "Not farming per se. I'm sure your Otzi grew grain and carried stale bread. The issue is the way we now go about it." She took a breath. "First, we alternate soy with corn on the same fields, fencepost to fencepost, for thousands of acres. To a farmer, milkweed is, well, a weed. So like a Clint Eastwood character, the farmer draws his pistol and pulls the trigger, but using Razor Pro, Roundup, Zap-It, or VPG Killzall. The milkweed keels over, along with a hundred other native plants. The bullets are one or another iteration of glyphosate, a gift of the Green Revolution. Which, if you're a wild species, isn't something you experience as green at all."

"They can't adapt, the butterflies I mean?"

"Their flight paths last swerved when the ice age ended. For monarchs, much of North America was a banquet then. Now it's a food desert. It's a similar story with moths and other butterflies, though their range is less so they have a better chance of survival in isolated regions."

She brought her glass to her lips and found it empty.

"But some are surviving, no? I've seen them. Maybe their adaptation is on fast-forward. So they'll end up fewer, but smarter?"

"Oh, insects, even butterflies, are tough and collectively they're able to adapt. They manage to find a way through hurricanes and droughts. Even the ice age was just a chapter in their history. But now they're losing."

"You've got the subject for a good documentary. Every school kid knows how to recognize a monarch. They're what calendar makers call charismatic fauna, like the koala and the polar bear. The public identifies with them. If your story got out, you could generate support for a string of natural refuges."

"Documentaries exist, particularly about the monarch's winter home in the fir trees of the Bioshere Reserve at Angangueo, Michoacan, near Mexico City. That is certainly a refuge. And essential. But even though it generates a lot of tourist dollars, each year illegal logging is still paring it down. You hit the nail on the head, though. Wildlife lovers look for what's cute and cuddly. The public is appalled by oil-soaked pelicans after an off-shore drill rig spill. But the problem is bigger than saving one species. And other than spectacular butterflies—monarchs, the blue morpho, the lunar moth—humans find bugs creepy. Yet they're essential to the food web in ways we don't completely understand."

"I can see that bugs have a PR problem. When I think 'insect' in New York, it's a cockroach on the kitchen counter. Sort of like mice. I could show you a cupboard in my apartment where those critters ate a hole through a half inch board."

"Right. So you set traps, buy insecticide spray, and wipe 'em out. But if we want butterflies, we can't treat nature like a countertop."

"You said 'food web'. I thought you were into diversity for its own sake." Ed adjusted his leg and wondered just where on her body she was hiding a butterfly tattoo.

"Like art-for-art's sake? No. It's a practical matter. Insects pollinate seventy percent of our crops. Without them you'd have to give up on apples, blueberries, almonds, figs. That coffee in the Krupp's brewer over there on the side table, stale as it probably is, wouldn't exist without bees working the coffee blossoms. Maize is wind-pollinated, true, and legumes—the peas, the lentils—are self-pollinating. But fruits, nuts— most anything that flowers—needs insects to reproduce. Bats and birds help, but they're a minor factor. The super pollinators are bugs." She caught her breath.

"So flowers are serious business?"

"Damn straight. From an evolutionary perspective, they co-evolved with pollinating insects. They're a team. Now we're ripping that fabric apart."

Her cheeks were flushed. She unfastened the buttons on her sweater.

"The best case for caring about insects turns out to be the food argument."

"And you don't mean eating dried grasshoppers?"

"No, thought that's a significant protein source, in Mexico at least."

"Then there's the worm in my bottle of mescal, back in New York."

"You're such a cosmopolitan," she said.

"I may be conventional about food," Ed said, "but I'm with you on flowers. I've always appreciated naked Tahitian beauties with flowers in their hair. Only in art, of course."

She raised her eyebrows and wiped her lips with a napkin. "I'm onto your game. First you encourage me to get lost explaining my research, then distract me with a tidbit from your last trip to an art museum." She buttoned her sweater. "But this is serious. Speaking of mescal, without insects you won't have agave cactus or any mescal at all. As for Tahitian beauties," she continued, "do you think it's an accident that flowers play such a huge role in human affairs?" They both looked at the rose on the table. "Including death?"

"Death?"

"Yes. Courtship, weddings, and funerals. It's all one piece. At some level of consciousness, we recognize flowers as an affirmation of life, maybe because they wither away so quickly."

"Point taken." It was clear she was on home court and pressing her advantage.

"You've seen 'Jurassic Park', the robotic T-Rex and all? That world came into being 180 million years ago when earth's continents were a single plate, Gondwanaland. Most plants were conifers. Then, over the next 80 million years, the pace of change picked up. The Cretaceous saw the first flowering plants." She waved her fork at the rose. We think most insects came into being at that time, co-evolving with flowering plants as their pollinators."

"Because?"

"We know about this from bugs caught in amber, which is fossilized tree sap. A flowering plant, an angiosperm, has enclosed ovules. If you want to create a viable seed, you need a mechanism to unite the pollen with the ovum. And that mechanism is our friend, the bug. It was tree ferns that first worked this out."

Ed was back in a classroom at Tufts. A more attractive teacher, though.

"As the pairing proved successful, other plants got into the game, along with their specialized insect pals. Now jump ahead to modern times, say 3000 B.C. when Otzi was hiking around. I know, giving the big eye to someone else's wife. At the same time over in the Americas, people were domesticating squash, maize, and beans. Then came chiles and tomatoes. As humans bred changes into these plants, the insects adjusted in order to continue to scavenge nectar and pollen. Especially the solitary varieties of bee. There's 5,000 types in North America, all dependent on flowering plants. They make their rounds collecting their lunch, and make it possible for edible plants to produce seed."

"And for us to eat."

"Precisely."

"You didn't think I was paying attention, did you?"

"Did I get into the zone? Apologies, but you set me off with that bit about mescal and agaves. But just because you're a journalist and not a scientist, you don't have to play cretin."

"'And gladly would he learn, and gladly teach,'" said Ed.

"That a quiz?" she replied. "Chaucer's clerk, from the Canterbury Tales. You see, I'm not just a laboratory rat."

"You win another round." He licked a finger and made a check in the air.

"Stop trying to distract me. You take the yucca. It was essential to humans in the Southwest during the first period of agriculture. It provides food, fiber, rope. Also soap, as the natural cosmetics industry has recently discovered. But, ta da! You can't have yucca without the yucca moth. This critter allows the yucca to reproduce. The female extracts a ball of pollen from the flower, places it back in the stigma, and lays her eggs. The pollen fertilizes the ovum to produce seeds. Then the larvae of the moth hatch, eat some, and scatter the rest."

"Messy eaters."

"Which reproduce the plant. Co-evolution at work. There's lots of examples of sole pollinators like this. The hawk moth for another. No hawk moth, no hawk moth orchid. And speaking of orchids, there's one in Africa with a twelve-inch nectar tube. Even though no one's found it yet, there's a moth lurking out there somewhere with a twelve-inch tongue."

"So, in economic terms, we humans are free riders on the work of all these busy bees?"

"Give the boy an 'A'. But here's the thing. Evolution can also run downhill. Now that we no longer understand our natural surroundings, including the role of insects, we're all city folk exterminating rats and roaches." She swept her arm around, taking in the room. "We're oblivious about how our food comes into being. And as with milkweed, we tear apart the whole evolutionary web."

Ed thought of his minibar. Gingerly, he stood up and located a one-glass bottle of Cabernet Sauvignon, pouring it into Aisling's glass. She watched his shaky ballet without moving, a progressive parent letting the child learn from his mistakes. It wasn't merlot but she brought it to her lips.

"Try this imaginary experiment. Say you're a worker bee—you'll need a sex change for this."

"No problem."

"You're comfortable roaming half a kilometer from hive to flower. But you're a smart little bugger and know that going much farther means you'll burn more energy than you'll get from the nectar and pollen you find. You also have food preferences. Now really stretch your imagination and think of yourself as a bee that's forty years old. What's been happened to your meadow over your lifetime? I'll tell you. A lot of what you ate is now gone, done in by tractors and chemicals. And monstrously inedible weeds have taken their place."

"That's a downer."

"It is. The 2006-2007 period was so bad that beekeepers talked of total colony collapse. With so few wild bees, commercial production of almonds, apples, and blueberries came to depend on bee keepers trucking in hives of domestic bees. But now there isn't enough of those either. There's a mix of causes, Varroa mites, for one, but the key pathogen is a new family of agricultural pesticide, neonicotinoids. Europe banned them and stabilized their bee populations. The USA didn't. Even Vermont, which is a center of organic production, only imposed some use restrictions. So the bees keep disappearing."

"I see an army of lobbyists out there," said Ed. He'd have to quiz Bart's wife about which industries she represented.

"Not my area, but sure. Maybe psychologists can tell us why we can't see our own collective interest."

"Is this what you'll be talking about at the conference, the bee Armageddon?"

"Broadly speaking, yes. And I confess, I've been using you to rehearse. But my specific assignment is to tell the food industry they need to do what's necessary to keep pollinators alive. I'll be polite, but they need to see that it's in their own interest as well as ours. The boat we're all in is sinking fast."

"You want change around the edges or a paradigm shift?"

"I'm saying we can't treat crop production like a factory process."

"I take your point about bees. But at the same time, you can't deny we've ramped up the food supply. There's no Irish potato famines anymore. We must be doing something right."

"You can play devil's advocate but you can't erase the problem." She was suddenly tired, her ferocity spent.

"Welcome to the Titanic, eh?"

"With the iceberg just ahead." She stifled a yawn. "On that cheerful note, I need to leave and get some sleep." She pushed back from the table. "You know I do teach? But my students aren't generally as sophomoric. Still, you've made the time fly." She looked at her watch. "I did enjoy our evening, Edward Dekker."

"And it was great seeing you today, both times." He struggled to find his feet.

"Stay put," she said. "If they left the food cart in the hall, I'll bring it in and clear this up. That way you can sleep late." Within moments she'd loaded up the trolley with the plates and pushed it outside before returning.

"Keep the flower," he said. "Will I see you during the conference?"

"I hope so. I'm going to need supporters when I make my presentation." She hesitated, then leaned over and kissed his forehead. "Get well."

Chapter Six

THE MORNING BROKE CLOUDLESS, sunlight glittering off the icicles that draped his window. By nine-thirty he'd managed to shower, dress, and make his way to the lobby for something to eat. The reception area was crowded with well-dressed men and a few women, sleek and pink-cheeked from the outside cold. Silver-haired dignitaries pushed imperiously through the crowd, their attendants following along holding brief cases and overcoats while hotel staff pushed trucks of luggage. It was also old-home week. People greeted one another and laughed in small groups close to the huge stone hearth. Navigating the jostle with care, Ed made his way to a small restaurant, one of three the hotel provided. He grabbed a plate at the buffet bar and moved down the line. The room clattered with silverware and boomed with good humor, guests shouting out and slapping backs. Hooking his cane on his arm, he managed to steer his tray to a window table. He hoped the knee brace, black like his trousers, wasn't too conspicuous. This was not a crowd likely to sympathized with cripples. A waiter, circling with coffee flasks in each hand, filled his cup.

He slipped his scarred leather messenger bag from his shoulder and thought about the day ahead. The bag held his interview kit: a compact recorder no bigger than a cigarette pack, a cell phone, a digital camera for better quality photos, a notebook. He'd also packed research reports and news clippings useful in framing his questions. He made short work of eggs, sausage, and potatoes as he studied the day's agenda. Three cups of coffee later, he felt briefed on what lay ahead.

During the next few hours, he met with a pump specialist working in the Sahel region of North Africa, an area with a huge but diminishing aquifer. As much a salesman as a development consultant, the stout South African clearly was there to attract investors. Then he spent a half hour with the Greek minister of labor, a short, balding man in his sixties whose eyes looked as if they hadn't closed in a week. Yes, retrenchments in the public sector were continuing, the European Central Bank still deaf to human misery on the streets of Athens. Pensions? They'd have to be reduced again. "Can I interest you in the purchase of a small island?" the official said in a rare moment of humor. "But seriously, if the Germans don't ultimately see reason, it's going to be the World War Two occupation all over again."

"Including the resistance?" Ed asked.

"More like mass migration, I'm afraid."

Ed shuffled toward the main ballroom where the first plenary session was about to begin. By now his leg was seriously aching, and it was hard to keep a neutral face. If he could sit, he just might survive. Functionaries on either side of the entrance discreetly checked hangtags and nodded obsequiously. He was reminded of the staff at an Atlantic City casino, all hospitality until you ran out of credit. He flipped the tag on his lanyard so that his name and photo were visible. Embedded within it was a weird hologram and the image of a typewriter. Quaint. It marked him as a member of a subordinate caste. But not playing favorites, the receptionist at check-in had given him a folder bound in real leather containing the week's program and early press releases. Finding a seat at the back, he ran through what was there and noticed that large areas were left open. It seemed there was much he wasn't entitled to attend.

Punctuality was clearly subordinate to gregarious chit-chat. As sitting didn't seem to help his leg recover, Ed struggled to his feet and grabbed coffee and a cheese Danish from a nearby buffet table. Not that he was hungry; he wanted the red porcelain mug. It had the hotel's icon, a stag's head, printed in sliver. Finishing the coffee, he wiped the mug with his napkin and slipped it into his shoulder bag. He'd have to snag another to make a pair. Then again, Molly, Bart's young daughter, might like one. He'd have to nab three. He looked around but there was no sign of Aisling.

The speaker's lectern was on a low platform. The moderator, his head bald and sun-burnished, reflecting light from the chandeliers. He was talking casually with dignitaries seated at the elevated dais. Did the guy wax his pate? Eventually the moderator moved to the lectern and rapped on a crystal water glass with a pen. Two hundred conversations slowly subsided and stragglers found their seats. The reporters, self-segregated like Ed toward the back, took out notebooks.

"Let me welcome you to the second annual meeting of the Global Economic Directorate, what we are proud to say has become the premier forum for efforts to manage our shared burden. My name is Gunnar Sorenson and it is my pleasure to preside over this year's convocation. It is our conviction that most problems—from violations of human rights to eroding environmental quality—can be alleviated by market forces combined with enlightened economic management. While we seek ways to shore up the foundations of financial growth, our vision is broader. And so will be our discussions over the next four days. You will hear from many voices—experts from academia, government officials, and corporate leaders—as we seek consensus on both problems and solutions. Our conclusions will be directly communicated to the World Economic Forum and ministerial trade talks at the World Trade Organization."

Having stroked his audience, Sorenson continued. "To start our conversation, let me introduce our first speaker. A Nobel Laureate in Economics, he has done groundbreaking work on sovereign debt restructuring. Formerly an advisor to Presidents Clinton and George H. W. Bush, he is presently chief financial officer with the venture capital firm

Gilmore, Street, and Stone. In addition, he lectures at the London School of Economics, preparing the next generation of world finance specialists. Those of you with an interest in South Asia will know him from his most recent publication, *The Micro-Lending Miracle: Capitalism for the Poor.* Please welcome Dr. Norgood Bjorne."

Rail-thin, Bjorne was slightly stooped which lowered his six-and-a-half-foot height. He loped vigorously to the lectern and adjusted the microphone. Ed made a note: Victorian mortuary attendant, and put a tiny speaker into his ear to check the sound level on his recorder..

"My friends," Bjorne began. "Thank you for your kind invitation and for the chance to visit a place I haven't seen since college days. Then, trekking was a rite of passage for Scandinavian boys. While we conquered the peaks, our real hope was to meet and overcome the proverbial Tyrolean milkmaid." There was scattered laughter. Bjorne grinned and Ed noticed his teeth were yellow. Yes, an undertaker caste to type.

"The way to stay grounded in economic reality is to notice the landscape, the houses people build, the food they eat. Here that includes the brown Swiss cows that will groom these hillsides come spring. Herded, as we know, by a massive EU subsidy." Laughter rose again. "I say this to remind us that the test of economic policy is how it effects everyday life."

Ed made another note. Was this a lead-in for a story?

"Economists in their grandeur—may I say hauteur?—often overlook the cheese and chocolate. Once I was such an economist. Now my concern is to see how our ideas can enrich daily life. And there is no time to waste. The lives of ordinary people are becoming more difficult. Not just the two billion who scratch out existence on two dollars a day, but the one-in-four Europeans facing permanent unemployment.

"Yes, CAT scans are ubiquitous, the most remote regions of China have broadband, and skyscraper-cities dot the Arabian desert." He turned as if looking toward Abu Dhabi. "But we have more refugees than at any time in world history, many simply escaping economic stagnation. This despite our aid programs and bank bailouts. Yes, the economies of the global North and South are converging, but not as we'd hoped.

"It is the North that is approaching the South, not the reverse. Oh, not here." He looked around in an exaggerated manner. "But the rail yards and underpasses of Madrid and Paris have become the refuge of migrants from Africa and Southeast Asia. These are only the more visible of marginals. What of our own younger generation? They may not be living under bridges, but more than a quarter of them have university degrees they can never use. And this is after recovery from our most recent recession." He paused, filling a glass from a pitcher on the rostrum and taking a drink.

"The Greek economy contracted 3 percent in 2012, then again in 2013, 2014. It barely rose in the years since. Italy and Greece have sovereign debt burdens equal to 120 percent of their GDP, twice the debt load economists consider sustainable. Some say this is just Mediterranean malaise. Then what of France, where the situation is similar and, as we speak, protesters in their *gilets jaunes* are in the street? Or the United Kingdom, coping with economic contraction by reducing state support for health care and burning their bridge to Europe? Then there's the mighty United States, with a debt burden equal to 100 percent of GNP.

"When the masses last faced such a bleak reality, democracy collapsed into dictatorship. And dictators launched war economies fueled by oppression and pillage." He grinned. "And speaking as the descendant of Vikings, I understand pillage economics."

"Is the present century so different from the last? Are not parliaments allowing global mechanisms to hide private fortunes from tax collectors and allowing the European Central Bank and the IMF to wield the flail of austerity? Even those Parisian taxi drivers know austerity is less to restart growth than protect speculators in sovereign debt." He paused for effect.

Many in the audience had turned to side conversations, some slipping out of their seats to replenish their coffee. Oppositional chatter rose from a trickle to a noticeable stream. Bjorne ignored it.

"Our civic culture is unraveling. France deports the Roma, Italy closes its shores against migrants from North Africa, and Australia sends its refugees to appalling island camps. And the United States cowers behind its Great Mexican Wall.

"I offer no simple solution to such unraveling. But I know that we, the creditors in the global system, will have to compromise. Debt levels, individual and national, are unsustainable. It is magical thinking to count simply on economic growth." He delicately pounded the rostrum. "Where repayment is impossible, we must cancel sovereign debt."

Chairs scraped on the floor, throats were noisily cleared. The conversation in the hall rose above the sound of Bjorn's voice.

His long fingers wrapped around the edges of the lectern. "I know this is not welcome news. But at times, the correct medicine is bitter. I thank you all for your attention." As he stepped back, the applause was barely discernible.

"Are you telling us that an Athenian hair dresser should be able to retire with a full pension at age 50?" shouted a thick-necked man with a British accent. "Are we to give in to car-burners?" said another in French. While English was the lingua franca at such gatherings, this man was overwrought, likely due to his attachment to his Mercedes, Ed wrote.

With no way to address what were rhetorical questions, Bjorn lumbered from the stage, handing off the chaos to the moderator who closed the plenary with a wave of his hand.

Ed jotted down the more colorful audience comments, some beyond the reach of his digital recorder, and threaded his way out with the crowd. His leg now ached from inactivity.

Chapter Seven

VENDORS HAD SET UP exhibits in a secondary ballroom. Each promoted some service or system: fluids for hydro-fracturing shale oil deposits; chemical solvents to extract gold from low-yield ore. One booth announced, 'Municipal Water: a Public-Private Partnership'. Its flat screen contrasted a rusty tank-truck with *Para Uso Humano* on the side to a gleaming purification plant. Ed worked the aisles, collecting pamphlets and brochures. The UN table offered book-length academic studies. Most of this he'd leave in the waste bin of his hotel room but some might be grist for an article. He ignored the complementary pens but dipped into the free chocolate. Most booths were worked by a tag-team of attendants, often an attractive woman in boardroom attire shadowed by an older male in British tweed. Contingent academics, thought Ed, professors of English or French on break. Times are tough.

An agricultural display sponsored by a GMO trade association touted novel crops as the bulwark separating well-being from famine. The old Malthusian argument was alive and well, Ed noted. Our irrepressible urge to reproduce—depicted here as crowds of the dark-skinned and poorly-dressed—would draw the world down toward squalor or worse without scientific intervention. Climate change flooding the coastal fields and burning up the prairies just raised the stakes. But hope lay in genetically engineered crops. Resistant to drought or frost, able to poison insect pests, they could even deliver vitamin supplements to children.

Posters showed weathered hands holding seedlings and women in laboratory blue injecting plant tissue using gene guns.

Naturtek had a double booth. Their message was not just about seeds but the whole package: germ plasm plus fertilizer plus pesticides combined with soil-monitoring technology and custom harvesting machinery. Naturtek even offered weather forecasting and humidity monitoring from orbiting satellites. Those making the pitch for this company were women. While dressed in conservative skirt suits, their smiles were bright and their blouses only casually buttoned. Contrapuntally, the pamphlets they handed out were heavy with data. Their designer seeds had not one but a 'stack' of traits with all the qualities a farmer might need in a hostile environment. The subtext on elevated flat screens was the aesthetic of modernity—sterile laboratories and precise crop rows. No migrant pickers here. Like a panzer force invading Belgium, a phalanx of machines were shown injecting gaseous nitrogen into the soil followed by trucks rolling out plastic mulch. Then harvesting equipment turned it all into rivers of yellow kernels or green globules, filling hopper trucks. From lab to silo, all was precise and sweat-free.

Now it was after four, a break when participants could choose among several corporate-sponsored receptions. Ed studied the array. Which buffet would attract the more interesting crowd? And where would Aisling be? As a bee and butterfly person, she'd go with the 'Agro-Revolution Fiesta'. He gripped his cane and set off.

The seed and chemical companies had reserved the Alexander von Humboldt suite. Humboldt, he remembered, was the botanist who had mapped plants in the Peruvian Andes in the early 19th century. He'd brought the poinsettia to Europe, or so Ed learned in the second grade. The teacher had showed them that poinsettia petals were something of a fake, actually tarted up leaves attracting insects to the true if tiny flowers they surrounded. Only years later did he realize how genital-looking the female parts of this bi-sexual blossom were and wondered if his teacher hadn't been slyly salacious.

According to the map of the facilities, he'd have to take the north elevator. On the way he thumbed through an alphabetized list of conference participants and found 'O'Keefe'. He still couldn't reconcile the two images he had of her—his taciturn rescuer on the slopes and the evangelist for bugs she'd been last night. There on the page was the time and location of her session, tomorrow afternoon. She was part of a panel on plant pollination. He figured her angle would be why that pollination wasn't happening. Was she hunkered down in her room now, talking to her mirror? Or would she be mingling with the ag-chem bunch, sizing up the opposition?

A cluster of people spilled out from the Von Humboldt suite into the corridor. Peddling toxic sprays seemed no deterrent to cramming down shrimp from an open buffet. Or was it the free booze that drew the crowd? Ed shouldered his way inside and headed toward a credenza where a waiter poured hard liquor. Then, catching himself, he asked for seltzer with a slice of lemon. Moving carefully, he loaded a tiny plate and found space to lean against a window. He'd just finished off several bacon-filled truffles when he heard a cry of outrage and a glass shatter. A vortex opened in the milling crowd and there was Aisling, glaring. Dark liquid pooled at her feet.

"Touch my ass again and I'll brain you with the ice bucket," she shouted. There was nothing girlish in her tone. The offending party, a portly man of about fifty with one of those pink and fleshy faces that remained unchanged from high school backed out of range.

"Don't go all PMS on me," he snickered, and held up his hands as if she was rabid. Then he faded from sight. Show over, the crowd reclaimed their conversational circles. From the glances of several men, Ed gathered that Aisling's value as a trophy had just risen, but so had the risk. But for the moment, she was left an outcast hysteric. Ed hobbled over, glass crunching under his feet. A bartender arrived with a towel to mop up the mess.

"Just another Saturday night at the local," he said, scanning her face to see if she'd calmed down. He paused at a safe distance. At least she wasn't waving the stem of a broken wine goblet. "Hello, Aisling."

"It's red wine," she said, pointing to the spatter on her white blouse. "Did you think I'd stabbed him? Now this fucking blouse is ruined." She exhaled and brushed at her hip as if removing fingerprints. Her body was now sheathed in a black pencil skirt that flowed down to opaque stockings and three-inch heels. "Captains of finance, my foot. Frat boys with arrested development. I pity their secretaries." Then, connecting with his gaze, she smiled demurely and cleared her throat. "Would you mind getting me another merlot?"

She was Lauren Bacall with freckles. He lurched off toward the bar, pushing hard through the crowd. Moments later he was back with wine, a glass of soda, and a bar cloth.

"I forgot about your leg. I should have gotten that myself." She'd looked down at his knees. "How are you getting along?"

"Not bad. But I'm saving up my pain pills to sell on the street in case they hit me with the clinic bill." He wet the towel with soda and extended it to her. He'd caged it from the bartender. "Airline stewardesses say this works like magic. Can I give you a pat-down?"

"You too? Oh, I get it. You're still doing standup." She didn't sound amused. "But thanks for the thought."

He grinned. "Bloodied you may be, but your honor is intact."

"It's worse than taking the "T" to Downtown Crossing during rush hour. People think they can feel you up and if they don't catch your eye, it never happened." She watched his eyes for a moment. "But not you?"

"The thought never crossed me mind," His voice lilted with dialect again. "No offense meant; *bean álainn*."

"Oh, Jaysus!" She gave him a sidelong glance. "I'd guess that's all the Irish you know, right?

"Tending bar, you pick these things up."

By now she'd calmed down and led him over to the buffet table where she filled two small plates with shrimp and caviar on points of garlic toast and took him down the hall where they found two chairs. "I'm famished," she said, sliding one of the little sandwiches into her mouth and leaning forward to avoid crumbs falling on her blouse. "Where are my manners?" she added. He was still holding the drinks. She fed him a bit of shrimp from a toothpick, then took the damp cloth and tried to wipe down her blouse.

"It's hopeless," she said, giving up, "but I'll not be needing help, thank you." A smile played across her mouth. "Let me guess. From the state of your jacket,"—she plucked some loose threads from his lapel—"I'd say you're not new to living off an hors d'oeuvres table. At the odd wedding or funeral, maybe?"

"I prefer art gallery openings. What we call dumpster diving in SoHo. But don't let this outfit fool you. It's the fashion carelessness of old money."

"Seriously? I don't smell old money." She leaned into his shoulder and drew a breath, almost touching his cheek with the top of her head. "More like a musty library. Or a newspaper morgue. Do you people still have morgues? Or has it all gone soullessly digital?" She remained leaning toward him, holding her plate to the side. He wondered how much she'd been drinking.

"Or maybe it's dust from your last assignment in the Middle East. Either gunpowder or moth balls." She fingered the lapel. "At least no bullet holes."

"Did I mention that the secretaries at work say I remind them of Johnny Depp?"

"I'd have thought your fantasy self was more Sean Connery." She leaned a foot or two away and he resumed breathing.

He pointed to his jacket's patch pockets. "If I hadn't had to rescue you, I'd be loading up with cheese cubes and crackers."

She flared her nostrils. "You are a stray dog." In the softly-lit hallway, her lips were red-brown, her eyes smoky blue.

"So art openings are your hunting ground?"

"I'm realistic. I'm not creative enough to attract bohemian women and too ordinary for the collector crowd. So I drift in the middle latitudes, ignored but ready to pounce. While everyone else is talking prices, I get tomorrow's lunch."

"Not true. I think you have a serious thing for art." She sounded as if that was an affliction. He noticed a slight dip in the center of her upper lip, which he liked. "You see the world through paintings. Or is this just part of your charm offensive? Next you'll be saving the whales. Or the butterflies." The noise from the reception down the hall grew louder so they moved farther on to arm chairs placed to give a view of the town square.

"I'm glad you brought up your fragile friends. I didn't get the chance last night to tell you my butterfly story." He crossed an ankle on top of his bad knee and stifled a yelp before he could untangle his legs.

"It happened in Guatemala. I was researching an article on the collapse of coffee prices. Officially, Audubon International had paid me to work up a piece about over-wintering birds and the conditions they liked, but coffee was what caught my attention and I began looking around for other stories while I was there. The historic plantations, for example, were being deserted. Just as had happened in the late '90s, coffee prices had collapsed again and land owners were letting the coffee cherries rot on the trees. For the poor, work had dried up. Back in the 1980s, President Reagan had blown up the international pricing system and since then, speculators on the New York coffee exchange had been bouncing the futures market like a basketball. Up, down, then below the cost of production. Even subsistence farmers were hardly bothering to ship out a bag or two a season. And with the plantations deserted, no one was caring for the trees so pathogens flourished. Then came *broca*."

"Broka?"

"The coffee worm. That and a mold-like coffee leaf rust called Roya became a double whammy for anyone trying to stay in the game."

"I don't understand. Isn't world demand constant?"

"More or less. Coffee drinkers don't easily switch to tea. But production was up world-wide, thanks to USAID and the IMF. They'd given cheap loans to peasants in Vietnam and Indonesia to encourage them to enter the coffee trade and beat down prices in Columbia. At the same time, Brazil was expanding their low-grade, full-sun plantations. So Maxwell House didn't need the expensive mountain varieties, the arabicas."

"You're saying that development agencies deliberately glutted the world market?"

"Evil or ignorance, it amounts to the same thing."

"Wait, wait, wait. I don't want to sound callous but I drink coffee. Didn't I benefit?"

"Sorry, no. Like the rest of America since the 1930s when the big roasters merged, you've been weaned on substandard beans. And the reduced costs never made it to Joe's diner."

"You're saying those urns at Joe's were full of crap?"

"Were; are, I'm afraid so. And left to simmer for hours didn't help, either. Anyway, I'd been wandering around the backcountry, poking into haciendas that German immigrants had established a hundred years earlier. Feudal places, but now often deserted. I'd walk up a grassed-over road and past an empty gate house and there would be a mansion, dark and sagging. Sometimes a caretaker was around, maybe an aged aunt. But the *padrón* was long-gone to Madrid and the jungle was reclaiming rows of unpruned coffee trees.

Ed paused. "It wasn't all bad. The vacuum in the supply of premium coffee created a market for small farmers able to bundle their crop through cooperative marketing systems. But that's another story."

"And this has what to do with butterflies?"

"Ah, well. So there I was, poking through derelict coffee estates and empty *beneficios,* the processing plants once stacked with 100 pound sacks of raw beans, when one evening I'm sitting at a patio table outside a restaurant in a small village. I was doodling on my laptop, tweaking a story about misguided economic 'development' to send back to New York. I'd been on the road for weeks, feeling rundown and itching from bed bugs."

"Delightful."

"Across the dirt road was a tree-shaded plaza, what you find in most of these towns." He drew in the air with his hands. "If it had been a holiday there'd have been a band playing but that night, just a few couples strolled around under a string of paper flags left over from *Dia de los Muertos.*"

"Day of the Dead. I know."

"It's late November, the rains gone and grass in the plaza is brittle-dry. I'm on my third coffee, in no hurry to get back to a moldy mattress when a breeze moves through the square. One tree then another starts swaying. Dust devils spiral up from the street, chasing plastic bags. A few streetlights on the plaza blink on but they just make everything surrounding them darker. Suddenly the air is filled with these winged things. First, I'm thinking bats, and tense up to duck. Maybe some were bats but then this critter lands next to my coffee cup and I see it's a huge moth. It's mottled and the color of tree bark. Its wingspan is as wide as my hand." Ed splays out his fingers. "It's there on the table, kind of leaning over, and looking like a flattened sparrow. I'm thinking this guy is in distress. Then it crawls to the edge of the table and falls to the ground and I see the sidewalk is covered with these moths. Some are crawling, some making it to takeoff, others waving their wings as if they were breathing. It was spooky."

After a moment she said, "What you saw was the black witch, one of the few migrating moths. They're found in tropics from Brazil to Texas. Males can have as much as a seven inch wing span so they are definitely spectacular, in size if not color. They breed year 'round, but it sounds like you caught the end of a generational cycle. This usually happens in the fall, around Todos Santos. Or as you noticed from the flags, *Dia de los Muertos*. Maybe for that reason, they're considered evidence of the deceased returning from the underworld to visit their living relatives."

"I don't know about that, but yes, I felt I was bumping up against another world."

"The actual Day of the Dead is happy, if subdued," she went on. "But as you weren't seeing the crowds and piles of flowers from the day itself, I can understand why the moths would seem eerie. Their adult life is only three or four weeks. At that stage they travel, no one is sure how far. They're searching for acacia or mesquite to lay their eggs. When that job is done, they die. In the process they become food for bats and birds. Locals call them the 'Butterfly of Death,' *mariposa de la muerte*."

"They were like living leaves floating down all around me."

"Falling from life into death." She finished his thought.

"It made me think the whole town was spectral."

"They're harmless, to both people and crops. But because they're active nocturnally, mythology associates them with death. The Maya believe that if one enters your house—and this happens a lot because they're looking for places to rest during the day—and touches the four corners of a room, one after the other—anyone sleeping there will die."

She rested her chin on her open hand, looking at him. "It's folk religion, a mezcla of Catholicism and earlier ideas. But you shouldn't think of the *miraposa* as a curse. When it touches the four cardinal points—reflecting the cosmos—it's centering the soul of people nearby, helping them on their final journey."

"Good to know my fate wasn't sealed."

"Not to worry." She gave him a fortune-teller look. "But for the locals, death and life are in a close relationship."

"So, you know this culture?"

"I'm no anthropologist. But in my field, you need to understand how humans and insects live together."

"It was like being caught between two dimensions. Moths with battered wings trying to take flight, then smashing into walls and falling to the ground. Others, perfectly intact but motionless, as if they welcomed death."

"The *mariposa de la muerta* are pretty common but seeing a mass death is unusual. I'm jealous. But I'm glad you were there and could tell me about it. Now you can understand my passion for these guys."

"I can." He shook away the memory. "Let's get out of here."

They took the elevator to the lobby, Aisling explaining that she was working on her presentation for the next day so she had to skip the formal dinner. "Thank God for those shrimp," she said. "If I'm hungry later, I'll grab something from one of the restaurants." She brushed his cheek with the back of her hand and lightly touched his mouth with her lips. Then disappeared.

Chapter Eight

TABLES FOR EIGHT SET for the banquet now dotted the ballroom. They glittered with silverware and wine glasses. An usher checked Ed's tag and steered him to the press section. So much for eavesdropping on the table-talk of the finance ministers.

His table gradually filled. To his right was a reporter for the UK's *Guardian* newspaper, a balding, academic type, his mouth lost in an untrimmed mustache. On Ed's left sat a sharp-nosed woman from *The Australian* who introduced herself as Charlotte Cooper. "It's Australia's national newspaper," she said, like your *Toronto Globe and Mail,*" She'd pegged Ed as Canadian and he didn't bother correcting her. Anglosphere comrades, all. Explosions of boisterous laughter erupted across the hall. That and the buzz of a few hundred voices made it difficult to hear beyond his own table. While the press weren't the last to get the attention of the circulating waiters, they were well down in the queue.

Between mouthfuls of grilled salmon he apparently swallowed with-out chewing, the *Guardian* correspondent kicked things off. Sovereign debt across southern Europe was apocalyptic, he declared. In Greece it had reached 175 percent of GNP. Such a government had to fall. And with the Brexit fiasco, Europe too was about to fragment. It was all the fault of that sadist, Angela Merkel. "She wants nothing less than a hun-dred pence on the pound for bond holders. And who the hell won the war, I ask!"

The Englishman choked on his food, allowing the Aussie to move into the breech. "Quite wrong," she said. "It's all the fault of the 'PIGS' themselves."

Ed counted off in his head: Portugal, Italy, Greece, Spain. Or was the for 'I' Ireland?

Then Ms. Cooper glowed over the budget cuts her country's conservative government had 'courageously' made, while putting coal exports into overdrive. She gave Ed a conspiratorial wink, taking for granted his equal passion for the production of fossil fuels and that Ed was at least a Trudeau Liberal. To seal their alliance, she rubbed her knee against his leg.

Not only was the antipode flourishing, she explained, it was encouraging immigration. "Not boatloads of riffraff, but solid European stock. If Greece itself was failing, Greeks are doing very well in Sydney, thank you very much." Ed pictured streets lined with coffee shops, their patrons holding blue paper cups with the Greek design. And café proprietors working ninety hours a week.

Ed smiled complicitly. Hadn't the US followed Canada's lead in creating a visa category for millionaire investors?

"Of course, unlike Europe," Charlotte continued, "we have a happy relationship with China," she explained to a table of faces bent studiously over their plates. "They love our wheat, our iron, our coal."

Ed imagined her as a dancer in "Cabaret", her face bleached white by the footlights.

"I'm not revealing any secrets here when I say that our off-shore oil deposits will prove substantial. They'll come into production just as the Saudi wells are sucking up mud." She pursed her lips, mimicking the sound of a straw in an empty milkshake.

"You say 'our oil' but don't you mean East Timor's?" said the *Guardian* correspondent, using his napkin to wipe his mustache while reaching for his flan.

"There'll be a partnership, but the bulk of the reserves are well within

Australia's territorial waters. And we have the capital to get them out." She folded her arms and challenged him. "Would you hand over the gas fields off the Falklands to Argentina?"

Just to provoke her, Ed made a thrust. "Aren't you assuming we'll never get to a global tax on carbon? With your 'outback', as you call it, on fire, isn't the financial advantage shifting to solar collectors?"

"Oh, you are naughty!" Her leg moved up and down against his. "The serious people won't be restricting carbon use. And leave trillions in assets underground? My dear boy." She coyly shook her fork at Ed.

"Stranded assets," counterpunched the *Guardian* reporter. He looked around the table for support, or perhaps an untouched flan. "It's happened before. Aren't they fumigating fields of perfectly marketable Colombian cocaine?"

"Either way, we win," Charlotte continued. "Name another continent with more potential solar capacity than Australia. Our energy costs are below the rest of the world's and we'll still be shipping coal to China. God bless the Queen, my boy, but your day in the sun is long past."

Ed's mind wandered. He didn't feel moved to defend Exxon-Mobile. Was he surrounded by national cheerleaders? As he refocused, Cooper was still holding court, now on the challenge of learning Chinese from CDs, "Thank God for air travel," she said.

Just then the rapping of a knife on glass drew their attention to the dais. A man with a sheen on his cheeks announced the evening program: 'Global Assets and National Tax Policies: A Collision Course?' He then introduced the dinner speaker, an American economist from Harvard's Kennedy School. After Ed took a few notes, it became clear that the speaker was bent on a rather crude denunciation of any global tax on financial transactions, something the British Labor Party had proposed before they lost the last election. His passion ignited a buzz of harmonic resonance; the crowd was in his pocket.

Ed went through some reportorial gestures, writing down a few quotes for his daily update on the proceedings. As a second speaker was introduced, Ed mumbled apologies to his table mates and limped off to his room, much to Ms. Cooper's obvious disappointment.

Chapter Nine

WITH THE HELP OF mineral water and an icepack, Ed hammered out copy. This would be an atmospheric piece describing the isolated locale, the self-satisfaction of the participants. The measure of the latter was their view on debt relief. Bank heads and hedge fund mavens, he'd learned, were unanimous in rejecting 'haircuts' for investors in government securities. There would be no sharing the pain. Norgood Bjorne's warning was entirely lost. With the example of the Trump administration's pathetic response to the Puerto Rico hurricane, it was clear that the U.S. was in synch with the Europeans. Ed decided to tell it like it is and let the re-write scribes in editorial tone it down.

The encryption program built into his laptop flashed its operational status and Ed sent off his article. Looking at the 'sent' message, he wondered again about transmission security. While he had the assurances of the paper's tech office, Bart was more credible. Nothing was hack-proof. Hadn't Edward Snowdon told the world that the NSA monitored everything? Not to mention Google. He typed in a new address and sent a second copy to a different state-side server, something Bart had helped him set up years ago. Until now he'd never used it. Then he copied his file to a zip drive and wiped his laptop memory.

At nine the next morning he was waiting in the Naturtek suite for his interview with their representative. Unlike most of the corporate faces here, this guy was an actual scientist, a bio-engineer working in agriculture. Naturtek had a spacious suite. There were no lab coats in the welcome area but the atmosphere was still one of sterile intensity. The receptionist, a chunky woman sporting grey hair in a bun and with half-glasses hanging from her neck, switched her gaze from his identification to his face. If he'd expected friendliness, he was mistaken. Checking the time, she led him to an inner room.

"Our director of crop research is not presently on-site," she explained without turning around. "However, Dr. Gabriel Hammersmith is a senior investigator on several of our projects and can respond to your questions."

"'Respond', he noted. Not answer.

Hammersmith seemed to know he was a sacrificial lamb, a guy dragged from his lab to placate investors or, in this case, to confound the press. He'd barricaded himself behind a pile of reports and his pencil was flying over what he continued to read. Ed wasn't close enough to see the title. Hammersmith's round glasses, sharp nose, and brown tweed jacket gave him an owlish appearance.

After an awkward delay, the scientist glanced up and motioned for Ed to sit. Then he returned to his reading. He was either making a statement or very focused. Ed looked around. The room, a generic office space, was stripped down to the essentials. Temporary shelving held boxes of glossy reports and press releases. Half-drawn drapes obscured a view of the mountains. A double-screen computer array idled on Hammersmith's desk, faced well away from Ed's sightline.

Hammersmith could have been forty years old, or sixty. His shoulders were slumped, his face pallid, and his bare head ringed with grey brush. Every so often he mouthed what could have been Latin terms. Ed had the impression of a monk bent over his copy-book.

After two long minutes—Ed knew because he'd glanced at his watch—Hammersmith set his reading aside and asked Ed what he wanted. He didn't offer his hand.

"I'm told you are the press. Before we begin, you should know that I am not accustomed to dealing with journalists. We have public relations people in St. Louis for that. I'm a scientist. Why I'm told to give interviews here in," his arm made a circle, "the North Pole, I do not know."

"I understand," said Ed. "I'll be as concise as possible."

"This is not my element." Hammersmith sighed.

Still, something of a closet showman, thought Ed.

"But enough about my problems. What do you want to know?" The researcher's teeth were like old ivory.

"I'm with New York's *Business Chronicle* and we're very interested in breakthroughs in the area of plant genetics, particularly food crops." Ed leaned forward and laid his business card on the desk.

"I appreciate your time, Doctor, so I'll be brief. Rumors are circulating about advances in genetic engineering applied to an expanding list of crop varieties. While this would be scientifically interesting to the general public, our readers are more specialized. They are looking for investment opportunities, 'the next big thing', as it were." Ed gave an ingratiating smile. "What can you tell me about innovations in the crop sector that would appeal to venture capitalists?" Ed decided to skip the pursuit-of-knowledge line. This event was all about money.

"Innovations in the crop sector?" Hammersmith chewed on the idea and on the inside of his cheek. "I am, of course, not a flogger of stock. Still, I am authorized to say that Naturtek is pursuing a number of promising avenues." Ed scribbled in his notebook, 'corporate script.'

"As it happens, the more fundamental of these innovations arise from my own work. And that of my colleagues." Hammersmith was rising to the bait. "The corporate reach at Naturtek extends to pharmaceuticals, which I don't touch." Hammersmith shook imaginary contamination from his fingers. "Also, there's fuels and fibers—coaxing hydrocarbons and paper pulp from bio-mass through genetic manipulation. An interesting area, but not to me. And, as you say, you're here about food." He cleared his throat.

"Crop improvements stand at the end of a chain of interactions beginning with research and ending with commercial feasibility. I only do the research step but, as I say, my work is germinal." He rolled the pun around in his mouth. "It's all about the seed."

Ed smiled with appreciation while Hammersmith settled back in his chair.

"In the middle of the last century, certain philosophers insisted that God was dead. The task of modern humanity became filling that void, crafting ourselves and society according to our own design."

Ed's attention sharpened. If this was a script, it wasn't coming from company public relations."

"Well, I don't want to bore you with Nietzsche and Sartre, but I can assure you that in a similar sense, nature is dead." He paused to let Ed absorb this.

"I shock you? What I mean is that the framework of natural limitations that have constrained humans from the beginning, what I call the environmental absolutes, no longer exist. Poof!" He exploded his fingers. "For the timid, this is scary. But for those among us who can create the environment anew, it is emancipating." His eyes traced an invisible horizon of possibilities.

"At the beginning of human time, we were rude foragers, opportunists digging grubs from rotten logs and jumping for the lowest hanging fruit. All the while, of course, trying not to become fruit for others." He grinned. "Why the morphology of our hands and arms, after all, if not to bring things to our mouths?" He demonstrated. "And we have legs, of course, comprising nearly half our body weight. They're useful both for chasing down prey and running to save our own lives."

Half-baked philosophy could be a dangerous thing, thought Ed, especially in a natural scientist.

"Then, having developed agriculture, we brought recorded history into being. We could now grow the fruit we wanted, raise as livestock what we once hunted. All this was followed by clockwork looms and the whole mechanized apparatus of industry. This led to the chemical revolution, allowing us to peer inside material things. At each point we modified the environment, bent it to our will." Hammersmith used one hand to grasp and bend down the other.

"Oh, I see what you are thinking. What about the downside? Let us be honest. Our creativity released a flood of toxins. Lead-based paints and gasoline additives alone have probably depressed our collective IQ by ten percent. Then there's the radiation from power plant effluent and bomb tests. Coming up to the present, we find that the natural systems within which we evolved—soil microbes, the wild populations of the land and sea, are collapsing. Extinctions abound. What to do?"

"Our problems are not trivial. The systems that make nutrition available to us and allow us to dispose of civilization's waste are fragmenting. These are what economists call 'natural services', essential to life, but breaking down. Like the residents of smog-filled Beijing, we soon may all be wearing surgical masks." He gestured toward the valley. "Bit by bit, the Europe of chocolate, cheese, and brown cows is dying. Yesterday we faced Chernobyl; today it's Fukushima."

Ed jotted down notes, what Hammersmith certainly expected, but it wasn't necessary. The light on his recorder, angled in his shoulder bag, was on.

"Then there's the geometric increase in the human population. Notice I said geometric, not arithmetic. As it accelerates, it generates ever-more toxicity, even as it consumes a finite store of resources. Until," here Hammersmith snapped his fingers, "there goes the biosphere. Wherever you look, our natural systems are overwhelmed. You've heard of the 350 Movement, I'm sure. In 2007, James Hansen of the Goddard Institute published a paper saying that more than 350 parts per million of carbon dioxide in the atmosphere would destroy the climate as we know it. Now we've breached the 415 level. T.S. Elliot was wrong. Instead of the world ending with a whimper, there'll be a bang, a stupendous weather event."

Hammersmith paused. "Yeats was closer to the truth. 'Things fall apart, the center cannot hold; Mere anarchy is loosed upon the world.'" Ed again checked the green light on his tape recorder. If Hammersmith was unhinged, that in itself was grist for a story.

"But just in time," and here Hammersmith's eyebrows and pointer finger rose together, "humans found the solution: synthetic nature. Let me repeat; synthetic nature. We're not there yet. But if we can map, slice, and recombine DNA sequences, we can build a substitute environment to serve our needs. Yes, as the journalist Elizabeth Kolbert has so eloquently put it, we are in the midst of a 'sixth extinction.' But that's no reason to despair. The new plants and animals we need are on the way. They will be robust, bespoke, as it were, suited to our purposes and tolerant of our environmental mistakes." He opened his hands. "The solution is in our grasp."

"So, the world that evolved over the last five billion years, we can do without it?" Ed asked.

"No, of course not. We need a place to stand. And that is the inventory of fauna and flora that now exists." Hammersmith chuckled, banging his feet on the floor. "They are our building blocks, their DNA the legos for new creatures. We'll never reproduce that range of amino acids from their chemical elements. We need nature's storehouse. But why accept the existing architecture?" An inner glow lit Hammersmith's otherwise pallid complexion. "And we have such a DNA warehouse."

Hammersmith was now tapping on his desk with the eraser end of a pencil, marching ahead with each point. "Out of this inventory we can engineer our own environment. And, I might add, our destiny."

The researcher caught his breath. "If I weren't working for Naturtek, I'd be with NASA developing the synthetic food systems we'll need for space travel. There is your metaphor. "He pointed upward with his pencil. "Humans in space will carry their environmental components. Here on earth we'll do the same, creating worlds *de novo*."

Buck Rogers with a gene gun, Ed thought. This interview was sliding toward a case study in mental illness. How much does Hammersmith represent Naturtek? "But if nature is collapsing around us, surely that means our Walmart of organisms, our raw materials, is also disappearing."

"Try to keep up. By the end of the twentieth century, natural systems were crumbling. We'd hit the wall of sustainability. But we'd also discovered the tools to manufacture what we need, including our food. True, we require the raw material of the past. But even if the earth becomes a rubbish-strewn parking lot, we have that inventory." Hammersmith's eyes sparkled.

"You've lost me."

"Where did you say you went to college? In the 19th century we created 'zoos' to house exotic animals that tickled our curiosity, just as they were disappearing from the wild. We did the same with plants. Each center of empire—London, Brussels, Paris—had a plant research station for improving commercially-valuable varieties: tea, bananas, rubber. The imperial powers took them from one colony to another. At the end of the Second World War, research demanded something new: seed repositories. The seeds of every flowering plant in the British Isles are now tucked away in the Millennium Seed Bank at Kew Gardens. Fifteen such research stations—the CGIAR consortium—the Consultative Group on International Agricultural Research—now archives wild and domestic seeds. That's your Walmart for DNA, They're plant cowboys rounding up every known edible species. Now there's a World Fish Research Center as well."

None of this was new to Ed, but the argument was. Why bother with species conservation if you've got them all freeze dried?

"The crown jewel in this system, for plants at least, is the Svalbard Global Seed Vault. It's safely out of reach on a Norwegian island above the Arctic Circle. They call it the "Doomsday Vault." It's a genetic Library of Congress. Ultimately it will contain all cultivated food plants and their wild relatives. Ongoing species extinction just means we have to pick up the pace."

"So, no worries about rising sea levels?" Ed interjected.

"Not at Svalbard. Or pillaging hoards of the displaced. Whatever happens—and the transition won't be pretty—we scientists will have what we need to build the food humanity requires. This is more important than even the first agricultural revolution. Now you can see why I said the natural world we once knew is dead. Our future lies with synthetic nature."

Ed was visibly stunned.

"Look," Hammersmith continued. "We both know that the trillions of tons of carbon left in the earth will be burned. That's the way markets work." Ed recalled the words of the Australian journalist from last night. "Do you expect Exxon-Mobile to abandon their bank account? And that's what petroleum deposits are. The climate will degrade," the scientist continued, "and unless they're in a zoo, most critters will be roadkill. But on the bright side, we will have become architects of our own destiny."

"Excuse me if I'm not exactly dazzled."

"Would you prefer to live in a cave when you could have a house of your own design?"

Ed gathered his thoughts. "You say science will have access to this library of DNA. Don't you mean a handful of corporations?"

"Well, research needs funding and funders need incentives. But who can deny the social benefits?"

"Which would be the demand side of the equation?"

"Exactly," said Hammersmith. His pencil was now a baton, moving to silent music. "Your phone, your automobile, these are discretionary. But food? Given a choice, people will not go hungry. I don't mean just securing the necessary calories. They want what's tasty and attractive. I'm creating a menu for the restaurant at the end of the universe."

Hammersmith slumped back in his chair. Maybe you had to be a true believer to get through years of experimental failures. There was definitely a story here.

"That's interesting background," said Ed, "but can you be specific? Readers want to know what crops you're now enhancing, and how. What's the timeline for their commercial application? And what about costs?"

"We now have effective solutions for a wide range of insect infestations. We've spliced *Bacillus thuringiensis,* or Bt, into cotton, maize, soy, canola, and potatoes, among other plants. These plants have also been made impervious to the herbicides we use to control weeds. We're making advances in systemic resistance to the fungi and molds that devastate, say, strawberries. We can combine these enhancements with those that impart environmental rigor— drought tolerance and salinity resistance. Theoretically, there is no limit to the re-design of plants. We even have apples that don't turn brown when you slice them open. But it's not all strawberries and cream, so to speak." Hammersmith paused to enjoy the image. "Genes interact in unexpected ways, so we must proceed carefully. Sometimes we find our bells and whistles have come at the cost of plant vitality. You remember the first generation of cloned animals, Dolly the sheep? They were sickly creatures. Then there's taste and nutrition to consider."

"Assume you can work this out. There's still the bill," said Ed. "Won't the cost of new crops put them out of reach? There's billions of peasants who sow their micro-farms with saved seed. Can they afford your miracle plants?"

"Let's be frank. There's no place for peasants in the world that's coming into being. They are inefficient, too dependent on physical labor. Historically speaking, they've had their day. Innovative farmers will always purchase attractive inputs, whether from John Deere or us. Seeds are just another input. If they enhance market value beyond their cost, they're a good investment."

Ed toyed with his doubts. Still, the point was to get something concrete and Hammersmith hadn't given that up. "So, what should investors look for?"

"Can't tell you." Hammersmith set his lips together.

"You don't know?"

"Of course I know. I do the research. But I'm not going to tell you what's on our drawing boards. You're asking for proprietary information."

"Can you speak in general terms?" Ed prompted.

"Not beyond what I've said." Hammersmith shuffled the papers on his desk. Ed had shown himself to be an unworthy student; the interview was over.

"Well, a final line of inquiry, if I might. We know that the 'green' and the 'gene' revolutions were predicated on cheap petroleum to run equipment, produce fertilizers, and stock the shelves."

"With all those frozen dinners."

"Exactly. But a few years ago, oil hit 150 dollars a barrel. Doesn't a high price indicate scarcity, and won't this bring an energy-intensive food system to a halt?"

"You are talking about peak oil? In a word, no."

"I don't follow."

"There's more petroleum and natural gas than anyone thought existed just a few years ago. Now the Arctic is coming on line. There's 5 billion barrels under the South China Sea. Oil won't be a limiting factor for a long while and when it is, we'll have a work-around. And your numbers are way off. This week oil is closer to 40 dollars a barrel."

Hammersmith could slip from poetry to geo-politics.

"You're surprised?" Hammersmith asked? "'Peak oil' was always just a marketing slogan. As science, it was crap, which proves my point. Just as the technology of petroleum extraction has outstripped demand, innovation will do the same for crops. Count on it." Hammersmith got to his feet.

Taking pamphlets and reports from several shelves and boxes, he handed a stack to Ed. "These will answer your question on the energy demands of agriculture. We are making our crops efficient users of every input, including oil. I foresee a day when tractors pass over a field just once to plant and a second time to harvest. That's it. Genetics will take care of the rest." He passed his hand over the desk as if it were a field. Now, on your way."

Ed scribbled down a last note. This would work. Not the specifics but Hammersmith's 'big picture', his prediction that science would solve what politics couldn't.

"Remember, the bottom line," said Hammersmith as he ushered Ed out of his office. "People have to eat."

At the same moment the receptionist appeared. Ed wondered if she'd been just outside the whole time. She announced the scientist's next appointment was here and Ed found himself standing in the corridor.

Chapter Ten

It was past noon. Aisling's panel was at 2 pm. Using a house phone in the lobby, Ed called her room but was sent to voice mail. As he started a message, she picked up.

"I thought it might be you. I've been ignoring most everything—the other panels, TV news, even phone calls—while I beat this talk into submission. Now I need a break." She sighed.

"Having any luck?"

"Too much luck. Ten pounds of potatoes in a five-pound bag, as we say in *tha ol' sod*. Each panelist has twenty minutes to sell their idea. The moderator holds a stop watch and the audience is easily bored."

"So many ideas, so little time. And the *ol' sod* being Boston?"

"Yes, or the far west of Ireland, as we think of it. Forget your vampire stories about boxes of Romanian earth. We Irish can't sleep without the thought of home, or at least its taste in a glass. But seriously, what have you been doing?"

"Why don't I tell you over lunch? Meet me in that café off the south end of the lobby, *Die drei Mädchen*. It has a great view of the valley."

"All right. I need to get into my party threads. Give me fifteen."

"I'll snag a table."

The restaurant was crowded, but after ten minutes he was led to a table just cleared near the front window. Sunlight poured down from the mountains and the snow glittered. The village was a confection. After being inside all morning, Ed was restless. But with the knee, he didn't trust himself to walk on an icy sidewalk. At that moment the sun slipped behind lead-like clouds and the day darkened. Where had those clouds come from? he wondered. Fresh snow from last night lined the window sill and swirled up in gusts. The fireplace on the far side was reassuring.

He was fending off the waiter for the second time, a thin undergraduate-type in a black vest, when Aisling dropped into the opposite chair.

"Am I late? I had to dry my hair." Strands that were wiry on the slope were now electric, clawing at a beige hair ribbon. A copper aurora framed her face. Ed drew in his breath.

"I just sat down."

"Why so surprised?"

"Here it's the dead of winter and you're warming the room."

She blushed slightly but seemed calm for someone about to go on stage. Her blouse was silk, teal under a brown linen jacket. Other than a touch of blue on her eye lids, she had no visible make-up. Her lips were naturally pink.

"If the sun was still out, you'd burst into flame."

She laid a hand on his arm. "Steady, boy. I can see you're easily distracted. Either ADHD or," she looked around, "the restaurant decor." On the opposite wall three zaftig girls ran across a field of alpine flowers, their hair blowing in the breeze. "Which *Madchen* were you ogling?" It was back to conversational tennis and she easily moved him around the court.

"I know," she promoted. "The blond about to bounce her treats out of her dirndl."

Ed tried to focus on the menu. "Actually, I go more for the slender types. And what would the two of us talk about?"

"Edelweiss? Primroses? Judging from the setting." She scrutinized the mural. "I think I see some monkshood. They're quite poisonous, you know. When a lover proves untrue, these girls could really push back."

"Oops! I'm out of my depth again with flower talk. But be assured, my dream girl is very different — the wench in Schubert's *Röslein auf der Heiden*. But as this conference drags on, I'm beginning to settle for *Der Tod und das Mädchen*."

"I don't know the *Röslein* but I love the second piece," she said softly. "Ever since high school. Not that I understood it back then. Or now. But youth encountering death as something inevitable, there's frisson there." She feigned a shiver. "Do you think Schubert was a tortured soul?"

"So they say. He seemed to know that happiness is ephemeral, something you can't bottle up."

"You're sensitive for a newsy," she said, raising a pale eyebrow. "Of course, the thing about music is that it can be repeated, am I right? How many times have you heard *Death and the Maiden*?"

"Not enough. But it's never the same." Each time I bring to it a different mood. One time happy, another lonely. How a person feels colors the experience."

"I guess. Who can recreate, say, a first kiss?" She mercilessly touched her upper lip with her tongue. "Do you think of Schubert as a philosopher?"

"As in, what is the meaning of life? I suppose. But here you are, a student of flowers. You must know everything there is about what's transient."

"Flowers seem fragile, but considered in evolutionary terms, they're ruthless. Not to be girlie, but they're just a party dress. They come in countless styles, but each one gets the job done. Then the plant dumps them. If it's a day lily, last night's gown is gone by morning and the plant moves on to the business of generating a seed. At other times, a plant will hang on to brown and wrinkled petals for a few days, like the memory of something lost."

"Nice image." He wasn't unaware that she'd changed her own outfit from yesterday's.

"So maybe the impact of a Schubert piece comes after it's over."

"And before," he continued. "There's the anticipation."

"So, you'd have the maiden thinking, what will I lose when I meet with death? I have to say, though, flowers are more level-headed. Then of course there's the bee. She's the ultimate realist."

Just then the waiter appeared and took their orders, leaving three types of *brotchen* in a napkin-wrapped basket with a mini-tub of herbal butter. They dug in.

"Are you ready for the big time?"

"Hardly, but another day wouldn't make a difference. I have to sum up a lot of research, not just my own, and it's a moving target. I've written 'Draft, not for quotation' on my handout to give me wiggle room. They didn't pay me enough to write a publishable report, after all. The funders just want a hint of science, a little mud tracked in from the research field." She snagged the last piece of bread. "Your riff on flowers made me think of something."

"My riff? It was yours."

"Whatever. Brazilians say some people can't reconcile themselves to happiness. They don't trust it. The line goes, 'I'd rather eat the bee than taste the honey.'"

"Are you describing me?"

"I wouldn't presume to with a near-stranger." She widened her eyes. "Just a random thought."

"Or are you talking about yourself? In my experience, such chronic mistrust comes from disappointed idealism. Did you have a painful childhood?"

"No, my childhood was fine. No orphanage, no selling matches on the street. I had two wonderful brothers who protected me all through high school, almost as if I were a princess. Of course, I didn't deserve it, but hey, it's easy to take things for granted." She lifted her head regally.

"Not that we were rich. We lived on the top floor of a Boston triple-decker. My father cut grass for the city in the summer and drove a snowplow in the winter, a man for all seasons. But he was laid up a lot, one illness or injury after another. Mum was a nurses' aide, so that was handy, but it didn't bring in a great pay packet. So as far back as I can remember, I worked: babysitting, cleaning people's houses, work-study in college. If I wanted books or clothes, I earned them. Summers, I wait-ressed at a local diner, not at a fancy place like this." She looked around in mock awe. "Just a neighborhood spot where I'd set down coffee and a donut and expect a quarter tip."

"You were tough on that mountainside. I was thinking you were state-raised."

"State-raised? I love it. Such fake toughness. No, I was the first in my family to go to college. I wasn't sure if I was acting out my parent's dream or my own. Probably both. Graduate school got me further away. My brother Dave is actually the smart one, but he got into construction out of high school and couldn't give up the money. The younger one—they're both older than I am—is Raymond. Always "Raymond," never 'Ray'. He works for the Mass Bay Transit Authority, originally as an electrician fixing the trains, now as a supervisor in one of the power stations. My whole family is solid, except maybe me."

"I see you with two feet on the ground," he said.

"I always feared settling into a predictable groove. You know, becom-ing a secretary, marrying a fireman."

"But you didn't."

"No; too restless."

"Driven, perhaps?"

"'Driven' sounds ugly. But maybe. For whatever reason, my family picked me to be the one to keep climbing." She looked into the bread basket but it remained empty. "Then again, the neighborhood was sketchy. It was the Irish against the Italians. Or both against the Puerto Ricans. Girls had a choice. Be smart or be pretty. I wasn't pretty."

"I'm supposed to rise to that bait?"

"I'm serious. They called me 'Raggedy Ann', my hair sticking out every which way." She brushed the sides of her head with her fingers.

Having thought the same thing, he kept silent.

"Since I had brothers, guys weren't a mystery. Or very interesting. So I studied. That was something teachers didn't really expect at St. Joseph's and then South Boston High. I paid my religious dues by going to Boston College on a partial scholarship. Not for teacher training or nursing, which my parents expected, but in science. It turned out to be a longer road to a paycheck."

At that point the food arrived and they each dug into a beef ragu over sweet potato noodles.

"Well, things stayed tight. I balanced loans and grants with summer work but eventually managed to get a graduate fellowship at Northeastern. By then I'd discovered biology. You said I was driven; you should have seen me then, researching every possible scholarship and tuition deal." She was scraping her plate.

"But one way or another, I funded my doctoral work. And now, whoopee! I have a postdoc to keep my research going and very little debt. So, instead of teaching five sections of introduction to biology at a community college, I can spend every other semester in the jungle looking at insects."

"No teaching?"

"Some. Summer and midwinter semesters. And I take graduate students to Mexico. They help out and maybe learn something. I'm poor but holding it together."

"More than that."

"Because we're at a ski resort? Ha! Can't complain, but in the back of my mind, I keep thinking about next year and the year after. I'm living one post-doc grant to the next, with the teaching income pretty minimal. But without it, there goes my medical. What you see is a borrowed life. My office is on loan from someone away on sabbatical and the department secretary wonders who I am when I come in for my mail. Sure, the field work gets me away from department politics, but it still ain't tenure.

What I should be doing is applying for every open job in my area but I don't have time. Now, if my research pans out, that could change things. But for now, it's *la selva*."

"And your family is okay with this, you being out of the country so much?"

"They worry, I suppose, but hey, I'm 'the professor.' They're proud. Still, when I do come home, there's the usual interrogation—'You're thirty-four. When are you bringing a nice guy for us to meet?' But I guess it's different for guys."

The waiter cleared the table. They chose lemon squares from off of a rolling desert cart.

"We have at least something in common. Not that I'm an intellectual, but I'm out there with you on the edge. When I call myself an 'independent journalist', that really means I'm looking for a job."

"I'm an intellectual? I like the sound of that. But starving scholar is closer to the truth, not that this wasn't a fine meal. And right now I've even got a new pair of shoes." She held out a leg to display very red, very shiny pumps. "What do you think?"

"I envy the salesman."

"Fetishist!"

He looked away from her leg. "How does skiing fit into the gritty streets of Bean Town?"

"It doesn't. But I've always been an outdoor girl. In college there were always guys wanting to take me into the mountains."

"I'll bet."

She tossed her head. "But I made the best of it—within the behavioral guidelines of a Jesuit college. And learned to keep ahead of the guys both on and off the slopes." She laughed at memories she wasn't sharing. "Does that answer your question? And why here? My grant supervisor makes the occasional demand. This time it was go to Austria and show the flag for the Tropical Conservancy. Which just happened to give me a free day on the hill. Or glacier, as it turned out." She gave him a look. "Now I can go back to campus and tell my wizened colleagues that I've skied the Alps."

"Again, sorry about cutting that short. But does this trip mean you're getting recognition?"

"Well, not to brag, but I was paid $5,000 to attend this conference, beyond the room and airfare. And with you buying me meals, I'm doing okay." She smiled. "Of course, I had to dress the part." She held out the hem of her skirt. "Full disclosure; this is the nicest outfit I've got."

"I should have asked more from *The Chronicle*."

"I guess you'd say I'm working for the Tropical Conservancy. But life is complicated They're a conduit for the Green Foundation. And Big Green, as I call it, has ties to industry, including bio-tech. I know what you're going to say." She held up her hands. "That I'm a huge hypocrite, doing their 'green washing.'"

Ed kept a neutral face. "Any particular gen-tech?"

"I looked into it, but not very hard. There's a collaborative that supports the Green Foundation, but one funder is Naturtek, out of St. Louis. They're a symposium sponsor here, as you know. Actually, they're all over the map—conservation, recombinant research, commercial applications. As for habitat preservation, they're big on maintaining *in situ* populations of plants and insects. Anyway, I deal with the Conservancy, not the Foundation directly, and certainly not with the companies that support it. As for conflicts of interest, all I know is that no one has ever interfered with my projects."

The waiter checked on them and Aisling pointed to her coffee cup.

"What are you funded to do, exactly?

"Tropical Conservancy is serious about plant pollination, exactly my field. They have an interest in Southern Mexico because it's one of the seven greatest centers of biodiversity on earth. When I heard about their call for proposals, I answered. It didn't hurt that I had an article last year in *Nature*. So we're a good fit. And because the area down there is socially conflicted, there were fewer competitors."

"Dangerous, you mean?"

"There's the peasant insurgency that began in the '90s and is still going on, and corresponding army repression. Then there's the drug gangs. We're talking about an area that's the drug corridor from Columbia to the U.S. But so far, no problems." She rapped the table.

"Maybe I should interview you?"

"Isn't that what you've been doing?" She gave him a lidded glance.

"If I were, I'd ask what Naturtek gets out of supporting you, albeit twice removed. Besides the tax write-off."

"Like I said, they promote species diversity. And when I come across something novel, an insect or a plant, I send a sample to the Conservancy. They catalogue it for future research and, I suppose, Naturtek ultimately gets access."

"The odd grasshopper in a baggie?"

"The local people use a lot of natural materials as medicine—poultices, infusions—and as food. If something is interesting from that point of view, I make a note of it when I send off the specimen. This only happens once or twice a semester. Collecting is just a sideline. Mainly, I document the food chain for *lepidopterans*. Since there's at least 175,000 species of moths and butterflies in the region, the pollination process involves a great many plants."

Suddenly, Aisling glanced at her watch. It was 1:30 but she eased back in her chair.

"How'd you get into the newspaper racket, Clark Kent?"

"Ah, the rag trade. Would you believe I grew up mucking out the stables at Belmont Park in Queens and selling tips to the punters about which horses had sore feet? Picture a truant from middle school, a cigarette behind his ear."

"You've been reading too much Dick Francis," she said. "No. I don't believe it."

"Seen through again. Actually, I did grow up near the track but it wasn't my world. And I'd have trouble deciphering a racing form. We lived on a quiet street where my brother and I could throw around a football. But when I was seventeen, that ended. Mom was diagnosed with cancer and lasted just a few months after that. It was a difficult time and thinking about it now, I used every excuse possible to be out of the house. Mom's illness knocked out dad as well. He'd brought his business preparing tax returns home, so he lived mom's illness every day. When she died, he just folded up. By then I'd escaped to college. I was a sophomore when dad passed and Bart was eighteen, just old enough to join the military. We each found a ticket out, you could say. After we made arrangements to get rid of the house, Bart and I continued in our separate directions."

"You cut loose?"

"After graduation, I worked at one thing or another around New York while Bart was usually off at some base in the South. Fort Bragg mostly. Or deployed overseas. We'd email or exchange a card at Christmas. I think we both wanted to put our childhood behind us."

Aisling put her hand on Ed's wrist. "In a way, you were the orphan."

"Without even a dog named Sandy. But let's not be melodramatic." Ed exhaled. "To wrap this up, Bart eventually left the service, married, and moved to D.C. I've continued to kick around in the New York area so we've stayed at arm's length."

"He's got a family?"

"He does. Including a daughter, Molly. I play the mysterious uncle, dropping by once a year. But don't get the wrong idea. My brother and I get along. Actually better than we did in high school." Ed thought for a moment. "Back then, he was the athlete and our friendship circles didn't overlap. Still, I was older and with a driver's license, which sometimes proved useful."

"You were the brain?"

"I think the current term is 'nerd'. Through default, I'd become a writer. As much as one could be working for the high school newspaper. And more often than not, getting my stories panned by the faculty advisor."

"You insulted people?"

"I just asked obvious questions. Like how was it that the mayor owned a downtown commercial block where the zoning was changed to allow taller buildings? Or, why weren't *Catch* 22 and Baldwin's *Another Country* in the school library?"

"You were an anthropologist of high school life."

"And more smart ass than smart."

At that point the waiter materialized with the check which Ed grabbed without opposition.

"How little we change." She gave him a long look. "But now I'm out of here.

"Knock 'em dead."

Chapter Eleven

"STRUGGLE AND I HURT you bad." The voice had an indeterminate accent. Central European? It didn't help that Ed's head was stuffed in a bag. Lying on the floor, he felt himself dragged across the rug and slammed into a wall. He could hear a second person breathing.

"I'm a news junkie." The pitch was low, throaty. A smoker's voice. "You're going to educate me. I want copies of everything you've written since you got here. Even notes to your mother." There was a guttural laugh.

"I haven't written anything." Rebreathing his own air, Ed was on the edge of panic. He shook the fabric away from his mouth. At least is wasn't plastic.

"Don't lie, arsehole." Pain lit up the side of his head and hands pulled him to a sitting position.

"Check my computer", he mumbled. "I only got here two days ago. Things have just started." Ed tried to gesture toward what he thought was the desk with his laptop and realized his hands were tied. He had to hope they hadn't found his backup zip, tucked under the empty ice bucket.

"Oh, we did. There are no files there. Nothing, which is strange for a journalist. But there is email."

Ed drew in his breath.

"Don't be surprised. A school kid hiding porn would have a better access code. You sent out messages, all but one to the *Business Chronicle* in New York. But clever bugger, you encrypted them. Now you're going to give me the originals." Ed keeled over again and was kicked in the ribs. "Don't lie. It's tiresome."

"The paper gave me this computer. It encrypts automatically. I have no idea how." There was a rustle of fabric, someone kneeling down. Ed's head exploded again. "If you even think about yelling, I split your skull like a melon."

The best Ed could do was moan. Then he found his tongue.

"Yes, I turned in one story, just on local color and the opening plenary. Descriptive stuff. I don't have copies." Ed flinched, expecting another blow. " Once I hit 'send', the program automatically encrypts the text and deletes the file from my hard drive. It sounds crazy, I know." He tried to draw in breath through clogged nostrils and tasted blood at the back of his throat. "I can't save the sent files."

Cloth was sticking to the side of his head. "Take the computer. I'm sure you can figure this out. Maybe everything's still in there."

"Oh, we will. But we thought you'd like to help."

'We.' So there were two assailants. Or did he mean people he was working for? Ed sensed the guy in front of him was big. He wasn't going to argue. Bart might have known some tricky move, not Ed.

"That's all you can say to stay alive?" The second voice was gravel sliding down a metal chute. Or wet concrete. Then fireworks lit up the inside of the bag and Ed lost consciousness.

He awoke to pounding on his door. Still tied and blind, he tried to yell but his mouth was full of sandpaper. Using his shoulders and one knee, he wormed across the floor in the direction of the banging. "Help!" His own voice came from far away. He collided with a wall and shifted right. At the door, he found the handle was out of reach. Carefully, he pushed his back into the wall and got one foot under him. The higher he rose, the more vertigo he felt. Finally he was able to feel the levered handle with his bound hands. When the door flew open, it knocked him back onto the floor.

"Oh, my god." It was Aisling's voice. She slid down beside him, her hands cradling his head. Then she worked to loosen the cord around his neck that held the sack. When she tore it off, the room light was blinding. Freed from a double layer of pillowcases, the gash on his temple began to bleed. Aisling gasped.

Lowering him carefully to the rug, she ran to the desk and fumbled through a drawer. Then she was in the bathroom, breaking glass. He felt a sawing motion at his wrists as she cut what turned out to be plastic flexicuffs. He brought his hands in front of his face and tried to work circulation back into his fingers.

"Good thinking," he wheezed, seeing a broken drinking glass in her hand. She took his hands and began to kiss them.

"What happened?" Her voice was in a panic octave.

"They were here when I came in," he croaked.

"I guessed that." She helped him sit so his back was again against the wall. She probed around his scalp. "Christ, you're covered with blood!" She left and returned with a warm washcloth and began to dab at the side of his head.

"I was going to change the batteries in my tape recorder. I wanted to get your session down so we could talk about it. Someone—two guys at least—grabbed me. They asked me things and when they didn't like my answers, knocked me around. With that pillowcase on my head, I couldn't see them."

"What did they want? This can't be a robbery."

"No. They wanted what I'd sent to the paper." He reached around. The bulge of a wallet was still in his back pocket. "Looks like my money and credit cards are here. I guess all they wanted was my laptop." He could see the top of the desk was bare.

"What were you writing?" she asked. "This is crazy!"

"Just routine stuff, describing the place, last night's plenary. I can't understand why anyone would be interested." He shook his head to find focus. "What time is it?"

"Four-forty."

"This happened just after I left you. That was before two. They grilled me for a while, then hit me till I lost consciousness. You roused me from the dead. Again." He grinned, only to find his lower lip was cracked.

"You might have a concussion." She ran her fingers lightly through his hair. "I'll get the house doctor. And the police."

"That won't be necessary." Two men in blue blazers with the hotel crest stood just inside. In her confusion, Aisling had never closed the door. "We got a report of a disturbance. We're hotel security. If someone is injured, we'll get a physician up here."

"Oh, someone is definitely injured," said Aisling. He voice was hard. "And you've got yourself a world of grief. Two men broke into this room and assaulted one of your guests. And robbed him. How could this happen?"

How indeed, thought Ed. Given the pedigree of participants at this conference. "And it took you, what, three hours to get here?"

"There was just a report about shouting, so it wasn't a priority. Tell us what happened here, sir." The taller of the two men took charge. He helped Ed to his feet and walked him to a chair. The second man turned away, talking into his cell phone.

"I unlocked my door—it was definitely locked because I had to swipe it with my card. Just as I opened it, someone pulled me inside and knocked me down. I blacked out for a second. When I came to, I had that thing on my head." He pointed to the bloodstained cloth on the floor. "Then they beat the shit out of me and I went back under. I just woke up."

"No money gone, I heard you say? Just the laptop?"

"We don't really know," Aisling broke in. "But he has his wallet. And I saw his passport on the desk." She was in pit bull mode, glaring.

"And you are?", the man in charge asked, looking through Ed's passport.

"Edward Dekker, a reporter accredited to cover this conference." He groped for his identification pass, still on a cord around his neck. "This is a friend of mine, Aisling..." He couldn't remember her last name. He was still shaken up.

"O'Keefe," she filled in.

The second man held up pictures of each of them, retrieved on his cell phone. "Yes, I have you here. And you, Ms. O'Keefe. Were you in the room at the time of the, ah, robbery?"

"It's Doctor O'Keefe. And of course not! I only arrived five minutes ago and found him on the floor. Somehow he managed to get the door open. Then he collapsed."

To be precise, I didn't collapse, thought Ed. She knocked me down.

"You saw no one leaving?" He addressed Aisling.

"No. I was at a session downstairs all afternoon."

"You say two men?" He turned back to Ed. "Can you identify them?"

"Just their voices. One had a slight accent, maybe Romanian or something. The other had more conventional English but his voice was deep and gravely. The light was off when I came in, and they had that pillow case over me right away. So no, I didn't see any faces. Or clothing." Ed gathered his thoughts. "For an instant, though, I did see the arm around my neck, in some sort of smooth wool, dark blue, maybe." Ed was trying to be methodical. "They tied my wrists." He held out his hands. The skin was deeply chafed and one wrist was bleeding slightly. Ed wondered if it was from Aisling's shard of glass. He looked at her and she grimaced.

"Sorry," she mouthed.

"They asked me questions and then they knocked me out."

"Do you still have your other valuables?" The house detective in charge seemed confused.

Ed fumbled through his wallet. "I have my credit cards. And you're holding my passport." It was all about the computer. "Before they hit me the last time they asked what I'd sent out to my paper. They wanted copies. I said I don't keep copies once I file a story. And that everything on the laptop was encrypted. They weren't happy with that. Then they bashed me in the head. That's all I know."

Aisling was now sitting on the arm of his chair, still probing his head with her fingers. "This is his second concussion since he's arrived. He really needs medical attention."

Just then a man in a police uniform walked in followed by a small man in a creased blue suit wearing steel spectacles. Behind them was a red-faced and portly man in the hotel's blue blazer with the deerhead crest. He forced himself into a room that was already crowded. "What is going on here? I'm the manager." He glared at the group, focusing on Ed who was slumped forward in the chair. Aisling pulled Ed upright.

The man with steel glasses waved the manager back. Not to be put off, the fat man began a visual survey of the room, paying particular attention to the condition of the furnishings. Whatever had happened, his look implied, it was clearly Ed's fault.

"You are the guest who two days ago had trouble on the slopes, are you not?" There was no sympathy in the manager's tone.

"One thing at a time," interrupted the small man and pushed the manager into the hall, closing the door. "I am Lieutenant Rolf Schröder." Black notebook in hand, he took Ed through his story. At the end he was not optimistic. "Herr Dekker. This is virtually a public place. There is no point in looking for fingerprints. Even in luxury hotels here, robberies occur." He gestured toward the valley beyond the window. The drapes were now open. "You have the serial number of your computer?" Ed fumbled in his wallet and took out the claim sheet he'd had to present to the IT office in New York to borrow the computer. The detective copied the number. "If anything turns up, you will be notified."

He then brought in the manager, gripping his upper arm and ignoring the man's agitation. "What I don't understand is how these men got in," he said quietly. "The door shows no sign of being forced. Her Dekker says he didn't let them in. So, they had a passkey." He stared at the manager, who blew out air through his lips.

"Many people have key cards. The housekeeping and security must be able to access every room. But we vet our employees thoroughly. It is done by me, personally." He poked himself in the chest. "When a room is vacated we wipe clean the entry code. If a prior occupant retained a keycard, it would be useless." He shrugged free of the detective's grasp. "This is not my problem."

"We'll talk to housekeeping and your security people. But it is very much your problem if someone is in your hotel with a handheld electronic code reader. Sad to say, these are now common among a certain class of professionals. You may be due for an expensive security up-grade. Then there's Herr Dekker's legal action." He winked at Ed.

The manager's face had darkened. His problems were growing. Then, with surprising obsequiousness, he apologized to Ed on behalf of the hotel. When Ed pointed out that he needed a computer to continue his work, the manager promised to send up a new laptop immediately. "Well, not brand new, but one from our business center. Nearly new." He asked the police officer if that would be enough to erase the theft report, but was told no.

At that point the physician arrived, Ed's old friend Dr. Krobber. First swiveling Ed's head like a doorknob, he then passed a penlight in front of his eyes.

The detective stepped back, scanning the room.

"So, Herr Dekker, we meet again," said Krobber, smiling broadly. Today's sweater was a grey and white Icelandic, almost angora. He'd left the lab coat behind. "Life continues to challenge you I see, both on and off the slopes." Holding Ed's chin in one hand, he palpitated the back of his head, then ran a finger along a small gash on Ed's temple. Finally he massaged the scalp, almost like a barber at the conclusion of a haircut. Ed remembered seeing fighting cocks in Guatemala being checked mid-battle, caressed but then put pack into the arena. "How's the leg, by the way?"

"Much better. But to be honest, it's hard to think about that just now. My head really aches."

"Of course." Reaching into a black bag that hinged open from the top, the doctor took out a tube of salve and some pills.

"I don't want to give you anything that might set off internal bleeding, so you'll have to endure the head ache. But this ointment will dull the itching in your scalp and the pills will help you sleep. From the discoloration on your neck, it seems you were hit just below the occipital bone where nerves are close to the surface. Very professionally done." Krobber continued to manipulate Ed's head. "It doesn't look to have been a hard blow, a good thing because otherwise you would be dead. How long were you unconscious?"

Ed felt like he was testifying at his own inquest. He looked at his watch, still on his wrist. "It's five-of-five. I got back here about two. I was knocked out within ten minutes and woke up maybe fifteen minutes ago." Ed was becoming more coherent.

"That means he was out for three hours," said Aisling, "Is that bad, doctor?"

"I don't know. An MRI on the gentleman's head would show any internal bleeding. What do you say, Herr Dekker?" He looked again at the back of Ed's head. "But I don't think the blow caused this loss of consciousness." He continued probing. "Look at this?" He pointed to a small wound low on Ed's neck. The detective, then the manager, drew close to look.

There was a puncture wound four inches below Ed's left ear. "I think he was injected with something after he was struck. In a way, that's better than having a blow cause the blackout."

"This is getting interesting," said the detective. "Smash and grab artists with hypodermics? Are there drugs that could bring on uncon-sciousness like this?"

"Oh, yes," said the doctor, "a number of them. But as he's awake now and apparently lucid," the doctor smiled at Aisling rather than Ed, "my guess is that whatever it was has been metabolized. In such a case, it is not likely a blood test would tell us anything."

Ed was just the cadaver, not even Krobber's audience. "You're going to have to keep him out of trouble," continued the doctor, looking directly at Aisling and shaking his head as if the task was impossible. "And let me say, it is a pleasure to see you once again."

Krobber would hit on a widow at her husband's funeral, thought Ed.

The detective moved things along. "We'll begin with the guests on this floor." He pointed to the manager. "Room service and housekeeping next. Perhaps someone saw men leave this room in the last few hours. But I'm not hopeful." He turned his attention back to Ed. "The clientele here tends to focus exclusively on their own lives."

"You will be discrete," said the manager, unsettled. "Our guests will not enjoy being interrogated. I must ask that hotel security accompany you."

"I think you have more pressing problems," Schröder answered. "You're being worked by a professional team with the capacity to open locked doors and inject guests with knockout drugs. Gather up all your video footage so we can check facial images against the photos I know you have of guests. Now."

"As you wish," mumbled the manager.

"Is there CCTV on this floor?"

"Only in front of elevators and in the stairwell. The lobby and front desk are, of course, fully covered. We do record the faces of our guests so our staff can address them by name."

"And in case there should be a question about billing," said the detective.

He handed Ed a business card. It was limp and looked recycled. "Call the station in a few days. The number's there. We'll let you know if your laptop turns up." Then the forces of law, private and public, swept out of the room, the manager trailing. As he closed the door, Ed could hear the detective chatting with Krobber about the effects of various sedatives. The doctor was suggesting veterinary drugs used on horses.

Minutes later, a bellboy arrived carrying a laptop in a travel case. While not factory-fresh, it was a recent model, thinner and apparently more expensive than the one Ed had lost. "Yours to keep, with the compliments of the management," the bellboy said as he backed out. The situation did not call for a tip.

"Now what," said Aisling, once they were alone.

"I don't know. On top of it all, I missed your panel. I'm sorry." His grin was weak. "Could you get me some water?"

Aisling found a tumbler and filled it from the sink. No one had swept up the glass which crunched under her feet.

"Did you arrange all this to keep me away from your presentation? Shy thing that you are." His grin was lopsided. He wouldn't be whistling anytime soon.

"I talked about the recent dieback of pollinating insects in Central America and Mexico, data I've put together over the last year. It's a complicated story and I'd rather tell you about it when we have a couple of hours. Following me was the director of the Svalbard Seed Bank, this Rowling guy. You would have been interested in his remarks."

"Damn!" said Ed. "What'd he say?"

"I was still wrapped up in my own spiel and so nervous that I didn't absorb much of what he said but I remember he gave a timeline on the decline of cultivated crop varieties. Of the hundreds of apple types common in 1900, nearly all are now extinct. Same for potatoes, outside of Peru, anyway. Even with new varieties coming out of the ag schools, the picture is bleak. The culprit is the industrial food system, he said.

That fits into what I was telling you earlier. A zillion fast food restaurants want a specific potato for their French fries, so that's what farmers grow. Still, when I looked out at the audience, I couldn't see them at a McDonald's take-out window. So maybe the market for good stuff won't completely disappear."

"No. The rich eat from their own table. I remember reading somewhere that President Reagan only allowed Coleman's beef in the White House, grass fed and organic."

"Rowling's main pitch was to corporations," she continued. "He wanted donations for his seed vault, his 'refrigerator in the Arctic', he called it. It's supposed to save civilization from collapse."

"I've heard that story, Here, in fact." Ed thought back to what Hammersmith had said. "My guess is Rowling collected some checks."

"Well, his slant was, '*Soit nous, soit l'inondacion.*'"

"Modest of him. Did he distribute a paper?"

"Yes, and I have a copy. Now that I think about it, his bet was on genetic crop innovation and his poster child was winter wheat. During the last wheat blight, rust wiped out half the Russian crop. Remember when bread prices shot up a decade ago?"

"Yeah The commodities traders made a killing."

"Well, according to Rowling, now we're better prepared. Researchers have juiced up resistance to wheat rust with DNA from a heritage Turkish variety. So biotech will save us."

"That fits with the theme of this conference." She rummaged through her bag and found handouts from her panel and Ed skimmed over the titles.

"I think I can do something with this," he said. "Got to sing for my supper." He pursed his lips and grimaced when he felt the skin tear.

"Anything of interest turn up in the question period?"

"No. And audience comments were held to the end. Not to sound superior, but the other presentations bored me. And since I kept expecting a hardball question that never came, my attention was kind of narrow."

She shrugged. "There was one thing, though. Rowling was asked about intellectual property rights. With seeds reproducing naturally, the question was how could companies get their investment back beyond the first sale?"

Ed struggled to set aside the throbbing in his head throb. "You mean, what's the point of research if a farmer can just replant what he bought last year?"

"Exactly," said Aisling.

"And Rowling's response?"

"He said the courts in the U.S. and Canada give corporations ownership of anything containing their patented DNA. You might buy hi-tech seeds but you don't actually own them. It's a rental arrangement. And the rent comes due every season. Weird, huh?"

"So, if a farmer replanted without paying a royalty, the company could sue?"

"Could and does. For theft of property. When someone in the audience scoffed and said legal systems in the global South are a joke, Rowling had an answer to that, too. Terminator seeds."

"Meaning?"

"Plants that bear sterile seeds. Industry calls it a biological patent. The concept originated in the 1930s with hybrid corn. Hybrids reproduce but so poorly that farmers have to go back to the seed companies every year."

"Nature is the policeman?" said Ed.

"Yes. But not every plant can be hybridized, a process that involves the manipulation of pollen but not the DNA directly. What's on the horizon are crops that simply won't grow if you replant their seed."

Ed mulled it over. "I thought that technology was illegal. There's this UN convention, isn't there?"

"Sure, but now the genie is out of the bottle. When the audience absorbed this, they became really excited and that topic dominated the rest of the question period."

"So, birth control applied to nature," said Ed.

"More like involuntary sterilization."

"And food's not an elective purchase," said Ed. "Control the new technology and you have a global choke hold. First commercial farmers are on the hook, then backyard gardeners, and finally peasants."

Aisling looked disgusted. Her collaborators in Mexico were peasant communities.

"And Rowling was promoting this? Did he use the term 'terminator technology'?"

"No. He was all about 'crop improvement'. But the audience could see what was happening."

"Christ. I'm sorry I missed that." Ed tried to pace but the pain in his head made him sit down again.

"You're the walking-wounded. Relax." Aisling brushed his shoulder. "Are you going to survive after I leave?"

"The room?"

"No, the conference. I'm due back in Boston to wrap up my winter course. Then it's off to Mexico. My funding for this little jaunt has run out and I'm not paying for one of these thousand-dollar-a-night rooms." She looked around.

"You could stay here?" Ed looked over at the bed.

"You thought I was a charity case? Good luck with that. And with a bunch of thugs walking around with your room key, really. No, my reservation has me flying out of Innsbruck at midnight. Don't look so depressed. We have a couple of hours. I'll pack up and we can do dinner."

Ed struggled to his feet, more successfully this time. "The upside of being hit on the head is that my knee hardly bothers me." He flexed his leg. Then drew her to him. "Steady me. I feel dizzy."

"Well, if it's a medical emergency?" They held each other, passing a kiss back and forth.

"There's no denying that the Pulitzer I'll be getting from this gig will be great but it won't compare with having met you."

She rubbed her lips on his ear. "Aren't you afraid I'll add you to my butterfly collection?"

"And pin me to a cork board? I surrender."

Side stepping in unison, they moved toward the bed.

"God, you men are all alike. At least I hope so."

His hand slid over her thighs, keeping his balance. "What drew you to me? My athleticism?"

"Your resilience." She rubbed against him. "And your stamen is impressive."

"It's just a biological imperative. Nothing personal."

"I'm sure." Together they fell back onto the bed. His knee wrenched awkwardly but he hardly felt it. "Coming down the mountain, leaning against you, it was very erotic."

"Maybe making you suffer is what gets me off?" She slipped her blouse over her head. Her skin was a Milky Way of freckles swirling around two pink nipples. No tattoo, though. When she straddled him, her pubic hair was soft on his finger tips.

"Am I hurting you?" She was rocking, her breath rhythmic.

"Only in a good way."

Eventually they lay quiet, glued together with sweat. When she rolled away, it was like opening the pages of a wet book.

"Let's order out, shall we?"

"One of us will have to get dressed, answer the door," she said. Her fingers trailed over his flaccid penis.

"Maybe later."

Chapter Twelve

HOURS LATER HE AWOKE with Aisling gone. The evening color was long gone from the sky. She'd left no note. To keep from thinking about what he'd gotten into, Ed began to put together a story about declining crop diversity using what he'd gathered so far.

For thousands of years, small farmers had coaxed wild plants into something edible but all this was about to disappear, he wrote. Lab workers in white coats were building a new food system. And like it or not, this was 'the next big thing' for the investment community, the opportunity of the century.

A few years ago he'd done a piece on commercial fishing. The days of rugged individualism were over there, as well. Very few small boats heading out of Gloucester and St. John's these days because the cod were gone. The void was being filled by genetic mutants raised in off-shore pens. They hit plate-weight at the Boston market in half the time of wild fish. His lead for that article had been 'Swim with AquaBounty', the company leading this transformation. His counter-point, though, was less sanguine. 'Get this stuff labeled so we can avoid it.' Looking back now, he realized that effort to kick over the cart of food modernization hadn't worked. He'd only normalized the situation and whet the appetite of investors. Someday soon, children's books would be describing the antics of designer pigs.

How could he keep beating the drum for investors while telling himself he was writing cautionary tales? He was a fraud. He wasn't even doing advocacy journalism. His head still ached as he struggled to get dressed.

And now there was a new complication, Aisling. She'd left as if she was just going to the corner to fetch croissants. Why had neither of them mentioned meeting again?

He finished the article and staggered down to a small restaurant off the lobby, the only place still serving. Alcohol remained out of reach so he washed his burger down with cider. In the dim lighting, his bruised face didn't seem to shock the waitress. Pushing thoughts of Aisling aside, he went over what he'd just typed on his "new" laptop.

He'd laid out the standard argument for applying bio-chemistry to food—the need to feed the billions. This was industry's rationale for dumping regulations and fast-tracking global trade. Then, he'd moved on to genetic drift. Just as super fish would inevitably escape to doom conventional species, enhanced seeds would contaminate traditional crops and displace wild plants. The evolutionary canyon would narrow. New pests would inevitably appear, setting the food system back again on the pesticide treadmill. And with salvation in the hands of a few seed sellers, the old Standard Oil would look like the corner store.

Despite the garnish of mushrooms, bacon, and cheese—even a dash of horseradish—his hamburger was tasteless.

His immediate problem was his laptop; it was anything but secure. How could he get his pieces into press? What if he opened a Yahoo account in a phony name, then emailed the article to his brother and had Bret courier it over to the *Chronicle*? Convoluted, sure, but it would work.

Ed left the restaurant and used one of the business center computers to open an email account in a phony name. Back in his room, he copied what he had to a backup thumb drive, the one he'd hidden under the ice bucket, and returned to the business office. At least he'd have his own file. The glassed-in enclosure, accessed by room card, was deserted. The trick was to get Bart to pay attention to an unknown sender. For a subject header, he typed in 'Daisy Red Ryder'. That was the name of the BB gun they'd played with as kids. At least until they broke a window and their mother had taken it away from them. His brother would remember.

He instructed Bart to Fed Ex the attachment to the *Chronicle* by secure courier. He'd pay him back. Briefly, Ed explained his most recent mishap and the loss of his computer. If worse came to worst, he wrote, his brother could look forward to owning a fine Bowery co-op. And if so, please remember to water the plants. He hit send.

When day came, Ed managed to get back on his feet and cover several meetings, dutifully rather than with any real interest. He sat in the back so he could slip out when aches or boredom seized him, always keeping as many doors as possible in his line of sight.

Between sessions, he wandered the lobby checking name tags and looking for interesting people to chat up. Sometimes a casual conversation was more informative than an interview. Checking in at the security office, he found no progress made in the search for his computer but Detective Schröder had left him a message. "Villains still at large." It was just as well. He couldn't return here for a trial, if that's how things worked. He knew there was malware that could transmit keystrokes to an off-site location so if his laptop did turn up, it might be toxic anyway.

Late in the afternoon he visited the hotel clinic. Krobber performed his ritual, moving a penlight in front of Ed's eyes and probing his knee and neck. And none too gently. No obvious brain or bone damage. And would Ed remember to return the wheel chair and cane? Without Aisling around, Krobber was all business.

After catching the last session of the day, Ed went to bed. At five a.m. his phone rang. Still groggy, he answered "Aisling?" Instead it was the *Chronicle's* feature editor, Percival Hardy. 'Percy', but never to his face. Hardy worked late and was famous for ignoring time difference between New York and wherever his reporters were located. He spoke with characteristic slowness, suggesting deep thought and disdain for any Walter Winchell freneticism.

"Edward? Your latest piece reached my desk by an unusual route. Care to explain?" Right down to business. Ed heard a sepulchral silence. Hardy was slow but relentless.

"Explain?"

"Not the article. It appears adequate. I'm concerned with the mode of conveyance." In Hardy's scale of affect, 'adequate' was praise but 'concerned' approached 'going ballistic'.

Ed recounted the assault and the loss of his laptop.

"I take it from your continuing output that no lasting damage has been done." To me? thought Ed. To the paper?

"I didn't send you there as a war correspondent." War correspondents had a better death package, Ed thought. "Please assure me that your personal experiences are not warping your reporter's vision." First-person journalism, a glimpse of the writer speaking through a story, was not the *Chronicle's* style.

Wondering what to say, Ed hesitated but Hardy continued.

"Setting that aside, I can't decide if this last piece is overblown. Would your intent be to panic the markets, provoke the SEC regulators?"

Was it possible to live life in the subjunctive case, Ed wondered? "No, of course not. Traders will see this as more opportunity than risk. But I wanted to add a note of caution. As Alan Greenspan always said, 'Avoid irrational exuberance'. Anyway, I kept the red flags till the end. What I'm seeing here, as far as the food sector is concerned, is a consensus that underplays long-term problems."

"Thought-provoking is good; crying 'fire' in a theater, not so much. 'Pesticide treadmill?' Bit Apocalyptical, don't you think?" Handy would have the piece toned down, but he'd run with it. "Stay even-handed, Edward. As far as the financial community goes, we, not the Grey Lady, are the newspaper of record. And we're not competing with *Rolling Stone.*"

Wall Street a 'community'"? thought Ed. More like plutocrats pummeling one another in Fritz Lang's *Metropolis.*

Hardy continued. "What we print is on the wire services thirty minutes later. And in your case, also the environmental press. To suggest that the fundamental paradigm of crop development is flawed will get amplified. I'm not saying it's wrong. But let's not make a generation of IPOs into still-births. You'll recognize your piece but you've given re-write some work."

Ed had anticipated this. But not Hardy's next remark.

"I want you out of there before you drive up our insurance rates. I have the conference schedule in front of me. There's not much left other than the final plenary, which is ceremonial. We can get all we need about that from Reuters. You've squeezed the juice out of this lemon. Time to come home."

Was this actual concern on Hardy's part? "I'll be bringing a medical bill. I've had to put everything on the paper's credit card."

"But not your funeral." Hardy was actually making a joke. "As legal reminds me, our backing for you is not unlimited. We'll cover the bandaids, but I'm pulling the plug. Mona will book you on a flight out tomorrow." Mona was the dragon queen who guarded the door to Hardy's office. She also scrutinized expense accounts for creative fiction. "And Ed? Never again submit an unencrypted piece, even if it is hand-delivered. See me as soon as you're back."

PART TWO: THE UNITED STATES

Chapter Thirteen

"THIS IDEA OF 'SYNTHETIC nature'," said Percival Hardy. Ed was standing in the editor's wainscoted office, the oak paneling the color of leather. Photos of old New York hung on the walls. One showed the long-gone Six Avenue elevated train line. Ed remembered that John Sloan had painted a similar scene. The office was on the mezzanine above an open-plan newsroom, walled off with glass panels and wooden blinds. They were on the 17th floor. Palladian windows looked toward 52nd Street, mostly cornices and rooftop water towers. The *Chronicle* had downsized in recent years to a half-dozen floors but continued to brand the entire building. Rumor in the newsroom was that the edifice was up for sale. Ed imagined a condominium conversion, with the Palladian floor getting a premium. Despite adding an internet edition, management was barely holding readership numbers while ad revenue bled away. It was the same story across the industry and it meant that work spaces weren't up for renovation, Hardy's office included. Ed looked at furniture that likely dated from the LaGuardia era.

While running the features section, Hardy wasn't the top of the pyramid. He jostled with seven other department managers for page-space while above, like invisible gargoyles, crouched the general editor, the vice-president for finance, and the publisher himself. As a family enterprise, at least there were no investors.

Hardy wasn't a tall man and his corpulence made him appear even shorter. He ruled from an oversized desk, Edward G. Robinson style, but without the cigar. Only the flat screens in front of him clashed with his '40s appearance that included suspenders and a permanent expression of incredulity. He studied Ed till the younger man dropped his gaze.

"Not a bad term. It makes me think of that synthetic diesel that almost saved Hitler's hide. Your phrase or, what's his name, Hammersmith's?" Ed was in court and Hardy was the judge. Once head of Columbia's Butler Library, the editor was nothing if not methodical. If much of what now passed for news was just flash and bang, that was a problem for cable news. Here, Hardy held the line. A platoon of fact-checkers—Ed thought of them as Melville's scriveners —kept the reporters honest. As long as the publishing houses continued to churn out English majors with no better options, this wasn't a problem.

"Plants re-engineered for functional utility—protein content, available fiber, bio-mass." He tapped on the copy he read from the screen. "This has potential. But we have to handle it carefully." His eyes zigzagged down page after page.

Not for the first time, Ed wondered why someone would leave academia for newspaper work. To influence public policy? Hardy had bypassed street reporting on his way up—moving from Columbia to management at the *Los Angeles Times* and now the *Chronicle*—but his archival skills still served him well. He probed every crevasse and lost nothing. Ed imagined Hardy, bib in place, dissecting a boiled lobster. As editor, he rode herd on a dozen investigative reporters, contingents with specific assignments who reinforced a few full-timers. Contingents competed with each other for attention while any promotion would require a heart attack among the salaried staff. The rivalry was Shakespearian.

Hardy's job was to harvest the Pulitzers on which the paper's prestige depended. Even with a tight budget, that task gave him room to maneuver. His shop wasn't like metro where deadlines were life or death. If

Hardy thought your story had possibilities, you got gas in your tank. But only once, if you bombed out, that was it.

The north light from 52nd Street was diffuse, the windows streaked with rain. Hardy's shoe covers leaked water onto a rubber mat beside his door. Ed remembered his dad called them 'half-moons'.

Without lifting his eyes from the screen, Hardy pointed toward a chair and Ed sat down. The chair was heavy maple, covered in cracked green leather, and too deep for comfort. Maybe that was the idea. Ed glanced again at a rooftop water tower. Further west was what remained of the elevated train tracks, now the trendy High Line esplanade.

Unlike the sputtering fluorescents in the newsroom, the lighting here was from milky globes on chains. A photo caught Ed's eye: the mayor and the publisher breaking ground for the *Chronicle's* Long Island City printing plant. Each dignitary held a shovel, way too shiny to actually have been used. That was ten years ago. Once completed, it marked the end of the rotary presses that had throbbed for nearly a century in the basement and gave the workday a touch of edginess.

"Develop the hook. Your followup is still blurry." Hardy's voice brought Ed back to the moment. His sleep on the plane had been spotty.

"Nail down the direction of research." Ed should have sharpened his pitch.

"And what about the major environmental organizations? Where are they in this conversation? And your conclusion? Our readers want to know where to put their money. As I'm sure the business editor will remind me. What's the bottom line for seed company stock?"

Hardy scribbled out the sub-heads he wanted on a pad. "Support this here and here with additional interviews," he added. I know you're not a geneticist but neither are our readers, so show the implications of this by examples. How far along has this research gotten? We could be looking at a series here."

Even one featured article would cover his bills. "That I can do. I'll contact the EPA along with the major conservation orgs. The big one's have accepted the idea of a market solution to environmental destruction—carbon trading and plantations of mutant trees. So I don't expect much push-back against gen-tech there."

"Mutant trees? Aren't you wandering off topic?"

"Just broadening this out. You mentioned a series. Labs are reducing the lignin in trees by manipulating their DNA. The idea is to lower the cost of paper making. But lignin is what keeps a tree from falling over like a stalk of limp celery. Big Green thinks this kind of thing will save natural forests from clearcutting, so they're embracing the idea."

"One thing at a time. Will the biotech solution work with food?"

"There's more critics here, but they're not getting funded. Playing skeptic is a rocky career move."

"I want both sides, with attribution. Credible sources. We'll let the reader decide." Hardy offered a thin smile. "That way you won't be totally wrong."

And we won't face a liable suit, Ed thought.

"Frame the piece as a debate. I'm good with your small farmer reference but don't put your heart before your head. Wall Street won't. But if tinker-toy crops are a dead end, investors need to know."

"So, my hook is..." Ed trailed off.

"Synthetic foods. That merits attention. And at an unconscious level, it brings up Mary Shelley and the hubris associated with creating life. It's the perennial nightmare of modernity. Your job is to put it in genetic terms. Now, get to work; vacation's over." Hardy waved his hands, shooing flies off of a pie. "See Mona about your on-going expenses."

"On-going?" This was as close to a blank check as Ed was likely to see. He left before Hardy could reconsider, handing a wrinkled stack of receipts to Mona, who ignored him. On the main floor he dumped his things into a vacant cubicle. Along with a coffee-splattered desk computer, it held a phone and a few pencils, none sharp. The waste basket overflowed. Using the internet and the paper's electronic archives, he trolled the academic literature and corporate press releases. Then he called environmental NGOs headquartered in the city: food processors; small seed companies. By the end of the day he'd accumulated a few phone interviews but nothing substantial. He needed more

Contingents had no secretaries, no copy boys, no runners. Not in this century. But printing was free and the company's search engines sophisticated. Access to U.S. government databases got him into the Patent Office archives.

As the afternoon faded from grey to black, Ed saw that Manny LaRock's trench coat was dripping from a cubicle partition across the room. Manny covered sports and was full-time. That entitled him to his own work station. It wasn't enclosed—no one should feel too secure—but Manny had locking file drawers and shelves. Other than business, sports was highest in column inches at the *Chronicle*.

Like price-earnings ratios, sports could be reduced to statistics. But that wasn't how Manny told it. Pitching hot stocks to investors eventually grew tiring and brokers were bored. Especially with numbers. They wanted to smell the locker room, see the sweat. And that's what Manny delivered. He covered anything that could affect a team's performance—drug scandals, divorces, shoulder surgeries, and locker room confrontations. In covering the frail humanity of athletes, Manny was acknowledging the fears as well as the dreams of his readers. He also wrote well, if you liked opera. With forced trades, free-agent negotiations, aging quarterbacks and Russian oligarchs owning teams, villains and heroes abounded. And according to Manny, brokers were inveterate gamblers. His column, 'In the Bleachers', not only captured eyeballs, it shifted the odds in a thousand office betting pools.

All that took a string of informants—trainers, ticket scalpers, and retired pros who doubled as talent scouts. To keep the machinery oiled, Manny had a budget and the freedom to spend it. With the on-line edition, management could track which stories were opened, creating journalism's new box score. On that basis, Manny always placed high. Even in hard times, he got an annual raise while many of his colleagues took severance payments and considered themselves fortunate. As a result, Manny felt guilty. As penance, he rarely traveled for pleasure and wore the same suit year after year. More important, from Ed's point of view, Manny was bored. What did the thirtieth all-star game matter, after all? Manny envied Ed's forays into the more consequential and Ed wasn't too proud to push that button.

The sports reporter was shaking his wet coat, getting ready to leave, when Ed pulled over a chair. "Haven't seen you around much," said Manny. "Figured you'd drowned in the Bahamas. That's where you were, right? Reef swimming or something?"

"Cavorting with the sharks, yes, but not in the Caribbean. And hello to you, too. But I'm back, as you see, and sporting a skier's tan."

"And a skier's limp and bruises. Couldn't help noticing."

"Well, that's what a week in the Alps will do."

Manny looked at Ed through half-closed eyes, unimpressed.

"Did I mention a world-class resort?" Ed prompted. "On the paper's tab?"

"You made your point. I applaud your good fortune. Then again, I don't ski. I did hear they'd sent you to Austria. I was pulling your chain."

"I count on you to know everything."

"And on the company tit? This their way of packaging compassionate leave?"

"I was on assignment. Earning my keep."

"And how were you kept? There is that limp."

"Limp, gimp, I'm in recovery." Ed held up his hands. "Look, Ma, no cane! I took a slight fall on the slopes, but no problem. Just the price for upping my game."

"If you say so."

"I was lucky there were no ski dorms there or that's where they'd have sent me. This conference was in the Tyrol, something like Davos. Global players bent over like watchmakers, fine-tuning the world economy."

"And tightening the screws on the rest of us, I'm sure. Like I always say, the only thing you can trust in the paper is the ball scores. Your articles excepted. So, you had fun? Found distractions?"

Anticipating the drift of the conversation, Ed faked right and moved left.

"Not among these players. They were armpit deep in the money bin, not much interested in anything else. But look, I've turned in my travel vouchers and touched base with Hardy so I'm done for the day. Why don't we go for a beer?" Neither of them were comfortable chatting in Manny's 'dugout.' Not with the managerial mezzanine looming over them.

Without words, they headed for Snooky's Place on the next block. Aggressively grungy, it had fended off the corporate renewal that was reclaiming most of Manhattan. Stale Guinness scented the air and the floor was grey with ancient sawdust. There was nothing here to draw in tourists from Times Square so it remained an oasis for clerks and maintenance workers in no hurry to catch the 5:38 back to White Plains. As a tribute to *Chronicle* regulars, management had framed a few newspaper front pages—John Lindsay staring down Nelson Rockefeller in 1967 over street closures the governor needed to build the World Trade Center; stunned workers carrying cardboard boxes out of Lehman Brothers. And inevitably, the Trade Towers burning like chimneys.

Behind the bar, Lenny had mounted a few of his personal favorites. The prize was a yellowed news photo of the Easter Rising of 1916, Irish Volunteers proclaiming the republic in front of the General Post Office which they held for six days. And then saw 16 of the survivors executed. As Lenny liked to say, flashing teeth in need of dental work, "It was a miracle; a handful of heroes going in and thousands coming out."

Faded café curtains kept the street at a distance and framed a line of desiccated snake plants. It had been years since the city had banned smoking in public accommodations but the news had yet to reach Snooky's. The air was hazy. Lenny, his vest loose over a concave chest, was complaining to a regular about a new atrocity, talk of an E-cigarette ban. "If ya drink, ya smoke, and I sell cigarettes. Then they banned 'em. Now they're even takin' away the fake ones."

Ed held up two fingers and Lenny broke off long enough to bring a couple of drafts to their booth.

"Besides the bruises on your face, you got some color." Manny downed half his glass and wiped his lips with the back of his hand. "So, what's up with the masters of the universe?" He was in beagle mode, hunched over the table and gripping his glass like a microphone.

"The big thing was sovereign debt, banks getting bailed out with public funds while the pensioners are getting whacked. The underbelly of Europe is stagnating but to get an EU "rescue loan", you have to almost close your schools."

"It's like that all over," said Manny. "Did you hear that in Detroit, people who can't pay their water bills are being shut off? So much for public health."

"I missed that but, as I said, I've been skiing in Europe."

Manny guffawed.

"What I was getting into at Oetz was the precariousness of the global food supply. You have coastal land flooded, new plant diseases popping up, Australia on fire. But the thing is, these people are jumping all over it as a chance to get even richer."

"I'm not surprised."

"I'm talking real hardship on the way, not your Dean and Deluca closing down."

"Where's Alfred E. Neuman when we need him, the 'What me worry?' guy," said Manny, and pulled down the last half his glass of beer.

"That character dates from the Cold War. Now it's actually worse."

"It wasn't great then either. You're a bit on the young side but for a while in the '60s it looked like politics by assassination. Oh, and did I mention Vietnam?"

"Many times." Ed held up his hand for Lenny to bring more beer.

"So, you rubbed shoulders with the elite, did you?"

"The thing is, bad as things may be getting, the boys in charge never betray uncertainty."

"Did Bernie Madoff?"

"My point exactly."

"It's easy to be confident when you never have to say you're sorry." Manny began on his second glass.

"They love volatility, though. What really bothers them is stasis—a flat market. Global warming means everything is up for grabs and there's tremendous opportunities."

"And their grip will remain on the tiller, even if the ship is called 'Titanic'," added Manny.

"By the way, you'd have loved the architecture, all those half-timbered houses. It was like a holiday with the German general staff."

"No dissension?"

"Just the odd Cassandra. That's obligatory at these things, but nothing they took seriously."

"So, where can we ride out the storm? Assuming I can get a good price for my bungalow in Bensonhurst?"

"That's the thing. These guys are retrofitting the entire world."

"Nothing like modest ambition," Manny scoffed. "By the way, that Cassandra thing works. Slip it into your article while you hold your readers over the abyss."

"I'll keep it in mind. My focus, though, is on crop engineering and the coming food monopoly. Getting breakfast takes priority over paying your cell phone bill."

"Let me understand what you're saying." Manny began to draw

on a beer coaster, his huge fist dwarfing a pencil stub. "You've got a soccer match, Manchester United versus Leeds, the 'Mighty Whites' on their home pitch. The clock begins to run down with Manchester ahead, so the Leeds fans riot. They can't accept a loss. Manchester fans run for their lives while police and hooligans are going at it. If this happens once, the league survives. But at every other match? The sport would collapse. Who'd buy a ticket or place a bet? You see what I'm saying?"

"Ah, not really."

"Perpetual mayhem is bad for business. Even for the stock market."

"So you're saying they must have a plan," said Ed, leaning back in the booth.

"Has to be. Maybe in Victorian times hungry people would stand outside restaurants looking in. Never happen now."

"That's not what they think at Oetz," said Ed. At that moment two police officers walked past the window. No helmets, but they wore bullet-proof vests.

"Can the cops protect the penthouses?" asked Manny. "Remember Katrina? It took the National Guard to sort that one out. And that was one city."

"You have a point. I was down at Zuccotti Park once when the Occupy movement had the brokers afraid to go out for lunch."

"When things seriously unravel, your Masters of the Universe will have a plan to impose stability." Manny dug stale peanuts from a plastic bowl and rolled them between his palms. The broken shells littered his shirt. "And let's not forget the guy on the balcony at St. Peter's. He's saying food is a human right." Manny followed religious news, which always surprised Ed. If Manny graduated from a Jesuit college, he'd never say. "That impress anyone in Nordic Land?"

"I think Latin is a dead language, to them at least. But I did get a whiff of a plan: patenting every crop on earth."

"Fat chance." Manny waved Lenny over for another round and the bartender replaced the peanuts. "Here's to the underclass," said Manny.

Ed began to sing softly, waving his glass back and forth. Exhaustion alone was making him drunk. "We want our rights, and we don't care how! We want a revolution, now!"

Manny raised his fist.

"Look, I've got to crash. If I don't sleep, I'll fall in the street."

"And there goes your Pulitzer."

"And my MacArthur," said Ed. "My time will come."

"Absolutely. But remember, they put fact and fiction on different shelves in the library."

"I know. But hey, as long as you and I agree…"

"The first duty of a drinking pal is to be agreeable." Manny watched Ed push back from the booth. "And I've got my own humble column to write." He stood, more solid on his feet than Ed.

"Wait. Can you check something out for me?" Ed fumbled in his pocket for his notebook. "Hardy's after me for more interviews so I've got to leave town in the next day or so."

"No guarantees, but I'm known for turning over a rock or two. Where are you headed?"

"St. Louis, if it works out. I need to reconnect with this genetic engineer, Gabriel Hammersmith. But any info—past employers, grants, patents he's registered—would be a big help. I need to know who owns him."

"His compromises and contradictions. Got it."

"He works for Naturtek and he's on at least one National Science advisory panel."

"And you're wondering if his girlfriend ties him up and beats him with spaghetti?"

"You can let that go. But the rest, yeah."

"I'll get on it, compadre. Now, adios."

Manny shouldered into his rumpled trench coat and tried to lay some bills on the table. Ed pushed them away and put down two twenties. Once on the sidewalk, they headed in opposite directions, Ed stumbling toward the subway. He wondered why he hadn't brought up the rifle shots or the room invasion. And he'd kept Aisling out of it. A puddle washed over his shoe, and he resolved to watch his step.

Chapter Fourteen

AISLING—WHERE WAS SHE? HE dropped eggs into a hot frying pan beside browned onions and chopped peppers, and turned off the gas. The residual heat would do it and the rice was ready. He'd sobered up enough to shop on the walk home from the subway. Flipping the eggs, he remembered a story he'd begun to work on to send to Molly on her birthday. The idea came to him in Oetz after he talked with Bart on the phone. And the story? Bits and pieces he remembered hearing in a bar. Not Snooky's, but a neighborhood place in Medford where he worked weekends during college. There was this one regular, an old guy always ready to trade a tale for a beer. On a slow night, it was an even exchange. Setting his half-empty plate aside, Ed began to write.

Seems there was once a Queen of the Fairies living in the netherworld that parallels our own, according to the Gaels of folklore. Her face was pale, her hair long and auburn, and her name was Mab. As such creatures do, out of idle curiosity if nothing more, she wandered into the human world. On this spring day, Mab was keeping to the crooked byways to avoid attention. With the sun directly overhead, she came upon the village of Cloonsheerevagh. It wasn't much, even those who lived there would tell you that. A mere widening of the road. And there she spied a blacksmith's apprentice at work. Young was the boy, but huge with arms to match. She watched as he wrestled the leg of a plow horse under one arm while he nailed on a shoe. It looked as easy as tying up one's laces. Shirtless and glistening with sweat, he was impressive.

Taken unaware, the usually disdainful Mab felt her chest tighten. In spite of herself, she was smitten. Well, what's done is done, and now to make something of it, she thought. So she sashayed past the forge, not once but three times. Her step was indifferent while she feigned a fascination with the cows across in the pasture. Yet he took no notice. Confused, Mab retreated into the woods to think things over. Weren't her sisters the ones to rave about her beauty? Didn't every forest pool tell her she had no equal? Perhaps a less direct approach would work.

As is well known, each fairy has a special gift. Her's was the power of song. Her voice could bring down birds from the sky. Surely this would net him as well.

That night she crept up to the stable where he slept and sweetened the air with an echoing melody. First it throbbed with past love, then with longing, and finally the madness of desire. Roused from his bed, the lad thought he was dreaming. He'd never heard such a voice. It curled around his head like morning mist from the nearby lake, drawing him outside and toward her.

Ed's eggs were now cold, the story coming together in his mind.

What did the blacksmith see? Not Mab, for she'd taken the form as well as the voice of a bird. Speckled she was, befitting the Gaelic name of the village, sleek and long-tailed. But when all was said, a bird. Instead of the songstress, the blacksmith's eyes fell on Earline. She was the miller's blond and blue-eyed daughter. It was dawn and she was just starting for the local fair, leading two ponies loaded with wheat. Perhaps it was Earline's eyes as she glanced at him through golden ringlets. Or it was Mab's song. But the boy was undone.

As all knew in that part of the world, and perhaps ours, what happens in such a way can never be undone. Mab could only watch as Earline let the ponies' reins fall to the ground. The girl floated across the muddy road, never once soiling her bare feet, and into the boy's arms. As happens in a small village, they'd known each other forever. Maybe they'd learned their letters on the same school bench. Or he'd left garlands of flowers at her door, each being too young to celebrate Beltane in the way of adults. But at that moment, the ice of childhood melted. While the ponies nibbled on the grassy verge, the youngsters hurried off to the stables to make a feast of one another.

Exploding into human form, Mab spun seven times around in anger and laid down a thunderous oath. She cursed the village, all but the blacksmith and Earline who were protected from her jealousy by a circle of love. And so from that day to this, the women of Cloonsheerevagh are destined to be both exceedingly beautiful and utterly fickle. They break hearts the way a cook chops tomatoes into sauce. To those who love them, they are butterflies in a meadow, iridescent but always out of reach.

Who suffered the most, Ed wondered, the men of Cloonsheerevagh or the women?

Ed knew a bit of calligraphy. Later he'd copy this down on handmade paper, roll it up in a ribbon and send it off. It would be more interesting than the usual book. And if it caused trouble with Elizabeth, Molly's mother, that would be part of the fun.

Aisling had given him her cell number, even as she explained that in Mexico, she was rarely reachable. But for the next few weeks she'd be in Boston finishing up her teaching. It wasn't as if they couldn't get together if he acted fast. Or was the smart thing to let it mellow? What would he feel when she returned to Mexico in a few weeks? Perhaps he'd be on a new assignment, the both of them having moved on. He finished the meal, rinsed his plate, and tried to focus on the work ahead.

Hauling out his new laptop where he'd recorded his notes—thank you Schnalstal Lodge—he found Hammersmith's business contact. He'd told Manny he needed another interview and it was true. For Hammersmith, salvation lay with Our Lady of Technology. She wouldn't save us entirely,

Hammersmith had acknowledged, but she pointed the way out of chaos. Would he continue to be forthcoming?

Ed shaped his message, larding in a bit of flattery. Thinking he needed a more candid conversation than he'd likely have at the scientist's place of work, Ed accessed Google and found a personal contact on LinkedIn. He opted for the private one.

When Ed awoke the following morning, he had a reply. If he could get to Missouri in the next day or two, Hammersmith would find time to see him. It had to be at his house though. And no earlier than 7 pm. Wednesday was best, which meant tomorrow.

Ed called the *Chronicle*, got authorization from Hardy's office for airfare, and Mona booked the flight without comment. Hardy must have pre-cleared Ed for reasonable follow-on expenses. By 2 pm, Ed was over Ohio and plotting his questions on a yellow legal pad. The point wasn't just to get more detail on the scientist's research projects. He wanted Hammersmith's take on the big picture. With drought, floods, and super weeds, would designer seeds really be the answer?

For early February, St. Louis was surprisingly warm. But the wind around the terminal still held a hint of winter. It roared in from the Great Plains, an irritable presence that had made the plane flight a challenge. The pilot couldn't seem to get above or below the turbulence. He explained via the intercom that the jet stream was in an unusual configuration, bending south into the Midwest as far as Texas. After one pass down the aisle, even the cabin attendants buckled down.

Ed's rental car was waiting in the Avis lot. It had no GPS but the clerk provided a map of greater St. Louis. Before Ed left New York, he'd Googled a map to Hammersmith's address and printed out directions. Driving time was listed as just over two hours. As it was barely four in the afternoon, he had time to spare. An interview at the Naturtek lab would have been revealing in its own way, but a private conversation might be more candid. Ed thought of the mezzanine looming over the reporters' cubicles. Odd, though, the biologist insisting they meet at his house.

The airport was surrounded by a tired factory landscape. Within minutes it gave way to double-deckers, pre-war worker housing, punctuated by strip malls and fast-food drive-ins where old men pushed shopping carts from one dumpster to the next. The bottle-redemption economy, thought Ed. What was it his mother would say toward the end? "I will sing of my Redeemer, and his wondrous love for me." Nor was "redemption" working out so well for these gleaners, combing through the detritus of industrial decline. Where factory gates had been chained shut, their loading areas were reclaimed by brush. Eventually the tattered urban fabric thinned out to box stores and low-budget motels clustered at highway ramps. It was a relief to finally get to farmland. The undulating hills of worked earth were edged in a rind of snow. Here commerce still clustered at crossroads, but took the form of truck stops and diners. The smell of manure being winter-spread on frozen fields told him he was in dairy country. Rather than little red barns, these were huge operations, the cows tucked out of sight in long steel sheds. The land in between them was dotted with old-style silos, some ceramic brick, others the Harvestore towers that some called 'blue tombstones' when their operations went under. Too many of them, along with federalist farmhouses of wood or brick, had subsided into skeletal remains. It was a history of rural America in the last century. Tall wind turbines on hilltops ground out the latest chapter. Melville had written about Nantucketers plowing the sea; here they farmed the wind.

Along with free-stall dairy barns as wide as airplane hangers, the newest structures were mega-churches. At midweek, their huge parking lots were empty. From time to time, Ed passed a boarded-up school.

Leaving the highway, Ed followed the map onto county roads that offered more scenery. The town greens here were a relief, their ancient trees black and spidery while steepled buildings suggested a community might still exist. After a while the roads became lined with small, shingled houses, firewood piled loosely on lawns, pickups in driveways. The school day was over and lights were on in living rooms and kitchens.

Without enthusiasm, Ed selected a diner that advertised "Breakfast All Day!" He slid onto a stool at a Formica counter and ordered eggs, fried potatoes, and the local sausage from a middle-aged waitress. Noticing her spattered apron, Ed figured she was working the dogend of a long shift. His stool creaked and leaned while the muted TV on the wall ran the same banner he'd seen in the airport terminal, "White House official refuses subpoena to testify." The food came quickly and wasn't bad, especially the sausage. He sprang for a second cup of coffee.

Back on the road, he soon approached Hanover, site of the sprawling Naturtek campus. Housing stock was better; lawns were larger, and cars outnumbered pickups. He'd made good time. If Hammersmith wasn't home yet, Ed would wait. On a low hill, McMansions looked down over cedar hedgerows. As usual, the well-off liked to take the long view. Or not. Then came what appeared to be a new development—the ornamental shrubbery still small, the occasional stone wall from a past era making the vinyl siding of capes and garrison-designed houses beyond look insubstantial.

As quickly, he'd left suburbia behind and was on old roads that worked with the hills and valleys rather than obliterating them. There, coming up fast, was the sign he was looked for, Brighton Farm Road. It was a well-maintained gravel track, running between century-old sugar maples. Come March, he figured, people would likely be setting out sap buckets, if only to show the kids how things used to be. Here and there was a brick farmhouse, carefully restored. Horses in jackets stood motionless behind paddock fencing. Where he came to an intersection, there was a one-room school, now designated a county museum. "1871" was written above the door.

He drove slowly now, watching for Cheese Factory Road. He found it flanked between even stands of red pine, their height suggesting they'd been planted by the Conservation Coups during the Depression. He checked mailboxes. Hammersmith's was in front of an arborvitae hedge and a wall of fieldstone. The house, visible up the drive, was brick with the federalist symmetry of the 19th century. Meadows on either side and trees further up the hill gave it privacy from neighbors. Understated columns flanked the front door, but judging from the grassed-over walkway, it was no longer in use. Driving around to the side, Ed came to a barn-like structure of red clapboards. Apparently new, its rooftop held a solar array. Attached was a greenhouse, aglow with interior light.

Ed parked beside a new Range Rover. He was twenty minutes early. As the house was dark, he walked toward the outbuildings. A security light snapped on but no one answered his knock. He looked into the greenhouse and saw waist-high tables and trays of seedlings. Other plants grew from hydroponic tubs on the floor, climbing toward the ceiling on trellises. But there was no one in sight. Ed went back to the driveway and put his hand on the hood of the Range Rover; it was slightly warm. Back at the barn, he knocked again, louder, and called out Hammersmith's name. There was no response but the door rattled on the latch; it was unlocked. Announcing himself in a loud voice, Ed stepped inside. He faced a large room with work benches along the walls, brightly lit by overhead halogen lamps. Various pieces of equipment—autoclaves, racks of laboratory glassware, and refrigeration units—were scattered on benches. A centrifuge stood in one corner, its lid open. Inside were a dozen test tubes, stoppered and labeled. One wall held an array of active flat screens displaying pulsating graphs. If Ed were to guess, a DNA analysis was running. Somebody was at work.

Blinking under the bright illumination, Ed approached a large table in the middle of the room. Just beyond were two legs in brown trousers stretched out on the floor. It was Hammersmith. The biologist wore a white lab coat and was sprawled face-down in a still-liquid pool of blood. Not knowing what to do, Ed crouched down and felt for a pulse.

There was no discernible heartbeat. He rolled the body onto its back and checked for breathing. Still nothing, but the cheeks were warm. What were the right CPR moves? Chest compressions; then exhale into the mouth? Ed pinched Hammersmith's noise and breathed into his mouth. At least Hammersmith hadn't been a smoker. After twenty cycles, Ed's pants were covered in blood and Hammersmith hadn't responded. All he seemed to have accomplished was to deepen the pool of blood. Somewhere there was a wound, probably in the stomach. It was hopeless. Ed wiped his own face with his arm and found his hands were sticky and there was a metallic taste in his mouth.

"Jesus H. Christ."

He'd come too late. But only just. Wondering what happened, Ed parted Hammersmith's lab jacket and pulled up his shirt. The scientist's stomach had been punctured, that was obvious. He hadn't passed out and fallen on something sharp; he'd been attacked. And within the last few minutes. Ed rubbed his fingers on his own pants and got to his feet. Just beyond was a filing cabinet, its draws open, papers strewn around. And there was a telephone. Trying to step quietly, he moved to the phone and dialed 911. All he could hear was a fan in the adjoining greenhouse.

"What is the nature of your emergency?" said a female voice, calm, robotic.

Ed gave the address in a hoarse whisper. "A man has been killed. I just got here and I don't know if I'm alone. There's been a murder. Please send the police."

There was a pause, Ed supposed while the system scanned for an address. "Stay on the line. A patrol will be with you in ten minutes. Are you in danger?"

"Jesus, I don't know."

Just then a motorcycle revved to life behind the barn. It circled around to the front of the yard and roared down the gravel drive. Dropping the phone, Ed ran to the door. All he could see was a hunched figure silhouetted by a headlight and the bike's brake light flashing as the rider met the road. Then he disappeared.

"What is your name, sir? What is your name?" In shock, Ed replaced the receiver and collapsed into a chair, out of sight of the body. He looked again at the open filing cabinet. Clutching a bench for support, he made his way to the open drawers. Was this messing up a murder scene? He was here anyway. He wrapped his right hand in his handkerchief and poked through the draw with a pencil. Most of the paper seemed to be research reports, some with Naturtek letterhead, others just raw records of lab results. These were handwritten in columns with comments in various boxes. Strips of printed mosaics were stapled to several—blue, red, yellow. Ed supposed they were DNA sequences. Titles on some reports indicated they were growth projections for a variety of crops under varying conditions—humidity, light, and the application of fertilizers. Hammersmith hadn't been growing Christmas poinsettias; he was carrying out basic research. And running trials in his greenhouse. Why not at Naturtek? Why duplicate thousands of dollars of equipment?

Kneeling down and continuing to prod with the pencil, he flipped through the dump of documents. More lab reports and journal articles. Test subjects were labeled in shorthand: D78 soybeans; F360 maize; S44 alfalfa. According to the comments, pollinating insects had been introduced—honey bees, mainly—with ovum formation measured. One chart tallied the population of dead insects—flies, moths, bees—confined with the plants in plastic cloches. In some cases, death rates approached one hundred percent and fertilization zero.

Ed was tempted to take the reports but that really would be tampering with evidence. Instead, he took out his iPhone and photographed anything that looked interesting. The light was perfect. He concentrated on insect deaths, plant germination rates, and fertility. By the time he heard sirens approaching, he'd photographed more than seventy pages.

What was the killer after? Had he found it? Those drawers were more empty than full, even considering what was strewn on the floor. Maybe by banging on the door or just driving up, Ed had frightened him off. At the back of the lab, a doorway led to the greenhouse. It was half open. Ed cautiously stepped inside and saw rows of plants under lights, some in individual plastic enclosures like dry cleaner bags. Trays of seedlings and potting soil had spilled from a bench onto the concrete floor. An outside door stood open, moving back and forth as the wind blew through and rustled plant leaves. This was the killer's way out. If there hadn't been this exit, Ed would have had him cornered. Not a pleasant thought.

Just then, red and blue strobe lights lit the green house and tires crunched on gravel outside. Not sure where to go, Ed returned to the lab as the police officers burst in, weapons drawn. Ed stood with his arms raised, his hands open.

Chapter Fifteen

THE POLICE THREW ED to the floor, wrenched his arms behind his back and slapped on handcuffs. Two officers led him outside where he was patted down and made to watch while his car was searched. They found the blood on his hands, shirt, and pants of particular interest. Feeling lucky he hadn't been shot, Ed didn't protest.

Eventually a detective arrived and took Ed's statement while a forensic team set up lights and began to photograph the scene. Once the body was cleared for removal, an ambulance backed into the yard and the police forced Ed into a cruiser and set off for the station. It turned out to be in Jefferson City. There, serious interrogation began, but at least they uncuffed him. As the officers shot questions at him, technicians took samples of the blood from his hands. Finally he was allowed to wash up. Led back into the interview room, he was introduced to Detective Royco, a squat man in his mid-fifties with a sparse comb-over.

No, Ed hadn't touched anything at the scene, just rolled Hammersmith over trying to resuscitate him. Oh, wait; he had opened the door and put his hands on a counter. Had it been more than one counter? And the telephone. Of course, the telephone; he'd called 911. No, he hadn't taken anything. No, he hadn't seen the shooter. Could he describe the motorcycle? The yard light had been on but the rider was well away from it by the time Ed had gotten to the door. And he didn't know much about motorcycles, not enough to tell them apart. But it looked like the rider was dressed in black leather and wore a shiny black helmet. The bike had a configuration of four brake lights that flashed brightly as the driver turned onto the street. They handed Ed paper and pencil and he diagrammed the brake lights.

And what was his business with Hammersmith? Ed explained he was a journalist interviewing the scientist for an article. Yes, he had talked previously with him—once—but didn't know him in any other context. He could tell by Royco's expression that the detective wasn't much interested in the conference at Oetz or Hammersmith's apparent role in GMO development. "Not our jurisdiction, thank God."

After two hours, Royco's initial hostility flagged and he stopped what had become a loop of repeated questions. The station desk had contacted the *Chronicle* and the data bank of New York Motor Vehicles, confirming Ed's identity. Finally, the Jefferson City police were done.

"Who knew you had this appointment?" asked Royco as Ed stood and looked around for his coat.

"The paper, of course. No one else. We'd set it up by email." Royco's point slowly dawned on Ed.

At that moment two new suits entered the room and pushed past Royco. Neither were senior detectives or prosecutors with the DA; they identified themselves as attorneys representing Naturtek. Nonetheless, they were permitted to take over the interrogation room, crowding Ed until he had no choice but to sit down again at the steel-top table. Royco and the uniformed officers slipped out, closing the door behind them.

Ed went through his story again. These may not have been cops but he was still locked in a police station. But he still owed Hammersmith, even dead, some degree of protection. He wasn't going to mention being surprised when the scientist agreed to the interview or his supposition that the man had some motive in talking to the press. Maybe a crisis of conscience.

Ed explained that he was just a reporter looking to complete an interview begun in Austria. They knew about Oetz but kept returning to the details of his visit to Hammersmith's farm. Had the dying man said anything? Perhaps given him something? No, Ed explained. Hammersmith was dead when Ed found the body. He'd taken nothing. Nor, he said, had he understood anything about the lab. He was, he said, still in shock.

They were an odd pair, thought Ed, neither bereaved about the murder nor solicitous about Ed's brush with a killer.

"We still don't understand the point of your interview," said the older attorney, a frail man with skin wrapped tightly around the bones of his face. "You'd already talked in Austria. What more were you looking for?" The second lawyer, whose neck was as wide as his shaved head, leaned close and stared into Ed's eyes. "And why not a meeting at the company? That would have given you a chance to look around, see some work in progress. Wouldn't that have been more useful?" His lips were a thin line. His shaved head made it hard to guess his age. Was Hammersmith intending to give Ed any documents?

Corporate secrets? thought Ed. "Like I say, I'm a feature writer. I'm working on a piece about the social impact of engineered plants. When we last talked, Doctor Hammersmith had been enthusiastic about their potential. But as I blocked in the story, I discovered I had more questions than answers. And I have to admit, with much of the science I was hoping for a little help." Ed tried to sound naive, a cub reporter. "I'm no geneticist, but the *Chronicle's* readers include an important part of the investment community." Dropping the name of the paper couldn't hurt. "Hedge funds are always on the lookout for the next big thing."

The two men exchanged glances. "So are the Chinese," said the bald one. The aged lawyer scowled at his colleague's remark. The rule must be to give nothing away.

Ed didn't know how to bring the conversation to a close. "I'm shattered by what happened. But there's another problem; now my story is incomplete. Could you guys hook me up with someone else at the labs, a senior researcher?"

"That's not why we're here," said the cadaverous one, moving slightly away. He exchanged a look with the Bruce Willis look-alike that said, can you believe this guy? "Again, did you communicate with Dr. Hammersmith at any time after Oetz?"

"No. Just to arranged this appointment. That was it. I had initially wanted a phone conversation but he said that wouldn't work; there were things he wanted to show me." Then Ed played a card. "I also got the impression that he didn't think phone lines were very safe. So I hoofed it out here." Ed was turning out his pockets. If these guys were suspicious of Hammersmith, it was best to convince them no leaks had taken place.

"Naturtek has a large public relations division." The muscle had passed the ball to the old guy. "As to your further questions, you'll find the company most cooperative with journalists." He said this as if he were reciting a script. "After you agree to allow the company to preview what you write, of course. Hammersmith should have insisted on that in Oetz. Why he didn't follow standard protocol, we'll never know." The attorney looked at his watch. "Understand Mr. Dekker, we're dealing with cutting-edge science here. There's a great deal at stake."

Taking his time, he wiped his glasses with a pocket square. "If the next billion people are going to eat, the world is going to need Naturtek's innovations "

It was a line from the speech Hammersmith had given Ed,

"Direct contact with our research staff outside of a controlled setting is not permitted." Skinhead was taking control of the ball again. He spoke as if he were detaining Ed at a border crossing.

Silence seemed the least antagonistic response. One thing was clear. This was not a wake for a beloved colleague. Finally, the senior man reached into his briefcase and handed Ed a form, the afore-mentioned non-disclosure agreement. "Sign this and you can go, at least for the time being."

Who was running this police department, anyway? thought Ed. Beneath the edge of the table, he closed his fingers into a fist. He didn't touch the offered pen. "For the record, no interview with your employee took place yesterday or at any time since we met briefly in Austria. When I arrived, the man was dead. He told me nothing, showed me nothing. He gave me nothing. And I'm signing nothing. I've been patient, but if you persist with this line of questioning, you'll have to have me arrested and take up the matter with the *Chronicle's* lawyers." Would Hardy defend a stringer? Ed had no idea.

The two suits shared a glance; it had been worth a try. They'd never encountered such an unreasonable person, they seemed to say.

Tired of the charade—they weren't cops, after all—Ed made his way to the door and pounded on it with his palm. A uniformed officer opened it immediately. Royco was standing behind him. They'd been just outside, no doubt listening. Probably watching as well. One wall was a sheet of mirrored glass. Ed wondered if Missouri prosecutors out-source their interrogations.

"If the real police have no more questions," Ed said in a loud voice, "I'll be leaving. Unless you arrest me, in which case I'll need to contact my attorney."

A uniform pushed Ed back into the room while detective Royco and the Naturtek lawyers conferred in the corridor. A minute later, Royco appeared and walked Ed out to the station parking lot. There was his car. His brief case and suitcase were on the back seat. It was clear that someone had pawed through his papers, not bothering to repack them. For some reason, they'd never sequestered his cell phone.

"We know where to find you," said the sallow-faced detective. He gripped Ed's arm, reasserting his responsibility for the case. "We'll talk again."

Chapter Sixteen

ED WAS BACK IN New York. It was late afternoon as he rode the train in from Kennedy. What had he actually learned? No way was Hammersmith the victim of some casual robbery. The killer must have been in the process of questioning the scientist when Ed showed up. There were two visible knife wounds, one superficial on Hammersmith's neck, the other causing the blood flow that soaked the man's stomach. Torture was a real possibility. But with Ed at the door, the killer had panicked. The search of the files looked hurried, maybe a fallback. The motorcycle had sounded throaty and expensive. This was no street kid from St. Louis.

The key had to lie in Hammersmith research, carried out in private, away from Naturtek. Based on the grilling at the station house, the company wasn't happy about it. If they tried to control their employees' press contacts, they'd keep research information in their tight little fists as well. Sending attorneys to question him just hours after the crime smacked of panic.

On the other hand, this was an age of start-ups, scientist-entrepreneurs jumping from universities or corporate labs to found their own companies. All it took was a bright idea and a hedge fund. Had Hammersmith spirited away a piece of Naturtek's intellectual capital? Did Hammersmith himself own patents? Perhaps Manny had already found this out. And had the man reached out to investors? Selling off a vital formula was always a possibility. Hadn't the lawyers mentioned

China? Of course it could be a red herring, dropped to confuse things. One thing was clear: Hammersmith's setup was no hobby lab.

On impulse, after leaving the police station in Jefferson City, Ed had returned to the dead scientist's house. It was three in the morning and the crime-scene floods and blue blinkers had turned the yard into a movie set. In addition to parked patrol cars, a van with the Naturtek logo was parked in the yard, its doors open. Workers in overalls were loading plants from the scientist's greenhouse. And neither the crime scene techs still visible inside the laboratory or the cops outside were objecting. Ed slowed his car but didn't stop.

In rural Missouri, Naturtek was the big fish. If it wasn't controlling the investigation, it was certainly being accommodated.

Climbing up to the street from the 42nd Street station, Ed phoned Manny. They agreed to meet at Bickford's luncheonette on 48th. One of Manny's quirks was patronizing old-style diners, the kind that stayed open 24/7 and tolerated the homeless. Down-market and anonymous, they were a great spot to meet a shy source. And the food was cheap. But with rising rents in the area, it wouldn't be long before this fixture of Depression-era New York would disappear. Or it might become another Merchant's Lunch, the diner in the West Village where a female impersonator played a grand piano.

Taking a seat beside the window, Ed pushed his carry-on against the wall. The window was steamed up and greasy, making it hard to see Manny approach. Leaving his hat to mark his place, Ed went to the counter and chose eggs, bacon, fried potatoes, and toast from heated trays. Only after he'd paid the cashier did he realize this was his third breakfast in a row. But short of a heart attack, a safe choice. Back at his table, Ed found the sports reporter in the opposite chair, warming his hands on a thick mug of coffee.

"Like the hat, but don't be leaving your suitcase around."

Ed put him in the picture.

"So, they killed Hammersmith. Where does that leave us? And can you believe this fuckin' cold?" Manny had kept his trench coat on and was hunched over.

"Did you get started on that patent search I asked you about?"

"Yes, and no. There's nuthin' there in the last five years, at least registered in Hammersmith's name."

Ed shrugged. "That's most of his time with Naturtek. They claim your intellectual output so I'm not surprised about that. I had the guy down as a true believer, not a crook."

"Believer in?"

"The brave new world of synthetic biology." Ed made quotation marks with his fingers. "Course he could have used a front company for patent applications. Is that possible?"

"Sure, but if he did the work for Naturtek and it came to a scrap, he'd be bound to lose. The company's a behemoth. An under-the-table sale to a third party is more likely. But never rule out passion," continued Manny. "People aren't always rational."

"So maybe he was pissed at his boss and wanted to punish the company?" said Ed. "I wonder if motive even matters at this point."

"Just the facts, Ma'am." Manny grinned.

"What I saw was someone torturing Hammersmith to learn something."

"A conversation you interrupted. So we'll assume Hammersmith wasn't forthcoming or the perp was too enthusiastic. Hence the hasty departure." Manny reached across the table and used Ed's knife to spear his last sausage. "You gonna eat this?"

Not now, thought Ed. "But wouldn't pros have taken him off to a black site for questioning?"

"Things get outsourced these days," responded Manny, shrugging. "And when you use contractors, your quality becomes uneven. I've got a cousin in Bay Ridge that takes the odd job as an enforcer and I wouldn't trust him to take out the garbage."

"So, we can rule out the CIA. But the timing is suspicious. Who would have known I was on my way?"

"And how? You said your computer was ripped off in Europe. I'm thinking you were hacked and your communications decrypted. Looks like someone knew you were coming."

Ed digested that in silence. He'd filled Manny in on Austria. "Could they have timed it so that they'd do their thing and I'd be found with the body? But then I got there too soon?"

"With the perp planning to call the cops on his way out? Not bad, Sherlock."

"But I phoned 911 and hung around."

"Good citizen that you are."

"And slipped the noose. As far as I could tell there was no weapon there, which must have helped."

"If it had been me, I'd have planted it. Say in your car. You may have lucked out with a real amateur. These guys aren't geniuses, you know."

"Why not kill me, too? That would have wrapped things up."

"Not if you were supposed to be the chump. And you being killed while on assignment, your editor raises a ruckus. But if you're indicted, you're off the case. Wouldn't matter if you beat the rap. You're compromised." Manny scratched a scab on his ear."

"Because?"

"Conflict of interest."

"Still, could some doofus crack my emails?"

"This is a post-Snowdon world, boy. The skill set is out there. And didn't their legal team show up awfully quick?"

Ed looked gloomy. "So my life's an open book?"

"However boring. I'd worry more about a hit team waiting to sweep you off the board, now that you're still in play."

"Hit team? You not only look like Columbo, you've got the same script writer."

Manny waved it away. "If you dropped all this, they'd know that, too. You sure Hardy has your back?"

"I told him about guys breaking into my hotel room over there. That was what made him fly me home ahead of schedule."

"Let's see how long the love lasts. I always doubted the plot line in 'All the President's Men', you know where the *Washington Post* saves the day." Manny squinted at Ed. "Got anything else up your sleeve?"

"As a matter of fact, yeah. I used my phone to take a ream of pictures of stuff in Hammersmith's files."

"The phone we just determined was hacked?"

"I haven't emailed them anywhere."

"Yet."

Ed looked at the ceiling. "It was the best I could do before the cops arrived. I still have to go through them. If the perp did grab the goodies, it may add up to nothing."

"The cops didn't seize your cell?"

"No. I kept it with me. Seems you can be cuffed but not actually busted. I was just a 'person-of-interest', as they say."

"Let's look them over. But the question remains; why did Hammersmith agree to talk with you? He had to know it was risky."

"In terms of his job, yeah. But getting whacked probably didn't occur to him. Inconvenient, anyway you look at it."

"Spoken like the heartless reporter you are."

Ed thought for a moment. "You were checking him out. Find anything shady? Unexplained income?"

"No. He was a salaryman, as they say in Tokyo. Not even speaking gigs in the last few years. He's got that property in Jefferson City, thirty acres, developable, I'd say worth three mil on a good day. And no mortgage. But as a senior researcher, Naturtek would have been handing him near two or three hundred thou a year. I can't see evidence of any outside income. Course he could have tucked it away overseas."

"So, not obviously corrupt."

"Course as Falstaff said, or should have, 'Appetite hath no limit'." Manny chuckled. "But to be sure about patent royalties, we need his tax filings."

"What about patent envy?" Ed asked.

"If not greed, then pride, you're saying?"

"Say he makes some breakthrough discoveries but the company claims all the credit. By talking with me, maybe he was trying to get affirmation from the press."

"Seems thin." Manny folded his arms across a considerable stomach. "Which brings up that girl you met, Eileen was it? And under unusual circumstances. You still making a play for that?"

"It's Aisling, and not everything has to fit. You're changing the subject." Ed shifted in his seat. "What we know is that Hammersmith was so serious about his research that he built a considerable home laboratory."

"Point taken." Manny pushed back from the table and went to the counter, bringing back more coffee and two slices of apple pie. "You get cheese with it here. Nice, huh?"

Ed ignored the pie. "I think we're stuck."

"When they're out of ideas in the cop dramas, they wait for the next murder."

"Thanks for that. I'll sleep better."

"You said the cops were letting Naturtek clear out the crime scene. Could it be the company was allowing Hammersmith to work at home? Maybe Naturtek was actually lending him the equipment?"

"I'm sure that's what they'll claim."

"And what the cops accepted. Were these town constabulary or the staties?"

"Does it matter?"

"I don't know." Manny put down his fork; he'd eaten both slices of pie. "It could show how high their influence goes. And try this: Naturtek has the deceased working on something sketchy and they want deniability if it goes tits up."

"I know he wasn't cultivating orchids," said Ed.

"That's how I'd play it," said Manny.

"Devious. But take a look at this." Ed handed over his phone. "It's from Hammersmith's files. Sorry about the small print."

Manny squinted at the screen but gave up. "Glad you spared me the gore, but I wouldn't understand this, even if I could read it. We need a real scientist. And maybe a real detective."

"I know we can't catch the killer," said Ed, "but we can expose the bigger picture. You keep digging into the guy's financials; I've got contacts with real scientists."

Manny cocked his eyebrows, doubtfully.

"One I can trust, anyway. I'll share these documents with her on a confidential basis and see where that leads us."

"Just so you know, you're on thin ice with a second-hand computer. Treat it like a Trojan horse. Same with your phone."

"There's a limit to paranoia; I'm keeping the phone. But I could turn the laptop in to the paper. They could pass it on to someone in Lifestyle or Real Estate. I hate to see a $5,000 machine trashed."

Manny reached into his briefcase, a musette bag that appeared to date from the Battle of Gallipoli, and took out a computer. "Do that. But while the paper is scaring up a replacement for you, use this. It's a spare. And it will keep you off the one in the public library."

"Thanks, and thanks for the pie," said Ed. "Now I'm dragging myself home."

"My pleasure."

Chapter Seventeen

In the lobby of his building, Ed pulled a folded stack of junk from the slot in his mailbox—supermarket circulars, fast food flyers, a package delivery notice. That last was interesting. No return address but a St. Louis point of origin. Dumping the rubbish in a bin, he climbed up to his apartment long enough to leave his suitcase, then headed down the block. The pickup point for packages was five blocks away. He took a place in line and was eventually given a padded manila envelope. Still no return address. Back at his flat, he slid a thumb under the flap and dumped out the contents: an academic article by Hammersmith, printouts of journal papers on cell biology by other scholars, and a handwritten note from Hammersmith. Stuck to the bottom of the envelop was an unlabeled DVD.

"My dear Dekker," the note began. "I am sending you this in the event that we are prevented from meeting. If so, and you don't otherwise hear from me, use this information wisely. Release what you wish to the media, but wait at least a week. You are now my leverage, my guarantee of safety. I realize this may be awkward for you. Let us hope it all proves unnecessary."

"Thanks a lot," said Ed. "Now I'm a human shield. Or was."

"Meanwhile," the letter continued, "study this material and if necessary, make it part of your story. With this in the public domain, it becomes pointless for anyone to harm me. I'll explain more fully when we meet. Yours, Gabriel Hammersmith."

Ed could see Hammersmith sprawled out on his laboratory floor.

The package was posted a day before their scheduled meeting. Hammersmith hadn't put this into company mail so he must have posted it in St. Louis himself.

The articles were too dense to scan and as with the material Ed had photographed, he'd likely need help. How had Hammersmith gotten his mailing address? Of course, the business card Ed had given him in Austria. He'd written both his phone number and home address. And that card would that have been in Hammersmith's wallet when he was killed. Not a pleasant thought. Ed glanced over at his door, secured with a police lock. This was a steel bar that fit into a slot in the floor and angled up to a spot above the knob.

Ed phoned Manny. Not surprisingly, his colleague wanted to see the package. As he lived in the Italian South Village, a mile from the Bowery, it seemed safer to meet there than in Ed's apartment. After showering and getting into fresh clothes, Ed headed out.

The Bowery, once lined with flophouses and stores selling used restaurant equipment, was now Chinatown-North. So was Little Italy. Ed passed piles of food store refuse stacked along the curb. The crowd, largely Asian, pushed past him with indifference. It proved easier to walk in the gutter. As the neighborhood transitioned into SoHo, a hundred-year-old industrial zone, the pedestrian texture changed. People were taller, whiter. Rather than push shopping carts, they carried tote bags. Their companions were more often dogs than children.

In the decades after World War Two, SoHo had exploded as an artist area based on cheap loft living. Now it was another bedroom suburb of Wall Street, an aerie for bankers and lawyers too hip for the outer 'burbs and still too poor for the Upper East Side. Though the artists were now priced out, the store designers crafted their shoe boutiques and dress shops to mimic the art galleries they'd displaced.

Manny lived just beyond SoHo's metallic glitter in a walk-up built for immigrants. The neighborhood had been a thriving Italian community, but gentrification, first oozing south from Greenwich Village and then west from SoHo, had consumed it. The facade of the sports reporter's building still shouted 'tenement' but the old tub-in-kitchen layouts had been demolished to make floor-though flats. Ed knocked.

The interior was modish given Manny's disdain for fashion in his clothes, and Ed took a seat on a Breuer chair.

"When I first moved here, the paisanos ran the neighborhood," Manny explained, "But it was a neighborhood. The restaurants paid a gratuity to the mob, which eliminated all street crime. Fact is, this precinct had the lowest crime rate in the city. Reported crime, anyway. Eyes on the street and all that. Even now, if weird people knock on my door, I hear about it the next day."

An open-plan kitchen and dining table filled the front area where the light was best. The floors were replaced, now smooth oak like the countertops. At home with the decor was an elaborate espresso machine. Manny fiddled with valves and gushed steam, then set two cups of latte on the table.

"So, what 'cha got?"

Ed handed him the letter. Manny read it carefully, then looked without interest at the set of articles. "These are your problem."

"Can we play this?" said Ed, holding up the DVD.

Manny slipped the disk into a computer port and an oversized Mac came to life. For thirty seconds they looked at nothing. "This Hammersmith guy blazed a trail to your door, believe it." Finally, the picture flashed on.

Hammersmith was speaking into a video recorder, apparently part of his laptop. From the equipment visible in the background, Ed recognized the laboratory in Missouri.

"Welcome to my world, Dekker. I'm going to explain things in simple terms. Consider it a trot for the papers that may puzzle you. First,

I apologize for not being forthcoming in Oetz. I assumed our discussion was being recorded by my employer and furthermore, I hadn't come to the conclusions I've now reached." He drank from a white coffee mug.

"Eight years ago, I isolated the gene sequence that controls maturity in a number of common crops. I was principally interested in rape seed, also called canola. I was able to remove a portion of the chromosome sequence, inhibiting the maturation of a fully-viable seed while retaining all of its nutritional characteristics. The enzymes I removed regulate ovum formation after fertilization. Not to bore you with details, I ended up with a plant that puts its energy into a single generation of seed, one that actually contains a surplus of amino acids compared with conventional plants. But these seeds are a reproductive dead end. For that reason, the plants must be cloned, a process still difficult to scale up to commercial volume. But in the test plots, the system worked. Later, I enhanced blueberries and four varieties of bean in a similar way. I'm now convinced we can replicate the process with tree crops—figs, almonds." Hammersmith sipped from his cup.

"As you might guess, my employer was enthusiastic. I enjoyed considerable if not commensurate financial rewards, but no public recognition. Naturtek avoided all publicity about this breakthrough while the patenting and commercialization phases ran their course. The lawyers were fearful that adverse publicity whipped up by the vegetable right-to-lifers would stop us cold. That is why we adopted the term 'biological patent' rather than 'terminator seed.' But complications arose. In field tests, we couldn't consistently reproduce the greenhouse results. Plants that grew well in a sheltered environment failed in the open air. Eventually we found that the problem lay with pollination. Plants maximize the vectors that bring about pollination through the morphology of their blossoms, exploiting wind effects and attractiveness to insects. Their one desire, so to speak, is to transfer pollen from the stamen to the pistil, producing seeds which are the edible, though in this case sterile, component. Are you following me?" Hammersmith offered a smile, his teeth more yellow than Ed had remembered.

"Where insects are the significant vector—honey bees, stingless bees, flies, wasps, and butterflies—seed production crashed in our engineered varieties. But let me backtrack. Consider *Bacillus thuringiensis*, or Bt. Getting plants to produce this soil-borne toxin internally was industry's first real success, and seed reformulated to include this systemic bacterium now dominates the market in maize, cotton, and soy. But these crops are self-pollinating or wind-pollinated. Insects play little role. With such plants, the fact that Bt is an insecticide doesn't matter. In the case of our newly engineered varieties, bees continued to be attracted to the pollen. Otherwise they'd simply forage elsewhere. But as our field tests continued, we found that the rate of bee reproduction declined. By the third generation of bees feeding on our plants, the viability of their larva was down by half. Ultimately, we found hives deserted and workers dead.

"Why? We weren't sure. Colony collapse in other locations was being attributed to mites and viruses. Or to the insecticide neonicitinoid. But we weren't spraying our test fields. Without any hypothesis—many things could have caused this problem—we did not report the results to the Department of Agriculture. Which, by the way, does not conduct studies of its own. They use our data. Our concern was keeping this potential problem away from the crazies that have been plowing up experimental GMO crops here and in the UK. Imagine the backlash if it turned out we were killing masses of pollinating insects?"

Hammersmith rubbed his face with his hand. Sweat was visible on his forehead. Manny paused the video to reload his coffee maker.

"It was obvious that we had to go back to the lab. We'd either removed more DNA than we intended or altered the integrity of the entire genetic code. I was sure a technical solution existed but we needed time to find it.

"The bosses at Naturtek thought otherwise. They wanted to rush the commercial release. All they could see was share price and bonuses from a product launch. Many of our older patents had expired and competitors were mimicking those engineered seed lines. At the same time, the natural food movement was demanding GMO labeling. The company wanted to saturate the market quickly enough so that there would be no alternative to our product.

"I stalled the suits for a while. But once they sent me off to Austria, I realized they made the decision to commercialize terminator technology." Hammersmith licked his lips.

"I was boxed in. Research staff aren't allowed to meet with the press—you were the exception in Austria. Perhaps it was a slip-up but as a result, you are the only reporter I know. So I'm handing you the makings of a story. In it, please make my position clear: I'm not trying to kill the industry. I want to save it from making the one mistake that could turn the public against genetic engineering forever."

Hammersmith took out his handkerchief and blotted his forehead. "I wasn't born in a lab. My family farmed for three generations in South Dakota. During the Depression, my grandparents nearly killed themselves keeping a dairy operation going. It was a time of milk dumping and farmer suicides. We were north of the dust bowl but not of foreclosures. When my parents took over, they balanced the books by selling off road frontage. But it was clear to me that farming on a small scale with conventional plants—corn in our case—had no future."

"When the chance came, I ran off to ag school at Cornell and I've been in research ever since. It was my salary that kept my folk's place out of the bank's hands for nearly a decade. Now my brother runs the operation but the pressure is relentless. With the right crop, farms like his can pay again, I'm sure." Hammersmith sighed. "We'll talk soon, Dekker." He raised his hand and the screen went dark.

Manny wandered over to the window and looking down onto Sullivan Street. "So he's saying he's the victim?"

"Looks that way," responded Ed. It was a message from beyond the grave.

"And you're supposed to pick up the pieces." Manny ejected the disk and handed it back. "You can camp here, you know."

Chapter Eighteen

At corporate headquarters in downtown St. Louis, Naturtek's board room glittered under a modernist Scandinavian chandelier. Fragments of light reflected onto mirrors and crystal glasses. With its leather-topped table and sleek chairs, it was a comfortable aerie above the grey clouds and grayer city below. Christopher Addison, chief financial officer, and Marvin Lustig, head of the legal division, were joined by the director of company security, David Luff. The Naturtek team sat on one side of the oval table with Matthew McCord from the U.S. Office of Trade Representative. Like a government inspector at a mega-slaughterhouse, McCord was permanently assigned to Naturtek to facilitate patent applications, regulatory issues, and to liaise with the wider biotech industry. The real outsiders, clustered across the table, were Detective Royco and Dee Sturdivant from the FBI.

After inviting everyone to help themselves from the sideboard, Addison opened the discussion. "With Dr. Hammersmith's death and his lab ransacked, we may have lost control of important research innovations. What more can you tell us, detective? Are we closer to apprehending this killer and getting our property back?"

Royco tapped the folder in front of him. "For such a violent crime, there's surprisingly little evidence. No fingerprints from the assailant. No saliva, no hair other than the victim's. We have size 10 footprints in the blood-pool and on the earth outside the greenhouse but they're from a common brand of boot. If we were to find the footwear, we might be able to match wear patterns but that's largely conjecture. Part of the driveway was muddy so we have motorcycle tire tracks. They're from a Michelin Commander, a mid-range model, very common. The tires are worn so there's no point in checking recent purchases. Again, if we could find the bike, we would have a match. The instrument used to slash the victim—apparently after some minutes of duress which we take to be an interrogation—remains missing. The kill wound is consistent with a six-inch blade, fairly broad. It could be some sort of survival or combat knife. From the direction of the slashes, the perp is right-handed. That's all we have." He laid his hands flat on the closed folder.

"So, a crime of opportunity by a random psychopath?" Addison didn't try to hid his skepticism.

"Nothing of value that we know of was taken," continued Royco. "Victim's wallet, watch, all present. Machinery left intact. There was no entry into the house itself so the killing isn't likely to have been part of a larger robbery. Unless the perpetrator panicked and fled before that took place."

"What you're saying suggests that the object of this—this atrocity— was data. Paper work. That, of course, has been the company's fear from the start." Addison folded his hands.

"We agree," said Royco. "That's the reason we allowed the company to inventory Hammersmith's papers and possessions." The detective was addressing the table but shooting Luff a resigned glance.

"And the FBI?" Addison continued to control the conversation.

"This appears professional," said Sturdivant, "especially with signs of an interrogation. I'm speaking of the neck cuts. We have no one in our regional data base known for this sort of thing—torturing and then kill-ing using a knife. Nor does the motorcycle narrow things down, at least in the Missouri area. We've widened the parameters of our data search to a national basis. So far, no leads. I need to make it clear that we're not the principal investigators here—he nodded toward Royco—but we're lending support. Local police are doing everything we'd do if we were in charge." That earned barely a nod from Royco.

"And what's your take at this point, Mr. Luff? Anything useful on the missing papers? The point of this meeting is to pool our information." Royco spoke in almost a monotone.

The company security head rubbed his hand over a bristly grey crew-cut. "Here's the problem. We don't know what Hammersmith had there. There's no index to his files. If we were dealing with his office at the Institute, everything would be logged electronically. What we're faced with are unlabeled document drawers. We did find two folders, emptied and tossed on the floor. The titles were 'Project 237: run 56', and 'Project 350: run 7'. If he kept a master list of what he was up to, we haven't found it. From the look of disconnected cables, one laptop appears to have been removed. And let me add, we've reviewed the personnel files on each of Hammersmith's co-workers and found no past history that raises concerns. Hammersmith was a loner and his team, from all over and of various ages, didn't appear to socialize outside of the lab." Luff passed down a pile of thin folders. "Here they are, but I believe we've ruled them out."

"Just so we're all on the same page," interjected Addison, "we have no internal leads on the killer and no way to recover data from any missing papers, even if we could identify them. Did you find that samples had been removed from the greenhouse?" Addison pinned first the company security head and then law enforcement with his gaze.

"It's possible," answered Luff. "Tables were knocked over and speci-mens—whatever you call those little plants—were scattered on the floor. Could the killer have grabbed some on his way out? Sure. But it didn't look like a methodical search."

"Not methodical?" Addison drew some degree of satisfaction from that. "And the hunt for the culprit?"

Royco, uncomfortable with the whole idea of meeting on private turf, caught the ball. "Within sixteen minutes of the 911 call, we had units on the scene. Before even questioning this Dekker character, I dispatched teams to block state road 37A, 10 miles north, and fifteen miles south of the location. There are side roads, more accurately farm roads, but 37 is the most direct way to and from the interstate. Did the assailant outrun our check points? Possibly. Just in case, we sent up a bird from state police headquarters to scan for any motorcycles on the interstate. Just one copter was available so we prioritized east. We have 7 photos of possibles, including plates. We're going through the list now, locating and questioning riders. So far, nothing suspicious has turned up."

Lustig, the company council, broke in. "If I may, gentlemen. Motive seems to be the key here." Royco sighed; another amateur sleuth. "As the detective implies, we have to discount a crime-of-opportunity. Hammersmith's personal valuables were ignored. So it's a matter of intellectual property—lab reports or samples.

"That's our working assumption," concurred Royco. "We're familiar with violent crime in the county—meth-addled dopers pulling together the means for a fix—but none of that fits. This was deliberate, methodical if a bit sloppy, and with an escape plan. If we're talking about a professional, he could have had a box truck parked five miles from the scene, driven the cycle inside, and driven off into the sunset." Was he sounding glib? Too fucking bad.

"Or dropped the bike off a bridge near where he'd left another car," Royco continued. "That's less likely given that any vehicle is a hotspot for trace evidence, but we're checking ditches and streams."

"So, it's in our lap?" To Royco, Lustig's disgust seemed feigned. "We will proceed on the basis that data have been stolen and only we at Naturtek can figure out what that might be. We expect the FBI and the police to continue with their own line of inquiry."

What was this, a BBC crime drama, thought the detective.

"Naturtek appreciates that you are giving this the highest priority," Addison said, moving his chair back and winding down the meeting.

"And the man you arrested on the scene?" This from Luff in security.

"A reporter from New York City. Not arrested. We grilled him. Your people did so as well. It's his voice on the 911 call. He could have disappeared but he waited for us to arrive. He had opportunity but no obvious motive or means. And his demeanor didn't fit. As he had nothing obvious from the lab, we released him."

"Nothing, as in seeds under his fingernails? Photos?" It was Lustig, playing district attorney.

"We found nothing," repeated Royco. He'd be damned if he admitted that they'd never checked Dekker's phone. Besides, taking on a New York paper, in this case the *Business Chronicle,* in a prosecution that might have hinged on an illegal data search wouldn't have been pleasant.

"If I may ask," said Royco, "what's the government's interest here?" He'd never gotten a straight story from Agent Sturdivant and now was his chance.

McCord, the man from the trade office, jumped in. "I don't see the relevance of the question. For what it's worth, the government shares patent ownership with companies in the private sector—often as a result of public funding. That's the case here. So we could be looking at a loss to the taxpayer as well as to private investors."

Royco looked at Sturdivant and exhaled loudly enough to puff out his cheeks. His hope for useful information had dried up and blown away.

After Royco and Sturdivant left, the other participants remained seated. "What a fuck up!" said the CFO. "As of now, we have no idea how much of ours that shit, Hammersmith, had, and what we lost."

"It was you who authorized him to work at home," said Lustig with malice. "As I said at the time, it was dangerous."

"It was a calculation. It motivated Hammersmith to think he was in charge. We promised him company stock if he hit pay dirt." He turned to Luff. "It was your job to check up on him."

"We inserted cameras in his lab, like you ordered. No bigger than nail heads. But they focused on his work benches and screens. We had nothing around his filing cabinets or the door. The audio, unfortunately, proved defective."

"And the cops didn't notice these cameras? What about images of the killer?" Lustig asked.

"He passes through a video field in a couple of frames. But only when he's dragging Hammersmith toward the file cabinets. And he's got on a fucking helmet."

"But you didn't share this with Royco?"

"We had to see what was on the camera feed first, and that's taken time. What we have is a guy dressed in black, face covered, so what's the point?"

Addison asserted control again. "I want those cameras removed in case the cops want to take another look."

"Already done," replied Luff.

"I concur," said Lustig. "And wearing a helmet? You'd almost think he expected cameras. Or he was leaving his options open in case he decided to leave Hammersmith alive."

"I know that's not what we authorized," said McCord. "How did things get out of hand?"

"And I never expected this to lead to murder." Addison was shouting. "What kind of a clown did you hire? And pulling this off just as Dekker was set to arrive? What a clusterfuck!" He hit his own forehead.

"Hammersmith was going rogue," said Luff. "The point was to scare him as much as it was to recover our research. But you have to leave room for flexibility in these things."

"Flexibility? Try incompetence," continued Addison. "If this gets out, we're all looking at jail."

"Calm down, everyone. You're the big picture man, Christopher," said the Trade Representative. "And the big picture is the future of agriculture. No one person can be allowed to put this in jeopardy. And, I might add, push our balance of trade deeper into the shit,"

Addison settled down. "Alright. Maybe we can be proactive here. Luff, I want you to tell Royco that we just discovered video from a camera that Hammersmith must have installed. Just give him the one feed. We'll let him examine the images in our office so that no bench data gets out. Since they didn't notice any cameras at the scene, it will be a shared oversight."

"But it will clear Dekker," said Luff.

"Can't be helped. We'll have to address that problem later," said Addison. "But keep in mind, the second interview never took place and all we have from his talk with Hammersmith in Oetz is philosophical mush." The color in Addison's face was changing back to normal.

"Still, it piqued that reporter's interest. Allowing him access to Hammersmith in Austria was a mistake." Lustig didn't want Addison to become too comfortable.

"Getting that guy out of the lab bought us time. We minimize damage and move ahead." Addison stood. "That's it, gentlemen."

After the meeting broke up, he took Luff with him to his adjacent office. "Now, where are we with the contractor? You don't think he took anything, do you?"

"His brief was to make it look like that way, which he did," said Luff.

"We have to contain this now."

"We already have."

Chapter Nineteen

AFTER A NIGHT ON Manny's Mies Van Der Rohe leather sofa and a breakfast of coffee, Ed and Manny started uptown. Their first stop was a computer store in the Village where they burned two copies of Hammersmith's confessional DVD. They also reproduced his articles and printed the photos Ed had taken of the deceased's files. Using them would be tricky. They were, after all, stolen. But they might point in the direction of additional evidence. If the cops hadn't thought to download his camera, that was their problem. Manny took half of everything and Ed tucked what was left into his knapsack. At West Fourth Street, they parted company. Manny had a meeting with an expert on sports concussions at NYU and Ed took the subway uptown. Working from the newsroom seemed the safest course and Ed needed to touch base with Hardy.

Mona, Hardy's assistant, had him wait twenty minutes, eventually motioning him toward the inner office, her eyes hardly leaving her screen.

The feature editor watched him enter. "You need to look at this," said Ed, holding out the disk. Hardy rolled back his chair and slipped the disk into a port on his computer. They watched the confession in silence.

"Let me see if I have this right. Hammersmith develops one-generation seed for common crops, the agricultural advantage being that they resist diseases and maybe yield more than conventional crops."

"But only for one season," said Ed.

"The system works in controlled conditions, but not so well in the field."

"Right. Where plants rely on natural pollinators. Why? Hammersmith doesn't know. Maybe his super plants poison the bugs? But something affects bee fertility and hive populations collapse. That leaves Naturtek with a marketing problem."

"But the company doesn't let it go," broke in Hardy. "They've signaled new product in the pipeline and stock prices already reflect this."

"So they downplay the problem, plan to market everything anyway, but the good doctor won't have it. There's a face-off and when he doesn't get his way, he threatens to go public."

"By working with me, as it turns out."

"And now he's dead, right?"

"Pretty much. Hammersmith thinks he can save agriculture from the coming apocalypse of climate change but if he goes too fast…"

"He brings on famine, the fourth horseman. Revelations Six."

Ed jotted that down.

"Let's talk about evidence," continued Hardy. "If we were a tabloid, I'd say we have enough to go on: a mad scientist, a corpse in a laboratory, a potential food catastrophe. But we're not. So, what can we substantiate?"

"Well, with the video confession and the research notes he mailed, we have him on the record." Ed paused, then decided to leap in with both feet. "And I have data from his files. The killer was apparently going through them and they were scattered on the floor. I took photos." Ed handed over the stack of pictures. "I can't be certain what they mean yet but they could back up what he says on the video."

"This one, on company letter head, is to the CEO, what's his name, Radford?"

"Yes. And Hammersmith is demanding more time."

Hardy stroked his chin as if he had a beard. "I can go with an in-depth piece on the GMO problem. Let's hope more of this new material supports it. But you're also implying the company has committed murder. Legal will stop the story on liability grounds." The editor squinted at Ed. "As for these phone shots, we need to share them with the police."

"I left all the papers as they were so the cops could have taken possession but more likely passed them on to Naturtek. You really think I'm hiding evidence?"

Hardy mulled that over. "Any leads on the killer?"

"I phoned Detective Royco this morning. He said they'd issued an APB on the bike but no results so far."

"What does Royco think is going on?"

"He's keeping things close, including holding off the local reporters. I did a web search of area newspapers and nothing turned up. Not even a death notice."

"Speaking of which, spend an hour with Cellers, our obit guy. Help him with the Hammersmith bio. There'll be investor interest. Write a separate eye-witness account of the death scene and the ongoing investigation. We'll run that as stand-alone, but it will set up expectations for any continuing revelations. What looks like a police lid on this could be part of the eventual story."

"From what Naturtek's lawyers said—or let slip—the company is afraid of corporate espionage. They mentioned China."

"More to work in. It could have diplomatic implications if they make this charge publicly. We'll assume the Feds are involved at this point, so check with the Department of State. Maybe it's State gagging the cops. It's happened before." Hardy tapped his teeth with the end of a pencil. "But you think the crime is closer to home?"

"Well, Naturtek's lawyers weren't shedding any tears. And their cleanup crew stripped Hammersmith's lab that night. Whatever happened, they could have anticipated it."

Hardy tapped the pile of documents. "This may be the only example of his research that outsiders will ever see." Turning away in his swivel chair, the editor began tapping on his computer. "We've got something. The *St. Louis Post Dispatch* is reporting a motorcyclist found dead on a farm road in Jefferson county. A blowout suspected. The bike collided with a stone wall."

"Very convenient, if that's our guy. Anything about what he was carrying?"

"Nothing reported. And no I.D. given."

"So, we might be looking at a closed case. If they pin the scientist's death on this guy, we'd be dealing with another Lee Harvey Oswald—no apparent motive, no accomplices."

"Can a motorcycle fatality be arranged?" asked Hardy.

"Sure. You hit a tire shredding device on the road, you loose control. But if they were trying to retrieve documents, that might be messy. If I were setting this up, I'd do the exchange, pay him, then erase him later. No one wants exposure to potential blackmail." Where had this come from, Ed wondered. From his two years covering crime in Newark, he guessed. "Manny calls these professional killers 'mechanics.'"

"I've heard 'button man'. But don't get me started on the JFK assassination." Hardy seemed to deflate. "You're working with Manny on this?"

"Unofficially."

"He's close to a lot of things. But you may need more regular assistance." Hardy eased away from his desk, the rollers on his chair squeaking. "I'll have sports assign a quarter of Manny's time to your project. We'll say for two weeks. He's got contacts I've never heard of, but you're still the lead. So keep me in the picture."

"That would be great. Manny's already looking at possible financial friction between Hammersmith and his employer."

"You're enjoying this, aren't you." It wasn't a question. "But remember, a crime story may lock in readers but it isn't as important as the business ramifications."

And you're enjoying it too, thought Ed.

"On the motorcycle accident," said Ed. "If no papers were found at the scene, and he is our guy, it could mean someone's cleaning up."

"Or there was no robbery at all and the murder was a charade to get rid of Hammersmith while misdirecting any investigation."

"Well, Hammersmith certainly was expecting trouble."

"Yes, but from where is still a matter of speculation. Biotech is a key to our national competitiveness, has been since the Clinton administration. But if Hammersmith was seen as unreliable, I can see a federal interest in this."

"You're scaring me."

"Just giving back what you told me. By the way, I vouched for you when the police phoned at some ungodly hour. I hope that hastened your release."

"Thanks for that."

"Now, when can I have that murder piece?"

"Almost ready. I just need to touch base with Royco again."

"And the feature piece on food engineering?"

Ed hesitated. "Two weeks? I've got to decode some of this." He tapped the folder containing Hammersmith's material.

"On your way out, have Mona make additional copies of all this, including the CD. I'll buzz her now. We need expert opinion. Hammersmith could be fantasizing. But if he's right about either the longterm potential or the short-term fiasco, there's a ton of money at stake." Hardy talked on his intercom for a moment, then waived Ed off.

"One more thing," said the reporter. "What about Asiling O'Keefe, the woman who pulled me out of the snow at Oetz? Plant fertility is her area. Plus she's in love with bees. Can I get her comment on this?"

"As a paid consultant?" Hardy paused. "If she's willing, we can give her a contract. It may not be easy for her to remain objective, and I'm not talking about her knowing you. Criticizing Naturtek won't do her career any good."

Ed mulled that over. "Or it could work in her favor if she uncovers something startling."

"Just make sure she understands how you obtained those documents, including what you photographed. We'll pay our standard rate. I suppose we owe her something for saving us from having to repatriate your remains."

"There is that. Oh, and I bought her dinner a couple of times. I'm thinking, a business expense?"

"Don't quibble, but we'll let it slide. Now go."

Ed stood in front of Mona's desk as she sorted though the material in his folder.

"Should fit on one zip drive. I'll make several. Better our files than trusting this to the electronic cloud. So much for living in the 21st century." She looked Ed over.

"You're thinking NSA?"

"Everyone collects data, including Amazon. Who knows we have these?" She splayed out the documents.

"Manny LaRock. I've been bouncing ideas off of him. Hardy says we're to cooperate."

Mona raised her subtly painted eyebrows. "So Hardy just mentioned. When our ducks are all in a line, we'll go to Naturtek for comment, but not before. We don't want to telegraph our moves. I'll call you in fifteen for the pickup."

"Ta da!" He handed her one of the zip drives he'd made in the Village. "This should speed things up. But check to see if everything's legible."

Office manager? Editorial assistant? She was behaving like his boss. He watched as she took the material into another room. Probably in her early thirties. More 'nubile' than 'zaftig,' he thought, if someone were to ask. Then he clattered down the steps to the reporters' pool.

Finding a seat, he thought about his next move. Before he could decide, his cell rang; it was Bart. His brother explained he'd just arrived in New York on a quick job and when he'd finished, dropped by Ed's apartment. "Stay calm, bro. Your place got ransacked."

"What?"

"The door was jimmied, the place tossed." Bart went on to say he'd already phoned a locksmith who also repaired doors '*immediatamente*', or so the ad said. "Got to love New York. We agreed on something solid, wood laminate over a steel core. You're going to love it. Strong, but respectable. Your neighbors won't think you're a drug dealer."

"Jesus, I'm glad you showed up. You should have given me a heads up. Are you in town for long?" .

"I can supervise the repairs. I've got a few free days and it would be good to catch up with you, maybe see the city. Oh, the workers are here now. Got to go. I'm also having them install an alarm with a contact on the jam. You'll sleep better knowing that if someone comes in, at least you'll be awake."

"Very reassuring. I need to clear up a few things at the *Chronicle* but I'll be there in an hour or so. That work?"

"Fine. No hurry. I noticed your building doesn't have a super. I wanted to report this to someone other than the cops who, by the way, have yet to respond to my 911."

"Supers disappeared with the corner newsboys. At least in this part of town. If the law shows, could you start the paper work? When I get there we can see what's missing."

"Got 'cha." Bart broke the connection.

Ed sagged against the desk. Maybe Hammersmith had given him up?

Chapter Twenty

OKAY, ED THOUGHT, BART has things under control; no point panicking. Just move ahead deliberately. After a couple of deep breaths, he opened an internet search for Aisling, beginning with her faculty webpage at Northeastern. A brief CV listed her degrees, mentioned her campus entomology course, and highlighted her work with students in Mexico. She'd told him there was a group there now, and that that was where she was headed next. The Tropical Conservancy and the Green Foundation were credited with providing support for her work, illustrated with a few photos of tropical insects. JSTOR showed five journal articles she'd written, one using insect population counts to map pesticide drift. Moving from Tropical Conservancy to the Green Foundation, he found its biggest backer was Ecological Solutions, an industry partnership supported by the Porter Foundation. Shells within shells.

She'd given him an email address but it wasn't what the Northeastern faculty page listed. Going with her personal email, he wrote that he had a stash of research documents he'd like her to look at on a paid basis. Did she have time? He needed to know if the data was valid and what it meant. If so, he could get it all to her with a short-term contract. He omitted any mention of Hammersmith.

As he hit 'send', a runner appeared with an envelop holding four zip drives. No telling how many Mona had made. Thirty minutes later he was climbing the stairs at the Bowery subway stop. At his building's lobby, he heard hammering above his head and when he reached his floor, two workers nodded to him. Bart was sitting on the couch amid debris. A shelf had been ripped from the wall, desk drawers dumped. Bart held a cup of coffee. "I made myself comfortable. Like the door?" The workers were now reinforcing the jam.

Bart got to his feet and the two awkwardly hugged. Six inches taller than Ed, Bart enveloped his older brother, catching him in a vice.

"Great to see you, especially, now." Ed stepped back, crouched, and put up his fists. Bart darted left and hit Ed lightly on the shoulder. "Glad one of us still has the moves."

The banging continued for another hour while the brothers righted furniture and began to restack shelves. The kitchen was the worst, with food and flour spread all over the counter. The neatest part of the apartment was now the new door. It had eight panels in a wood tone and texture. The lock and plate were massive. There were four rather than the usual three hinges holding it to the jam.

"And notice, no peephole," said Bart. "The camera scans the hall but it's mounted to the side where it won't be noticed. They'll put the display screen to the left of the jam. What do you think?"

"It's great. But aren't you overdoing it?" Ed was thinking about the bill.

"Well, imagine a knock on the door. You look through the peephole and bang, there goes a bullet through your eye. You'll wish you had a camera then." Bart had made a pistol out of his hand and flicked his thumb.

Ed winced. "Ouch."

"Besides, you own the place. This is a capital investment. And your front door is your face to the world."

After they worked a while longer cleaning up trash that had once been Ed's belongings, they looked up to find the workers had finished.

They were Asian, befitting the neighborhood. After they carted out the old door, they returned and handed Bart the invoice. "Three thousand, six hundred and seventy-seven dollars," said the lead carpenter in British English. "That includes the CCTV. We had the door in stock so we discounted it down from four thousand five. Installation included." Ed looked around in the mess for his check book but Bart held up his hand and handed the workers a credit card. They swiped it through a handheld reader.

"I can't thank you enough for the fast work," Bart said, collecting the receipt and a manual on the intercom camera. Ed found a couple of twenties in his wallet for each of the workers and took the keys. As they carried out their tools, one whistled the Colonel Bogey March.

"This could be a growth business, given New York," said Bart. "But the price was right."

"About that," said Ed. "I can't let you pay for this."

"Sure you can. I'll shift it off to the company. I was up here for work anyway." Ed wasn't fooled but recorded the favor owed.

The brothers played with the activation mechanism for the videocam, then swung the door open and closed. It was heavy but moved smoothly. The four oversized hinges made sense.

"Now we'll both sleep better," said Bart, settling back onto the couch and ignoring the remaining debris. "Fill me in, big brother. Is this just a regular Saturday night event in your neighborhood or have you pissed someone off?"

"Let's finish the inventory first." Ed's head was spinning. They returned to the bedroom, picking things up as they went along. The kitchen required a broom and trash bags. Only the bathroom was intact. A handful of used zip drives were missing from a desk drawer, along with paper file folders. Actually, all his file folders. But because most of his data was stored in the cloud and accessible via his laptop through a code, he wasn't shut down. The missing zips were just back-ups.

"I already checked," said Bart. "Your CD collection didn't interest them. Course they might have stolen a Vermeer off your wall." It took another hour to reposition shelves and replace the music disks and books. Shattered pottery, things handmade in Central America, crunched under their feet until they'd swept each room a second time. "Too bad about the notes." Bart gestured toward the milk carton that had held paper files.

"They were mostly old stuff," Ed said. "Everything current is on-line or here." He unzipped a compartment in his shoulder bag and showed his brother. "But more importantly, I'm carrying the good stuff, information I just received from a source, a Dr. Hammersmith. I have a copy for you. The more hands holding this, the safer I'll feel."

"Whatever it is." Bart tossed the zip drive a few times, catching it before tucking it away. "So, lay it on me bro, and don't spare the details. You can never tell what's important."

Ed recharged the Mr. Coffee with grounds, glad that hadn't been smashed. "I'm working on the potential for genetically engineered crops. That's primarily why I was in Oetz. As I told you on the phone, while I was skiing, someone took a shot at me. Several, actually. It would have done wonders for my slalom time if I'd stayed upright."

"That's when this Aisling person turned up?"

"Yeah."

"Convenient?"

"You weren't there. She saved my bacon, and at no small effort. That was the beginning. Over the next few days, we kind of connected. She's a serious person." Ed realized he'd never tried to describe Aisling and now he was talking about her in the past tense. "And did I mention the red hair?"

"I think you covered that on the phone. Go on."

"For the next few days I limped around the hotel, attending events, doing interviews, sending reports back to the *Chronicle*. Most significantly, I talked to a Dr. Gabriel Hammersmith, an employee of Naturtek. He was both excited about his work and evasive. At the end, he went off in a grandiose direction hinting that his research could save mankind from a Malthusian collapse."

"Malthusian?"

"Yeah, the guy who said population growth always outstrips the food supply so famine is inevitable. Hammersmith's take was that climate change would make this happen faster. But not to despair, genetic engineering would save the day with super crops."

"A technological optimist."

"But a political pessimist. To continue—and here's a bit of déja vu—the next day someone broke into my room and assaulted me. They took my laptop and gave me what you'd probably call 'enhanced interrogation'. But it lasted only a few minutes before I passed out. When I came around, my visitors were gone."

"They?"

"They put a hood on me as soon as I came in the door, but yeah, two at least. One did the talking, sounding middle-European. Later, the doc there found I'd been injected with some drug, hence my blacking out so fast."

"And Aisling came to the rescue? Again."

"Fuck you! You're professionally suspicious. It was hours before she came by. The computer they stole was from the paper, one with the latest encryption, or so I was told. That's all that was missing. From that point on, I used a machine the hotel gave me. Which, by the way, I just switched for one a colleague lent me." He gestured to his bag. "After that beating, I was gunshy. That's why I sent in my last piece of copy through you."

"And chaos has followed you home."

"So it appears. But there's more. I'd set up an interview to follow up with Hammersmith out in Missouri. Minutes before I arrived, someone stabbed him to death. If I'd been on time, well…"

Bart absorbed that for a while. "What's happening with the investigation?"

"Not much. At first I was the obvious suspect and people from

Naturtek as well as the cops braced me at the station. Eventually, though, they let me go."

"I'm learning more about corporate behavior every day. Whether it's a machine or an employee, when it's obsolete, they throw it away. I'm surprised you got off."

"Me too, especially as I had got blood all over me."

"So now you have this Hammersmith's information. Is it valuable?"

"I can't be sure. I need to show it to the experts. But someone may think so." He gestured toward a broken chair.

"So, what's our next move, partner?"

"I like the 'partner' thing. On my side, I have two tasks. First, I need to finish a story on Hammersmith's death, easy since I was in the middle of it. And thanks to you, it looks like I have a safe place to write it up."

They fist bumped.

"The second is long-term. I have to know what Hammersmith was working on. According to his video statement—that's in here, too— he'd become a reluctant participant in Naturtek's drive for profit." Ed went on to explain what he could about Hammersmith's research.

"So the guy thinks going to the press will buy him security?" Bart shook his head. "And now you're the target."

"So to speak."

"You armed?" Bart's voice was mater-of-fact.

"No. Do you really think I can shoot my way out of trouble?"

"If you put it that way, no. Sneakers and 911 on your speed dial are better bets, now that we've buttoned up the front entry." Bart smiled. "Things being as they are, I'm thinking you need my assistance. I don't have the right get up for a funeral."

"You sure you've got some time?"

Bart nodded.

"I appreciate this. The faster we figure things out, the sooner I can stop looking over my shoulder."

"While you're deciding on our next move, I'm hungry." They'd binned up the contents of Ed's refrigerator which had been dumped on the floor. "I saw a Whole Foods a block or two north. I'll pick up a few things and we can eat here. On the way, I'll look for an electronics store. Your visitors may have left you a present behind so we'll need to do a sweep. And not with a broom this time." Bart grabbed his coat and was gone.

Ed sat at his kitchen table and rolled a chipped mug between his palms.

Just then Ed's phone vibrated in his pocket. It was Aisling leaving a text. "In Boston for the next few days. Would love to look over the info. Let's connect."

If Ed and his brother could catch Amtrak's Acela in the morning, they could be in Boston by mid-afternoon. He checked the schedule on-line and made reservations. Then he texted her back. "Meet at North Station," he wrote, "I'll be arriving on the 3:18 tomorrow afternoon." He didn't want to ask for her address over the phone. No point in implying he was bringing roses.

Barely a minute later she texted back. "No. Meet at my office, 316 Cargill Hall. The Biology Department. As close to 4 pm as you can make it."

So much for discreet, Ed thought. But maybe it was good that her colleagues would be around. But at least she was interested!

Chapter Twenty-One

"The good part is you'll be out of town," said Bart after he returned and Ed mentioned he'd connected with Aisling. "What's iffy is that anyone hooked into your phone knows your schedule and who you're meeting."

"I hear you. Everything's a risk but don't let your imagination run away with you."

"I'm just saying, it might be better if you kept your distance from this woman."

"She's already involved. The *Chronicle*'s hiring her to decipher what Hammersmith sent me. There's always the chance he's hallucinating."

"Cheese and crackers, as Mom used to say. I'm sure that getting her involved was your idea."

"Speed is our friend. Once the article's out, going after me will be pointless."

"All right. But we go together. Call Amtrak again."

"I already booked for two."

"One nice thing about rail travel," said Bart, revealing his teeth, "you get to carry a gun."

They caught the morning train. Ed had spent a restless night on his couch, and as soon as the brothers found their seats on the train, he settled into sleep while Bart surfed the web. With the Acela you got Wi-Fi. Bart was sure he could find something linking Aisling directly to

Naturtek. By New Haven, all he had was that an industry consortium, Ecological Solutions or EcoSol, was funding a number of university projects at Northeastern. One was in cell science, another in entomology. Entomology, he knew from Ed, was Aisling's area. So EcoSol could be the John D. Rockefeller. It had a philanthropic tax status and described its mission as "preserving biological diversity". Interestingly, its last annual report mentioned projects in Mexico to "monitor diversity in *criollo* crop varieties." Had to be Aisling. And this convoluted funneling of financial support was suspicious. All Naturtek seemed to directly subsidize was the Salvard seed bank. For a gentech company, that figured.

Bart moved on to Aisling's faculty page. The photo was small—like a grammar school shot—but her face was striking. He'd need help here. Without hesitating, he emailed Tom Buckley, the tech guru at Executive Action. Tom owed him from way back and wasn't averse to wandering off the invoice. No point in involving the company officially, Bart said. Using level-three encryption, he asked Tom to hack into Northeastern's servers and get Aisling's employment history. Same for her graduate transcript. For Tom this would be as challenging as putting peanut butter on toast.

They'd left Providence behind when Tom texted back. Ed, wrapped in his coat, slept on. With a BC undergraduate degree, Aisling O'Keefe had entered Northeastern six years ago on a 'full-ride'—a complete scholarship with a teaching assistantship. With her degree in hand, she was now listed as 'Adjunct Instructor'. There'd been a couple of departmental prizes, then grants from Tropical Conservancy, an arm of something called the Green Foundation. Getting curious, Tom had also looked at her high school years. These were less straight-forward. She'd withdrawn from a parochial academy at one point—there was a year missing—but she turned herself around and finished well enough to get into BC. What happened? Illness, breakdown, jail? Impossible to say. "Should I look further?" Tom asked.

"No", responded Bart. "Looks like ancient history. The main thing is, she's never worked at Fort Detrick making plagues." Clapboard double-deckers and idle brick factories slid past as they slowed to urban speed. Ahead lay South Station. "Well done, Tom, and thanks."

It was funny how things had changed since high school. Then Ed had been the big guy, the one who'd gone through it all first: sports, girls, that sadistic English teacher they both suffered under. Then they'd both sobered up, confronted with a mother home from the hospital with inoperable cancer. She'd seemed to shrink, finally disappearing under her blankets, just a white and waxy face. Both Bart and Ed had moved her a few times from her from bed to a chair and she'd weighed almost nothing. Then their father had gone AWOL, leaving Ed to parent. Or try. When the army beckoned, Bart couldn't leave fast enough. For a while, the military was a good fit: housing, a schedule. And while other guys were only the next bunk away, they left you alone, especially during deployments. Finding focus, Bart had moved up the enlisted ranks. Even Afghanistan had proved negotiable, at least in the first few cycles.

Now Boston was sliding past the window. No, the Middle East wasn't his first encounter with death.

And weren't the services flush with money after 9/11? The in-theater bonus pay was great to a young guy and promotion fast. Less interesting were the landscapes. Iraq, Afghanistan buzzed with unintelligibility and there was never a front you could see on a map. After a while, the job narrowed down to just keeping his men alive. A stint at officer training at Quantico was a relief and toward the end, he'd commanded a platoon. A second lieutenant's uniform still hung in his closet. But the mission? What was it, really?

Then he'd stumbled upon Elizabeth that evening at the National War College. Thinking about it now, he had to admit he'd caught her in a moment of rebellion. She'd just finished Georgetown Law and was at a talk given by some historian on the Geneva Convention. Part of his training, too. But the guy was so dull. They found themselves together during a break, looking for a graceful exit. She was on assignment from her K-Street lobby shop and he was on a Pentagon rotation, a 'comer' needing the polish of an in-service degree. And Liz, well, as the song says, she was burning just like kerosene. Two weeks later they were over in the Eastern Shore of Maryland standing before a justice of the peace. Then, more soberly, they remarried at her family estate in Virginia. He'd been the gypsy stealing the princess, no question. God knows what they'd said to her in private, but they went through with the ceremony. Probably keeping one eye on the silverware. But then Liz found her groove, proving adept at turning her clients' 'suggestions' into actionable legislation on the Hill, and they found themselves in a very comfortable three bedroom in Arlington. 'An investment', her parents said, handing her a check. But then Bart had deployed to Afghanistan, yet again. Even the surprise arrival of Molly didn't keep him home. And Liz had hired Consuela as nanny and housekeeper, not to say a predictable presence at the end of the day.

Not that Liz wasn't a great mother. While Molly moved from day-care to private day school, it was Elizabeth who vetted the teachers and hired the tutors in math or tennis. Here and then not, Bart had begun to think of his life as someone else's home movie. Finally pushing back, he resigned from the service and joined Executive Action. Hell, he could research the best orthodontist in northern Virginia as well as Liz. But driving home from work each evening, he was haunted from time to time by the fear that he wouldn't recognize his house. That he'd just keep going.

They'd tried counseling. And that had become a "cooling-off period" with him living in a small apartment in Crystal City. For the last six months, it was the new normal.

ExAc had been started by a major under whom he'd once served. Private security was a growth industry in the new century so their enterprise found solid footing from the beginning. Getting the balance right between overhead and income was always a challenge, though. It wasn't like working for the government. Bart still cringed remembering a time when he rented a bus to take Molly's entire fourth-grade class to the National Aquarium. It was her birthday and he wanted to come up with something impressive. Then, with the kids lined up at the ticket booth, he found that his credit card was maxed out. One of the other parents had to bail him out.

As he and Liz stumbled toward joint custody, there was one bright side. He'd never have to spend holidays with her parents again.

As the train slowed, the sound of the wheels increased. The continuous welding on the rails wasn't holding up, he thought.

Nothing was final. They agreed that Molly should keep things familiar—the same house, her school. Bart couldn't care less about dividing their assets. And hey, wasn't the house hers anyway? He was happy with the ten-year-old Jeep and having Molly a couple of weekends a month.

No, Elizabeth hadn't finalized the divorce. So much for her being decisive. Every so often they'd meet over lunch in the District to sort things out: should Molly take Spanish or French? If Spanish, couldn't Consuela help? If she transferred to the Gurney School, she could start off in Mandarin. But that would mean making a new set of friends. Then there was the coming summer. Soccer or violin camp? They'd let Molly decide.

Seeing Molly every 12 days was like watching a time-lapse photograph. Her visits made the rest of his calendar grey. He was providing counter-surveillance for CEOs worried about competitors, checking their offices for listening devices, at times going abroad to escort them on remote site visits. He was using skills he'd never learned in the army. Once he'd even carried out opposition research for a political candidate. None of it resembled what he'd been taught in high school civics.

Molly would love Boston, he thought, the museums especially. What was that place made famous by the art theft, the Gardner? That would be a twofer, fine art and larceny.

He opened his wallet and glanced at Molly's photo. It was out-dated now. The braids were gone, but the braces were still there. Like her mother, she was a beauty.

On the window side of the seat, Ed finally woke up. He looked around as if someone else had put him on the train.

"Five minutes to Beantown, bro. You sleep well?"

"Like a corpse." Ed put his hand on his heart. "They say when a woodchuck goes into hibernation, its heart beats only twice a minute and they're nearly dead. That's how I feel."

"No surprise. You got the shit beaten out of you in Europe and back here you trip over a dead body. You need a vacation."

"I just wish I could sleep on planes. The thought of being in an aluminum cigar tube thirty-thousand feet in the air is unsettling. Give me the thump, thump of crappy old railroad tracks."

Bart smiled. "And a chance for quality time, if watching you sleep counts."

"Right." Ed shook himself upright. "I never asked, but how's your life going?" The train had slowed to a crawl.

"Executive Action is, well, weak on the action. And I'm not the chief executive. But no one is shooting at me. You want a hardened vehicle? A secure conference venue? Call us. The real fun is chasing the occasional bookkeeper who's run off to Vegas with accounts receivable and the receptionist. Then we get a finder's fee."

"Nothing boring. And I see you're up on surveillance."

"You mean sweeping your apartment for bugs?" Bart shrugged. "I find white-collar crooks boring. They have the same weaknesses as you and me—drugs, gambling, sexual fantasies. They just carry them a little further."

"No terrorists in your sights?" Ed lowered his voice theatrically. "Or is it forbidden to say that word in public?"

"We're not at an airport. Free speech reigns, which is another advantage of train travel. Then there's this." He patted the holster under his arm. "Lately I've been managing a small team. I've been out to Bahrain twice. But after you've seen Baghdad's Green Zone, the Emirates aren't so exotic. Just ludicrously over-built."

"Ah, but the women." Ed pulled his scarf across his mouth and batted his eyes.

"They're just another set of complications. Do you bow? Do you shake hands?"

"Speaking of which, how's Elizabeth?"

"Funny you should ask. The divorce thing is still in limbo. But we're two strangers connected by a small child and school bills."

"I didn't know things were that bad. You can't un-parent."

"I know. But we're becalmed in the horse latitudes. But my nightmare is coming by for Molly and confronting a strange guy at the door."

"Think you can contain the violence?"

"I'll try."

"I've thought of you as a model family." Ed shook his head. "Compared to my own sorry state. How's Molly taking all this?"

"Okay, I hope. We get together, do fun things. If she blames one of us more than the other, she's not saying."

There's the bonus of two Christmases. But Ed smothered that remark. "Counseling?"

"Petered out after a couple of tries. She picked a woman who naturally wants to talk about our sex life. If I say nonexistent and Liz says just about right, how's that helpful?"

Ed let that pass.

"If Molly becomes a kleptomaniac, we'll try the shrink again. Seems that at her school, divorce is just another phase of life."

"And I thought living like a hermit was a problem."

The buildings were taller now, the triple-deckers and factory yards replaced by office towers. Occasionally the ocean glinted off to the right.

"Liz said she felt like she'd married a cop, always waiting for that midnight phone call from the ER."

"Even after you switched to private security?"

"Emotional habits are hard to change. And I was still locking up a gun in the home safe."

Now the train bucked.

"Molly's what, nine?" Ed asked.

"No, you doofus, eleven and in sixth grade. She's a little ahead of her age group." They passed a line of stationary freight cars. Or the cars were moving and they weren't. "Did I tell you we actually have a maid? A Salvadoran woman Liz found through some agency. She comes in the afternoon, straightens up, picks Molly up at school, and gets dinner going."

"Is Molly calling her 'Mommy' yet?" Ed regretted the words a moment later."

They sat in silence for a long minute, the train limping forward in stops and starts. "Speaking as someone with no stable relationships," said Ed, "maybe you're over-hasty in calling it quits with Elizabeth."

"Sending me back to the shrink, eh, and torture by a white-noise machine?"

"Your divorce will ruin my holidays."

"You never visit anyway. Or hardly." Bart looked beyond his brother to something that was no longer there. "To be honest, I may not have a lot to offer her."

"The diagnosis *de jure*, PTSD and all that?"

"More like I'm on edge. Even at night."

"You go for help?"

"Can't have my chart saying nutso'. It's a career-killer, civilian or military."

"Fake name?".

"A fake mustache?" Bart's smile broke the tension. "Not a bad idea."

The train stopped dead still short of the station. Workmen wearing florescent vests wandered around outside. Must be some sort of track work, Ed thought. He looked at his watch.

"You have to tell Aisling about Hammersmith, that he was murdered. It's only fair."

"I know. She needs the chance to back out. I'm bringing her a check from the *Chronicle,* though. You think I'm luring her into a trap?"

"I think you're starry eyed and in a trap." Bart raised his eyebrows. "But don't worry. I won't rain on your date. While you're getting reacquainted, what should I do?"

"Manny located an old colleague of Hammersmith's, a professor at MIT. One of us should talk to her, see if Hammersmith mentioned having any enemies. Or problems with his research."

"That I can do. But first I'm seeing you off to your meeting with the passion flower. I want to make sure no one's tailing us."

Chapter Twenty-Two

THEY CROSSED THE STATION'S concourse to a taxi stand. The outside air was bitter, swirling their breath like cigarette smoke. Bart checked the street, then they slipped into the back seat of a cab. In minutes they were registering at a nondescript hotel in an industrial section of Cambridge. Leaving their luggage, they walked to the subway and rode together until they crossed the river back into Boston. "Here's where I get off," said Bart, running his eye up and down the car before heading for the platform. "Call me as soon as you can. Otherwise, I'll see you tonight at the hotel."

With one transfer, Ed arrived at Huntington Avenue station twenty minutes later. A posted campus map sent him to Cargill Hall. It's probably named for the big grain trader, he thought. Somehow the phrase 'America's largest privately-held company' echoed in his mind. Or was that Walmart?

Aisling's office was on the third floor, the door open. Backlit from a window that looked out on the Fens parkland, she was bending over a stack of papers on her desk. The sun set fire to her hair.

"Thank god you're not here to protest a grade," she said, registering his presence as if they'd seen each other yesterday.

"I didn't realize you were still teaching."

"Finishing up the J-term. Then I'm out of here to balmy Mexico and a different set of students. Different and better." She patted the pile of papers. "This bunch of wankers!" She pantomimed tossing the stack into the air. "Let's just say their ambition exceeds their competence." She put down a red marking pen and began to work her way among chairs and boxes toward Ed. "I also have to vet a new batch of field work applicants for next year. Everyone wants to get away from a Boston winter." She held out her arms and they embraced.

"Or they want to work with a great teacher."

"Well, my grant covers their expenses but they better not be expecting a vacation." She laughed. "No side trips to Puerto Escondido."

Ed stepped back and struck a surfing pose, holding a Manila envelope.

"Don't you wish. But what's happening with the leg? No crutches, I see." Aisling closed the door and worked her way back to her seat.

"Just stiff from the train ride, but as long as I bite down on a pencil..." He settled into a rocker embossed with the Northeastern crest.

"They give you these instead of a raise," she said. "If you get one with a cushion, we call the chair 'well-endowed'." Hers was bare wood. "So, what have you got for me?"

Ed noticed lines around her eyes he hadn't seen in Austria. He held out Hammersmith's article and DVD confession. "Remember I interviewed Gabriel Hammersmith at the conference? And you said you knew him?"

"Of him."

"He agreed to a second interview in Missouri. But—and this is a shock—just as I arrived at his place, someone was leaving out the back after killing him." No point beating around the bush.

"Jesus, Mary and Joseph." She gave a seated jump. Back on her feet, she was pacing. "Just as you got there? You could have been killed!"

"Wrong place at the wrong time, as they say. It happened in a lab attached to his house." Ed went on to describe what he saw and his night in the police station.

"They gave you the third degree?" She slumped against the edge of her desk.

"I'm being over-dramatic. No 200-watt lamps or rubber hoses, but as I was the last person on the scene…" He cleared his throat. "It gets more complicated. When I got back to New York, I found a package waiting for me from Hammersmith. This." He gestured to what was in his hands.

"I don't understand."

"He thought this would be some sort of insurance policy, a deadman switch, as it were. He could say that if he were to die, the word would get out. Unfortunately, the gambit failed."

"He was under threat? By whom?" She squinted at him.

"His employer, apparently. They weren't seeing eye-to-eye on the direction of his research. He wanted to go slow; they had the pedal to the metal."

"Unbelievable."

"Turns out someone wasn't willing to play by his rules because shortly after that, my apartment was broken into. My brother, Bart, happened to come by for a visit and helped me straighten things out. Now he's become my extra set of eyes."

"You have a bodyguard?"

"That term is alarmist. His regular job is in security. So he's helping out. In fact, he's up here with me in Boston."

Aisling glanced at her office door, wood with a large opaque glass panel. "Doing what?"

"Right now?" Ed looked at his watch. "He's about to check out a lead at MIT. One of Hammersmith's old colleagues is there. She might be able to tell us more about his work."

"Don't take this in the wrong way, but you are a walking disaster." She stepped toward him and hugged him again, this time tighter. "It's too fucked up."

"I agree. But I'm not just telling war stories. I want you to know what you could be getting into. The *Chronicle* will pay you to interpret what Hammersmith sent me, his paper in particular, but as far as I'm concerned, we can just do dinner and that's it."

"You're looking for what we academics call 'informed consent'?" She looked him up and down. "Who knows about this trip? Who knows about me?"

"My editor and a colleague at the paper. Then there's Bart, of course. That's it."

Aisling took the papers from him with two fingers, as if they were contaminated. Reluctantly, she looked over the titles of the articles.

"There's a check in the envelope, if you're on board. If not, absolutely no problem."

She was thoughtful for a moment. "If they tried, they could probably find me through you. Whoever 'they' are."

Ed wasn't sure how that worked but he stayed quiet.

"So, what the hell? I'll take the money and run. I'm leaving the country soon anyway."

"You're the expert we need. Then again, I did want to see you."

"I figured that." She rubbed her tongue around in her cheek. "I'm serious about leaving for Mexico. It won't be tomorrow, but once I'm gone, only the department secretary will know how to reach me. And she hardly knows my name, anyway. I can swear her to secrecy." She found the check and waved it as if the ink was wet. "So, you want me to evaluate Hammersmith's research, or what's here at least?" She flipped through the pages. "I won't be able to get to it for a few days."

"No problem. But sooner is better. There are also some photos I took of his papers. I can email them to you if you're interested in getting in that deep. But that part would have to be off the record."

"Because you stole them?"

"Looked at them, while I was at his lab. It's just that the data there might give you a line of attack on what he sent me. Which isn't stolen."

"You're having me walk a very fine line here, because none of this is published work."

"There are some journal articles, so that much is on the record."

"Also, this isn't exactly my area of expertise."

"I just need the big picture, the implications. And if you can tell me the numbers seem valid, that's a huge plus. And it is biology."

"So's infectious hepatitis." She looked him up and down. "The only reason I'm even considering this, other than the money…"

"Of course."

"Is that you've already blazed a trail to my door. And given Austria, I feel involved."

"The quicker I get a story out to the public—assuming what you find holds together—the safer we'll all be." Without thinking, he leaned forward and kissed her.

She pushed him away, holding him at arm's length. "Neither the time nor the place. Here's what we'll do. My apartment address is in the college system, so I'm not anxious to go back there. But I've been watching out for a friend's cat for the last week and I have the keys. It's closer, just down Huntington Ave. If I need to, I can even borrow her clothes while I get this course work finished and start on your little project." She stopped for a moment and seemed to listen. "If we leave from the side door of this building, we can avoid the lobby."

Ed was impressed. "A reasonable precaution."

"We pass a Stop 'n Shop on the way. Eating her food would be a little over the top, don't you think?"

"Sounds like a plan," he said. "I would have been happy to buy dinner but takeout will work. Who is this friend?"

"Just a colleague. I've been checking on her cat for a while, and I can assure you the cat is all you have to fear."

"Let's hope." Ed crossed his fingers.

"But while we're coming clean, this animal is very protective." She shrugged. "Maybe hunkering down is the best way to go." The sun was losing out to leadened sky, the room resolving into shadows.

Aisling packed a briefcase, pulled on her coat, and wrapped a wool scarf around her neck. The coat had a hood which she pulled up. With Ed hunched in his leather jacket, they slipped out into the corridor and down a back staircase.

Aisling took the lead at what turned out to be a Whole Foods. Stop 'n Shop was a generic term in Boston, like Kleenex. They went straight for the prepared buffet and ended up with eight plastic boxes of assorted stuff, two bottles of mineral water, and a good California red. A restaurant meal might actually have been cheaper, he thought as he took his credit card back from the cashier. Fifteen minutes later they were on the third floor of a pre-war brick apartment house. The door was doughy with repainting but the building looked sound. And they'd needed a key to get into the lobby. She took the food into the kitchen while he threw the deadbolts. Before they did another thing, she fed the cat, an orange monster that circled around her feet.

"Maine coon," she said. "Name's Charleton. He likes a lot of attention."

"Charleton? Odd name." Ed reached out to establish diplomatic relations but the cat had eyes only for its dish.

""It's something of a joke, Charleton Coon was an American anthropologist from the last century who believed in the natural supremacy of Europeans. The cat believes in species supremacy."

Ed gave the animal plenty of space and looked around. The room was comfortably used, books and more books on the floor, the furniture ill-matched in a way he read as male. Aisling laid out plates on the kitchen table and brought in bowls into which she'd off-loaded the food.

"Feeling normal?" she asked, opening the wine. "Last time you were teetotaling."

"I'll push the envelope for at least one glass." They touched goblets. "Think this will be enough?"

"Enough for what?" She smiled.

"To let us forget the headless horseman on my trail."

"Wrong state. In Massachusetts, think witches, though we strung up a few Quakers on the green, as well. But take a clue from Charlton. Eat, and then you can go to sleep on the couch." The couch, he noticed, was an inch deep in animal hair.

The wine gave out before the food was gone. "Are you two actually doing the job of the police? I can see you being motivated, having found Hammersmith. I mean, the way he was."

"Absolutely not. But here's the thing. The cops don't seem interested. They have a suspect, a motorcyclist. They're going with the idea that I interrupted a random break-in. The owner challenged the thief and got killed for his trouble."

"Which you don't believe?"

"Not for a moment. This was targeted, something Hammersmith seemed to expect. Hence the stuff he mailed."

Aisling was now sipping coffee. She'd found ground beans in the refrigerator and worked the plunger on a French press. Ed realized she was quite at home here.

"Look. I have to get back to New York tomorrow to work on this story. But if you want, I can ask Bart to stick around for a few days to keep an eye on things. When are you off to Mexico?"

"A week, I hope. Can you really see him sleeping on that couch?" She grinned. "Or is he the good-looking brother?"

"He definitely is, but don't tell his wife that."

"Now, now. Don't go all competitive." She looked at him with flirty eyes. "But who would watch *your* back? No. At this point the bad guys may not know I exist. I've got all I need here in the apartment, including plenty of work." Her briefcase, propped against a chair, was bulging. "If I need something, I can slip back to the office after hours. I've got a building key. Our host," she gestured to the entire apartment, "is a forensic anthropologist who works across campus, when she's here. You've heard the term silo? That's what academic departments tend to be. Not even our secretary would know her."

"A forensic anthropologist? "

"Unfortunately, I haven't had the time to ask her about Oetz, but I will. We're just friends. You were thinking lovers?" She grinned. "I met her through her former boyfriend, someone I was also close to at one point. Then I realized she was the better conversationalist."

"They shared this place? I have the feeling there's a male lurking around."

"Long gone. But quit pissing on hydrants."

"Goes with the chromosomes."

Just then the phone in Ed's pocket vibrated.

"You were supposed to call," said Bart.

"Ah, sorry about that. All's well here, but I got a little tied up." He looked toward Aisling and she feigned deafness. "Why don't I meet you back at the hotel later. I could be running late."

"So you made your connection?"

"We'll compare notes then. How about you? Did you catch up with Hammersmith's associate?"

"She postponed. I set something up for tomorrow on the MIT campus. The quicker we wrap this up, the sooner we can get back to NYC."

"Did you get any sense that we'd been followed?"

"No, but if someone is good and part of a team, it's impossible to spot them. Why?"

"Let's get into it later. I'm just concerned about my colleague here."

"Later it is." Bart rang off.

Aisling had moved to the sink and was cleaning up from the meal.

"So, how is he, your brother, I mean."

"He's at loose ends. He showed up at my place as if he didn't know what to do with himself. Keeping him busy was my idea."

"At loose ends?" She raised her eyebrows.

"Frustrated, then. He just separated from his wife and it looks like it may become permanent. That raises the question of their daughter. So much for perfect families."

"So he flees into derring-do. You said he was a military guy?"

"Yeah, but working private now."

"How's that make you feel? I mean, aren't you the older sib?"

"But not necessarily the wiser. Like I told you, our parents died when we were both young. When Bart eventually set down roots, that was actually reassuring for me. Now, it seems, 'All that is solid melts into air.'"

"And man is at last compelled to face with sober senses his real conditions of life."

"I'm impressed."

"You think my life is all microscope slides? When you cat-sit, you can discover some interesting reading. Besides, I have to sound better educated than my students."

"Actually, I was thinking that you picked up on Bart's emotional state pretty quickly."

"You can't be thick-skinned and work with undergraduates."

"On that note, I guess I should go. You seem all set up here."

"I do have Charleton for company." She was drying her hands. "But his vocabulary is limited and he doesn't carry a gun."

He was on his feet when she wrapped her arms around him.

"You think I do?"

"I'm sure May West would have an answer to that."

Chapter Twenty-Three

THE NEXT MORNING, BART walked north on Cambridge Street, scanning the crowd behind him. Ed hadn't shown up at the hotel, but no surprise. What had cinched this appointment with Dr. Ciobanu was dropping the bomb, telling her that Hammersmith had been killed. She'd been about to hang up. They'd agreed to meet today in her building, Life Sciences. Bart's muscles felt tight and he needed some exercise so he decided to walk there. But not directly. He could cross the Longfellow Bridge into Boston, circle around to the government center, and then retrace his steps. The walk would also reveal anyone showing him any undue interest.

A rind of jagged ice rimmed the Charles Basin. Runners in brightly colored tights pounded along paths by the shore, splashing through salty snow. Once up on the bridge, Bart found he was alone. Cold gusts from the bay told him why. The noon sky was dull, the sun a silver wafer so dim that the ornamental lights along the walkway had blinked to life. Leaning over the railing at one point, he caught a side view of a Viking ship carved into the stone pier. According to a signboard at the entrance, this was fanciful history. Back when the bridge was being built, a Harvard scholar had convinced the designers that Leif Erikson had rowed up the Charles, half a millennium before Columbus. Intent on applying to Harvard, thought Bart. A fantasy to be sure, but the conceit had ended up carved in granite.

Once he'd returned to the Cambridge side, the MIT campus opened up on his left. He was soon on pedestrian paths. There was a Parthenon-like building, probably a library. Nearby was Kresge Auditorium. One of the odd facts he'd picked up while checking out the university web page was that the auditorium was said to have perfect acoustics. What else would you expect at MIT?

A sign pointed the way to Life Sciences. Were there death sciences? He'd been in Washington long enough to answer that. DARPA, the Defense Advanced Research Projects Agency, covered that base. He suspected that more than a few of the imposing buildings held laboratories fueled by DARPA contracts. The wind had picked up. Students on the walkways were wrapped in puffy coats, scarf ends flying from their necks. The New England *hijab*.

A thin woman in her mid-fifties was standing in the foyer to Life Sciences which opened onto a large but empty lounge. The stone fireplace, dominating an arrangement of easy chairs and sofas, was cold. Above him, tiers of balconies drew the eye to a large skylight, now dappled with snow.

"Bart Dekker," he said, extending his hand. Hers was icy.

"Daria Ciobanu." Her Eastern European accent gave her voice an edge. With a nod, she led him to a pair of armchairs.

"Gabriel is dead, you say?" Her gaze bore into his face. "I have trouble believing that. And you are?"

"I'm working with a journalist at the *Chronicle*, Ed Dekker, helping him with leg work. He spoke with Hammersmith in Austria a week or so ago, then arranged a follow up interview in Missouri. But when he arrived, he found your colleague dead. I'm very sorry for your loss."

She seemed rigid, impassive.

"This was near the Naturtek facility, but actually at Hammersmith's home. Police suspect the assailant escaped by motorcycle. Perhaps it was a botched robbery, or something else."

"And you want to talk with me, why?"

"We know you two collaborated some years ago. If his murder had anything to do with his work, we thought you could suggest where we might look for a motive."

She settled back and folded her arms. "You say you work for a newspaper, but I think you are police. Yes, you are really police."

"No, but a good guess. I'm in private security." He showed her his Executive Action identification. "It's my brother who's the reporter. I'm giving him a little informal help. Before this, I had a career with the military. That may show."

"The world is a complicated place, and not just academia. Little surprises me. That you have a family tie to all this is in your favor. If you'd flashed a badge, I wouldn't continue this conversation."

"I appreciate your help. My brother, Ed Dekker, will be filing a story in the next few days about Hammersmith's death. It will be an obituary, but will honor his work. Anything you can tell us that would help with a profile of his life, perhaps even suggest a reason for his, well, his murder, would be helpful." No point in beating around the bush.

She remained impassive.

Was he losing her? "Ed thinks there's more to this than a random robbery. It could involve a dispute over intellectual property or the direction of Hammersmith's research. It appears that toward the end, he was conflicted about the way his discoveries were being used."

"Conflicted?"

"I don't pretend to understand it. Hammersmith wanted to talk with Ed. In private. It would be good to know why."

"Gabriel, wanting to talk with a reporter?"

"As I said, they'd met in Austria. Ed interviewed him about Naturtek's new products. I guess they hit it off, I don't know. When Ed asked for a more detailed discussion here in the States, Hammersmith was receptive. As I say, they arranged a talk but it never took place."

"I'm sorry to say there's nothing I can do to help. Gabriel and I did work together on several projects in the late '90s. Nothing since. At that point he was on the faculty here and we were colleagues; more than that, we were friends." She took a breath. "After he moved to the private sector, we remained in contact, but only now and again. Emails, lunch at conferences. So I don't know the details of his recent work. When he joined a private genetics company, he signed all sorts of nondisclosure agreements. I told him that was a mistake, that he was putting his own publishing career in jeopardy. But he went ahead. Apparently, the money was very good."

"I know you teach here, but have you made similar arrangements with the genetics industry?"

"Contract research, you mean?" Her eyes narrowed.

"Where a company might own the results? I'm just trying to understand this relationship."

"Never. It happens, too often maybe. But for me, it would be academic suicide." She rose up in her chair, then settled back. "Perhaps that's putting it too strongly. The expectation here and at all research universities is for faculty to bring in grant support. Some is from the government—NIH or the Department of Agriculture—some from corporations."

Bart thought of DARPA again, but kept that to himself.

"With the private sector, the relationship model can be a consultancy—looking at a specific problem—or underwriting what you're doing already. There are stipulations concerning royalty income and patent ownership. Ultimate control of the raw data can be contested, and there might be prescreening of publications."

Bart jotted this down in a notebook.

"Companies want the objectivity a university affiliation conveys so they rarely prohibit publications of research results. Rather, they may delay things, or frame the research question to begin with. You understand me?" She looked out through the plate glass windows of the lounge.

Light snow was falling. "Since funders often pay for equipment, off-set our university salaries, and fund post-doc assistants, the relationship is very tempting. Still, you can negotiate terms. But once, like Gabriel, you move fully into the private sector, well, they own you."

She sighed and turned away from Bart toward the view outside. The paths had become mere creases in dimensionless white, .the trees black skeletons against the snow.

"You sense my unease," she went on, turning back toward him. It was a bird-like gesture. "I have spoken too much, yet I must be honest. In the past I did proprietary research and found the oversight—the 'suggestions', shall we say—stifling. Now my focus is protein development in planktonic marine bacteria, the key to the ocean web of life. It's all very basic and without any industry interest, thank God. At least so far."

Bart continued to scribble down notes. Which of them was the more disenchanted realist, he wondered?

"My innocence may lie in being overlooked." She fished a handkerchief from her bag and blew her nose. "Once, twice a year, I have the chance to evaluate a product for its potential environmental impact— pesticides, animal food additives, that kind of thing. Some offers I accept; others, no. I'm walking in traffic here—that's a Romanian expression, opportunity or catastrophe coming at you from all sides. But the major industry ties that the administration here loves? I'm not interested. I came to this country to do my own work." Her voice became stern. "But you will not quote me." She raised her finger at him.

"Of course." Bart took his pencil off the page.

"I'm hearing you say it might be his research that got him killed, no?"

"That's what Ed thinks. But I have to tell you, the police see it in simpler terms: a botched robbery."

"The police! They are the same the world over, I know. And behind them there is always the politician." Her accent thickened.

"Where was his research going?"

Dr. Ciobanu took a breath, coming to terms with something. "Fertility. More precisely, interrupting fertility, something I was never comfortable with. But then, I'm Catholic." Her thin lips pulled into a tight grin. "You create a superior seed line that agriculture will want but it is only viable for one planting. The result is called a biological patent. So the next year, there's more sales. I usually don't see any conflict between science and religion, but this line of research, it seems something like..." She paused. "A sin."

Bart resumed taking notes; she ignored it.

"What is the most basic impulse of life, in all forms? To reproduce. I told him so. Maybe that's why we became distant these last years."

Bart wondered if she had children. Or had lost children. "Anything else you can tell me?"

"No." She wrung her hands. "Gabriel, Gabriel, Gabriel." Then she composed herself. "First, we never had this conversation, you and I. My name must not come up in your newspaper. I'm at a distance but my career would be dead if I was associated with libel against Naturtek."

"I understand. And I appreciate your frankness."

"Wait." Ciobanu was leafing through a small, red address book. "I made a note during one of our last conversations. Where is it? Ah, yes. He was calling from an unfamiliar number so I had my book open to make a note of it. He said it was a secure line, which I thought strange. He wanted my advice about finding a lawyer who could advise him on his rights to certain discoveries he'd made."

"If he were to leave Naturtek?"

"That's what I gathered. But I don't know such people. I said, you're making three times my salary, why leave? That was mean, I know." She brushed hair from her face.

"He said he was afraid he might lose control of his lab. They'd re-assigned some promising research he'd initiated to another team. And they'd 'foisted'—that was his word, foisted—a new assistant on him,

208

someone he hadn't selected. He thought he was being, how you say? sent out to pasture."

"Sidelined."

"Exactly. He'd come in mornings and find things rearranged on his bench, slides missing. His assistant denied anyone had been there, but Gabriel was very uneasy."

"Did you know he had his own research facility at home: a greenhouse, DNA sequencers, gene guns?" Ed had brought Bart up-to-date on what he'd seen in Jefferson County.

"He mentioned working at home. I didn't realize it was so elaborate, his facility."

"If he'd lost control of his work, that would be disquieting."

"But still, his story was vague. Things rearranged over night? Who remembers where you put down a book the day before?"

Bart thought she'd know exactly where she'd left every pencil.

"He also said he'd had a strange encounter at a bar in St. Louis. A woman came up to him, beautiful, he said, and much younger. I joked he was boasting. Joked, because Gabriel was no looker, and he knew it. But he brushed her off." The scientist shrugged. "I didn't think he wanted to make me jealous. That wasn't Gabriel. But he'd found it strange."

"Hookers happen, even in Missouri."

"This was something else. He said she was well-dressed and knew technical terms. She claimed to be studying biotechnology and recognized him from a conference somewhere."

"He though she was a commercial spy?"

"That was his thought."

She brushed off imaginary dust from her dress and stood up. "That's all I can share. I appreciate you telling me about the death of my friend." She looked around. "I can tell you nothing more."

"Again, I'm sorry for your loss."

She gave him another handshake, still lifeless, and disappeared into an elevator.

Bart watched the lounge area for ten minutes. People passed in and out of the lobby but no one had taken an interest in them. Or appeared to follow Dr. Ciobanu. He finished writing down his recollection of what she'd said and put away his notebook. He also switched off the recorder in his pocket. Belt and braces, as the English say. Shrugging into his coat, he set off toward downtown through four inches of snow. As he approached the Longfellow Bridge, a train, its windows bright, rumbled past.

Chapter Twenty-Four

AT THE COPLEY SQUARE Library, Bart found the internet stations and logged onto the MIT web site. Ciobanu had posted her class schedule and a vita. No photo. But she included a short bio. She'd arrived in the United States in 1986 to study at U.C. Berkeley, where she completed her doctoral work, then a move to MIT. Hammersmith was still on the faculty then, Bart knew from what Ed had told him. Ah, there; they were listed as co-authors in work looking at cell differentiation in plants. Bart found the paper online and read the abstract. Plant tissue in the cambium close to the outer layer or phloem has similarities to human stem cells. Under certain conditions, cells in that layer can differentiate creating buds, branches or roots. Gardeners have been stimulating this dynamic for centuries through air-layering, the authors wrote. The paper explored how this took place at the cellular level. Bart thought it sounded harmless.

Anyone looking at Hammersmith would have come to Ciobanu. If that person was cleaning up loose ends, that could represent a problem. Bart drummed his fingers on the keyboard. Should he call her? It couldn't hurt. He'd wait though; posted signs forbid the use of cell phones.

Taking out his recorder, he put on ear buds, transcribed his interview into his laptop, then sent it over to the reading room printer along with Ciobanu's vita. A reference librarian charged him twenty-five cents a page. Highway robbery.

It was now after six o'clock. Standing on the library steps, he punched in the professor's number and got only a generic answering service. He left his name and said he had one more question. No point in spooking her. Down the street to the right glowed a restaurant sign. He set out toward it, automatically looking for patterns among the pedestrians, perhaps a face he'd seen before.

As he sliced around the bone of a rubbery steak, his phone rang. Not his brother, or Ciobanu, but the Cambridge police. Where was he now and would he stop by the station for a conversation? They would send a car.

Not a request.

Bart weighed the alternatives. Getting into the back seat of a patrol car with no inside door handles wasn't inviting. But they had his name and number. It wouldn't be hard to find him through Executive Action. As a licensed operator, his picture and prints were on-record. The question was, what had happened in Cambridge?

He agreed and within twenty minutes he was back across the river, in an interrogation room. The police were polite; they always were at the beginning. He declined coffee. A Detective Ballancio was the OIC, officer in charge. He was short, his face flushed. Probably a heart attack risk, given his weight. The detective walked him through the situation. Bart's phone was the source of two recent calls to Dr. Ciobanu. No, he wasn't a 'person of interest,' not yet. His last call had come within minutes of the event in question. A GPS trace on his phone put him across the river at the time, seemingly away from the scene. Seemingly.

"And the event in question?"

"The professor fell over a balcony railing, four flights down to the stone floor of her office building lobby. Her neck was broken."

Bart remembered the grey slate floor. Calmly and without prompting, Bart outlined his behavior that day, his appointment, the connection to the death of her former colleague, Dr. Hammersmith. He and Ciobanu had met in a very public place, that lounge where she'd been found.

When they parted, he explained, she was not overly distraught. All the while they talked, a number of people came and went that might recall seeing them. And seeing him leaving.

"Why did you call the last time?"

"I'd just looked at her web site and discovered she'd collaborated with Hammersmith on at least one project. It was in the public record. Since he'd been murdered, possibly for reasons related to his research, it seemed prudent to let her know that she might be in danger. True, Hammersmith had left MIT years previously, but from our talk, I knew they'd stayed in touch. Maybe they continued to collaborate? Or someone might think so."

"And you wanted to warn her." It wasn't a question.

"I thought she might ask the campus police to keep an eye out, maybe check on her office from time to time. Or she might consider taking next week off. I told her that my brother is working on a newspaper story related to Hammersmith. If that gets into print, any threat might evaporate."

"But you didn't leave a message." The lieutenant suppressed a yawn. It looked to Bart like he'd been on duty too long, this shift or this lifetime. Or was it misdirection?

"She didn't pick up. It seemed alarmist to say 'Someone might kill you'. I mean, I didn't have any facts. If she had picked up, I could have eased into it."

"But you said you had a question." The police had read her e-mails.

"Just to say something. So she'd return the call."

"As it happens, your call came too late. We have time-of-death established: 5:48. Campus security was making rounds at that time, checking offices at the end of the day. They found her almost immediately."

"Shit. What a waste." Bart sighed. "Did you check her office?"

"Yes. First thing when we found she worked in the building. And she'd just been in there."

"And you know that why?"

"Because that's where her coat was hung up and she had on only one black flat. Not something she'd wear in the snow. The other shoe was on the fourth floor balcony." Together they digested this fact. "Seems unlikely that she'd take off one shoe before she dived."

"Any closed-circuit surveillance? Anything taken?" As long as the lieutenant was answering, Bart was asking.

"No, to both. In fact, her door was ajar, no forced entry. But like a lot of academic offices, papers and books were scattered all over. We can't tell if anything is missing."

Bart said the doctor struck him as meticulous. Ballancio absorbed that.

"Another thing," the lieutenant continued. "She'd have visitors, students there, right? But no fingerprints were found on the door handle, either side. Not even hers. Oh, and her purse was inside with nearly a hundred bucks and keys. She wasn't leaving for the day."

"The door was wiped?"

"Looks it. All things considered, we're leaning toward homicide. Still, the hallway railing was only four feet high, so suicide or a slip and fall are possibilities. The MIT administration will be all over this, demanding action. We're taking it seriously."

"She was short," said Bart, looking away from Ballancio. "Her center of gravity was well below the top rail."

"We thought of that. But hey, you'd just told her a friend had been murdered, right? Maybe she was despondent."

"She didn't seem so when I left, but I didn't know her. We'd just met the one time. I'd say she was more angry, in a contained way. It was clear she had a continuing relationship with Hammersmith, how emotional, she didn't say. I'd call her self-contained, not suicidal."

"And you know this because you're a psychologist?"

Bart could only shrug. "Were there other injuries?"

"Frontal neck abrasions consistent with a chokehold, one torn fingernail. But you fall forty feet onto rock, who knows? We won't have more until the autopsy. Give us your contact information. You may be called for the inquest. If so, take the invitation seriously. Coming after you in—what is it, D.C.?—will make us seriously pissed." He fingered the business card that Bart had given him. "And work against you at your trial."

"Message received." Bart held up his hands. "Am I clear to go?"

"After we type up your statement and you sign it. Now, about this Hammersmith thing; when you turn up anything—you see I have confidence in you—I expect a phone call *inmediatamente.*" He took out his own card and gave it to Bart.

There was no free ride on offer back to Boston, so Bart took a cab. By nine-thirty he was in his hotel room looking out at the lights shimmering on a slate-like Charles River. The snow had ended.

Had he been followed in the afternoon? Had he led some bastard straight to Dr. Ciobanu? My God, was he slipping that much?

Chapter Twenty-Five

WHERE THE HELL WAS Ed? Bart pictured himself standing on the bridge above the Charles, alone except for cars and a passing train. If—and it was still an if—they had been tracked from D.C., could the villains have followed them both? The face of the biologist came to him, angular, thin. The accent; an outsider in New England. She should have taken down her internet profile. At least encrypted her phone. It took the cops no time at all to metadata her calls. And so could anyone else.

Reaching for his phone, he speed-dialed his brother. After a suspiciously-long time, Ed picked up, his voice groggy.

"Worn out, are you?"

Ed groaned. "I'm not as young as I used to be. I need my sleep."

"I'll bet. Stick your head in the sink. Something's come up and you need to focus."

"I'm focused, I'm focused." Bart could hear the rustle of sheets. Another voice murmuring in the background.

"I interviewed Dr. Ciobanu at MIT. Shortly after I left, someone threw her off an internal balcony and ransacked her office. Or she ransacked her own office and then jumped off the landing, take your pick. I'm going with number one, and so are the cops. Picture someone barging into her office, knocking her down. She recovers, tries to run, and in the confusion gets tossed over the railing."

"Jesus. Or they were out to kill her from the get-go?"

"Let me finish. She died from the fall but may have had prior injuries. My guess is that she fought back. No one would want to kill her the way they did, so publicly."

Ed processed that. "So they were looking for information. You talked with the cops? What are they saying?"

"Yeah, they had me in for a conversation. Looks like they have nothing, no CCTV on the drop, no fingerprints in her office." Bart ticked off the facts point-by-point. "But Cambridge is an academic town, and they're motivated. In any case, her purse was there—wallet, money."

"Oh, shit." Ed was fully awake. "This business is way out of hand." Bart could hear an indistinct side-conversation.

"Ed, back to the issue. There's a possibility we were followed from New York. If so, I could have been tracked over to MIT." Bart's voice lost its power. "But damn, I was careful. I walked, and I swear no one was behind me. That leaves phones or a tracking device. I've gone over our trip and nothing comes up but maybe something happened on the train, someone slipping a tracker onto my coat while I was in the bathroom and you were asleep. I'll have to find a scanner to be sure. These gadgets can be small."

"Which means?"

"Which means they could know where you are. When we're done here, ditch the battery from your phone."

"Wait. Let's not panic." Ed was talking as much to himself as to his brother. He slowed his speech. "It's also possible that Ciobanu was already identified as Hammersmith's confidant. We found her, after all."

"Maybe. And they got into her emails and cell phone. I don't want to get technical but it can be done. If so, they now have my cell number and yours. Which means your location data." Splitting up had been a mistake. And not his only mistake. "Do you have a weapon in the apartment?"

There was mumbling just out of earshot. "Kitchen knives?"

"And your lock?"

"Just a minute." In a few seconds Ed said, "Two deadbolts and a chain. The door looks nothing special. Even I could probably kick it in."

"All right. You will need to get dressed, throw everything into a backpack. Don't tell me your address, but what's the closest street corner, some place you can see from your lobby?"

Ed quickly conferred with Aisling and relayed the names of two intersecting streets.

"I'll be there as quickly as I can. Watch for me at the lobby door. We'll figure out our next step but we have to move."

"Hold on." Bart could hear more conversation. "Aisling says the front door is locked and the foyer windows have curtains. It will take us a few minutes to get ready so you might beat us there."

"Put a chair under you door knob till you're ready to leave. Is there a peep hole?"

"Yeah, but it's painted over."

"Good. Lay a towel at the base of the door so no one in the hall will see light or moving shadows. If there's a tracking device on your clothes, it might only be accurate down to the block or building, not the specific floor. Now, get going. Oh, and junk the cell battery!"

Bart threw on his coat and headed for the street, tucking his gun in his belt. There was a taxi queue outside and a Yellow Cab was waiting; a stroke of luck. It was also lucky the driver spoke English and knew the town. Traffic was light, and Bart arrived at the designated corner within twelve minutes. Brick or brownstone apartment buildings lined the street. No cars idled, no figures lounged in doorways.

"Can you wait here for me?" he said.

"You pay the fare so far, then we'll see. I get a call, I'm gone." The driver shrugged; he'd seen it all.

Bart paid and got out. Of the few cars that passed, none stopped. After watching the block for five minutes, he saw a vestibule door opened four buildings down. His brother stuck out his head and waved. Bart crossed the street at a trot, holding his subcompact down by his side. Before he reached the building, the cab drove off.

The lobby was dimly lit and Ed and Aisling had retreated back to the stairs. Aisling clutched a bulky briefcase, her eyes very wide.

"Is there a back way out of here?" asked Bart. Aisling seemed frozen for a moment, then pointed to the rear of the lobby.

"We took the stairs. Ed didn't want us trapped in the elevator. I did see a door back there when I carried down trash one time. Beyond those barrels." She led the way and they were in motion. "I don't actually live here," she said in a stage whisper.

The lobby opened onto a service corridor holding barrels labeled "paper and recyclables" and "trash". Beyond was a door. Aisling pulled it open and they saw a narrow alley that ran between buildings. A street was at the far end but if it was gated, they couldn't tell. At that moment they heard a car screech to a stop, then pounding on the lobby door. Moments later they heard the front door being wrenched open and footsteps pound across the lobby, then up the stairs. At least two men.

Bart gestured for Ed and Aisling to move down the alley and began to ease the door closed behind them. Backing away, Ed banged against a stack of boxes, knocking over a case of empty beer bottles. "Go," shouted Bart, sending Ed and Aisling running down the alley. Before he followed, Bart pushed the stack of boxes over so they fell against the door. They almost reached the street when the door behind them was forced open and they'd heard shouting. Aisling gasped. The last in line, Bart grabbed the edge of an open dumpster and pulled it across the width of the alley, emitting a metallic shriek. Then a light came on above them.

"Keep moving. It's likely motion-activated." Their heads at least were now illuminated. The service alley opened onto a commercial street, now largely deserted of pedestrians. "Go left," shouted Bart, "Go, go. go!"

Three blocks later they took another left and began to slow down. Aisling, her briefcase clutched in her arms, was falling behind and Ed took it.

"Keep moving," hissed Bart.

Just ahead stairs descended into a subway station but Bart motioned for them to keep going. Who knew when a late-night train would come? An empty platform was the perfect trap. As they approached the next intersection, Bart still hanging back, footsteps began to slap loudly on the pavement behind them.

Going left again, they turned onto Boylston Street, a major artery. Bart motioned for the two in front to keep going.

"Get on the first bus you see. Switch to a cab when you can, cross the river and head for the Kendall Square Marriott on Broadway. Here's the key card and room number, Ed." He handed over a small envelope. "I never checked out. I'll be there as soon as I can or call on the room phone." He was panting, but not as much as they.

Turning back, he waited. Seconds later he leveled his pistol and fired at the sidewalk in front of a running figure. The person pitched to the ground, rolled between parked cars, and sent a shot skyward. Even with ambient traffic noise, the shots were loud. Advancing from car to car, Bart crouched low, then dropped to the ground. Three cars back, he saw a leg and took a second shot. There was a grunt. The figure collapsed, then hauled himself up and began dragging himself away.

He'll call his partner, thought Bart. There's probably a third guy circling in a car, but I've bought us a few minutes. They can't afford to leave an injured guy on the street. A minute later he turned to follow Aisling and his brother but they were nowhere in sight.

Slipping his warm pistol into a jacket pocket, Bart turned up his collar and slouched down Boylston Street. An hour later he stepped off a bus a block from the Marriott. He'd made two transfers to shake off pursuit. When he got to the room, he found Ed going over the coat he'd worn on the trip up from D.C.

"Smart move," said Bart, "but you may not find anything. You'll have to dump it. I saw you packed a sweater. There'll be a laundry sack somewhere in the closet. Put your coat in it and take it down to the street. I'll cover you."

"What? This is my favorite leather jacket! My only leather jacket."

"Oh, suck it up. Think of it as a donation to the homeless, like they say in the Bible."

"That was about a shirt."

"If it makes you feel better, I'll do the same. And I dress a hell of a lot better than you."

"Point taken."

Five minutes later, Bart watched as Ed located a trash barrel and hesitatingly stuffed it with a white plastic bag.

"Stop. Leave the bag outside with your coat visible. I guarantee you some penniless student will scoop it up." He couldn't suppress a chuckle. Ed slipped back under the hotel marquee and disappeared into the elevator. Five minutes later it was Bart's turn. He'd changed into his suit jacket as well as a sweater. By this time, Ed's coat had disappeared.

Chapter Twenty-Six

"Nice meeting you, by the way," said Aisling, offering a brittle hand. They stood awkwardly in the utilitarian hotel room. "I suppose the right thing to say is, nice shooting. I hope you didn't kill that guy."

"Likewise. But no. I just wanted to give him something to think about. I figured whoever was with him would have to take him to a hospital."

"Shot the gun out of his hand. This is turning into a real Western. But don't bad guys just shoot the wounded?" She looked at him with distrust.

"Villains, the smart ones anyway, avoid unnecessary complications, like leaving their partners bleeding on the street. But speaking of cleaning up messes, I understand you saved my brother's life in Austria." It was half statement, half question.

"Yeah, well, I do what I can. Right place, wrong time." Aisling was staring at Bart, a bird watching a cat.

"Let's talk about now," said Aisling, breaking eye contact. "I need to get to my apartment."

"No, you don't," said Bart. "We have to assume we are all compromised." He held up his cell phone, the back removed and the battery gone. "The opposition seems to have us in their electronic sights."

"What are you saying? That I should go back to Mexico because it's safer than Boston?"

"Other than the *narco trafficante*s, maybe," said Bart. "But at least on this side of the border, you don't have that morning ritual of banging scorpions out of your shoes."

"I've never been shot at there, you fucking racist. And what about this MIT professor thrown down a staircase? What have you two gotten me into?"

Ed could only absorb the hit.

Bart exhaled. "I'd just spoken with her. It was a horrible thing. We have to assume all this is connected."

She glared at him. "And you've put me on the run? What about the apartment you just drove me out of? These guys will tear it apart."

"No. They saw we were gone. And Ed's the target." He nodded to his brother.

"How reassuring." She still glowered. "At least I left Charlton with plenty of food." She brushed some cat hair off of her shirt. "I'll have to tell Maude, his owner, that I've been, what, called away?"

"Use the room phone. But first, we need to figure out our next move."

"Oh, right. There's people out there killing other people."

Ed weighted in, "Speaking of damage, you think one of the hospitals will have a report on a guy with a gunshot wound? At least we can tip off the cops."

"I can tell my new friend, Detective Ballancio, but chances are it won't help," said Bart. "This is a sophisticated operation. They'll have their own medic."

Ed imagined an alcoholic veterinarian.

"But let's wait till we're clear of the scene," Bart continued. "They tie us to this, we're not going to be able to leave the city."

"An anonymous tip, then," said Ed. "But I never heard any sirens. My guess is no one even reported this." He turned and looked at Aisling. "I'm sorry we got you into this. If you want to drop that contract job with the *Chronicle*, I understand. In fact, you should. This isn't your mess."

She stared at one brother and then the other. "You say they've already traced me to you, whoever 'they' are? I don't see a lot of options here." She seemed resigned. " You need to finish that article and get what you know into the public record. If I can speed things along, that's best for me, too."

Ed and his brother exchanged a look. It was her decision.

"We're safer together," said Bart.

 "In that case, I'll stick with you guys. For a while, anyway."

"Thanks," said Ed. "Which raises the question, where to next? We need a place to decode Hammersmith's notes."

Bart rubbed his hands together. "This is a little counterintuitive, I know, but your apartment isn't a bad choice, Ed. There's the new security system. Plus you'll be close to the *Chronicle*."

"I need a desk, a chair, and some peace and quiet," said Aisliing. She nodded toward her satchel. "If I'm not going home, I'm not hanging around deserted hallways at Northeastern. It's the break. So, we go to your place or you put me up in a hotel."

"I agree with Aisling," said Bart. "We do what's necessary so you both can work."

"Okay," Ed conceded. "We pool our resources and get this done."

They raided the mini-bar for beer and sprawled out on both beds and the desk chair. Aisling broke the silence. "What's our next move?"

"We probe Naturtek's research agenda. Find what they're bringing to market, what government agencies they're partnered with. I'm working with a guy at the *Chronicle* who's digging into their corporate records."

"And I have government contacts," said Bart.

"What's this guy's name?" asked Aisling.

Before Ed could answer, Bart interrupted. "Need to know, need to know. Let's not put people in any more jeopardy than they're in already."

"As luck would have it, I reserved two tickets on Amtrak for New York," said Ed, looking at his watch. "If that goon squad is still on the job, they'll be looking for two guys traveling together. Since you have the gun, Bart, and Aisling's the most vulnerable, you two should take those seats. I can fly out of Logan."

"In your dreams," said Aisling. "I'm not playing couples with that guy."

"They know the two of us by sight," said Bart. "Splitting up just makes us more vulnerable."

"I don't agree." Ed leaned back against three pillows.

"They can't cover every terminal, train station, and car rental place," said Bart. "But they have hacking prowess. They'll be onto those train tickets."

"Wait, you just said it." Ed broke in. "We rent a car. With cash."

"Rental agencies don't accept cash," said Bart. "They want your credit card to fix that dent in the front end."

"No, no, no. We're not stealing a car," said Ed.

"Can you think of anything else?"

"Can you even do it?" asked Aisling.

"It's worth a try. It won't be anything new, given all that electronic stuff, but I can work with, say, a coat hanger and an old Honda."

"I'm not hearing any of this," said Aisling.

An hour later Bart was behind the wheel of a 2008 Chevy Cruz and they were headed west on the River Street bridge toward Allston. "The garage   had no security," he explained. "And nice, low ceilings. This baby had the parking ticket left right on the dash."

"How'd you pay?" asked Ed.

"Had to use my plastic. If they locate it in the system, there's no way they can race this car to me without going through hours of camera footage. Even then, unlikely."

Aisling had claimed the back and was lying down, her face buried in her coat. "Wake me when we get there, or when the police pull us over." She was asleep before the car reached the Mass Pike.

At a rest stop on I-84 in Connecticut, Ed took the wheel. Once they'd settled down again, Bart turned and looked at Aisling. She was breathing regularly, her face pressed into the seat away from the passing lights. "You trust her?" he whispered.

"You're certifiably paranoid," Ed hissed. "I'm the one who approached her with this consultant job. Just because your own marriage has fallen apart, don't try to poison my relationships." Where had that come from, he wondered.

Like a rock on the shore, Bart was oblivious to this wave of anger. "So, you trust her?" he repeated.

"Oh, fuck. I'm just stressed out. Sorry. I shouldn't have brought up Liz. That was uncalled for. I know you're putting yourself on the line for me here. I'm a jerk."

"Your words. But think about this. She joined the team pretty fast."

"Did we give her any choice?"

"I'm not envious." Bart gazed into traffic. "You're right about Elizabeth. As a couple, we're history. But that's not why I want you to be careful. This is getting stickier. It's hard to see who's involved and who isn't."

"Granted. But she saved my life. That counts." His eyes tracked the passing traffic. "At some level, we're not that different, you and I, but I don't want my natural suspicion of people to make me a recluse."

"I hear you." Bart's face flashed between grey and white in the oncoming lights.

Ed was thinking about his father's withdrawal after the death of their mother from cancer. "And I understand why you split for the army. Hell, I hunkered down in college, doing almost the same thing. We each decided the known world was an uncomfortable place. But that was decades ago."

"You know what they say about paranoids?" Bart didn't complete the thought. "I'm glad you have that new steel door, though."

"Me too." Ed shot a look at his brother. "I've been thinking. Once we're back at my apartment, I want you to go home. See Liz, try to patch things up. And there'll be things only you can do for us in D.C. Tracing government ties to Naturtek, for one."

Bart was silent as they passed through the New Haven skyline on an elevated section of I-84, then merged with I-95. Streetlights pulsated off the windshield. "All right. But I intend to leave you this." He opened his coat and pointed to his shoulder holster. "You remember how these things work?"

Chapter Twenty-Seven

THEY DROPPED THE STOLEN car on 14th Street, careful to leave the doors unlocked, and grabbed a cab to Chinatown. They walked the last two blocks to Ed's building. It was now the morning rush; they'd made good time. Hunched over, they merged with a river of pedestrians threading past sidewalk vegetable stands and around sandwich boards advertising foot massages. Ten minutes for ten dollars. To Ed it sounded good. The lobby of his building, the stairwell, and finally his apartment were empty and unchanged.

Once they were inside, Bart turned around and said he'd see them in a few minutes. They'd just gotten a second pot of the coffee brewing when he returned with a package.

"Three burner phones. I was a dunce not to cover this base before. When we talk about anything connected to the case, this is what we use."

It took a few minutes to mutually program the phones with each other's number. "Now I'm off. I can sleep on the train," said Bart, refusing Ed's offer of a few hours on the couch. "We're all in this together. I'll do a pass around the block. If everything is cool, I'll head up to Penn Station. Trains leave for D.C. every hour. If I can get the Acela, there's internet and I can get to work. Till I pass out, that is. A guy in Homeland I know might help me see if there are any security companies working for Naturtek. I'm thinking firms that deal in corporate espionage. It could tell us who's doing this stuff."

"A cleaning crew?" said Ed.

"That's the term. If Naturtek's competition isn't our problem, it's the company itself."

"You're thinking Hammersmith tried to sell data, got caught, and Naturtek retaliated."

"Or the buyer decided that the cost of a mechanic was cheaper than paying the late scientist," said Aisling. Ed and Bart turned to look at her. Tough girl.

"When I find something out, I'll be in touch." Bart was buttoning his suit jacket back over his sweater. Ed had offered him a coat from his closet but the fit was off, even without the automatic. "You people do the same."

They had barely locked the door when Ed and Aisling looked at each other and shrugged. "Nothing like almost dying to make you want to savor the moment," said Aisling. She began unbuttoning her shirt.

"Mechanic?" Ed was wide-eyed.

"Just getting into the spirit of things."

Later, as Ed drifted toward sleep, Aisling shook him back to consciousness. "I heard you talking in the car. Bart said he didn't trust me."

"He's just being protective."

"I figured. Then again, you did speak up in my defense. That was sweet." She pulled away. "But what did happen to your family? You said something about your mother dying?"

Ed rolled on his side. "Nothing all that dramatic. It's not unusual to die of cancer. Mom fought it through a couple of surgeries, chemo. Nothing took. Toward the end she was going to sue the hospital."

"Classic Kübler-Ross."

"Whatever. But it was dad who ended up in depression. He was a CPA with a small office but quit to organize Mom's trips in and out of treatment. For a while he juggled things, worked at home doing the neighbors' tax returns. When Mom died, he broke like an old clock. In March we had one of those late snowstorms, thick, wet flakes. The way the state police reconstructed it, he drove to a parking area off the interstate and started walking, facing away from traffic. With the snow, it was impossible for drivers to see him. A guy hauling lumber down from Maine couldn't stop, knocked Dad fifty feet. The guy almost flipped the rig bringing it to a stop, but it was too late. Dad was dead. As he'd intended."

Aisling shook her head.

"I was at Columbia by then, in their masters J-program. Bart was tucked away in the army. I handled what was left of things—the funeral, prepping the house for sale. Then I tried not to look back."

"Bart was okay with that?"

"It wasn't as if he had control of his schedule. I signed the papers, paid off the mortgage, and took half of what was left. First I just let it sit in a bank. Then a few years later I bought this place."

"And Columbia?"

"Muddled through without distinction while I tended bar. Then scrounged up newspaper assignments here and there. Bad as things are, New York is still a newspaper town."

"So, you can write with one hand and mix a drink with the other?"

"We're not talking black-tie here. Place I worked on the Lower East Side was a mill delivering beer and shots. The regulars would start with Dewar's on the first of the month, that's when their disability checks came, then move down to draft beer as the weeks went by. I didn't get many calls for a Tequila sunrise."

She laughed. "What they call 'ladies' drinks'?"

"Back in the Depression, they did. And this bar hadn't changed since then. We stood on a rack behind the bar, supposedly to make it more comfortable but actually because the floor was rotted out. You'd have to say that the ambiance suited the patrons—same faces on the same bar stools, same songs on the juke box. And same bartenders, I came to realize, me included. It took away my taste for hard liquor, for a while, anyway." Ed, on his back, stared at the ceiling.

"You were healing," she said.

"At the time it felt like I was holding on to anger."

"At who?"

"At Dad, of course, for being such a wuss. Then at Bart for leaving it all in my hands." He sighed. "Finally, at myself for being angry. Does that make sense?"

"Yeah. Guilt and anger can feel pretty much alike."

"Worse, I blamed my mother for getting sick. Stupid, huh?"

She kissed him on the forehead but he didn't respond. "The guy I should have pitied was the truck driver. They cleared him of any fault but he never drove again. He went back to Maine and took a job on a lobster boat. Till one day when he disappeared at sea."

"You followed all this?"

"Through the papers. It was newsworthy, in a sick sense. I wanted some sort of closure, so I kept up. When I read in a Penobscot weekly about his disappearance, I let it all go."

"I'm beginning to see where you two are coming from." Her lips were dry and she licked them. "You know your problem, don't you?"

"Which one?"

"You look at a woman and see your mother."

He was quiet for a time. "You're saying I think of myself as an orphan?"

"I shouldn't have said that." She got up and slipped into one of his over-long tee shirt before wandering around the room. "Shall I make us coffee?"

"May as well. There's beans in the freezer."

"So then what happened?" She was holding her mug in both hands, her elbows on the wooden table. He sat across from her, not touching. "I found work at a paper in Paterson, New Jersey. Keep in mind I wasn't at the top of my class, but there was still a market for investigative reporters."

"The fallout from Watergate."

"Twenty years earlier. But 'All the President's Men' was still on re-runs. Do you know Paterson?"

"No."

It's pretty crapped out now with the mills closed and high crime, but it's got a great labor history. Alexander Hamilton located the first American factories there at the falls of the Passaic River. Industry was going to make the U.S. independent of England."

"That's a while back."

"It is. While it lasted, the city had a dramatic run, rapacious capitalists and big labor at each other's throats. There were textile strikes in the 1830s. By the 1870s, weaving technology was mechanized enough so the owners could hire children. They were even cheaper than the Irish. Picture kids in bare feet making silk ribbons for better-off kids to wear in their hair."

"Silk?"

"Silk as well as cotton. The big strike was in 1913. The IWW was pressing for shorter hours, better pay. But the strikers could never bring out the industry located in other cities, so they ultimately failed."

"Ultimately?" She said.

Ed nodded. "But for a while, Paterson workers were the heroes of organized labor. When they marched on the mill offices, they were led by Big Bill Haywood and Elizabeth Gurley Flynn. At one point two thousand strikers were in jail. It took the New Deal to get them the eight hour day. But by then, the investors were moving things to the South and finally overseas. That's when the phrase 'Going South' was coined."

"Now we say 'circling the drain'."

"When I got there, police corruption was soaking up what was left of the gravy. This was the late '90s. Hurricane Carter had been released after spending half his life in prison on a trumped up murder charge and there wasn't a bar in Paterson that didn't have his picture up. Except the cop bars, of course."

"All I know about that case is the Bob Dylan song."

"That tells the story. Carter fought back, and not just in the ring. He was a contender for the middle-weight title. By then the Irish had been replaced at the bottom by Blacks, but with a lot fewer jobs. Hence the brutal policing."

"And you wove that history into your stories?"

"When I could get away with it. Like I said, Hurricane happened before I got on the scene, but he was still a presence. My North Jersey experience left me a tad skeptical about the mills of justice."

"And then?"

Ed sank back in his chair. "I outwore my welcome so I moved on to a paper just down the road in Newark. I did better there and then landed this gig with the *Chronicle*. Tenement real estate was still cheap in Manhattan, especially here on the Bowery, so I fit right in."

"Fit in?"

"With the missions, the SROs, the day-labor exchanges."

"SROs?"

"Single room occupancy. Essentially flop houses. The beds were in wire cubicles but they were warmer than a sheet of cardboard on the sidewalk. Then, slowly immigrants crowded out of Chinatown and artists priced out of SoHo moved in. By then I'd taken my share from my parents' house and I bought this."

"And the location fit your mood. I get it."

"You make me sound like damaged goods."

"No, you do. But I'm discounting most of it as self-pity."

"Can't deny that."

"And Bart?"

Ed thought for a while. "As I say, we lost touch once he left for basic training. Then he was overseas. I was never sure where. He'd call, usually around Christmas, but we rarely got together. Neither of us were big on nostalgia. Eventually , though, he met someone, settled down."

"You attended the wedding?"

"Oh, yeah. In Chevy Chase. I was the Ancient Mariner among the wedding guests, none of whom I knew. And Bart had changed."

"How so?"

"There was the physical thing. He was taller, a lot quieter. I expect it was due to his experiences overseas. I'd never met Elizabeth, his wife. She seemed down to earth, but there was lots of money sloshing around, you could tell."

"That talk in the car about a divorce?"

"I have no idea where that came from. Hell, I was glad Bart settled down." He chuckled. "It sounds odd but I think she blamed me for Bart's imperfect childhood, like it was my fault."

"But she was going to straighten him out?"

"Or try. Her family's single-malt aristocracy. They expected a son-in-law who was a professional."

"But a warrior in uniform, that can't be bad." Aisling laughed. "You keep defining things in terms of booze. I find that interesting."

"Like a reformed drunk, you mean?"

"Maybe. You and Elizabeth—you eventually got on?"

"I've never found her warm spot but she's big on being polite. She made it clear that Bart had married into her family, not the reverse, if you get my drift."

"Do indeed."

"Not that she's all ruffles and a perfect smile. She finished Georgetown Law and lickety split, landed a position on K Street with a lobby shop.

She takes the asks of the trade associations—big dairy, the processed food industry—and crafts them into legislative language."

"Did they get off to a good start?"

"At one level. Her parents pitched in and helped them into a place in suburban Arlington. Heaven forbid they should live in a flat on the bad side of Capitol Hill, I suppose. Not that their place is ostentatious. I've visited a few times after their daughter, Molly, was born."

"To see the final piece of the perfect picture."

"You are harsh. No, I just wanted to see my little niece. Is that so strange?"

"And how was it, visiting I mean?"

"Bart had reached a respectable rank in the Army and finagled an assignment in Washington so as to be home more. And he was working on a college degree. But he knew he was destined to go back overseas. Maybe that pressure helped things unravel at home. So after one more tour, he cashed in and joined a buddy doing private security."

Light from the kitchen window caught Aisling's hair, which warmed the room.

"But maybe too late. They've been living separately for a while now."

She studied his face. "But this is his chance to reconnect with you, no?"

"The silver lining to murder and mayhem." He shrugged. "Now, what about that food? There's nothing we can trust in the fridge, so we'll have to shop."

"That door thing," she gestured to the front of the apartment, "It's too much."

"You're thinking the castle keep? Bart does lean toward protective. He took me to a firing range a few years ago, said he wanted to show me how to fire a pistol. It could be this pistol." Ed nodded to the gun on top of unopened mail on the table.

"All macho?"

"Not at all. It was strictly business. I was the client, and not particularly adept."

"No quick draws?"

"Just stable stance, left hand on right wrist, everything a triangle. I can show you if you'd like."

"I'll pass, thanks. She looked at the pistol. "Whose image of the world is correct?" Then she crossed the room and closed the bathroom door behind her. Outside, an ambulance screamed up the Bowery.

Chapter Twenty-Eight

AN HOUR LATER THEY had both showered and dressed. She was tying her running shoes, dry now but dirty from Boston snow. She slid out of reach. "None of that. I have a ton of work to do here."

He sighed. "I have to get going, too. There's data bases at the *Chronicle* I need."

"And your mysterious partner in crime?" She frowned.

"You're my partner in crime, but you mean Manny. His beat is sports but his passion is ferreting out crime in the suites as well as the locker room. A Russian oligarch buys an American team, and Manny's on it looking for money laundering. For him, the only things you can trust in the news are the ball scores."

"Not the weather forecast?" Aisling raised her eyebrows.

"You're joking?"

"Such a nest of cynics. Go." She picked up his jacket from the floor and tossed it over. "You abducted me from Boston, so now let me earn my pittance. But first bring me something to eat."

"Keep that pistol in reach." Holding it toward her, he dropped the magazine and reseated it in the handle with the heel of his hand. "You hear noise in the hall, check the CCTV camera, then stand away from the door. Here's the safety. Someone comes in, you chamber the first bullet, then point and pull."

Aisling hefted the Glock G30. "And I've got what, seven shots? Who needs a doctorate?"

After leaving a bag of delicatessen food at the apartment—bread, cheese, tomatoes, coldcuts—Ed was in a cubical at the *Chronicle*. There was nothing on the wire services about the Hammersmith murder beyond yesterday's vapid obituary in a St. Louis paper. "Died unexpectedly." The photo was a decade old and the piece dwelled on his time at MIT. The *Boston Globe* covered the death of Dr. Ciobanu but with equal lack of detail. It was "a tragic accident". He found nothing about gunshots on Boylston Street.

Ed reached Detective Ballancio through a patch from the Cambridge station house. The cop was annoyed. "Why is the press calling me? The PR office will give you a statement."

"Wait," said Ed. "I'm working with Bart Dekker, the guy you interviewed." Was it just yesterday? "We've been working on a related case for a while." He filled Ballancio in on the death of Ciobanu's former MIT colleague. "The two cases are linked, I'm sure of it."

"We know about Hammersmith. The FBI tipped us to her phone contacts with him. And we've talked to the Missouri cops. That's what we do. So far, there's nothing firm to tie the two crimes together. That is, if the MIT prof was actually murdered."

"She told my brother they'd been in recent contact."

"But apparently not on her office phone. Doesn't matter. Her cell and laptop are missing." This was new.

"Lots of people are leery of using their office phone," said Ed, "when it's a personal thing."

"If you say so. We'll get the content eventually but warrants can take a while." The detective shifted to a musing tone. "Remind me why I'm even talking to you?"

"We're still on the Hammersmith end of things," Ed replied. "He and Ciobanu collaborated in the past and may still have had a personal relationship. But I don't see this as a crime of passion. It's about intellectual property. Money."

"We have your brother's statement. Lucky for him, a phone call places him across the river at the right moment. Otherwise, he and I would still be talking."

Ed pivoted. "So you've discarded the suicide idea?"

"Yeah, it's murder, in my opinion. But I'm not the D.A. I'll be candid; we've got no suspects—no other suspects, that is. You want to keep that in mind if you turn up anything. Understand?"

"Absolutely, detective."

"And ASAP. We might be passing this on to the FBI. There's the interstate angle, and maybe foreign players."

"Meaning?"

"That company down there, they're talking about international patent theft. But you didn't hear that from me."

"When Naturtek interviewed me after Hammersmith's death, they dropped the same idea. But the Jefferson City police were happy with a random assault scenario."

"But you weren't?" said Ballancio.

"I didn't know what to think. Still don't. Hammersmith could have been ripping the company off, selling their research to a competitor. But I think he found out something the company wanted to bury."

"So they buried him? That's quite an allegation."

"I'm speculating. Remember I interviewed Hammersmith once before. This was a guy who believed in science." Time to share, thought Ed. He filled the detective in on the attack in Boston, describing Aisling simply as a consultant on the story. When he got to the package Hammersmith had mailed, he really had Ballancio's attention.

"We could subpoena that," said the detective. "Then again, you're already having it analyzed." Ed heard squealing, likely Ballancio's chair.

"Here's how we handle this. For the moment, you keep me informed and save the city some money. If your report gives us a lead, we'll move to seize the papers and the DVD."

"Understood." Ed wondered if this was a way to keep things in the detective's hands, rather than the FBI.

Ed heard a slurping sound.

"Boston doesn't share routine updates on shots fired, but I'll look into it." He paused. "You're in New York, right?"

"Yeah, back at work."

"Well, here's my direct number, should something turn up." Ballancio broke the connection.

Next, Ed called Royco in Jefferson City and got through immediately.

"What have you got for me, Dekker? It better be good because we're chasing our tails down here.

"How do you mean?"

"A major scientist bleeds out on his lab floor, and we've got nothing. Now we're sharing that nothing with the FBI. If you could turn up a new angle, our department could stay in the game."

"What happened with the motorcyclist?"

"Wiped out before he reached the interstate. But here's the gruesome part. Looks like a cable was strung across the road, maybe two feet high. It flipped him. We figure he was doing at least fifty at the time."

"So a party knew his route, and didn't want him wandering around. That is harsh."

"I agree. Course marks on a tree aren't an exact science."

Ed let this settle. "Any papers, I.D.?"

"None. What's really weird is that his prints weren't in any data base. My guess? The guy was a foreigner who slipped past Customs and Immigration."

Ed absorbed that. "So, a pro."

"Looks like it."

"Was he carrying anything?"

"Nothing in the saddlebags. If he was, it could have been taken. We did find tire prints for a half-ton truck, but can't date them or narrow it down."

"How far away was the crash?"

"Twelve miles. As for the bike, we have a VIN that tells us it was stolen in New Orleans. At this point, we welcome your contribution."

Ed could hear the sound of a teletype machine in the background. The *Chronicle* had discarded them twenty years ago.

"I just spoke with Detective Ballancio in Cambridge. He said the two of you are in touch, so this may not be new. The woman killed up here, a Dr. Ciobanu, was an old friend of Hammersmith. It's this connection that interests my paper."

Royco cleared his throat. "Yea, Cambridge talked to me. Are they saying Ciobanu didn't just jump four stories to a granite floor?"

"Not yet."

"What's your take?"

"I know it sounds like we're somehow involved, but only as investigators. My brother interviewed her, told her that Hammersmith was dead, in fact, but she had no idea who might have killed him." Ed didn't mention the package of documents he'd gotten from Hammersmith. Compared with Ballancio, Royco didn't seem to be his own man.

"I came by that evening and saw Naturtek scouring the scene. Was that normal procedure?"

"That was the D.A.'s decision. He claimed the company had a right to secure its property. They gave us an inventory, but it was just equipment."

And plants, but Ed let that go. "I was chased around Boston last night. Don't know by whom but they were interested enough to take a shot a me." There was no point in mentioning Bart and Aisling. "I'm thinking there's more to this than a guy on a motorcycle."

Royco processed this for a minute. "You think? Listen, keep in touch.

I'm more likely to get something from you than the *federales*." Royco's voice faded from angry to disappointed.

"Anything I write for the *Chronicle*, I'll make sure you get a heads-up."

"No. Well before that. And send it to me personally." He gave Ed a post office box number.

Chapter Twenty-Nine

ED POUNDED THE KEYBOARD for the rest of the afternoon, sending off his account of Hammersmith's death and context about genetic engineering to re-write by the deadline for tomorrow's paper. The apparent murder of the suspect would get attention. Switching to the Samsung burner, he called his brother but had to leave a message. Following Bart's caution, Ed then discarded the sim card.

Next, Ed blocked in the facts of Hammersmith's importance to science and sent that to obit so they could craft it into a respectful biography. At that point Manny called saying they should meet; they agreed on Puglia's, an out-of-the-way place in Little Italy in an hour. Aisling would be hungry now as well. A group sit-down seemed the way to go.

Ed caught a cab to his building and spent a few minutes standing across the street from his lobby door. There was no obvious surveillance.

He found Aisling agitated. "I replayed the video. What he said tallies with the research notes and both support his claim to have isolated the gene sequence for plant fertility. He'd gone past theory, at least for canola. He was growing it in an enclosure. Once the plants were in flower, he'd introduced bees. The idea was to see if the nutritive characteristics of the altered nectar and pollen would affect the vitality of insect larvae."

"He wanted to see if his plants were poisonous?"

"Or just producing empty calories. His time frame wasn't long enough for definitive results but he found higher-than-expected worker mortality compared with a second hive where bees had access to the outdoors. Suggestive, maybe startling, but not conclusive." She shook her head.

"How so?" asked Ed.

"Bees feeding on the altered genetic material experienced rapid aging. The larvae, which are voracious eaters, had high mortality before reaching the pupa stage. Put it together, it spells hive collapse."

"I can't see Naturtek being happy with that. Anyway, let's continue this over dinner. I've arranged for us to meet Manny in"— Ed looked at his watch—"ten minutes. That work?"

"Can't say I have much of an appetite. If true, this stuff is horrifying. But I should feed the machine. Besides, that sandwich stuff you left is getting old fast. The rest of what was in your fridge is in those garbage bags."

"Yeah, well, when you're on the road... We'll have to do some serious shopping." He made a mental note to pick up eggs on the way back. Oh, and cheese and ham. "No viable onions or peppers?"

"You're welcome to look in the trash."

"I'll take that as a no. Let's go."

"Can we get out safely?"

"We'll do a Boston. The basements and backyards around here are inter-connected. I found that out when I stored my bike in the cellar last summer. Despite a chain, it disappeared. Looking around for it, I discovered the alley led over to Chrystie Street. We can circle around from there and get to the restaurant. But get ready for a challenge. We'll be passing behind a fish market."

"No problem. And I won't be ordering seafood." She waved toward the desk. "Bring the gun."

Manny was standing outside the restaurant when they arrived. After quick introductions, they slid into a corner booth, avoiding the large communal tables in the center of the room. Manny ordered for them in Italian: white bean soup, pasta with sweet Italian sausage, and a salad with Balsamic dressing. Whether from hunger or fatigue, no one protested.

Between mouthfuls, Aisling outlined Hammersmith's research. "Admittedly from a small sample, but he's concluding the terminator sequence he developed is toxic. At least to honey bees." She sat back, folding her arms. "Imagine a monoculture of thousands of acres, and that's what you get with canola. Wild insect populations would crash. With both wild flowering plants and conventional crops depending on insect pollination…"

"We just cooked the goose," said Manny, finishing her sentence. "Time to stock up on Spam. But why would infertility spread?"

"Though infertile, these plants still produce pollen and nectar. But now it's funky. It screws up insect metabolism. With pollen drifting to additional plants, the trait could spread."

"Like a pandemic?" said Manny.

Aisling put down her fork. "There's no reason to think it would directly affect humans but for insects, think Ebola. Then birds eat insects… You get the idea."

"A downward spiral." Manny liked birds. He circled his finger in the air, then turned to Ed. "What'd you make of the video?"

"He wants Naturtek to give him time to continue to manipulate the gene sequences."

"That's my take as well," said Aisling. "He believed in the science but wanted to iron out the problems."

"Something Naturtek saw as a threat," said Manny.

"He made it in his home lab," Ed continued. "I recognize the shelving. And through the windows, you can see there are no leaves on the trees. So it's winter. The question remains, how would Naturteck have responded, assuming he gave them an ultimatum."

"It's more a confession than a threat," said Ed, "But if they saw a copy, they'd see both."

"The threat being to go public." Manny was rubbing the bristles on his chin. He looked more drawn than usual.

"It was a stupid move," said Ed. "The guy might have been a brilliant biologist but he was no student of corporate behavior."

"Naturtek would have assumed the worst," said Manny.

"But he'd have told them other people had copies. Maybe he mentioned you?" said Aisling.

"If he said 'press', they'd have your name, Ed," said Manny.

"If I'd gotten to Missouri a few hours earlier, things could have been different."

"Be glad you didn't." Manny mopped some sauce from his plate with a chunk of bread.

Ed shivered. "Let's take stock. I just filed a story that raises a question about what Hammersmith was working on. And two police departments are aware of what might be three murders. Sorry, I forgot to mention. Royco on the Hammersmith case thinks the motorcycle guy was also eliminated. With a rope across the road, no less."

"Decapitation?" asked Manny.

"I didn't ask for the details. But it means others knew his timing and route. Which suggests they hired him. If he took anything from the lab, they got it." Ed looked grim. "There's two police departments and the FBI on this. That leaves us with the science angle." He turned to Aisling. "What else can you get from the data?"

"With a lab, a budget, and six months, I could replicate his DNA sequence, clone tissue cultures, and see what grows. But I don't have that. Or, the inclination. It could be horrendously dangerous."

"What about Northeastern? Would they let you use their lab." Ed was pushing.

"And hope to get results before I was mugged? Sound delightful.

Beyond that, I'd need serious money and approval by three committees. That's how universities operate. Then Naturtek would hit me with a patent suit." Aisling sighed. "And did I mention I'll be in Mexico?"

The three were quiet for a while. It looked as if Naturtek held the high cards.

"Maybe there's something simple I can do in Mexico. Let me think about it. Course I have very limited equipment there." She was thoughtful. The waiter removed their empty plates and set down three orders of tiramisu. Ed refilled their glasses with a harsh house wine, emptying the carafe.

"What have you got, Manny?"

Manny thumbed through his note pad. "Naturtek applied for patents for 'fertility suspension methods'—their words—as well as for a procedure related to sequence splicing. But get this; parts of the patent application are redacted."

"Redacted?" said Aisling looking puzzled.

"Removed from the record. In other words, there's unspecified means and methods involved," said Ed. "What is this, a matter of national security?"

"Welcome to the deep government," said Manny. "But it's not so strange. Naturtek shares ownership of the genome with several partners, the key one being the Department of Agriculture."

"Your free market in action." Ed was whispering.

"A portion of company funding came from DOA via three land grant universities—Cornell, the University of Iowa, and the University of Nebraska." Manny licked his thumb and peeled through his notebook. "So don't expect FDA and EPA to look too closely at this little monstrosity."

"So I gathered," said Ed. "Ever since the Clinton administration, the feds have prioritized it as national industrial policy."

"Like drones and nanotech," muttered Manny.

"Well, it gave us corn ethanol and high fructose corn syrup," added Aisling. "Genetics is massive. So don't look to government to protect you from Frankenfood."

"That's what I'm learning," said Manny.

"Can you get me details?" Ed had been jotting down notes on a paper napkin.

"It's right here." Manny dug a sheaf of printouts from the pocket of his trench coat, which he'd kept on. Ed smoothed them out so he and Aisling could see.

"There's the FDA field trial approval," she said, "meaning the federal regulators have signed off."

"Leaving a newspaper scoop as our best bet." Ed wasn't entirely displeased. "If it generates public alarm, the environmental lobby should take up the issue. Then there's regulators in Europe and Japan. A lot of countries don't like the idea of a genetic free-for-all in people's cereal boxes."

"Glad we see eye-to-eye on the value of the press." Manny pushed away his empty desert plate. "Lost your appetite, Ed?"

"Before he could respond, Aisling split his portion in two and slid half onto her plate. Manny took the rest.

"For a scientist, you're geometrically challenged," grumbled Manny. His share was more like a quarter.

"We need to get this project finished. The piece on Hammersmith's murder should buy us time."

"What do you mean?" Manny was scraping his plate.

"It's like turning on the light in the kitchen. The roaches scatter."

"But not for long, if it's my kitchen. And if editorial bleaches it out?" Manny asked.

"They can't cut out all mention of Naturtek or the direction of Hammersmith's research. The company will have to deal with it."

Manny rubbed his chin. "Assuming they haven't already."

They were now the only customers and a waiter was putting chairs on the tables. They'd missed a chance at espresso. Manny used his phone to call a taxi.

"I want you guys to ride around a little with me before you go back to that apartment. We can look the street over."

"We're covered," said Ed, declining the cab. He slapped the bulge in his coat pocket. "And we can get into the building from the back."

Chapter Thirty

Ed and Aisling reached the apartment without mishap.

"You've knocked me off my schedule. I still need two days with these student papers." Aisling nodded toward the stack on the kitchen table. "Grades are due Friday and pressure is building for me to get back to Mexico. I've been away since late December. I can't have my interns alone down there much longer."

"How many interns?" Ed was reconciled to the inevitable.

"Just two this time. It's a graduate program so they're adults chronologically, but still…"

Ed flipped through a few of her papers, looking at titles. "I don't see the common theme."

"It's foraging behavior of social insects: ants, bees, wasps."

"Cockroaches?" Ed looked down at the kitchen baseboards, 'mopboards' his parents called them.

"Actually, no. Roaches are not as socially evolved. Termites, yeah. They're the smart cousins, derived from the cockroach but their behavior is more complex. Evolution is movement toward complexity."

"Like human civilization."

"If you say so." Aisling looked somewhat grim.

"You're suggesting evolution can run backwards? That maybe we're devolving toward our roach-like ancestors?"

"If we had their immunity to toxins, there might be an up-side. But there's no common antecedents. Humans are much more fragile. We only survive by cooperation. Unfortunately, we're forgetting that."

"I remember all that talk about the fallout from nuclear war, that only the roaches would survive."

"Certainly not the bees," she said. "But I'm sounding like a misanthrope. What with university politics and meddling funders, the ladders in my world are narrow and greasy."

"Seriously? You're an academic *wunderkind!*"

"I wish." She sighed. "The death of those two biologists has thrown me a curve."

"I understand." Ed glanced at his reinforced apartment door.

After a few minutes of silence, Aisling held him by the shoulders at arm's length. "Seriously, I need to leave soon. But I want us to be clear. It isn't healthy if we leave a bunch of emotional loose ends." In the harsh light from an overhead bulb, he could count the freckles on the bridge of her nose. She turned her face away when he tried to kiss her.

"I know this isn't much of a palace."

She relented and let him kiss her. Briefly.

"But you could stay, take on other assignments from the *Chronicle?*"

"Sharpening your pencils? Be realistic. There's my interns waiting in Mexico, and my local hires. I have to keep them all busy. The rainy season will be coming soon and we still need a month of dry ground to inventory insect populations and prepare the transparent bee hives we're working with to monitor the new queens." She gently pushed him away.

"Where exactly in Mexico?" The room felt colder.

"I fly to Tuxtla Gutiérrez, in Chiapas. I left specimens at a research facility there, ZooMAT. I think we identified a new variant of the blue morpho. They're helping with the identification."

"After that?"

"Then I bus down to the Lacandon and our research site."

"In the jungle? 'Lions and tigers and bears! Oh, my.'"

"I wish. It was a jungle in the 1970s. Then the civil war in Guatemala sent a hundred thousand refugees over the border. At the same time, the Mexican government was in its last gasp of land reform, telling their peasants to make a new life in the South. With most of the open land in Chiapas in the hands of cattle barons, that was a recipe for conflict. You had farmers whacking down the forest with the big landowners on their heels, bringing in zebu cattle."

"Some sharp differences there, I'll bet."

"You said it. The ranchers run the state. When they need to, they hire private guards. The new arrivals were pushed up into the highlands. Over time, they came to value the forest for what it supplied them—lumber, medicine, meat—even though they cleared a lot of it. Thing is, though, not having lived there for centuries, they weren't already beaten down. They were more militant. What resulted was a tense equilibrium. When the *latifundistas* forged titles and stole land from communities, the dispossessed would invade isolated estates. In areas where the elite began to lose, they used the state to buy them out."

"It helps to run the government. So the forest is disappearing?"

"There's original tree cover left, but not as much as I'd like."

"As you'd like?"

"For species diversity."

"I told you in Austria that I'd been down there," he said, "just as a journalist. I've seen the mist rolling over the hills in the evening like whipped cream. It's beautiful."

"You've got mountains separating valleys in a way that creates countless ecological niches. And rainfall varies. Some spots are near desert, others tropically humid. At the top are the cloud forests where bromeliads hang from the trees. That mist you mentioned originates over the Pacific as humidity. When it hits the mountains, it condenses, often into thunderous rain." Her eyes were shining.

"How come the ranchers tolerate you? Don't they see you as a spy for the Sierra Club?"

"'Tolerate' is the word. Northeastern has contacts at the state and federal level. So as long as we color within the lines, we get a pass. I tell the girls—women are more likely to study abroad than men, don't ask me why—we're not here to demonstrate. That's for the Mexicans. I also carry letters of introduction from SEMARNAP, Mexico's Department of the Environment. They don't always work when we hit an army checkpoint, but they help."

"Still, the cattle barons could have you thrown out."

"There's certain nuances. The bureaucrats want friendly relations with American universities, which helps when they ask for project support from the InterAmerican Bank. Or USAID. And they can use our data to build a case for NGO assistance. What I like to think though, is that what we do helps small farmers."

"Teaching new ag methods?"

"No. It's USAID that's pushing new seeds and chemicals. We help farmers validate what they're already doing."

"I hear a bit of skepticism about the experts."

"How to put this? Pretend you're Mexico and I'm the US." She tapped him in the chest. "When I promote 'development', it means I want you to be more like me. Then we can get along. And the next thing you know, you're hosting our open-pit gold mines."

"Which otherwise I wouldn't want?"

"Not if you're a farmer. If you're an elected official, you can count on a place on my local management team."

"I get your drift," said Ed, rubbing his chest.

"Or say you're standing in a field that's been in production for six thousand years. That's at least as far back as the history of maize and squash down there. My gold mine will produce for twenty years and with luck, you farmers will get shovel jobs. But in the process, we'll make your ground water permanently toxic." She was getting wound up. "Sound like progress?"

"Do I have a choice?"

Aisling rolled her shoulders and took a breath, a boxer between rounds.

"You can move to the U.S. Oh, wait a minute. Now there's that wall, isn't there?"

"So, you're telling people to stay put, continue what they're doing?"

"We're not telling people anything. That would violate our agreement with the authorities. But if we can demonstrate the value of what they've been doing for a few thousand years, it gives them a pat on the back."

"I thought science was all about progress." Ed couldn't help provoking her.

"Again, it's complicated. First, there's terminology. In Chiapas at least, we're putting new words to what folks have understood for countless generations. Which, by the way, includes innovation."

"Are you too modest? But what's second?"

"Second is power. You divide people into those who know and those who don't, the experts end up with the power. Especially when you're dealing with agriculture."

"Your students buy that perspective?"

"If they want to be missionaries, they've picked the wrong department. We aren't the Peace Crops. But some academics play that role. Ever since the 1950s, there's been outsiders studying community life there, pushing it in one direction or another. But here's the thing. Given the option, these people adopt only what is useful. Take Catholicism. It's been a force there for five hundred years, and not always constructive. But the people have re-worked it, made it part of the social fabric. And the flow goes both ways. Think of those missionaries in Latin America who joined insurgencies."

This was a side of Aisling that Ed hadn't seen. "I read somewhere that a priest led the original Mexican Revolution."

"Miguel Hidalgo y Costilla, but not the Mexican Revolution. You're a hundred years off. It was the War for Independence. But unlike the one in the U.S., Hidalgo called for land reform and racial equality. How about them apples?" She grinned. "Being there changes people, even priests."

"And you?"

"I wouldn't be much of a scientist if I didn't learn from my surroundings." She laughed softly.

"So this butterfly you found, who gets to name it?" Ed ended the philosophical duel.

"It's a novel variety, not a species. Some morphological differences— color pattern, wing shape. I doubt it will be recognized with a new name, but that's a matter for Tuxtla Gutiérrez to decide. It's their backyard."

"Say 'Gutiérrez' again. I love to hear you roll your 'r's."

She made a derisive sound through her nose. "You'd like seeing blue morphos, I could tell by your story about *mariposas de la muerte*. Morphos can be as big, up to eight inches across wing tips. In the sun, they're iridescent." Behind her, the window revealed only tenement roofs and the odd water tower.

Ed slumped down on the couch. "It's going to be a change with you gone. But maybe you'd be safer there."

"Nicely phrased, Casanova. That how you ditch all your old girl friends?"

"That who you are?"

She was quiet for a moment.

Ed moved to the arm of her chair but she leaned away. "We can keep in touch."

She sighed. "We can try. Phone lines in Mexico are iffy. When it rains, they can go out, even in Mexico City. So when cellular came around, the demand was huge. We even have a few cell towers in the Lacandon. So yeah, we can try."

"I detect a lack of enthusiasm."

"Just being realistic. It wasn't exactly in the cards that we would get back together."

"Which you regret?"

"Well, it hasn't been boring."

He was close enough to feel her body heat.

"We have Bart's disposables. I suppose they would work in Mexico."

"And be safe, as long as we keep switching out the sim cards."

Now she was leaning into him. When he began to graze on her ear, she moved her head away.

"That's the problem, isn't it? Tiptoeing around. You're what my mother would have called 'bad company'."

She got up and headed for the bathroom. When she returned she was wearing a long tee shirt and panties. "I'm packing it in. Don't wake me."

Chapter Thirty-One

OVER THE NEXT FEW days, Ed followed leads he turned up through the paper's data access while Aisling finished her teaching work. To Ed's disappointment, she'd become distant, getting to bed first and not wanting to be disturbed.

Too soon they were standing at a terminal in Kennedy. Aisling hadn't been able to pack clothes when they fled Boston so they'd shopped in midtown first. She was pulling a new red suitcase.

"Jesus, how unprofessional." She looked back at the roll-on with disdain.

"But easier to spot on the carousel. All the rest are black."

"That's what I mean." They were nearing the point where non-passengers faced a barrier. "I sent off a written report to your editor last night; things went more quickly than I thought. And my grades are in. It will take a day for me to get down there, which I'll use to think about you."

"Finally? At least I'm on your punch list." He smiled. They were standing in line for document check. As they inched ahead, Ed's throat tightened. "So, this is it, for a while at least," he whispered.

"You know you're allowed to visit." She did that thing with her eyebrows. "Provided no one follows you." Then she noticed his eyes. "You big baby."

"As soon as I get this Naturtek stuff out, let's talk about me coming down. By then, everything should be cool." They kissed a final time and she sagged into him. Seconds later she was flashing her passport and shuffling toward the metal scanner, her shoes in her hand. She glowed red in the crowd; then she was gone.

The terminal had a variety of bars and restaurants. At a loss, Ed wandered into an ersatz Irish pub. The paneling was plastic but the lighting comfortably dim. He asked for a Guinness and carried it to a small table with a built-in stool. Bart's number was programmed into his throwaway phone, one of the two he now carried. He called his brother.

"I'm glad to hear your voice. I tried reaching you but didn't want to leave a message." Bart seemed out of breath. "Where are you?"

"Kennedy. I just saw Aisling off for Mexico."

"How's that going?"

Ed paused.

"If you have to think, that says it all. Things stay quiet at the apartment? No unwelcome visitors?"

"No. We've been sneaking in and out through the back, so no complications. The new door is a comfort, but it got me thinking. Can't they go through the wall? And you never hit me with the bill. What's the damage?"

"Don't worry. My treat for those Christmases we missed. The wall, well. It's probably a hundred-years-old—studs, plaster, horse hair. I wouldn't worry. It would take them time and make lot of noise. But, yes, it's possible."

"I'm just antsy."

"Something else. Our crew down here? I turned them loose on Naturtek, focusing on recent contracts. It seems our neighborly seed vendor has a standing arrangement with Guardian Services. I'd describe them as a competitor but we're not in their league. As far as corporate protection goes, they're the gorilla, with lots of former combat specialists on their roster."

"Like you."

"I'm talking mercenaries. We bump against Guardian from time to time so I know how they operate. They charge top dollar and guarantee results. Their contract language is so vague that if laws are broken, nothing splashes back on the client. Naturtek hooked up with them last summer, well before your trip to Austria. The contract specifies 'investigative services, domestic and foreign'. Like I said, vague. Hammersmith isn't named, just 'subjects to be specified'."

"You got into their system?" Ed was impressed.

"Eventually they'll find footprints, but it won't lead them to us. But they'll know someone's watching them. It could make them more discreet."

"You think it was these guys who broke into my room in Oetz? The one who questioned me sounded German or Polish."

"That's standard. The foreign piece of a contract is often subbed to locals who know the terrain. Here they'd want coordination. New York, Cambridge, Boston—my guess is it's one group of operators. And from that mess in Boston, it looks like their B team."

"Cambridge really crossed a line. And in public."

"A very sloppy murder. Someone's either stupid or pressed for time." Bart paused. "Poor Dr. Ciobanu. I should have been more perceptive. Thinking back, I can see the fear on her face."

Ed let a moment pass. "So, if it's a single crew, fresh from one murder, we were lucky to get away on Boylston Street."

"And you're one cat-life down. Course I had your back. If I were a betting man, I'd say Guardian is implicated in both assassinations. Still, the amateurism bothers me."

"So maybe we're talking about the C team.

"Missouri, at least, was in Naturtek's backyard. So they'd want a very long spoon so as not to seem involved," continued Bart.

"And the motorcyclist?"

"You want speculation? A disposable subcontractor." After a pause, Bart continued. "Here's what we need to do."

"Glad you got to this part."

"You're still in touch with the cop in Missouri, right?"

"Detective Royco. You want me to call him?"

"Yes. Pass on what I said about Guardian Services but don't mention how you know it. Just say it might be an interesting area for him to explore. Then do the same with the Cambridge dick, Ballancio. I got the impression you built up a little rapport there. If either department runs with this, that will make Guardian nervous."

"What else? I was hearing a list."

"Your break-in tells us Guardian knows where you live. Assume they're tracking your route to work, where you buy beer."

"I kind of thought that already."

"Just sayin'. Has to have been them with us on the train to Boston. Or they had our phones covered."

"Is that possible?"

"The first? Yeah. You brush past someone, sure. You slept most of the way and I took a walk. I blame myself for not being more alert. As for phones, well, that's why I got us those burners. Their goal is to shut you down, on this subject, at least."

"And your solution is what, an armored car?"

"Next best thing. I'm on my way to Reagan International now. I can be at Kennedy in a few hours. Stay where you are. Airports are full of cameras and TSA. That makes them safe places."

"I don't know. I haven't heard a peep, no weird knocks, no dead birds in my mailbox. And what about your job? Oh, and did you patch things up with Elizabeth?"

"I have vacation time due and I like to think I'm too important to be canned, being partner and all. There's nothing I'm working on that can't be passed along. As for Lizzy, well, think East Coast/West Coast with a lawyer in between. The thing is, I can't work on that and worry about you. You know she likes you? Because you're a reporter, I mean. She told me you guys keep the government honest."

"Not so's you'd notice since Watergate, but tell her I appreciate the confidence"

"She'll go with the flow, is what I'm saying."

"This is all set up?"

"I didn't think you'd turn me down."

"I'm not. And I'm appreciative. Especially with her confusing me with Robert Redford."

"Or that other guy. Anyway, buy something to read and expect me in a couple of hours."

"Hold on. I'm running against the clock and what I need to work is back in my apartment. Meet me there. Like I said, I'm The Shadow going in and out."

"You're taking a chance. Look for me about 5:30."

As he walked from the AirTrain to the subway, Ed was light-headed. Okay, the needle had jumped out of the groove at the end but before that, he and Aisling had set up a rhythm. Hell, we were playing house. Now what? Fortunately, there was work to do.

The open-air train platform slowly filled with people, a few tanned and talking excitedly into cell phones. Probably back from places exotic, he thought. Grey snow was heaped in piles on the streets beyond a chain-link fence that boxed in the station. On the opposite side was a marsh. A duck plowed through the open water, skirting a dumped shopping cart with indifference. Could a duck be indifferent? Every few minutes the sun glinted off a silver airliner leaving it all behind.

Ed's backpack, hanging from one shoulder, was uncomfortable. He'd brought the automatic, as Aisling insisted. Bart had left a belt holster, but that seemed pretentious. And too visible in an airline terminal. He shifted the bag to his other shoulder.

The crowd grew, people flowing down the escalator from the

Skytrain, maneuvering roll-on suitcases. Then gazed up the tracks, bored, impatient. This was a no place on the way to somewhere else.

People jostled for a place near the tracks—couples in ski jackets, solitary men in business suits, faces of all shades. Three uniformed airport employees crouched behind a pillar away from wind, smoking.

As the train approached, there was a commotion on the glass-enclosed staircase leading down from the walkway. Two men moved faster than the escalator, pushing people aside.

Ed looked in both directions. There was only the tracks, concrete walls, and a chain-link fence. He leaped down four feet onto the rails and ran toward the on-coming train. There were two rail lines and he crossed to the furthest, betting this train would stop at the platform and create a barrier.

It did. The gust from the moving cars sent him to his knees. He wouldn't be hidden long. For the moment, the train was a wall of metal, smooth and without anything to grab. He ran toward the last car, seeking an escape. The crowd was shuffling through the open doors, stacking into the aisles. Then the doors closed. Ed saw the coupling that connected the last two cars could be a foothold. Above it was a narrow ledge. No handhold, though. He put his foot on the knuckle-like coupling and pushed up. The cars were separated by a ten inch gap, so narrow it looked like they'd grind together on the curves.

Now the train jolted into motion. With one foot on the coupling, Ed felt franticly for something to grip. The next jolt sent him hard against the carriage but he righted himself. Beneath his feet, the ties began flicking past. With care, he maneuvered up and put a foot on the threshold of each door. He felt like a rodeo rider. Then he looked back. Two men were tearing along the platform after the train, one with a pistol pressed against his side. Just clear of the station, the train began a sharp curve, giving Ed a better view. And giving the men the same. One fired, the sound barely audible as the train wheels screeched.

Ed pulled in his head and held on. Each vibration from the rails traveled up his legs and the wind tore at his jacket. He might as well be on the outside of an airliner. On the other side of the glass door panels, passengers swayed, their eyes in the middle distance.

In five minutes his hands were frozen. At one point a train blasted past on the opposite track, sucking him toward the void. Just as it vanished, he was hit with the shock from a switching mechanism that nearly threw him down between the cars. Buildings were flashing past; he guessed he was traveling at forty miles an hour. He tried to hang on for a count of ten. Then ten more.

When the train swung into another curve, he could see an oncoming a station. As he relaxed slightly, the brakes threw him forward and he gashed his forehead on a jagged strip of aluminum. A bullet had ripped a channel in the cladding, tearing it open.

The tracks were now elevated and the station was two stories above the street. He'd never looked closely at this part of the trip into Manhattan. Paint peeled from steel I-beams and posters advertised movies from a year ago. Signs on the stores down below had Asian lettering, Chinese or Korean. There was no one on the platform and when the train finally shuddered to a stop and he slipped to the ground. He was so stiff he could barely step aside as the cars jumped forward again. A few faces inside turned toward him impassively, then passed out of sight.

He leaned with his hands on his knees, then forced himself up onto the platform. He'd crossed the straps of his backpack across his chest and it was still with him. But there'd been no time to take out the gun. A moment later he was through the turnstile and down the stairs, a handkerchief pressed against his forehead. He needed a cab, and fast. These guys would be on the next train.

Luck was with him. A ten year old Buick with a taxi sign attached to its roof with suction cups swerved to the curb in front of him. Ed held up two twenties and said, "Manhattan". The Asian driver held up five fingers. Ed added another ten and after a moment, the driver nodded. The backseat was worn but clean.

He had just minutes to work out a plan. Bart had been right. Some group, presumably Guardian, was serious about putting him down. He took out his phone and dialed Royco in St. Louis. The fact that the driver could hear him didn't matter. Another language, another world. He left a message explaining that a firm called Guardian Security had signed on to do investigative work for Naturtek and could be involved in the Hammersmith business. It might be useful to check any internet traffic between the two companies. To add a level of urgency, he explained what was happening in Queens. Still happening. Even if the feds were in bed with Naturtek, he'd have to hope Royco was independent. He'd try Ballancio later.

The driver let him off at the Manhattan end of the Brooklyn Bridge. The taxi commission focused enforcement on the island rather than the outer boroughs, so the driver was playing it safe. Ed added a ten to his handful of bills. Cheap at the price.

He'd escaped from Kennedy, but now what? Bart was hours away. If there was a team tracking him, someone could be outside his apartment. Navigating the back alley alone no longer seemed attractive. Ed hunched down in his coat, his collar up. Better to work from the *Chronicle* and contact his brother from there. He crossed City Hall park and clattered down the subway steps.

Chapter Thirty-Two

MONA, FINGERS DANCING OVER her keyboard, explained that Hardy was in his office but busy. Ed should wait. She never seemed to look at an appointment schedule. Maybe she just liked to slow him down. Today she wore a silk blouse, the ivory color setting off a maroon jacket. From his seat, could see her legs. The skirt matched the jacket but seated as she was, it didn't reach her knees. He wondered if she was a runner. When he glanced at her face, her eyes jumped away from his. A minute later she took one hand off the keyboard and motioned him toward the editor's door.

Percival Hardy stood behind his desk in shirt sleeves and suspenders, not the red braces favored by power CEOs but wide brown bands attached to leather loops; a 19th century hardware store clerk. He put down his phone.

Ed smiled. "They say that Emerson worked at a stand-up desk, Puritan rectitude against sloth." He was beginning to feel at ease with the boss. Still, he should watch himself.

"Not Puritan. Emerson was a transcendentalist. If you were on the arts and culture desk, we'd have to dock your pay. So, how's it going? Your piece on Hammersmith's death was a bit long but it will be out tomorrow. You failed to get a quote from his employers so we did. Not that they said anything. Just the usual: remarkable researcher, great loss to science, and terrible accident.

"They called it an accident?"

"Hammersmith was in the wrong place at the wrong time when someone came at him with a knife. Or to that effect."

"Nothing about foreign competitors and company secrets?"

"We pressed them on that because foreign intrigue sells, but it was no-go. They couldn't imagine how the rumor got started. As far as they knew, probably a meth-addled psychotic took down their best employee." Hardy's monotone was meant to echo the Naturetek spokesperson. "They want this behind them, as far as the press is concerned."

The stiff visitor's chair was making Ed squirm. "So, case closed. Except for the fact that someone's still trying to kill me."

"Do explain." Hardy raised one eyebrow.

Ed related how he'd just seen Aisling off at JFK and what followed. "It's got to be the same team that dogged us in Boston, and maybe killed Ciobanu."

"You say you rode between the train cars, and people were shooting at you? Remarkable. Too bad we didn't have a photographer there. Not our cup of tea, of course, but we could have sold it to the tabloids."

"Your condolences accepted."

"I noticed you were in one piece. Or nearly so." Hardy took in the abrasion on Ed's forehead. "And the police, what did they say?"

"I didn't call them. I came directly here so I can work in safety. My brother's on his way."

"There will be closed circuit coverage of the station. You need to report this."

Ed shrugged.

"Don't go macho on me. And take care of that cut on your head. Mona can help with that. Then call the precinct from the outer office. In fact, give me a minute and I'll lay the ground work. I know people at Midtown West. I'll have them call you back at Mona's desk. Fill them in, then get back here." Ed got up. "Wait! Don't we have Dr. O'Keefe analyzing Hammersmith's research?"

"Yes. Actually, she's finished. Her report may already be in your email." Ed looked at his watch. "Right now she's in the air over Louisiana."

"And out of the line of fire, let us hope."

Ed tried not to flinch while Mona dabbed his forehead with alcohol, her mouth pursed as if she were restoring a painting.

"I thought I saw blood when you came in but I didn't want to feed your self-pity." She kept dabbing. "This sting? I could wrap your head in gauze but you'd look like Frankenstein's monster. Better to let the air get at this."

"Are you the paper's substitute for a medical plan?" He tried to sit on the edge of her desk.

"Watch yourself, Bub. We're done." She pointed to a chair as her phone rang. Before he could move, she handed him the receiver. It was a Detective Avaaz.

"Took your time contacting us. Before you ask, CCTV was down along the Skytrain. It happens. We do have a blurry picture of you taken from inside the station by a guy who saw what was going on and then ran back up the stairs. He sent it to us. I love New Yorkers. So helpful. Anyway, Transit is looking for damage to their cars but, surprise, they're not sure which train was where three hours ago. Your editor tells me you weren't hurt. So, what is your story?"

Unhurt? He let that pass and explained the incident. "Both medium height, one wide, one not-so-wide, dark hair, brimmed hats. And I hardly saw their faces."

"While you skipped over electrified tracks. They say being lucky is better than being smart. But you could have been fried chicken." Ed let that pass. "The transit police couldn't find bullet casings. Maybe these guys used revolvers. I'm told you're at the *Chronicle* now, right?"

"Yes." Ed had almost said 'holed up.'

"We're at 621 forty-second, just east of 10th Ave. Get over here and sign a statement. We don't do these things by telephone. I'll have some-one to drive you home afterwards and eyeball your building. And keep it on our watch list. It's on Bowery near Broome, no?" Hardy must have given him the address.

"That was interesting," said Mona, after he hung up. Somehow she could hear both sides of the conversation. The half-glasses she usually wore now hung on a chain from her neck. A spiral of brown hair cork-screwed down the side of her face. It hadn't been there earlier.

"We need a memorial wall," Ed said thoughtfully. "You know, like the CIA has to honor dead agents."

"I'd be happy to supply the obit." She smiled. "But don't forget our death benefit. Three hundred dollars as I last recall."

"That much? You could serve hors d'oeuvres at the ceremony. Only wish I could attend."

"It would have to be brief, though. Can't hold up the presses, you know." She stared at him, a cat watching a mouse. "I don't usually get this close to a story." She dropped a tissue, pink with Ed's blood, into the trash. "Nice talking with you Dekker." She checked her screen. "Hardy wants you again."

The feature editor asked for the rundown from the Cambridge and Jefferson City police departments; Ed filled him in. "There's not much for them to work with, but they buy the connection between Hammersmith and Ciobanu."

"I can't believe there's nothing at MIT from their CCTV footage," said Hardy. "This isn't Podunk Community College. They should be able to do a face recognition search of everyone who's come and gone, then filter out the staff and students."

"It's a big building," Ed responded. "Bart says there's no reception desk, but someone may have noticed a stranger."

"Hardy sighed and scratched the sparse bristles on his head. "You know, I worked at Columbia for years. I predict five minutes of faculty outrage and demands for new locks on office doors, but not much more."

"Locking up the barn door, and all that?"

"Precisely. Self-preservation tops empathy. We need you on Ciobanu's death. Or I can ask Metro. Your choice."

"I've got it. It's all related and I know something about her already."

"Talk to her department head, one or two colleagues. This isn't Stephen Hawking we're talking about, so nothing too extensive. As for faculty, don't expect much there. They'll have tunnel vision, especially in a place like MIT. They're researchers, and likely to be oblivious of anyone not on their project or even in their field. Treat this as a tragedy for science, work in a subtheme about campus safety. But don't make it a detective story."

"Will do. But another thing. I've had my brother looking into Naturtek's corporate behavior. He found they'd contracted with a private security firm, Guardian Services, for unspecified services."

"Your brother, in addition to Manny LaRock? You're building quite a team. I suppose you want him on the payroll as well?"

"He's taking time off to help. And to provide me some protection. He's former military."

Hardy thought it over, taking in Ed's forehead and grease-stained coat. "Let's do this by the book. I'll have our security people follow you back to your apartment and stick around for a few days."

"Bart can do that. And he's good looking into the dark corners of D.C. corruption."

Hardy paused for a dozen heart beats. "Okay. Your brother's on board temporarily. Once this feature is in print, there'll be no reason for you to be anyone's problem. Which means, get it done." He hit the intercom switch and spoke with Mona. Turning back to Ed he said, "She'll have legal write up a contract. You can pick it up from security when you go there to meet your escort. They'll wait with you until your brother shows up. Anything else?"

"I appreciate this."

"Just make us proud with the story. You're following up with NYPD?"

"As soon as I leave here. And my place is pretty safe. Speaking of which, I've had to get a reinforced door. You remember my apartment was broken into?" In for a dime, in for a dollar, thought Ed.

"We're covering the Boston trip and your brother, as of tomorrow. Buy your own door." He hit a button on his intercom. "Mona, help this guy with his expense sheet. That includes a trip to Boston—train, hotel, whatever. Make it for two, if he insists."

Mona helped him log the travel details. Several of the receipts were missing—the gypsy cab from Brooklyn for example. After giving him an are-you-serious look, she cut him some slack.

"We have things to talk about," she said. Her voice deliciously rough. Sometime in the last hour she'd darkened her lipstick and he could imagine her in a Weimar cabaret. "The boss wants me to keep you on track."

No question, she was more than just Hardy's receptionist-secretary.

"You need to pitch this feature to me before you bring it back to Hardy." She pointed to the intercom on her desk. "There's not much that gets by me."

As he left, he could hear the hiss of nylon stockings.

Chapter Thirty-Three

CHIEF GUMBLETON'S POST WAS off the main floor lobby, a small office with a large plaque on the door that said "Company Security". Television monitors bathed the interior in blue light. The chief wore a XXL blue blazer and was pouring coffee from a battered carafe.

"You want some?"

"No, I'm good," said Ed, anxious to get on with it.

"Features says we have to cover your back until you arrange otherwise. I have that right?"

"That's it. I have my own protection coming in tonight."

"And we're going to put this palooka on our payroll? I don't like that. Either I run the operation here or I don't. And who is this guy? How can I be sure he's not going to cause trouble?"

Ed explained the setup and Gumbleton said twice that the risk was on Ed.

"When I'm here at the *Chronicle*, my brother will take a walk. There'll be no interference. Persons unknown have twice tried to block my investigation, three times if you include a break-in at my apartment. Shots have been fired. So this is an unusual situation."

"I understand. I've called Rodriquez off his rounds. He can escort you to your place. He'll see you get inside and wait for your guy."

"I appreciate that. But I need to go home by way of the 42nd street precinct. That a problem?"

"None."

"That's great, Mr. Gumbleton."

"Call me Chief." The big man smoothed down his jacket. Letters on the lapel affirmed the title. "Ah, here's Rodriquez."

A compact man in a considerably slimmer blazer stood in the doorway. His teeth were edged in gold.

"Dekker here is a reporter whose gotten himself in trouble with… what did you say? Oh, yeah, persons unknown." He drew out the words. "See he gets home safe and stay until relief arrives. He's arranged for his own protection. Hardy, upstairs, is putting this new guy on our payroll so you'll have to get his particulars." He handed the guard a manila envelope.

On the way out Rodriquez chuckled, "Train or cab? I feel like a shotgun rider. A cab would be more secure."

Better a stroll in the sun, thought Ed. "We walk. It's not far to the station. Then a cab."

An hour later they were done with the precinct and climbing up to Ed's apartment. Rodriquez took the lead and walked sideways, a hand on his shoulder holster. The lobby, stairwell, and upper hall were empty. Reaching Ed's floor, Rodriquez marveled at the new door. Once he'd assured himself the apartment was empty, he swung it back and forth.

"Don't even say it," joked Ed. "It makes it look like a mob apartment, I know."

"Whatever rings your bell," replied the guard. "But I need to know where you got it. Where I live in Bed-Sty, things can get a little dicey, if you get my drift."

"I'll get back to you on that. My brother had the work done. What can I get you? Coffee, a sandwich?"

"Coffee works. Black."

"*Si, café negro sin leche.*" Always good to hone his restaurant Spanish, thought Ed.

"Hey, they hear you talk like a *cholo, la migra* will be asking for your *documentos*!" His teeth flashed.

Ed perked coffee and they sat for an hour. The guard explained he'd been born in Brooklyn but there were times he wished he carried a birth certificate. If it ain't ICE, it's stop-and-frisk," he explained. "Rousted for being tan. "But no complaints with the paper. I even have health insurance."

"Beats my deal," said Ed. "I'm a stringer. The technical term is 'contingent', hired by the story. When they don't need me, I'm on my own."

"They must want this story," said Rodriquez.

They fist bumped. "Speaking of which." Ed then launched into his tale of riding the outside of a subway car.

"City surfing? Fucking amazing! No story is too tough for you reporters."

Just then there was a knock at the door. Ed flipped on the video intercom and saw Bart's face, the nose close to the camera was magnified. "You need an intercom downstairs and a remote release for the lobby door," Bart said. "And who's this?"

"Bart, meet Diez Rodriquez, a security officer at the *Chronicle*. Hardy thought I needed a sitter till you got here."

The two shook hands. "Your brother's cool. We were just about to practice quick draw." Rodriquez lit the room with his smile. Then he handed Bart the paper work. "Sign here, here, and here and you're in that new Mustang outside. Oops! I mean, you're on the *Chronicle* payroll. You keep the pink copy."

"Hang on to that," said Ed. "Diez here tells me it comes with health insurance."

"Already got that, so I'll take the cash." Bart signed and Rodriquez headed for the door.

"You guys need me, I'll be at the shop. If I stay away too long, I raise Gumbleton's blood pressure."

"You kept me alive." Ed gave a wave. "But hey, I need your cell number. I'll let you know when I'm back in the office."

With Rodriquez gone, Ed brought his brother up to date. "Riding outside a subway car?" Bart shook his head. "That's crazy. But it makes the case for my being here."

"I'd like to say I felt like a character in a Batman movie, but in fact I was scared shitless."

Bart threw an arm around his brother. "You're a reporter. You just got a new story to tell. So, what do we do now?" As they talked, Bart unpacked his duffel. "We need to bring this to a head. While you're thinking, let me do a few things. I've brought the latest security protocols for your laptop and I can clean out any malware. I'll also look around for microwaves. Those break-in artists could have tucked a bug anywhere. I didn't have the right equipment last time. And there's this."

"How'd you manage to get a gun on a plane?" Ed was looking at the handgun that Bart placed on the table.

"I picked up a federal permit since I was here last. And my partner at Executive Action pulled some strings on the waiting period. I didn't want to stand under a bridge here to buy a Saturday night special."

Ed weighed the piece in his hand. "Light."

"This is the smallest Glock they make, the 42.380. With a full mag, it comes in under 15 oz. Easy to conceal. When you run, it won't bang against your chest."

"You're saying I need this?"

"What happened to the one I left you?"

Ed pointed to his backpack. "It's here. And I had it with me today but I was in no position to use it."

"Maybe it's better if you stick with your notebook and leave the artillery to me. Unless you're range-certified." Bart's voice dropped to the register of a drill instructor.

"Only for throwing a bagel, Sir!" snapped Ed. "Which reminds me.

You must be starving. I know I am. Let's find a place to chow down. I'm afraid that Aisling and I did more eating than shopping."

"I'm sure," said Bart with a blank face.

They headed for a steak house in Union Square. As cold as it had become, Ed wanted the walk. They passed Astor Place, Grace Church, and the 'World's Largest Bookstore'. Word was that after a century, it might be closing. It was after 9, but Leunig's was still serving. As Ed expected, Bart led them to a table against the far wall with a view of the door.

"Just a habit. My radar tells me nothing's going to happen until we poke 'em in the eye again."

"Which we're trying to do," responded Ed. "The transit police are reviewing the camera footage at Kennedy looking for facials. Gun shots near the airport are serious business. Maybe these punks will turn up in some data base."

"They get ID'ed, they'll be forced to lay low. Do the authorities have video of your train caper?"

"Guy at the police station said no. A camera maintenance issue. They're writing off my ride as a forgivable dereliction. They're not billing me for damage, anyway."

"At this point, where are we?"

"Aisling's review is done but I haven't seen it. My pal at the paper, Manny, got release time to create a business profile of Naturtek—research directions, patents, new products, competition. This might turn up a lead. I'm going to try contacts I have with an environmental NGO, the Earth Defense Fund. They won a couple of superfund pollution cases and they're here in New York. They specialize in seeing where industry is headed before it falls off a cliff."

"You're working with a budget?"

"For you, Manny, and the consultants. There's something for travel, within reason they tell me."

"Sounds like a plan." Their steaks arrived, taking up more space on the plate than the baked potatoes and green beans. The kraut was in a separate dish. The waiter set down big, wooden-handled knives, the kind you could wear on your belt in the woods. Bart asked for refills on the German draft they were drinking.

"Here's where I'm at. I can continue to hack into the Naturtek and Guardian Security correspondence. It pits our technology against theirs, but it's worth the risk. The guys in our shop make the NSA look like a junior college computer class, or so they tell me. They've set me up with some cool algorithms so I shouldn't get caught. But if I do trip an alarm, it will be on my head, not theirs or Executive's. Even then, it'll take days before they can trace the intruder." He emptied half his glass. "I'm thinking I can base the operation at the 42nd Street library, link into their Wi-Fi. That scatters the bread crumbs even wider."

They finished their meal in silence. Ed watched with regret as the waiter collected the oversized knives. On the walk back they stopped at a 24 hour supermarket to stock the kitchen. Not only did Ed pay, he had to carry the bags. Bart wanted his hands free.

Chapter Thirty-Four

By TEN THE NEXT morning, Ed was at the Upper East Side office of Earth Defense Fund waiting to see Janet Malcolm. Bart had walked him there and then gone off to the public library to continue his research.

Ed had worked with Janet on a story about the coffee business and the fair-trade labeling of beans grown by small farmers. She'd researched the law on whether a conventional roasting company—one threatening to bring a law suit against the labeling company—had a case based on the fact that food labeling was a federal prerogative. The suit had never materialized but the possibility had rattled the fair trade sector. He and Janet had got on well and coordinated strategy with one of the larger labeling organizations. Janet had been *pro bono* counsel, semi, at least, and Ed the embedded journalist. For a while, the two of them had walked a fence emotionally, unsure if they were just collaborators or something more. By mutual agreement, they'd ended up as colleagues.

After keeping him waiting for ten minutes, Janet appeared looking drawn but elated. She gave him a serious hug and led him back to her office. Files were piled on the desk, the visitor's chair, and the floor so they stood while he explained the current state of his research on Naturtek. Her face grew grim when he described Hammersmith's murder. He handed her a copy of what the scientist had sent.

Scanning it, she got right to the point. "You think the company is about to tank the environment?" She was wearing jeans and a black polo shirt that contrasted with her loose, grey-blond hair. It clearly wasn't one of her court days. Tension or overwork had kept her slim. "Oh, and I'm sorry. Move that stuff and sit down."

"Hammersmith thought so. Add crop sterility technology to genetic drift, you have to be concerned."

She paged through the notes. "And this Hammersmith—who we can assume isolated the terminator gene—backed away? Yet he delivered the results to his employer."

"Most of it. That was his job. But he warned them that the direction they were taking was problematic. With his death and the rifling of his files, we have to assume they now have the technology they need."

"Which would be patentable?" Janet's voice was detached.

"Or patented. Still checking on that."

"The press—meaning you—can go after them but the controversy will be settled on the basis of science. As things now stand with the government, you have the burden of proof. And frankly, I don't see enough here to make a case that all hell will break loose if Naturtek commercializes this line of seed."

"The fact that someone is trying to shut down any and all criticism has to mean something." Ed briefly outlined the facts surrounding Hammersmith's death. "Who would do this unless they were acting on behalf of the company?"

"I'd be worried if I were you. But we're not a criminal law practice. And you're not a cop. As scientists, our firm would need more detail on this gene technology."

Ed was losing her. "I'm not looking for an indictment. It's their ambition that worries me. If we're not talking about a significant danger, why did Hammersmith make an about-face? He was a true-believer in technology. In Austria he was spouting the company line—biochemistry will usher in a new world of synthetic nature."

"Synthetic nature?"

"His phrase. A week later, he's ready to meet with me and then he's murdered. I go back to New York and find he's mailed me these papers." He gestured toward what lay on a space she'd cleared on her desk. "It's like he was expecting to be killed."

She crossed her arms.

"The timing suggests he was killed before anyone knew he'd sent me this stuff. But it's clear he also mailed them a copy. There's his video. He says the company wasn't interested in proceeding carefully. Okay, the science is over my head, but I can understand remorse when I hear it."

"This is all troubling. Someone's likely to be chasing the package. You make me think of those physicists who worked on the Manhattan Project. They'd built the damn bomb but some of them thought it might incinerate the atmosphere. Truman, of course, didn't agree."

"I'll give you that being a whistle blower can make some people feel important, but the fact remains, he was murdered. And so was a former colleague of his at M.I.T." He explained.

She breathed out loudly. "I'll have our people look at this, okay?" She was bouncing the stack of papers he'd given her, blocking the edges. "I have a lowly law degree, but people here will know if this is a biological bomb. Earth Defense isn't the district attorney, but we could bring a civil action based on the failure to follow environmental regs or sue the government for not following the law. If someone's growing this stuff now, we could try for an injunction." She was thinking as she talked. "Aren't the police chasing the murder suspects?"

"I keep hoping. The cops are still involved but it's becoming an FBI matter. Problem is, if this turns out to be political, Naturtek is a big economic driver. And it shares patents with the U.S. Department of Agriculture."

"And the last four U.S. presidents were big-time on genetic crop research, I know." She shook her head. "This could eat up a lot of hours. Does that envelope hold a check as well?"

"I'll talk to my editor. He's signed up one researcher already and mentioned others. Why not you people? The more experts, the more persuasive the story gets."

"If there's consensus. I keep an open mind."

"Understood. I wasn't buying an expert witness. But the publicity could be good for Earth Defense, especially if down the line you become the plaintiffs."

"Slow down, Ed. We're small. We have to choose our battles. I'll take these papers on spec but I need board approval to do anything serious. And we're not accident lawyers, working on a percentage." Janet popped a stick of gum into her mouth. "I'm trying to stop with the cigarettes. If I'm caught lighting up on the courthouse steps, there goes my credibility."

"But you'll let me know if I'm on solid ground here? And by the way, snapping your gum gives you adolescent appeal."

"Was I doing that? You want youthful, hit on my intern."

Ed's mood lightened. She was moving in his direction. He laid out the rest of the situation. In for a dime. "The story, as they say, gets worse."

"More worse?" She raised her eyebrows. She was foot tapping.

"The day after Hammersmith colleague at MIT was murdered, our little team was getting ready to leave Boston and some goons chased us through Back Bay."

"Your team?"

"Yeah. I enlisted my brother on the case. He's in security. My paper put him on the payroll while I research this story. Also, there's a biologist at Northeastern. She's the other consultant I mentioned. She vetted Hammersmith's work but I still need to look at her report."

"A reporter, a body guard, and a scientist. Have I seen this movie somewhere? You continue to surprise me. If this holds together, it could shift things to a new level."

"In the courts?"

"Or the court of public opinion."

"Are you with us?"

She rocked slightly back on her heels. "All right. I'll do the legal research. We can access court records that aren't sealed, but in these cases they sometimes are. I'll get a preliminary opinion from our science people. If we take a step beyond this, Earth Defense will need a contract and a check. And you'll need to acknowledge our help in what you publish."

"Done. One last thing. Hammersmith was worried about GMOs impacting pollinating insects. It's in the notes. Can you look into that?"

"No can do. We're not an agricultural college. But to answer your implied question, seed companies do their own trials and take the results to the USDA and EPA. If these bodies determine that a modified organism is substantially equivalent to what's traditionally grown, the company gets a pass." She went on to explain the details. "And companies aren't required to tell local government where test plots are located."

"Who pays for genetic contamination?"

"Not the companies. They have no legal liability to owners of adjacent plots." She paused. "Where there have been law suits, it's the companies getting damages from the nearby farmers."

"For?"

"Theft of DNA."

He absorbed that.

"Okay, you got my attention. Now, I have things to do." She gave him a contract form and moved toward the door. "Watch yourself, kiddo. Get that back to us. Do I have your numbers?"

He dug out his *Chronicle* business card and penciled in the number of his throw-away phone. "Use that. And do you prefer steak or seafood?"

"You, at room temperature, but not today." She gave him a hug. It lasted longer than the one they'd exchanged when he arrived.

Chapter Thirty-Five

IT WAS AFTER ELEVEN. The deal was that he'd call Bart when he was finished but the day was sunny, the sidewalks crowded. It seemed pointless to interrupt his brother's work. Ed headed south toward the 42nd Street library. The curbside snow was going. Ed ducked into a sandwich shop for coffee and drew out his computer. Checking his files on-line, he located another NGO, Blue Water. Some years ago he'd done an investigative piece for them on brownfields in Newark, toxic areas left by departing chemical plants. For fifty years, PP Ireland had made industrial solvents on the east side of the Passaic River. In 1989 they declared bankruptcy and left a pool of seepage that would cost millions to clean up. EPA hired Blue Water to carry out testing and lay the basis for a law suit. While covering the story for the Newark paper, Ed helped the science guys craft a media narrative. While the company no longer existed, the story enraged local legislators and the site was given Superfund status. Unfortunately, cleanup took the form of an impermeable cap and two feet of fresh soil; any reuse of the site was a century away.

The process had left a sour taste in Ed's mouth. The municipality, teetering on the edge of bankruptcy, got no reparations and instead of property taxes, was looking at ten useless acres. Blue Water had done okay though from the tranche of federal funds. Their offices were in Midtown and worth a phone call.

After talking his way past the receptionist, Ed reached Bruce McLean, the project manager he'd worked with several years ago. McLean was available that afternoon.

Then Ed dialed Bart.

"I just discovered there's no cellphones allowed here", said Bart, speaking in a whisper, "but I had the thing on vibrate. You done?"

"At Earth Defense, yes. They'll help. I'm meeting with another environmental NGO, Blue Water. Their focus is chemical contamination. I'm hoping that includes genetic pollution."

"When's your appointment?"

"At 4, which gives me almost three hours. Should I come by and lend you a hand?"

"Good idea. Need an escort?"

"If I get lost, I'll ask a cop. See you in thirty."

Cab or walk? Ed stuck with the sidewalk. Keeping to the east side of Fifth, he caught sun most of the way. This was "Museum Mile", with Central Park on his right, the "Round and Round Museum" as people called it, on his left.

The sun had brought out a crowd in front of the city's largest library, sitting, lined up at taco trucks, or glued to cell phones. Ed found his brother in the main reading room, bent over his computer. Piles of books kept the adjacent seats free.

"Find anything?"

"Maybe. In 2018, Naturtek notified the Department of Agriculture they were about to field test three genetically altered crops: peppers, avocado, and mango. Then, get this, they amended the notice to include arabica coffee. Based on their in-house studies, which was all the USDA required, they got approval. Anything strike you?"

"All tropical plants, right?"

"My thought, too. But they're aiming at the whole vegetable aisle. There's a press release that references expected progress on almonds and apples."

"The whole megillah."

"Yeah. With that heads-up to investors, Naturtek bumped up their share price." Bart handed him the photocopy of a press release.

"This was two years ago. They don't say where the tests will take place. I doubt Saskatchewan."

"Not for mangos."

"I just learned that USDA doesn't require information on test plot locations."

"You're saying the Feds don't monitor these things? We're talking food. What we eat, for God's sake!" Bart's voice had risen in volume and was attracting stares.

"They inspect slaughter houses and check for puss in the milk, but GMOs? Only if there's evidence of allergens."

"In other words, first show me something's not safe." Bart was disgusted. "Makes their job a lot easier."

"And speeds up approval. Time is money. That leaves the company having to convince farmers the extra yield is more than the added cost. Which is the point of the field tests."

"So, the demand is there?"

Ed leaned closer. "It's not a level playing field. As the companies consolidate, it gets hard for growers to get the older seed. In corn, for example, there are fewer and fewer varieties sold."

"But yield is the ticket, no?"

"Actually, it's net profit." Ed grabbed a scrap of paper from his brother. "First, you pay a royalty for these super seeds. Then you have to follow a protocol in cultivation, use specified fertilizers and chemicals to maximize output. That's out of pocket"

"Why do farmers bother? Corn is corn." Bart scratched his head.

"It's a treadmill set in motion by the land grant colleges. After they put agriculture on a scientific footing, it's been all about innovation, protein content, and production statistics."

"A new language?"

"A new culture. If you're having breakfast in a diner out in Iowa, shooting the shit with your neighbors, you want your fields posted with signs that read, say, "Pioneer Hybrid—P9834AMX. That tells your friends you're on top of your game. And what's new is rewired genes."

"Slow down, bro, you're knocking science."

"Not holistic science, no. But if it treats plants in isolation, an improvement may not pan out on the farm. For eighty years, extension agents patted farmers on the back if they were 'early adopters'. That meant buying new machines, new seeds, plowing more acreage. The idea was, get modern or get out. The battering ram was hybrid corn. Once you bought it, you couldn't save your seed so you were tied to the supplier."

"I don't understand."

"Hybrids bump up yield but they don't reproduce well. So you'd be dumb to replant your own harvest. Now it's worse. Your grandfather's seed will die if you apply weed killer. His soybeans don't mature all at once so you can't use that new machine you just bought that scoops them all up in one go. If you're in potatoes, you plant what McDonald's tells you or they won't buy it. You're out there on your own land, thinking you're liberated, but you're caught in a web."

"Liz insists on organic. How's that fit in?"

"It's a contrarian market, growing, yes, but the industrial farmers are king. They supply the food processors and chain restaurants. That's where the American meal has gone."

"For you, clearly." Bart poked Ed in the stomach.

"Hey, do I have a wife?" Ed cringed. "Sorry about that." They were attracting hostile stares. Bart tried to tone it down.

"As an expert on meals-ready-to-eat, I say Naturtek has a dumb business plan."

"You wish. Think of farming like an addiction." Ed drew a diagram. "Super seeds give you an edge until the bugs and bacteria adjust. Now you're faced with super weeds and super insects. You go back to the store—what choice do you have?—for extra super seeds. And so it goes. And each time, the cash goes into the pocket of the suppliers. It's a great business plan."

A librarian was now standing beside them. They hadn't noticed her approach. So much for being a bodyguard, thought Bart.

"You are bothering people. Take this conversation outside." She stood there with her arms folded while Bart packed up his notes and computer. The sign said leave re-shelving to the staff.

"Actually, it was good they kicked us out," said Ed. They were standing on the steps beside the big granite lions. "I was about to miss my appointment at Blue Water. Shall we go?"

They grabbed a cab and headed uptown. "You're sure your computer searches aren't leaving traces?"

"State of the art technology, and I'm closing backdoors each time I leave." Bart wiggled his fingers like a piano player warming up. Or a safe cracker. "Quick in, quick out. But we have a problem. My guy at Executive tells me he's stopped rummaging around in Naturtek's system. Says it's too dangerous. I talked to him while you were uptown. From the bathroom, let me add."

"What's he afraid of?"

"Turns out Naturtek's cloud is the one used by the NSA."

"Is that unusual? And what about you?"

"I've switched over to look at their security contractor. Different risk factors."

"So, we get what we can." Traffic was gridlocked at fifty-seventh street. Ed watched pedestrians weaving through stalled cars.

"One thing though. While I was still looking at Naturek, there was something about a dropped project. Had to do with blueberries. Seemed like it hadn't worked out in practice."

"When was that?"

Bart opened his notebook. "Three years ago."

"I wonder if this was one of Hammersmith's projects." Traffic moved ahead a block and then stalled again.

"What we have to realize is that things are speeding up."

"Not this cab," said Bart.

"In genetic engineering. Around 2002, a new tool became available for gene splicing. They call it CRISPR. It uses enzymes to very accurately edit a genetic fragment. It makes adding and subtracting traits a lot easier. To be honest, I think the genie is out of the bottle." Ed sighed.

They'd arrived at an office building on sixty-fifth. Ed handed the driver the paper's credit card. This was a gusty corner and they pulled their coats tightly closed. "I shouldn't be long."

"I'll wait in the lobby, eyeball things."

Ed stepped off the elevator into Blue Water's reception area and introduced himself to a girl of high school age. Interns are everywhere, Ed thought. Yes, she said, he was on the list. He took a seat and stared at the art on the walls. It had a liquid theme: seacoast watercolors, tidal ponds, Adirondack bogs. One photo was of Arctic ice; no polar bears. The tone was up-beat, lots of muted blue.

A florid man in his early forties strode into the waiting area, his hand extended. "Ed Dekker! As I live and breathe. Great to see you again. Still doing good things at the *Newark Journal?*"

"Bruce McLean, good to see you too. Thanks for taking the time. Actually, I'm with the *Business Chronicle* now. I crossed the river from Jersey a while ago."

"A step up into the big time," said McLean, finally releasing Ed's hand. "Do you mind if we talk here? I have a client in my office going over a report we did for him and I ducked out. I only have a minute."

"No, this is great. I'll get right to it." They settled back in a pair of

Eames chairs. Probably two grand a pop, Ed thought. Business must be good.

"I'm trying to run down any environmental complications associated with terminator crops, plants that mature once but leave a sterile seed."

"Heard of them," said Bruce.

"I know this isn't a water issue, but as you people say, everything is connected. I'm hearing that pollination problems are cropping up around these things. Bees being poisoned, and where they're the fertility vector, crop yields fall. I'd expect the same problem holds for insects generally. Ever come across this?"

McLean passed his hand over very dark hair. "As you said, not our area. You have a company in mind?"

"I do. But if this is a problem, it's industry-wide. I'm saying 'if' because I'm trying to keep an open mind."

"As you should. But frankly, that technology—from what I've heard—seems like a dead end. It would conflict with every biological imperative I know of. Life begets life." He looked over toward the receptionist and lowered his voice for a moment. "All creatures want to procreate. But we're not entomologists here. True, we've surveyed insect populations associated with ponds or coastal littorals but as indicator species to gauge the toxicity of chemical spills." His hand seemed to be combing his memory without actually touching his head. "We've done wetland restoration studies for the EPA. And won superfund lawsuits, I might add. You were involved in one." Bruce patted Ed on the shoulder and grinned. "Big bucks there, eh?"

As Ed recalled, his paycheck for that job barely covered the timing belt for his Toyota.

"We need the big ones to support our other work. But genetic restriction technology?" He held up open hands. "Nothing."

"I see. But you're a Yale grad with a degree or two beyond me. What's your gut feeling?"

"Now you're sounding like an accident-scene reporter. 'How does it feel to be hit by a semi-trailer, sir?'" Bruce laughed at his own joke. "What I *feel* is that every problem has a solution. After, of course, someone funds us to look for it." He stood. "Sorry, but you're asking the wrong guy. And I've got to get back to work. Client waiting."

"Thanks for putting some thought into this. I appreciate the time."

"We've got to get you back on the rolodex. I'm surprised we haven't hired you recently. As I remember, you have a gift for telling a good story. Give your new number to my girl. I'll ask in-house on the seed issue. And if we can use you, I'll be in touch."

"I appreciate the thought. And your time."

Bruce waved his hand and disappeared. The receptionist entered his contact numbers into her computer. "Guess rolodexes have passed into history," said Ed. "Just desk clutter, eh?"

"Huh?" the girl said, puzzled. Ed retreated to the elevator and hit the button.

Ed had checked out Blue Water's last annual report. They were doing okay. But even nonprofit NGOs had to stay solvent. The vague offer of an assignment seemed like a distraction, though. And Ed didn't buy the argument, 'We only do water'. The tell was when Bruce asked him to name the target company. Well, nothing ventured, nothing gained.

Chapter Thirty-Six

THE DEKKERS RETURNED TO the city's central library. No one in reference seemed to care that they'd been ejected earlier. While Ed checked out journal articles on gene splicing, Bart continued with his forensic autopsy of Guardian Services; neither was turning much up. As closing time approached, Ed suggested a sit-down with Manny over dinner to brainstorm. He got through to the sports desk and Manny picked a seafood place in the Village close to his apartment. Shorter walk home, he said. He was exercising but why overdo it?

By seven they'd regrouped at a table for six, spreading out notes and laptops. The place wasn't crowded and the waiter didn't object to the clutter.

"First, we have to get the terminology right," said Manny. "I've been looking up patent applications on suicide seeds but the industry prefers "Technology Protection Systems.""

"I like 'terminator technology,'" said Ed. "It gives Arnie Schwarzenegger his due. But in polite circles, the term is 'GURTS'."

"As in Gertrude?"

"As in Genetic Use Restriction Technology."

"That trips off the tongue," said Bart.

"The second thing I discovered," continued Manny, "is that Naturtek doesn't own the recombinant genetic technology they're using to develop one-generation plants," continued Manny. "They're partnered with an outfit called Delta & Pine Land, which filed the first patent on self-destroying seeds in 1998. But get this. DPL has a partner as well, the U.S. Department of Agriculture."

Ed doodled USDA on his napkin while Manny paused for effect. "Now factor in the piece about the government writing regulatory standards and being a central player in agricultural trade negotiations and what do you get?"

"Bibbity, boppity boo? No, let me think. A conflict of interest?" Ed hit his own forehead in mock surprise.

"Try RICO," said Bart, referring to the Racketeer Influenced and Corrupt Organizations Act the feds used to go after organized crime.

"But unfortunately," said Ed, "the government isn't going to indict itself. I've known abut the link to USDA."

"It's self-dealing, for sure." Manny reclaimed the lead. "And doesn't this make the government the intellectual author of a crime under, I don't know—help me out here, Ed—the Endangered Species Act?"

"No, and that's too bad because the courts take spotted owls seriously. What you're thinking of is the Convention On Biological Diversity. It's a UN thing. It says governments can't field test GURTS. But unlike, say, intellectual property protection, the CBD has no sanctions."

"Naughty, naughty!", said Manny, wagging a finger.

"That's about it, a reprimand. The research goes back to the Clinton era when biotechnology was picked as America's new machine tool to dominate the global economy."

"Given that our factories were crumbling into rust." That from Manny.

"The claim was that information technology in agriculture would let us own the food system. Genes, after all, are just little information packages, really just software." Ed was on a roll.

"And speaking as a security professional, I'd say information equals control."

"Knowledge is power'," responded Ed.

"Okay, guys." Bart pushed his papers to the side. "Let's order." The waiter had been standing there.

It was mussels and pasta Fra Diavolo for the Dekkers, scallops and linguini for Manny. As they ate, Ed filled them in on his outreach to the environmental NGOs, saying one might prove helpful.

"We're facing an impressive opponent here," said Manny, "industry hand-in-hand with the federal government. It's the NHL against, well, …."

"Your local middle school?" Bart filled in.

Ed was mopping up tomato sauce with the last piece of bread when he said, "Assume other companies are rushing to catch up. That puts Naturtek on the clock. St. Louis needs a big score to keep investor confidence."

"Metaphors rule," said Manny. "From what I've found, the company isn't sitting on the bench."

"We think the federal government is supporting Naturtek, at least with their data security," said Bart.

"One play I am seeing," said Manny, "is Naturtek buying up feisty little competitors. Even overpaying. Then they soften up the rest of the opposition by threatening lawsuits for patent infringement."

"Monopoly has always been the royal road to profits," added Ed.

"And Guardian Services could just be another tool in their box," said Bart.

"Tomorrow I'll take a closer look at the competition," said Manny. Then he rumbled his lips. "As they say on Wall Street, we're swimming with the sharks." Getting the waiter's attention, he said, "Bring me a limoncello."

"Lee mohn CHEH lo," said the waiter under his breath.

By eight-thirty, Manny was gone and the Dekkers were walking down Chrystie Street, circling toward Ed's apartment from the back. As they neared the alley leading to the basement of his building, they had to navigate around vegetable crates and trash bags. The sidewalk was crowded and Bart took the lead. With a metallic hiss, the door of a van parked beside them slid open and hands reached for Ed's arm. Without thinking, he pivoted in a counter-clockwise direction and swung a closed fist. By chance, he connected with the face of his assailant, a lithe man in a black turtleneck. As the man leaped from the vehicle, his feet slipped on the pavement and he pitched over a stack of empty crates, sending his brimmed hat into the street. In seconds he was back on his feet and moving in. Bart, pushing his brother aside, landed a punch in the middle of the man's chest, a blow that forced him to drop the bicycle chain he'd been swinging. Then the door to the van's passenger seat banged open and a second figure emerged, waving a pistol. Ed grabbed a box of wilted bok choy and swung it, forcing the guy to recoil. As he backed into the side of the van, bringing up his pistol, Bart paralyzed his gun hand with a hard punch to the shoulder that spun him half-way around. He followed that with a roundhouse kick that sent the first attacker through the open door of the van. Now facing both Dekkers, the gunman leaped back into the front seat. The driver, unseen in the altercation, whirled the van into traffic, its sliding door gaping open. The entire episode had taken less than a minute.

"Go, go, go!" shouted Bart, pointing back up Chrystie Street against the flow of cars. "Where there's three guys, there might be others." The brothers loped north, threading through pedestrians focused on their shopping carts and children-in-tow.

This was the freedom of the city, thought Ed, that not-my-problem attitude that let you take care of business. The Dekkers continued on across Houston Street, slowing to a race-walk pace as Ed's leg cried out in protest. Half a mile later they were at Astor Place.

"You cocked him one, all right," said Bart after they'd slunk into a Starbucks. "Didn't know you had it in you." Ed moved his hands under the table edge, hiding the dried blood on his knuckles.

"I have been known to go to the gym, you know. You should see my work on a speed bag."

Bart drew in his shoulders and cracked his joints. "As for me, I could be in better shape. But, my bad. I let you fall behind me. When I heard that door slide open, I was out of position."

"All I saw was the chain. What's with that?"

"Probably to stun you, maybe to wrap around your neck and drag you into the van. They'd be wanting to question you. They may not have known there were two of us."

"Or they'd have sent a bigger team?"

"Precisely."

"Now what? We call the cops?"

"You're the victim; your choice. But there's nothing I saw that will help, beyond the letter 'B' on a New York license plate. From the one or two words I heard, I'd say two Hispanic males, approximately thirty, five foot six to nine, but where does that get you?"

"One lost his hat. What about DNA?"

"If it hasn't already been picked up, it's covered with who-knows-what from the street. I'd say forget about DNA."

"Question is, do we go back to my place or find somewhere else?"

"I doubt they'd expect us to return, at least right off. I'm for going back," said Bart. "I have faith in that door."

"And because you want to meet them again."

"Maybe. But your call." He grinned and looked down at the pistol on his belt.

This time they entered through the lobby on Bowery. The apartment was untouched. Ed's phone rang while he mulled over whether to notify the precinct. Surprisingly, it was Mona.

"You're the last person I'd expect to hear from, especially at this hour."

"Little do you know what it takes to put out a newspaper."

"I've heard rumors." Maybe she did run the office, thought Ed.

"I have a message from Hardy. You know he told NYPD about your break-in. He pulled in some favors and they're having their foot patrols in the Chinatown area keep an eye out."

"He mentioned something about that."

"What you don't know is that a few minutes ago the cops spotted two men scoping out your lobby, hunkered down in the shadows of the foyer. When the police approached, they ran off. One was nabbed and is being held. Hardy wanted to give you a head's up."

"Jesus," said Ed. "It doesn't rain but it pours. Actually, the evening has been interesting. We had a run-in with that crew an hour ago."

"Care to explain?"

Ed did, skipping over his own role.

"But you're okay?"

"And so are they, unfortunately."

Mona processed that. "Detectives came by your place to follow up on your initial complaint, but you were out. They admired your new door, by the way."

"My castle keep."

"The guy they caught is in the Chinatown precinct now, they say a local loser. They described him as on probation for car theft. Oh, and he tried to ditch a gun. That, and the suspicion of a B&E at your place, means they're taking it seriously."

The paper had his back, which was good to know. "It will be interesting to see who turns up to represent him."

"That's what they're waiting for. In the meantime, the guy isn't saying anything."

"And probably never will," broke in Bart. By this time Ed had his phone on speaker.

"You know my brother's here, right?"

"Bartholomew Dekker, of course. I just processed his paper work. Is he taking care of you?"

"I am," said Bart. "The name's one of the twelve apostles. My mother's idea. But go with the short version, would you?"

"Just verifying the paper work." They could hear shuffling as Mona talked. "So, this run-in?"

"Looked like a fumbled abduction," continued Bart. "We could do an identification but we have no physical evidence."

She mulled that over from a minute. "Any progress on the story, Ed? Something I can report to Hardy? You want to keep him interested."

Ed relayed Manny's discovery that there was likely a race on among various companies to lock up terminator patents. "Oh, and guess who has an ownership position in death-seeds? Delta & Pine Land. And through them, the US Department of Agriculture."

Mona exhaled, almost a whistle. "Things are getting interesting. Here's my personal cell." She recited the number and that of the downtown precinct. "Hardy says check in there and get back to us if there's more trouble. Day or night."

"Will do. Thank the boss for his help with the police. So they want another interview?"

"Keep them sweet. If you phone, they may pick you up. Best to get everything on the record."

"Okay, I'll do it." He clicked off.

Bart scowled at Ed. "Not likely these guys just wanted a place out of the weather to smoke. I'm thinking they couldn't get through your door."

Ed rubbed his knuckles. "Let's get down there and take a look." He made the call.

While they waited for the cops to buzz the door, they washed up from the fight. "I doubt these miscreants are on Guardian's payroll," said Bart. "Not how these things are done. Guardian will have hired a cutout for just this eventuality. Even if this guy is willing to talk, he won't have much to trade."

It worked out as Bart predicted. The perp turned out to be the guy with the bicycle chain. He'd also been armed. Through one-way glass, the brothers could see that his cheekbone was bruised. With nothing more to contribute beyond physical descriptions and the letter 'B' on a New York license plate, the Dekkers were driven back home in less than an hour.

"At least one guy's off the street," said Ed, locking the door. "Who's left?"

"The well is never dry," said Bart. "But now the cops are involved so I expect Guardian to lay low. We may have caught a break. If it's okay with you, I'd like to hop back to D.C. and take a closer look at Guardian. Also, I need to motivate our guy who's hacking into the Naturtek records. With the police looking in on things, you should be good for a couple of days. Just don't do anything stupid."

"Works for me. Anything to move things along. I'll keep bothering Royco and Ballancio. But it's that seed article that will pay the rent. I can push it ahead and still hunker down."

Bart was out before dawn. By noon Ed had checked with the out-of-town police departments and found nothing new. Ballancio had given up pretending that suicide or an accident were possibilities. "People who work in a place for years don't kill themselves in front of their colleagues." But there were no leads. In Jeffersonville, the dead motorcyclist remained unidentified.

Janet Malcolm at Earth Defense turned up no record of regulators or private parties suing Naturtek. In fact, it was the other way around. The company's arsenal of lawyers had brought more than a hundred legal actions for theft of intellectual property, mostly against farmers. The defense contended genetic material had simply blown onto their land. Or that genetic contamination had been deliberate. Faced with Naturtek's resources, the farmers mostly settled.

"When you're dealing with deep pockets, it's no contest," Janet continued. "The GMO market is worth fourteen billion a year in the U.S. alone and covers eighty-five percent of our cropland. Then there's sixty million hectares in Brazil and Argentina. If terminator becomes the new iteration of GMOs, the impact on the environment could be huge."

"You say 'if'."

"A lot remains experimental," said Janet. "Before they can roll out a commercial version of say blueberries, they need to be sure their line of herbicides and pesticides continue to function. That's also part of the business."

"So it's not game-over yet?" said Ed.

"No, but don't expect the regulators to be more than a speed bump."

"Hum. If you come across any specific horror stories, let me know."

"There's another angle," she went on. "These seeds are sandwiches. Think of a Big Mac. They're a stack of traits. One to address moisture issues, others for diseases and pests. And get this. They're working on varieties with root systems that sequester carbon in the soil at twice rate of ordinary plants."

"Taking carbon from the atmosphere?"

"It's their answer to fossil fuel pollution. They're betting big on the climate apocalypse."

"Doubling down, like Naomi Klein described," said Ed.

"Yeah, catastrophe capitalism. I have to say, we're getting more interested over here. So get me that check."

Late in the afternoon, Ed turned to Aisling's report. She'd emailed it to the *Chronicle* from Mexico and Mona sent it over as an attachment. Ed found it frustrating, evasive even. With no independent way to confirm Hammersmith's results, all she could say was pollen and nectar in terminator plants could be toxic to pollinating insects, most likely through endocrine disruption. Genetic markers had been used in the altered genome so theoretically the modifications could be located. Then she repeated the problems with Hammersmith's sample size.

More uncertainties, thought Ed. He needed a break. Front or back? He chose the lobby and went a block to a small, second-floor gym. It was bare of fancy equipment and smelled of sweat. In a good week he was lucky to get there once. After taping his hands, he borrowed gloves and worked the heavy bag until he could barely lift his arms. Then he jumped rope for another twenty minutes. He was Sugar Ray. He was Hurricane Carter back in contention!

Stepping out of the shower back at his apartment, he was just in time to catch a call on his burner phone, the one paired with Aisling's. It was a text message.

"Hope you got the report. It was the best I could do with what I had. I did some serious thinking on the trip down. You're a great guy and doing important work. But we have different trajectories. You're an exposé writer going after lies and deceptions. I'm not saying you're a sensationalist, but my focus is different.

Now that I'm at a distance, I see how much this has taken out of me. I've been tied up in knots since Oetz. Then there was Hammersmith's murder and Ciobanu's. Not to mention that nightmare in Boston. All the time we were together in your loft, I thought someone might come in through the window. I have to end this. I'm an academic. I've got a career to think about. I'm not made to sit in a foxhole.

I wish things could be different for us, Edward. One last word of advice. Be very careful. I'm shutting this phone down.

A

Ed reread the message. She didn't even know all of it. He grabbed a beer from the fridge and slumped down on his couch. If he could just talk to her. But what would he say? Wasn't he more or less still hiding out in his apartment? He glanced over at his desk and the gun Bart had left for him. With a sigh, he put his burner phone in a drawer.

Chapter Thirty-Seven

HE LOOKED AROUND AND tried to recreate her presence. Her scent. If she'd mailed this message, he could imagine her holding the paper. There was nothing.

His eyes fell on one of the academic articles Hammersmith had sent. It was by Ricarda Steinbrecher, a geneticist and critic of the industry. Ed glanced through it again, checking what he'd already highlighted. The scientist compared the standard approach used in genetic engineering to a lego construction, each piece a building block in isolation from the whole organism. One gene equaled one trait. Fish bits added to the genome of a tomato to lower the freezing point. The author argued this approach was fallacious. Genes didn't have hard edges. They express themselves throughout the whole organism. That's why those tomatoes tasted bad. And salmon reengineered for rapid weight gain had deformed heads.

Feeling like he'd run out of steam, Ed decided to call Mona. She'd want his take on Aisling's analysis.

Her voice, usually business-like, was low. Must be the evening hour. It was as though she was whispering in his ear.

No, she explained, Hardy wasn't interested in Aisling's report as such; whatever was there, it was Ed's job to weave it into his feature article. And that would be ready, when? His spot in the Sunday supplement was penciled in for the first weekend next month.

Mona, the expense account dragon, was turning out to be a key player. On the defensive, he outlined what he had and the angles he was pursuing. One was finding a dramatic example, something to illustrate the downside of this technology. And he was nailing down the risk factors. They both knew he was stalling.

"Here's what we'll do," she said, cutting him off and hardening her tone. "You'll outline the article as you have it now, even if you use a magic marker. Then you'll walk me through it. I'm Joe Reader. I want the story fast and punchy. The exercise will force you to pare things down; but I want both argument and color."

"You want an abstract?"

"What I don't want is rhetorical bullshit. Or scholarly pretension. More like a good TED talk." Ed had watched these popularized lectures that experts gave on Youtube. If Mona had a degree, he thought, it wasn't from secretarial school.

"Our readers veer off the business pages when they see something more exciting. They're smart, but impatient. You've got five sentences to draw them in, one paragraph, or they're gone. I'll supply the whiteboard and marker. Let's say done and down in ten minutes."

He was back in high school English. "I can do that," he said. "Shall we say next week?"

"Eight tomorrow tonight. Come to my apartment in the Village and make your pitch." She gave him the street address. "The office has too much going on and I want you in focus."

"I'll be there." Was there a choice?

Mona lived in a red brick townhouse on Barrow Street. The federalist building had three floors and from the buzzers, Ed gathered there were three floor-through apartments. Hers was the ground floor. It was good she'd said that because he didn't recognize any of the names. There was no nameplate on her desk at the office and she hadn't posted her full name on the bell. The tag read M. and J. Miranda. A little disappointed, he checked himself over. Husband? Wife? This was the Village, after all. An older child?

A magnetic lock buzzed and he entered a tight lobby with stairs leading up on the right. A hundred years ago, this would have been the center hallway to a merchant's house. Then the inner door opened. Mona stood barefoot wearing an untucked white shirt over jeans. A man's shirt. Without heels, she was shorter than she'd seemed at work where she ruled from behind a desk. She took his hand, surprising him, and led the way into a living area where a fire burned. The room was open-plan, most of the original walls removed. The lintels and crown moldings that remained looked 18th century, as did the fireplace mantel. But not the granite countertops and stainless steel appliances in the kitchen area. Ed's mental real estate calculator spun. He was looking at six thousand a month; maybe eight. French doors opened onto a small private patio. Be nice there in summer. No way a salary at the *Chronicle* could pay for this.

Mona pointed to a comfortable leather chair near the fire.

"Something to drink? I'm reheating a casserole in case you're hungry. Sausage and spinach in baked beans with onion and tomatoes. I'm saying this in case it affects what you'd like to drink. You're not a vegetarian, I hope?"

"Ah, no. It sounds, I don't know, savory?"

"I make these things up myself. It's like painting. Foods have colors and need to be served in the right combination. A Merlot?" she said, handing him half a glass, then refilled her own. "There's no coffee. It's easiest if we share the same wine and red goes well with the look of the casserole. When colors harmonize, so do the flavors."

They settled down around a low table, maybe an antique cobbler's bench. The room was warm and the air slightly acrid from old fires. Ed lay his coat on the back of a chair and loosened his collar. Jumping up, Mona disappeared into a side room and returned with a tripod holding an oversized pad of paper. "Sorry, no whiteboard, but will this do?" She noticed his reaction. "You thought I was kidding?"

"No." Ed fumbled in his briefcase for his notes.

"No crib sheet. This is your pitch to the editorial committee. They're into you for a pile of travel receipts and want to know if you're worth it." She smiled. Her lips were a glossy red. "They'll want you to stand."

"So, no pressure, eh?" He set his wine glass on the fireplace mantel. She folded her hands.

Once he got started, it wasn't as difficult as he'd feared. Occasionally he jotted down terms on the oversized pad. She looked at her watch two or three times but she never interrupted. He began with the events surrounding Hammersmith's murder, then used the intricacies of terminator technology to add mystery and social import to his thesis. What might this technology do to the food chain? To biological diversity? Was it an evil genie best left in a bottle? Was that even possible? He balanced suppositions, pro and con, but intimated a potential catastrophe.

"Nothing on human health?" She tented her eyebrows, the well-prepared student.

"That would be a related subject. Important, but a stand-alone."

A bell sounded in the kitchen. "Ah, the casserole." Mono looked at her watch a final time. "I've been timing the food, so don't be offended. You were eighteen minutes, though. Say 2800 words, maybe less because you were repetitious a few times. With editing, let's say 2000 words. Breaks down well into subheads. On the other hand, you'll need a tighter connection to the science for credibility, but not so much you bore your readers. That's always the challenge. We could put references in the on-line edition." She waved her glass, empty again. "Say we're up to 2400 words. Are you thinking illustrations? That's how things are trending, especially with the Sunday supplement. And the paper stock there is better."

Ed liked the sound of the supplement, a stand-alone magazine that arrived with the weekend edition. People kept it.

"I agree with what you said on the phone." Now she was talking over her shoulder from in front of the stove. "You need some actual genetic problem that people can visualize, something in the everyday world."

"I know," said Ed. "But I'm not Mary Shelley. I can't conjure up a monster."

"Forget lurid. Think graphic at-scale—drought, flood, famine." She'd returned to the dining table using oven mitts to hold a covered dish. The firelight played off her lips and eyes. "An example that worms into the reader's frontal cortex."

The bar was going up.

"So, ready to eat?" She set down the bowl on an iron trivet. When she removed the cover, steam billowed up to the coffered ceiling. "Now it's your turn to be critic. Tit for tat." With a well-used wooden spatula, she dug into the mix and filled their plates. He was relieved that it smelled quite good. He didn't mention that the colors had run together.

They removed their napkins from circular silver holders and she struck a wooden match on the underside of the table, lighting two candles. Her face, pale before, took on a warmer hue. Looking through the French doors, Ed could see small white lights on the branches of a leafless tree.

"Security," she said, reading his glance. "But nicer than a flood light."

The garden was enclosed by brick walls and strewn with grey snow and leathery oak leaves. Summer would be nice here, he thought.

"What's the verdict?"

He made a production of nibbling from the edge of his spoon. Before he could locate the right word, she said, "Needs broccoli." She chewed thoughtfully. "For a deeper green."

"No, no. It's fabulous the way it is. And the spicy sausage is fantastic. Fennel?" It was surprisingly rich.

"Exactly. Glad you noticed."

She was an enthusiastic eater and Ed matched her spoon for spoon.

He didn't refuse a second helping. This was a different Mona. Gone was the ice queen, the porcelain fashion plate. Except for the display board—a hint of a dominatrix there—she was now a homemaker plying him with food.

They finished with salad. "No dessert," she said, "not yet. I plan to take a Saturday course at the Culinary Institute on pies and puddings but I haven't had the time." She smiled. "So you'll have to come again."

He could imagine Indian pudding with a colonial rum sauce. It would go with the cottage table, the federalist wall sconces. This was a London tavern of the imagination, with Moll Flanders bending low as she refilled his goblet. Or sitting on his lap. Her starched shirt winked open and shut.

"Was this exercise helpful?" she asked, opening a third bottle.

"Very much so. But after this meal, I might forget what I said."

"Fear not; I taped it. Easier than having you carry home 17 by 24 inch sheets of paper. And I anticipated the effect of food and drink." She gestured him back to his feet and led him over to the fire. Were they about to dance? To his disappointment, they took facing chairs. The fire had settled to a deep maroon with spurts of blue flame.

Swaying between contentment and anxiety, Ed fumbled for his footing. "I don't want to pry, but how can you afford this place? And who is J. Miranda?"

Mona's laugh was like a tray of crystal goblets, lightly shaken. "Ah, J. Is for Jay. He's the best sort of roommate, ever agreeable and never leaves the toilet seat up." Her eyes glinted in the firelight. "No woman in the city advertises that she's living alone. And as for my income, how can you be sure that—to use a term out of Henry James—someone isn't keeping me? Hardy, perhaps?" With that, she leaned toward him and gave him an open-mouthed kiss.

She felt surprisingly slight under the billowing shirt. But determined. He wasn't sure if he carried her into the bedroom or she led him, an ox to slaughter.

By six-thirty the next morning, she was in the shower and he was sitting up in bed, head-in-hands. The room spun. When he was able to focus, she was lacing up knee-high boots.

"I could get used to this," she said, her mouth twitching to the side in a sly smile, her top lip curling slightly up. "But work is work. I'm going and so must you. Up and at 'em! But do clean up before you leave. And sorry, I don't do breakfast."

Clean up what, the kitchen? His act?

"Here's a key. Make sure you set the dead bolt when you leave. This quaint little block is also crime city." She came close to the bed, raised Ed's chin with her finger, and kissed him warmly. "It's been nice but remember — if you even think of flirting with me at the office, I'll skewer you on a letter opener."

Ed believed her. He heard the door close and fell back on the pillow. What had he gotten himself into? Did it matter?

Then there was Aisling. Well, he had an excuse, if only by the skin of his teeth. She'd dumped him in no uncertain terms. So, why did he feel tangled up, and not just in bed sheets? Last night floated, unmoored from past or future. Perhaps it had happened to someone else.

He showered. Seeing her shampoo and a safety razor, he felt even more like an intruder. There was nothing male in the bathroom. He dressed, trying to absorb every detail of her apartment in case this was the only time he'd see it. Then he thought what the hell? He wiped down the kitchen counter and stacked the dishwasher. It was a chance to linger. Poking around in a cabinet, he found a bag of ground coffee and brewed a cup. It tasted very stale. She must have given up coffee years ago. Sitting at the table with the cup in his hands, he was Goldilocks in someone else's house. There were no photos on the refrigerator door, no post cards from Ibiza signed in a big, sprawling hand. Not even crayon portraits from a five-year-old niece. Okay, he had slipped into reporter mode. He glanced over toward the bedroom but drew the line at opening draws. Or making the bed.

The morning light beyond the French doors was grey. He'd never transitioned from one woman to another in such a short time. And who was she? But Jesus, she'd been eager. He had to be a replacement for someone else in her life, a stopgap. A contingent, again. But there was no shadow of this other's presence, no size 12 boots in the hall, no cap on a peg. And Mona? How much of this Mall Flanders life was really her?

She'd be at her desk now. She had access to his personnel file. There was little equal about this relationship. He thought again about pawing through her wardrobe. Maybe he'd find a mask and manacles. He rubbed the bite mark on his shoulder where she'd broken the skin.

Chapter Thirty-Eight

He reached his own apartment a little after eight. To hell with height-ened vigilance. The streets were busy but no one paid him any attention. A police cruiser was parked down the block, maybe something to do with him, maybe not. He ignored the uniform sitting inside. His lobby was empty, the stairs silent. His door unlocked smoothly.

Bart had touched base by email saying he'd talked with "the tech-nician" and reported progress dismantling "the engine". With everyone hacking into everyone else, communication was getting cryptic. If Bart were to call, he'd use the burner so Ed retrieved it from the drawer. It still held Aisling's message. Up to now, Ed had thought of it as "the princess phone". Wait till Bart hears that "the princess" bailed. As he was holding the cell, it rang. He heard his brother's voice.

"My techie broke through pretty much all the encryption and here's what I have on Guardian Services," Bart began. "Their contract with Naturtek dates from last year. Billing reports indicate they've been carrying out surveillance of specified employees via their electronic com-munications. Also street surveillance of key people, unfortunately not named. There's a bill for work done in Austria."

"What we expected, but it's good to have confirmation. Can we say Guardian has broken any laws?"

"Beyond electronic intrusion, no. I doubt they bill for committing murder. As for Naturtek, the intrusion into their employees' communication could be legal if waiving privacy is a condition of the job. According to hiring documents, workers are supplied with handhelds and restricted to a company server. It's shielded but we found a back door. Their system's not all that sophisticated, as Guardian Services reminded them, fishing for another contract. We can't prove Naturtek has crossed any lines on this."

Ed was disappointed. "And Hammersmith in particular?"

"His calls and emails are archived by the company so we have them."

"Encrypted?"

"Like chalk letters on a sidewalk. Nothing too difficult, but nothing stands out."

"What about looking at Hammersmith's personal account? We know he used one when he contacted Ciobanu."

"Using her office records, we traced calls between the two, on his end from a noncompany account. But there's a wrinkle."

"Which is?"

"These records have footprints all over them."

"The cops?"

"No, because they could only have gotten involved a week or so ago."

"So, we're hunting the hunters?"

"You could say that. We don't know who, though. But assume we left our own traces there as well. Bottom line — on the surface, Hammersmith was a loyal player. But he was computer-savvy enough to shield his personal I.P. address—the code that identified his access point to the internet—and bounced it through a series of proxy servers and used a program that turns the text into gibberish."

"But Guardian broke through?"

"Not to the content of his electronic communications on personal devices, but Guardian could still get the metadata—time, duration, addresses—which is what we have as well. He could have hidden everything but he got careless. I'm thinking at some point he used a hot spot at an airport to call his squeeze at MIT. That's all Guardian would have needed. They could have bought the info from the trolls who monitor these places."

"If airports are a hacker's paradise, what about public libraries?"

"The Wi-Fi, sure. But an internet search would be anonymous. Unless you do something stupid like use email."

Ed mulled that over. "In any case, we can say that Hammersmith acted like he had something to hide."

"That's what Naturtek would think," replied Ed. "But we know more. Long story short, Hammersmith's calls to Ciobanu were frequent, suggesting a relationship or a common project. Maybe he was boasting about his latest breakthrough as a mating display. There is one call to her office phone that we can read where he asks about academic openings at MIT."

"So he's jumping ship."

"He'd worked at MIT once before, don't forget."

"Which Guardian Services would know?"

"Yes. You should get this to the Cambridge cops, but with discretion. Ballancio can get a warrant for her iPhone and computer accounts, if he hasn't already."

"I'll mumble something about the Chinese People's Liberation Army if he needs motivation. So, where does this leave us?"

"Your call, bro."

"I go with Occam's Razor," said Ed. "The simplest explanation that covers the facts is usually true. That means Naturtek, through Guardian, is our nemesis."

"That'd be my guess."

"If the company thought their star scientist was sharing secrets with someone at MIT, or about to join another team, they'd want to pay Ciobanu a visit." Ed paused a few beats. "The bright side of this, if there is one, is that we weren't responsible for putting her in their sights."

"Then why do I feel guilty?" said Bart.

"When you two talked, things were already in play," continued Ed. "Problem is, most of what we have is fruit from a poisoned tree. It's inadmissible in court because we stole it. We have to hope that Ballancio can confirm this.

Back in D.C., Bart grunted acknowledgment.

"I'm focused on getting out this article, but I also want to see justice done. I'm going to tip off Royco in St. Louis as well."

"And my mole? I don't want him compromised."

"You said he was cagey, right?"

"More squirrelly. And I'm running out of favors here so you need to shake loose a few thousand from the *Chronicle* to pay him."

"Will do. Maybe they can hide it in extra hours for you. Now my news. First, Aisling texted from Mexico. She wants nothing more to do with me, or this project. She was emphatic." Ed took a breath.

"What can I say?" responded Bart.

"I also have a copy of her report. At best, it's of limited use."

"You were smitten, weren't you?"

"I'd say that's the word. But we dragged her through the wringer. It's no surprise she bolted. She certainly loves those bees, but under it all, she's focused on the future."

"Which doesn't include playing cops and robbers. But will she rat us out to Naturtek, maybe challenge something you put in print?"

That hadn't occurred to Ed. He hesitated. "She cashed the *Chronicle's* check. She's our consultant, after all. I'll give her a draft copy of what I write, to say we gave her a chance to comment. Assuming she'll take my email."

"Sorry bro. Just when you finally found a dance partner. Still, I'd have expected to hear more pain on your end."

"And I'm hearing this from Dr. Phil?" Ed caught his breath. "Sorry, that was out of bounds."

"It was. I still think she's sketchy, but I'm not going there."

"You're there already."

"You need to take this more seriously."

"You know what? This is not working out. Do whatever you want in Washington. I'll make sure Hardy sends a check, but let's you and me open up a little space."

"You are such an asshole." Bart cut the connection.

Still angry, Ed threw the phone into the couch where it bounced intact. He got another beer. Got to stay focused, he thought. Calm down. Maybe Janet Malcolm has something more. Hardy's going to want visuals. He was melting down. He had to hope that with Mona behind him, he'd be able to squeeze out the funds to cover this tech guy. And now Janet Malcolm.

Chapter Thirty-Nine

ED DOVE BACK INTO the article. Around noon he phoned Mona. A call was more discrete than a tête-à-tête outside Hardy's door.

She picked up on the first ring. After banteri   ng about the key to her apartment—he could feel it in his pocket—they got down to business. "You want me to help you fudge an expense account, is that right?"

"We had Hardy's blessing to dig and the path led to Guardian Services. Bart found a way in, that's all, but we have to pay the guy."

"It's not the money, though that's always an issue. You're talking about the commission of a crime." Mona didn't raise her voice but she gave it an edge.

"All right. Have Hardy give me a bonus equal to what we pay this hacker and I'll send the guy a personal check. But getting a retainer to Earth Defense is a longer reach."

For a moment, there was just the usual office sounds—distant conversations, a keyboard. Finally, Mona said she'd talk to Hardy. "I was more worried about you. We need space between the paper and this caper but if he tries to stiff you, I'll threaten to quit."

"You'd do that?" On the basis of one, sort-of date?

"Not just for you. I need to establish control over this project. I can't have Hardy delegating things and then micromanaging."

"I'm in your hands, boss."

"Just in case you're still hung up on that 'kept woman' remark I made last night, I was just being mysterious. God, men are so easily threatened."

"No, no," said Ed quickly. "I'm just worried about my bank account." It was time to come clean. "I'm broke. And there'll be other costs." He was thinking of Malcolm.

"Which explains that moth-eaten jacket you wear. I've been authorizing your checks for the past two years so rest assured, your limousine-casual style didn't fool me."

"My aspirational wardrobe. Does that mean the coffers are opening?"

"Stall ConEd or whoever. I'll do what I can." She gave a throaty laugh and broke the connection.

By mid-afternoon, he learned Earth Defense had found a couple of court cases where GMOs had gone feral and contaminated nearby fields. Writing that up kept him busy. Over the next week, he assembled more information—dribs and dabs pried from Royco and Balancio, stuff from Manny's research into patent records, and snippets from Bart's government contacts in D.C. The brothers were pretending they'd never argued. Mona processed the contract with Earth Defense and came through with the bonus so Ed could send his brother something for the technician. Ed had never expected anything from Blue Water so wasn't disappointed there. Sticking close to his apartment, though, he was beginning to feel like a recluse.

By mid-afternoon most days, Ed would feel overcome with caffeine nerves and head to the gym. Who knew when there could be another altercation. As for Mona, well, she'd never asked for her key back. But their few office interactions were a charade of formality.

Late one afternoon he was taking his usual break, working the speed bag. He had a good rhythm going when his phone rang. This particular gym was handy but the lockers were long-broken. His clothes were piled neatly at his feet so he heard his ring tone.

It was as if the bag bounced back and hit him. It was Aisling on his business line. The burner they shared was back in his loft.

"Ed," she said. "Don't hang up. I was pissed about what you'd gotten me into and I was unforgivably crass. Please forgive me. But things have taken a turn. Can we meet?"

Meet? Was she in Manhattan? Sweat rolled down his arms and the phone almost slipped from his fingers.

She jumped into the gap. "I'm in Mexico. Is Bart still with you? I was hoping you both could come down here."

Ed regularized his breathing. "Why would I want to fly three thousand miles? To hear you apologize?"

"I'm not talking about us. Understand? I can't explain over this line, and I threw away the phone you gave me." Her breathing was audible. "But if you come, I'll be able to hand you an example of crop manipulation gone haywire. You haven't finished writing the article, have you?"

"No. It's framed but it needs shelf appeal, more villains. And less scientific uncertainty."

"The murders?"

"No arrests yet, and our legal department at the paper isn't going to support my speculation."

"I can give you villains." He heard her breath again.

"For real?"

"I can't go into specifics but the situation here has become unstable. Without the right kind of publicity, I may have to shut down my project. Then there's the small farmers here to think about."

"Look, I owe you for Oetz, but this sounds flimsy. And hold on, didn't you just run out on me?"

"I got on with my work. But will you listen? I'm not talking favors. But now that you mention it, without me you'd be dead on that mountain."

"I stepped into that."

"You need material for your story? I need time to finish my research, another month at least. I've got things in process I can't flush down the drain. If you were here, it would do us both good."

"I'm confused," he said, though he didn't think he was. "Who's helping whom?"

"We'd be helping each other."

Ed rolled this around in his head. Getting money to Bart's techie had been complicated enough and his bank account was still sucking air. Were his credit cards maxed out? Could he ask Mona for yet another advance on his pay? Then again, wouldn't this be project expenses?

"Not that I'm agreeing, but assuming I can pull this off, where would we meet?" Paper, rock, scissors. Guilt covered good sense, ambition beat guilt.

"You'll need to get to Tuxtla Gutiérrez, the regional airport for Chiapas."

"You're there?"

"No. I'm working outside of Las Margaritas in a small community in the Lacandon rainforest, El Encanto. It's fifty miles further south but Tuxtla's the nearest commercial air connection. It's an industrial city. But from there, the journey gets iffy."

Iffy. Ed could imagine.

"I might not be able to meet you. I suspect I'm on some people's radar and I don't want to make your visit obvious. When you book, send me the arrival date. If you don't see me at customs, rent a car and drive to San Cristóbal de las Casas. That's the old colonial capital up in the mountains. It's a beautiful place, you'll love it. Look in a guide book and find a small hotel. Try for La Casa de Mama, it's in-town and cheap. Text where you are and I'll meet you."

"This sounds tenuous."

"I'm asking a lot and not giving you much to go on, but can you at least think about it?"

"Yeah. Call me tomorrow. I need to see what funds I can get from the *Chronicle*." The line buzzed and died. He was listening to the ether.

Before he could change his mind, he found himself on the line with

Mona. Old business first. "That bonus was great, but it didn't put me ahead."

"Advance. It's just life support, I know. I'll need time with Hardy to work this all out but right now we're all really busy."

In for a dime. "Another thing came up. I'm thinking about an air ticket to Chiapas, Mexico. Would Hardy would go for it?"

"And that would be in regard to what?" She was all business.

Time to come clean. "This is strange, Mona, but I just got a call from Aisling, the woman we hired to analyze Hammersmith's documents."

"I know who she is."

"I thought our work together was over but now she tells me that what she's doing in Mexico has a bearing on my story. I don't know how yet. She couldn't explain over an open line. If I go there, she assured me she had something red hot."

"I'm sure." Her tone was flat. "I'm thinking second honeymoon? And so soon after Austria, imagine!"

"It's nothing like that. Didn't you tell me to locate some dramatic material? That's what she claims to have." Was he stretching it? "Besides, she implied she was in physical danger."

"Did you suggest 911?"

"Honestly, if she is in trouble, I should respond. She pulled my chestnuts out of the fire in Oetz. And she's kind of our employee?"

"You mean her consult contract? Over and done. And you as much as told me she'd delivered some thin soup. I can't help thinking about your chestnuts in her hands again."

Ed's chances were slipping away fast.

"Okay, try this. You add a thousand to my bonus or advance, or whatever. I'll get the air ticket myself."

"This is a pay-on-delivery shop. You're suggesting we go into uncharted waters here." He could hear her drumming a pencil on her desk.

"I can't stampede Hardy into writing you a check. He's already gone overboard with your brother's contract and with Earth Defense." She began clicking her teeth. "Call me stupid but I'll take a flyer. I'll personally advance you plane fare. Come by the office tomorrow and I'll give you a check. Treat it like an investment. So you're going to have to deliver." Then she hung up.

The walk home and a shower gave him time to plan. He'd have to tell Bart where he was headed. He certainly couldn't expect him to come along. Still, it wouldn't be a pleasant talk.

Returning to his article, his mind tracked back to Mona. Coming up with the money herself? And with Aisling involved? That was something he didn't expect. He got back into email and hit compose.

Mona, you didn't give me time to thank you, I know you're not doing this entirely for the paper. I've thought a lot about our evening together, the grilling you put me through, the dinner you cooked. And afterwards.

At that point his mind wandered to the curl in her upper lip.

In fact, you were very helpful and if problems remain, they're for me to fix. And Mexico could provide the answer."

Was he groveling? Sophomoric? Before he could censor himself, he hit 'send'. Within moments he had a reply.

All communications from employees on Chronicle devices or sent to company offices will respect official policy, avoiding workplace harassment and sexual innuendo. Now get the hell off email and back to work!

"Will do," he said to his screen.

Then he called Bart at Executive Action, first asking if anything new had been ferreted out.

"Nothing. But I doubt our techie would want to be called a rodent."

"Actually, a ferret isn't a rodent. It belongs to a higher order, I believe the weasel family."

"Whatever, Mister Science. Anything else?"

"I got a call from our mutual friend from Boston, now enjoying tropical sunshine."

"Kicking your sorry ass again, I hope."

"The opposite. She's remorseful. And needs a favor."

Nothing from Bart.

"Says she has information for our investigation, a perfect case study." Ed had slipped in the plural. "And that she's in an unspecified spot of trouble."

"And the castle churl wants to impersonate Sir Galahad."

"You don't approve, I understand. But she was serious. Calling me couldn't have been easy for her. I think she's out of options."

Again, nothing on Bart's end.

"It's not impossible, the idea of a perfect case study. She's doing environmental work in one of the most biologically diverse environments on earth. I know, I've been there."

"But?"

"But nothing's specified. It's the who's-listening problem."

"And you're calling me, why?"

"We're in this together. I just wanted to let you know."

Silence from Bart.

"It's really a picturesque place, southern Mexico. Colonial churches, Indigenous villages. Come to think of it, maybe you could use the break?"

"You want a bodyguard."

"Companion, research assistant. But only if you're free."

"Is the trip free?"

"I think the *Chronicle* will cover expenses. Salary, no. I have Mona's tacit approval for my ticket."

"Tacit being the operative word."

Best to come clean. "Actually, she's advancing me a personal loan. We're hoping eventually she'll get Hardy's okay. Once I'm in motion, it may be hard for upper management to scotch the thing."

"Listen to yourself, smooth-talking one woman into paying for a trip abroad to see someone else."

"That's really harsh." If accurate, thought Ed. "Anyway, how about it? Think mescal and chicken mole."

"When are you leaving? Work shouldn't be a problem but I've lined up a trip to the National Gallery with Molly. Her idea. And I've got a dinner planned with Elizabeth. I could leave late Wednesday." It was now Monday.

"I knew you'd come through, bro."

"Good to know you finally caught on to what people learned after a thousand years of playing chess."

"Never sacrifice your queen?"

"No. Back up your moves. Book us out of D.C. to save me the trip up. In the meantime, I have a life to glue back together."

Picking up the check from Mona took only minutes. Hardy's door was closed but Mona put a finger to her lips and walked him back to the elevator, an envelope in her hands."

"Turns out there were office funds I could tap into. You have two thousand. Use it wisely." It was in cash. "You need to sign this."

He did, without counting the money. He hoped this would cover two round-trip tickets and the cheapest ground facilities. When they reached the hallway, she continued to whisper. "And Bart?"

"Bringing him."

"Figured as much. His contract here closed out last week but I can fool with the date. Percival hadn't anticipated international travel as part of this, so I'll have to soap him up a little." Now they were alone.

"Don't you dare."

Ed leaned down and kissed her. She relaxed into his arms, then quickly pushed him through the open elevator doors.

"I can't promise the paper will go your bail, but if it's any consolation, our insurance covers the repatriation of remains."

PART THREE: MEXICO

Chapter Forty

By Thursday afternoon, their plane was approaching Tuxtla, Chiapas after a lengthy stopover in Houston. The airport meal there had lined Ed's stomach with grease. With that and fatigue, he was nauseous. As the sun sank over hazy green mountains, their plane settled down onto the valley runway. Five miles away city buildings reflected the yellow sun from towers of white concrete and glass. Closer in, the landscape was a jumble of dun-colored single-story houses and factory yards. Small farm holdings immediately surrounded the runway, donkeys sharing pasture with the occasional beef cow. When the brothers clattered down the aluminum steps from the plane, somewhere a rooster crowed.

The terminal was nearly deserted. Its walkways and plate glass were modern, overbuilt in expectation of commercial traffic that hadn't materialized. The installation was not purely civilian. A dozen olive-drab helicopters lined one side of the taxiway and rifle-carrying soldiers watched the passengers thread toward customs. More interesting to Bart was a pair of parked DC-3s. One had empty engine housings, and in the other plywood replaced the cockpit glass.

"Great plane," said Bart. "We actually used them in Afghanistan to bring supplies to remote areas. This model dates from the late '40s. In lots of places they're still flying."

"But not here evidently," responded Ed. "Must be tricky to get parts. And please, no war stories. My stomach is still turning."

After collecting their luggage, they crossed through a cavernous hall, passing booths that earlier in the day offered mescal and mariachi hats. Now they were shuttered. A sign pointed to the taxi rank.

"Do we dare risk more airport food?" asked Bart.

Ed looked at the winter-barren fields, empty of all but scrub. From ground level, the city had moved further away. Then he saw a single food cart at the curb surrounded by half a dozen people, some in uniform, some with suitcases. Perhaps it was the aroma but his queasy stomach righted itself. "Always follow the crowd."

They ordered thin slices of braised beef covered with *nopales con cebolla*. That and bottled beer brought Ed back to life. They over-paid in dollars and the vendor grinned.

"That's a point for you," conceded Bart, wiping his mouth on a minuscule paper napkin. They'd taken their meal to a bench and Ed dug out a tattered guide book. There was no sign of Aisling.

"It's ten years old but should still be useful," said Ed, flipping pages.

"And we're headed where?" asked his brother.

"Las Margaritas," Ed explained, "the largest town in cattle country." Back in New York he explained, he'd checked the human rights and environmental web sites. They described that area near the Guatemalan border as transitional. At about 5,000 feet, it combined jungle ecology with cloud forest. The tree cover had been fragmented in the 1970s by settlers claiming free national land. Because they'd came from various Mexican rural areas, they brought a variety of languages and customs. Some farmers were even from Guatemala, fleeing the civil war there. Outside the larger towns, daily life was carried out in dialects of Mayan— Tzeltal or Tojolabal—rather than Spanish.

Las Margaritas was upcountry from the Pacific coast where the oldest *haciendas* were located, largely sugar operations. On higher land, sugar gave way to coffee, its cultivation encouraged by the government in the 19th century to supply European markets.

While the international price of coffee had always been volatile, its recent collapse had convinced many landowners to switch to cattle, raw material for the voracious American hamburger chains. Having monopolized the valleys, the big estates forced recent settlers onto the hillsides. But even after the latest land rush, areas of the Lacandon rain forest remained, especially east of Las Margaritas around Las Lagunas de Montebello, a conservation zone. The current threat was illegal logging. A low-intensity conflict smoldered between tree rustlers and indigenous municipalities that managed their lands in common.

Ed broke off his monologue and looked at his watch. Still no Aisling.

During his trip to southern Mexico in the early 2000's, he'd encountered a group so interdependent with the jungle and so remote, they'd been able to ignore most of Western civilization. The Lacandon, both men and women, wore white cotton tunics and wore their hair long. Using spears, they fished from dugout canoes in marshes where even the army was reluctant to travel. Were they still around? If so, they'd likely gotten sophisticated fast.

"We're wasting our time. I don't think she's coming." They were now working on a second round of beer.

"She said that might happen. She knows our time of arrival but may not have control over her schedule. Okay, it's been an hour. Let's move on to San Cristóbal."

They got to their feet and Ed led the way to a taxi stand. He selected a newish Nissan Tsuru and used his rusty Spanish to settle on a price with the driver. San Cristóbal? No problem. They loaded their belongings into the small trunk and squeezed into a narrow backseat.

"I thought we were going to rent something?" said Bart.

"I know. But renting a car is like changing money. You get the worst deal at the airport." They watched the scenery. "Then there's the roadblocks. We've better off with a local driver who knows what's up."

"If you say so, *comandante*." Bart had been looking forward to driving.

A mixed landscape slid past, not especially picturesque. Houses of concrete block were surrounded by assorted building material—doors, construction debris, loosely piled gravel—every dwelling in some arrested stage of construction. Given the weeds and rust, progress was intermittent. Skeletal fingers of rebar reached above rooflines toward future levels. Densely planted cacti separated plots. His guidebook called them *Pachycereus marginatus*, living fences six or seven feet high, but they did nothing to confine the wandering chickens. Yet every so often an arched opening in a brick wall was outlined in luminous Bougainvillea—mauve, pink, white.

Signs on dusty streets offered car repair, school supplies, and beer. Fixing punctured tires appeared to be a local specialty. Now and again, their taxi skirted plazas marked by huge trees and well-worn bandstands. As the evening deepened, occasional balloon vendors appeared. What Ed hadn't seen before were the touches of suburbia —supermarkets with large parking lots, garden centers, daycare centers decorated with Disney characters. The side roads were still dirt, though. They trailed away into the hills where blocks of new white, blue, and pink houses were pushing back the primordial tree cover. Along the road, orange-red blossoms from tall, flamboyant trees vibrated optically against their deep green leaves. Everything was in-process—growing, being cut down, under construction, or in decay.

On his earlier trip, Ed had driven east through Veracruz and Tabasco where the mountains were wet, the foliage thicker. There the houses were often mud-wattle ovals, tucked beneath maize fields that climbed impossibly steep slopes. It all seemed unchanged for centuries. Here the dry season prevailed and the pavement, battered into submission by construction vehicles, throbbed with activity. The air reeked of diesel fumes.

Now sidewalks were crowded. Uniformed children waited at bus stops, old men carrying machetes trudged in from distant fields, while mothers walked with toddlers bundled up against the evening chill. Everywhere there were whip-thin dogs. They lay in doorways following the traffic with their eyes. At noon on the side roads, they'd be lying on the pavement, soaking up the heat. They were a breed unto themselves— yellow-brown, shorthaired, foxlike. Now, interestingly, he noticed something new—recognizable breeds. Perhaps their owners had turned them out when times turned tough.

If motion passed for modernization, this industrial heart of Chiapas was up-to-date. But Ed knew the reality was more complex. Even as NAFTA created an export market for flowers and tomatoes, it had decimated revolutionary Mexico. Government price supports that once propped up peasant agriculture were gone and the free market reigned. Those displaced were left to wander north to garment factories in Juarez or Chicago, leaving only their faces in photos on home altars.

After half an hour, the cab came to a modern toll road and began the climb into the mountains. If Tuxtla was the future, they were now moving backward, toward the old colonial capital. San Cristóbal de las Casas was named for Bartolomé de las Casas, the 16th century Dominican friar whose concern for the indigenous set him against the first feudal families. Outrage over continuing oppression boiled over again in the War for Independence, then in the Mexican Revolution. Most recently, resistance had taken the shape of the Zapatista armed rebellion and its rejection of NAFTA modernity. But through it all, a ladino oligarchy remained in control.

The virtual servitude of *los indios* was the constant. First it was to force them to gather cochineal, a dye highly prized for church regalia. Then the key to colonial fortunes became sugar, finally coffee and cattle. In the 1970s, lay priests, supported by the Catholic diocese in San Cristóbal, rekindled the message of liberation. *Los indios* stopped giving way on the sidewalks to the *ladinos* as they'd been doing since colonial times. When official Mexico acknowledged the 500th anniversary of Columbus' arrival in the hemisphere, protesters turned the commemoration upside-down. They re-named it the Day of the Race and in San Cristóbal, a singular event took place. The statue of Diego de Mazariegos, the conquistador whom the white population considered the founder of their city, was pulled from his pedestal and beaten to pieces by a crowd. To prevent his resurrection, fragments of his body were carried off to indigenous villages.

The wracking of Mexico to fit the global economy has remained brutal. In Guerrero, armed peasants challenging the government's neoliberal agenda were beaten down by the army and, infamously, 43 students from a rural teachers' college were 'disappeared'. In the Valley of Mexico, villagers were more successful, blocking the airport which the government tried to locate on their fields. When contract farmers in the north supplying Green Giant and Campbell's couldn't pay their debts, they closed down major highways. Resistance was sharpest in Chiapas. On January 1st, 1994, eighty-four years after Emiliano Zapata raised an army of cane cutters, indigenous farmers marched from their villages and occupied San Cristóbal itself. For a few glorious days, insurgents with sticks and ancient hunting rifles overran had the municipal offices and lectured the crowds from the town hall balcony. It didn't last. The Mexican army, equipped with helicopters supplied by the U.S., swept in and forced the peasants back. Then, at the point of annihilation, they were saved. The local Catholic diocese, along with university students from across Mexico, demanded a ceasefire. With the world watching, the government complied. In the following two decades, an uneasy peace prevailed, punctuated by army provocations and peasant invasions of isolated estates. Turning their backs on the state, the Zapatistas built their own schools, clinics, and economies in rural enclaves, reaching out through videos and conferences to a global audience.

As their taxicab climbed upward, Ed marveled at the highway. When he was last here, the road to San Cristóbal followed an ancient oxcart trail described in the novels of B. Traven. Then, teamsters had cracked whips and laborers groaned as they pushed wagons from one switchback to the next. History was now paved over. Bridges and slope cuts made the new highway indifferent to hills and ravines. And perhaps to insurgency. Never again would the army have to face downed trees and boulders in a race to San Cristóbal.

The brothers checked into a small hotel a dozen blocks from the zócolo, the central square. Ed found the city remarkably unchanged, still a dense collection of one and two-story structures, many of plastered adobe. Above an ocean of tiled roofs, church spires rose as they had for centuries. The noticeable innovation was a few streets at the center of town now closed to all but foot traffic. While the aim was to accommodate tourists, it allowed the ancient urban fabric to reveal itself. The streets themselves, their slabs of stone polished over the centuries by human feet, were narrow, the sidewalks narrower still.

Rising the next morning, the brothers looked out from their window at the limestone facade of a cathedral from whose niches saints peered down at market women in red and black *huipiles.* The cold air made the scattering of banana, palm, and Norfolk pines on the patios below appear incongruous. In a yard close in, huge blue-headed turkeys picked elegantly at a pile of compost.

By-passed by industry, most of the city's 17th century buildings were intact, supporting tourist-centered livelihoods. But it was also a center for NGOs that fiercely defended the Zapatista communities out in the countryside. Self-confident *Indigenismo* pulsated in the market stalls and traditional healing centers. The recorded voice of Subcomandante Marcos, international spokesperson for the 1994 uprising but a recluse in recent years, could be heard in the cafés and backpacker hostels where foreign and domestic activists argued about alternatives to modernity.

As always, land was the issue. It was the prize in a contest between the army and villagers for control of outlying estates and where new technologies using cyanide had made possible a revival of gold and silver seams. Periodically, the tourists found themselves pushed aside as San Cristóbal's streets filled with outraged farmers and banner-waving students.

Chapter Forty-One

"I wish I'd brought a weapon," said Bart, falling back on one of the two beds, "but I don't have clearance to carry on international flights. I feel empty-handed."

"When in Rome and all that," responded Ed. "Buy a machete."

Ed was tapping out Aisling's number on the phone he'd set aside for reaching her. After failing to connect at the airport, he was afraid they'd lost contact. He didn't expect her to answer, and he was right, but he could send a text saying they'd arrived and where they were staying.

"Let's find a real restaurant," said Bart, his eyes closed. "That micro-thin steak sandwich we had when we landed didn't stick with me. Remember the days of in-flight meals, those trays with the tiny compartments, the mayonnaise squeeze-tubes? God, I miss them."

"Just shows you're getting old," said Ed.

"I guess," replied his brother, standing up.

They made their way along the sidewalk to the city center. With their eyes tracking from one piece of revolutionary graffiti to the next, the inexplicable pits in the pavement were a continuous surprise.

It was a relief to reach the pedestrian streets. There they found several ATM machines and each took out the maximum in pesos.

They settled on an internet cafe tucked into the atrium of an old mansion. The alcoves around a central dining area held small *tiendas* that sold posters, photos, and other paraphernalia related to the Ejército Zapatista

Liberación Nacional. A woman's rural cooperative with an EZLN affiliation displayed weavings. Everyone fished in the tourist stream. Here the clientele was down-market, backpackers rather than retirees. The men were young and bearded, the women in skirts layered over jeans with bright indigenous shawls around their shoulders. Near the serving counter were racks of well-thumbed Mexican newspapers.

After a languorous pause, a young man brought them menus. Ed, using his Spanish advantage over Bart, selected for them both— tortilla soup followed by chicken mole. The soup wasn't bad but the mole— black and rich with spices and cacao—was intoxicating. Bart's skepticism about foreign food evaporated. "Not a convenient place to get to," he said, "but it just might be worth it."

Sated, they worked on bottles of beer. "You never said why you left the military," Ed ventured. "I know you wanted to be closer to D.C. and your family, but I always thought of you as an adventurer."

"The family was the main reason." Bart drew down his bottle. "But things happened in Afghanistan I couldn't tolerate."

"Like?" Was Ed being the reporter or the psychologist?

"The war was being out-sourced. You knew that, right? Every embassy and construction project had private security teams, contractors. But we thought of them as mercenaries. A major would leave Special Forces and a few months later you'd see him again but representing some private outfit."

"In business for themselves," commented Ed.

"Still takin' the king's shilling, but in this case, by the full bucket."

"But hey, isn't that the American dream, start a small business, watch it grow?"

"Except it wasn't business savvy they were selling but their contacts up the line. Thing is, these outfits didn't answer to us. As far as I could tell, they didn't answer to anybody. You heard about Blackwater shooting up those civilians in Nisour Square in Baghdad? That wasn't the only time."

"Were you ever tempted to jump ship yourself, go to the dark side?"

"Not there, not for a minute." Bart squared his shoulders. "Sure, they were making three times my salary as a lieutenant. And Probably their investors made millions. But the pay difference wasn't my problem."

"Every war has graft," said Ed, thinking about *Catch-22,* the novel that had gently shattered illusions about World War Two.

"I suppose. Though here it was institutionalized. Picture truck convoys bringing diesel and ammo out to our APCs in the boonies." He made a camera aperture with his hands, blocking the scene like a Hollywood director. "They'd unload the supplies and you'd see an unusual number of mercenaries. Then they'd be reloading, this time bags, pallets, duffels. So you ask yourself, what the hell could anyone be sending back that's worth guarding?"

"Besides the trucks themselves? I dunno."

"I dunno either, but you know how people talk. Then you're back at base and read a report that says Helmand Province is supplying most of the world's heroin. You don't need to be Einstein to put it together."

"Does make you wonder." Ed had read the same UN reports.

"It weighed on me. That and being away so much. I finally said, fuck it. This is all just a racket." Ed watched his brother lapse into silence.

"Something specific happen?"

"I'll say this once. This happened in Iraq, a previous deployment. We were in Anbar outside Ramadi. We'd integrated with a group of private contractors providing cover for a meeting of local leaders, tribal chiefs and imams. The mercs were covering the road, we had building security. Mortar rounds started coming in. I was directing everyone to a set of concrete blast walls behind the building when one of our APC's in the yard went up. Direct hit. Five guys were taken out permanently. Later I find out the contractors had fucked up. They secured the main road through the town but not the farm tracks. And they never told us how they'd deployed." Bart was flushed. "I had to put our dead in a personnel carrier, the pieces we could find, and get us out of there."

"You must have reported this?"

"Oh, sure, filed an after-action brief, talked personally to the CO. There was nothing anyone could do. That was the start of the hole in my gut. It took a while but eventually resigning made sense. That stuff stays with you." Bart looked off into space. "I can't fault Elizabeth for wanting more of a fun guy."

At that moment Ed's phone rang. Aisling, finally. She was in the city; she'd find the restaurant. By the time a second round of beer arrived, she was sliding into a chair at their table. No kiss, no hugs. She shrugged a canvas messenger bag from her shoulder and put it between her feet.

"You came, both of you." She looked from one to the other. Ed noticed her face was drawn. It had been only ten days since New York but now her wiry curls were matted and her clothes smelled of wood smoke. When the waiter returned, she ordered *pozole,* the large bowl.

"Before we start, let me catch my breath. It wasn't easy asking you to come, Ed, but I didn't know where else to turn." She looked around the restaurant as she talked. "What I said in that message about going our separate ways, that you were trouble, is true—you can't deny it. But I think we can help each other. Can I explain?"

"That's why we're here," said Ed. Bart wasn't helping either of them out.

"That wild ride from Boston, then hiding behind that armored door in your apartment, I couldn't take it. I expected Mexico to be a relief."

"But that's not how it turned out?"

"I have two longitudinal studies going." She moved her hands over the table, smoothing the table cloth. "A year ago, my team covered two areas of roughly three thousand square feet each with Reemay; that's this porous plastic fabric. We hung it over hoops, high enough to walk under. The structures function as greenhouses. Most of the sun's visible spectrum can enter, but not insects."

"I get the picture," said Ed, his voice flat. She sounded rehearsed.

"We planted one area in conventional vegetables—*maize*, squash, beans, some chili. We borrowed the plot from a community maize field. The second plot is our control, an overgrown area that local farmers haven't used in five years. The idea is to open up the Reemay for several days and let bugs in. We have cameras set up. This is especially important after dark when we use infra-red to catch night pollinators, moths and bats. After a week we button things up and apply a rapidly degrading, narrow spectrum fumigant. It kills the insects and we make an inventory."

Bart's eyebrows went up.

"The pesticides surprise you? There's no other way to do this. You were expecting catch-and-release? In the scheme of things, what we kill hardly matters."

"In the scheme of things," said Ed.

"We're adjacent to a jungle." She licked sun-chapped lips. "Anyway, our test plot gives us a census of pollinating insects—flies, bees, moths, butterflies—matched with the plants they're near and prefer. We've been doing this since July of last year in both the dry and rainy seasons. From time to time, we find insects no one's ever heard of. Like the morpho variant I took up to Tuxtla."

Bart was visibly bored.

"Here's the thing." She sped up. "We get a count of both the pollinators necessary for domestic plants and for the wider environment, including the wild relatives of domesticated plants. While insects have co-evolved with what's farmed, they need food when these aren't in flower. For thousands of years, farmers here have understood this interrelationship between the cultivated and the wild, and organized their fields accordingly. They've also addressed soil fertility. That's the logic of leaving some fields fallow. An Iowa farmer would consider idle land just wasted." She paused, willing Ed to understand.

"You're saying slash and burn isn't just a fertilizing system, it preserves insect variety as well?

Ed was drawn in; Bart sat back and crossed his arms.

"It's low-input agriculture. Commercial farmers don't fallow, so they have to purchase nitrogen by the ton. Or they rotate with nitrogen-fixing soy, which does support honey bees but not the wide variety of insects you see in a fallow patch."

"And the point is?" broke in Bart.

"Hold on." Ed held up his hands. "Do I have the picture here? You're documenting how unplowed land is essential for vegetable production."

"You got it. Insects are also food for poultry, but we ignored that. The data shows that swidden or so-called slash-and-burn agriculture makes a lot of sense, even if the idea is heresy in the ag schools."

"All those dead butterflies," commented Bart. "Reminds me of what they said about Vietnam, 'We destroyed the village to save it.'"

"I'm surprised you're so sensitive." She turned on him. "We can't get a count of bugs that die naturally. What hits the forest floor is immediately digested by a hundred varieties of insects and microbes. Everything gets recycled. Yeah, we're killing butterflies but we're making a case to save them."

Bart exhaled dismissively. "And this has to do with Naturtek, how?" he said, draining his Dos Equis.

"I'm getting to that. This is background."

"Gonna be a long night."

She gave him an exasperated look while Ed signaled the waiter for more beer.

"The community where we work has a honey operation. Honey bees are a European import, but their presence is a constant in the area and has been for centuries."

"Wait, wait, wait. Not to sound anti-intellectual, but did we come three thousand miles for an academic lecture?" Bart looked at his Brother but Ed ignored him.

"So, you're living in the community where you're working?" Ed asked.

"Close but not in the village. We have tents, a generator, and battery system to power our microscopes and cameras. We started out trying to be separate but over time, we've gotten closer. They gave us access and we hired two of their young guys as workers, a quid pro quo, though we need them. They're getting training in lab techniques and we'll fully credit them in anything we publish."

"Hearts and minds," said Bart.

"Every Sunday we eat with families, our one good meal of the week, I might add. For which we tried to pay."

"Tried?" said Ed.

"They won't accept money. It was an early lesson in cultural competence. Eventually we figured out they expected something in-kind. Now every Monday — market day — we go to a larger town and buy a dozen live chickens. Then at mid-week we cook a meal for the community. I say we, but five or six village women help out. Teaching us, really. And beheading and plucking chickens, well that's been an experience."

"You're getting your chops in as an anthropologist."

"It's great for my students as well. Now we can all slap out a mean tortilla." She pantomimed and smiled.

'Okay. So the village adopted you. But again, why do you need Ed and me?"

"Last summer, we started getting anomalies. Then in December, things got precipitously worse."

"Anomalies?" said Ed.

"Local insect populations were declining, up to fifty percent for some species of bees. With fewer pollinators, honey production fell off as did several crops—squash and beans in particular. In the fallow area, wild plants we'd seen before were gone."

"Nancy Drew and the missing plants," said Bart.

"Hey, fuck you. Did I ask you to come down here?"

"Settle down you two." He held up his hands. "Actually, you did."

She shrugged that off. "The community looked for answers. It turned out that shortly before we arrived, a cluster of large greenhouses had been erected at an abandoned cattle ranch ten kilometers to the north. At first, people thought this was a tomato operation. It's something USAID is promoting for export. But this was different. For one thing, the bosses brought in their own workers. Then there was the private plane traffic on a grass landing strip. Most alarming, the workers were regularly fumigating the greenhouses wearing full face masks."

"Nobody went and asked?" said Bart.

"Oh, yeah, they asked. But this crew wasn't friendly. At first men went over there looking for work. Then the mayor tried to look at their permits. Nothing doing. The next week they put up a chain link fence. Finally, they did produce some paperwork, documents signed in Mexico City. Or so I was told."

"I can see why the community was uneasy," said Ed.

"This village, El Encanto, supplies organic vegetables to San Cristóbal, everything from mushrooms to potatoes. They combine their honey with production from surrounding villages to fill a container and ship it to Germany. Because everything is organic, they get a premium price. But they won't if there's chemical contamination. And their bees are dying. So they sent over their community police — the committee of vigilance. And they were met with armed guards."

"What about the state authorities?" Ed asked.

"First they visited the state agricultural office in Tuxtla. That's where they learned the project was owned by a Dutch seed company, Inheld. As far as Tuxtla was concerned, everything was in order. But I had a contact at the university there. He traced this Dutch company and found it was actually a shell, essentially a name and a postal box. Guess who the real owner is?"

"Pepsi Cola?" said Bart.

"Naturtek."

Ed absorbed that. "Isn't chemical use regulated?"

"Depends. And operators are permitted to sterilize their greenhouses between crops. But this was something else."

"Something virulent?"

"Looks that way. But government oversight relies on self-reporting. They check the paperwork but rarely visit because— surprise, surprise— they're overworked and underpaid."

"Count on that," said Ed.

"A small community has almost no leverage." She blew her nose into a paper napkin from the table and looked depleted. "Chemical use is normal here. You'll see government promotions with an image of a campesino carrying a backpack sprayer."

"So, toxic fumes are drifting onto the community's land from these greenhouses." Ed rested his chin on his hand. "Or is it something more? You're thinking terminator plants, aren't you, Aisling?"

"Maybe in tandem with the pesticides. You see why I thought you'd be interested?"

Bart spoke up. "Not my thing, farming and all, but couldn't there be another explanation? Say, disease? Or El Encanto got its compost recipe wrong?"

"No disease is full-spectrum," said Aisling. "El Encanto has been cultivating this land for a long time. They're not some recently relocated population. They're feeling genuine panic."

"The state won't investigate?" asked Ed.

"They have one specialist team and it's working full-time against the coffee rust moved up from the Soconusco, the hot country on the coast. That's a much bigger money issue."

"Let's cut to the chase. You want Ed and me to sneak in and steal samples of what they're using, right?"

"Quick thinking, cowboy," she said. "Cans, labels, invoices, plant samples—the whole nine yards. And it won't be easy. Did I mention the armed guards?"

"That all?" Bart relished a challenge. "Give it all to us. CCTV?"

"At least on poles at the gate."

"And probably motion sensors."

"Which is suspicious in itself," Ed chimed in. "When are tomato plants worth bank-vault security? Unless they are genetically re-engineered."

Bart leaned across the table toward Aisling. "Assuming we're interested, can you draw us a map of the area, something showing the buildings and the cameras? A schedule of any sentries making rounds would be nice."

"I know people who can find this out. As I say, the community is highly motivated. I have binoculars I can lend them. No one would have to get close."

Just us, thought Bart. "We'll have to go in at night." Then he looked around the room. "You know, if I were running that operation, I'd plant someone in a place like this." He nodded toward a nearby mural of a masked Zapatista. "Especially with free Wi-Fi here and all these hippies."

Ed tried to swivel his eyes and not his head.

"You know our hotel? When you have the information, call from your safe phone. But still, be discreet."

"You think you were followed?" said Ed.

Aisling paused. "No. I rode in from the village on the back of a produce truck. For most of the way, we were alone on the road. Which reminds me, I have to get to my pick-up point for the trip back. But take this." She removed a small envelope from her bag.

"Which is?" asked Ed.

"Copies of the insect surveys I mentioned. On a flash drive. I'm more comfortable if someone else has a copy."

"Can I pass it on to our other consultant?"

Aisling paused. "If they agree not to use it in their own publications." Then she gave a wry smile. "I'm kidding, but not really." She stood.

"Hold on. If I were General Chemical running sketchy experiments down here, I'd keep an eye on the hippy-dippies." Bart lowered his voice. "The people like you."

"Yeah, well, I'll let you take care of that." She took her time wrapping a scarf around her neck. "But I do have a friend who works in the kitchen. I'll drop in there, say hello, then slip out the back."

"*Vaya con Dios*," said Bart. Ed looked surprised. "I got that from a song."

While Bart watched the crowd, Ed opened up his laptop. "Still got that security program I put on?" Bart asked.

"It's Manny's machine, and he says it's safe. And totally unconnected to me; the IP number is a fake."

"I doubt it's more secure than what I gave you, but let that slide. You're going to email what's on that drive, aren't you?"

"I'll send it to Mona, have her pass a copy to Janet Malcolm. But from the hotel. Right now I'm just making a copy." Ed then gave the drive to Bart. "Two pockets, twice as safe."

They ambled back to the hotel under a matte-black sky.

Chapter Forty-Two

"YOU'RE AWFULLY QUIET," SAID Bart. It was after eleven in the evening and they had the tiny hotel patio to themselves. A screen of bamboo and hibiscus separated them from the lobby.

"I'm wondering if I should call Mona. It's an hour later back in New York."

"You afraid to wake her or to find she has company?"

"You can be a real butthead, you know that?"

"Actually, I'm marveling at your new-found powers at juggling multiple women. And to think you were so shy in high school."

"Why don't we talk about your home life?" responded Ed. "How's that going?"

"Yip, yip, bro. The smallest dogs are always the noisiest. It so happens that Elizabeth and I are making progress. The other night we had a civilized dinner. I booked one of the places where we used to go before we were married. Had a veranda looking out on the Potomac and the city lights. Citronella candles, purple martins swooping up the mosquitoes. It was almost romantic."

"And?"

"She said we'd always have a common bond, meaning Molly. But our separation isn't doing the kid any good. She's showing anxiety symptoms, becoming less outgoing, more withdrawn. When Liz hugs Molly now, she says the kid goes limp."

"And you?"

"With me living apart, she's begun to act like she's visiting her uncle. Divorce can tear up a kid."

"So can domestic tension, or so I hear." Ed propped his feet up on the railing.

"I suppose. Sometimes the kid talks nonstop — about what she's reading, classmates. Trying to keep me in the picture but suspecting it isn't working. Then she'll go silent."

"I can understand that. She's likely to blame one or both of you. Or worse, herself. If Liz is openly on your case, that makes things worse."

"I don't think Liz knows which way to go with this. Us, I mean." Bart looked dejected. "Bottom line, we're still living apart."

"And she's keeping you hanging. What was she wearing?"

"Whoa! Let's talk about your two women, Casanova. Maybe you could lend me those testosterone pills you're taking."

"Sorry if I'm intrusive. I've always envied your family life—beautiful wife, lovely daughter, nice home—while I drift around."

"A jellyfish in the sea of life. I like that. And where did you wash up? Chinatown."

"The Bowery, actually. It's becoming trendy, which may mean my youth is behind me and I'm just another gentrifier."

"But you're right. She was a catch, Liz I mean. Better looking and smarter than me. I had to think she'd wake up to that eventually." Bart looked out at the flood-lit cathedral tower. Dogs began a chain conversation, the barking rising and ebbing. "She can do better."

"Oh, bullshit. You're a great guy. And now that you're working in D.C. instead of some hotspot, maybe you can get through this." Music played below them, faint, calming.

"She getting good grades, Molly?"

Bart struck a wooden match on his shoe and set fire to a skinny cigar.

"Her teachers aren't complaining. Molly's quick as a cheap firecracker. Always has been. Got that from Liz."

"But she's got your looks."

"God help her, no. My point is she could coast for weeks without cracking a book and I doubt anyone would notice."

"Cause the teachers are burned out? I remember Miss Peck from high school chemistry. You had her too. She couldn't end the class hour fast enough."

"Yeah. Retired in place, as they say. But Molly's school is solid. I'm just saying the girl is smart enough to fake it, till it all falls apart, anyway. This isn't Sidwell Friends where the Obama girls went, but it's good. Given the tuition, it better be."

"They have a counselor?"

"They call 'em life advisors, not shrinks or counselors. That way the parents don't have to say their kid is fucked up."

"Keeps the records clean."

"Oh, yeah. We had the same problem in the service. Can't let some army shrink label you 'batshit crazy' if you're angling for a promotion. So you suck up the nightmares or whatever." He drew deeply on the cigar. "If I were overseas, Molly might understand things better. As it is, we pretend it's all normal while we're bailing out the boat." He ground the spent cigar under his foot and flicked the butt into the darkness below.

"Then again, our schedule concentrates the mind. When we all lived together, days would pass and it seemed like we didn't really talk. Now I plan our weekends."

The dogs were at it again, a disparate pack re-establishing order.

"Did I tell you she has me playing tennis? She's on the school team, so now she's coaching me. More running my ass off, but that's fine. And get this. She showed me her notebook. She's keeping track of the museums we'd been to, made it into a school project."

"A guide to the Washington art scene," said Ed. "Very mature."

"No. It was an essay on museum shops and cafeterias. Best buys, best sitting times. Places where you should definitely brown bag." Bart laughed.

"She's telling you something."

"Indeed."

"Here's a thought. Give her a call. Then give me some privacy and I'll call Mona."

"I'll buy that." But Bart didn't pick up his cell. "You serious about any of these women?"

"My women. Now I'm Brad Pitt." Ed leaned back. "Aisling knocked me off my feet, but she ended that. Decisively. I think I was just her summer love."

"So why are we here?"

"I owe her. And then there's the assignment."

"There is that. And Mona?"

"Things are confused there. I hadn't processed Aisling's kissoff when Mona popped up. She'd always been a fixture in Hardy's office, candy behind the shop window. Only a fool hits on the boss's assistant. Then we began working together on this article and things started to develop."

"Her doing, it sounds like. I mean hell, you said she audits your travel expenses."

"She's Hardy's right hand. But here's the thing. After I outlined the story for her—all business—the gears shifted. She invited me to stay for dinner. One minute she's taking the lid off the casserole, the next we're mouth to mouth in a canopy bed."

"Always good to know CPR."

"Yeah. But after that, everything was back to normal, at least at work."

"Some things don't last. Anyhow, you need to play it safe at the *Chronicle*. If you want unconditional love, get a dog." Bart grinned. Then he got up and headed for their room leaving cigar smoke.

Ed hit a number on his phone and Mona's voice came through, low and husky. "You sound like Veronica Lake, or maybe Lauren Bacall. Let's switch to Skype. I want to see you."

Using the hotel's Wi-Fi, he powered up his laptop. As he waited for her to connect, he brushed back his hair.

"Greetings from La Selva. Surprised?"

"More like impatient."

She was siting cross-legged on her bed wearing a man's shirt, Her honey-colored hair was matted. "So, what's happening? You seem to be still alive."

"You look beautiful."

She cocked an eyebrow. "You're not bad yourself." Then she leaned into the screen and shaped a kiss, a slight upward curl to her top lip.

"Okay. What's going on?" She had picked up a pencil and pad.

"I'm getting paranoid about eavesdropping so I won't go into detail. I'll send an encrypted e-mail later."

"Probably smart. Do you miss me?"

"Jesus, you're a devil. Yes, I miss you. Here's what I can say. We're in San Cristóbal, found a hotel, and met up with you know who over a late supper. Now we're back at the hotel."

Mona flashed a tight smile. "Sounds romantic."

Ed slogged on. "This individual gave us some preliminary research results that may be useful. I'll include them in the email. You'll also need to send a physical copy to Janet Malcolm at Earth Defense Fund. We'll see what she makes of it."

Her pencil stopped moving. "Wait. And how was that supper? No, cancel that." She took a deep breath. "What's next?"

"This unnamed individual wants to show us an agricultural station that's near their field setup. It appears sketchy. The ultimate owner, a few shells back, is Naturtek. My guess is they're here because it's off the radar."

"Mexico is off the radar?"

"Or corrupting the authorities here is cheaper than in Kansas. Bart and I expect to obtain evidence of what they're up to."

Mona paused in her note taking. "Obtain. I see. Now, listen while I read you the paper's standard precautionary statement—'Do nothing illegal; take no personal risks; if you do, you're on your own.'"

"Our informant here found significant crop damage at some distance. It could be from a number of things—chemicals, some new disease. My guess is that suicide technology has escaped the cage. The samples will tell us."

She tapped her pencil against her teeth. "Significant. But risky."

"We've probably gone too far already for a Skype connection, but yeah."

"Is your 'informant' maybe jerking you around, playing maiden-in-distress? They say a snake will crawl into your bed down there, just for the heat. Learned that in the Girl Scouts." A non-smile. "What do I tell Hardy?"

"Tell him this will take a few days but when I get back, I should have what I need for the piece."

"Promises, promises. At least then you'll have my assistance.

"It's a thin line between motivation and distraction," he said, letting out a breath. "I'll get that e-mail attachment to you right away. If Hardy has lined up other experts, give them zip drives as well."

Ed stared at her face. "I've missed you since our dinner."

Mona leaned back and stretched up her arms. Her shirt fell open. "We each suffer in our own way. 'Night, stud." She blew him a kiss and the screen went dark.

Chapter Forty-Three

WAITING FOR AISLING TO make contact, the Dekkers explored the city. It was hard to pass through markets without loading up on indigenous artisania but they resisted. They'd likely have their hands full leaving. Then they hailed a cab and made a deal with the driver to show them the surrounding region. At one point the driver took them to the army post south of town which the rebels had stormed twenty-five years earlier, trying to secure weapons.

"Always a good idea in a war," said Bart. "Too bad the assault failed."

As evening approached, the brothers were back in town. As they walked past the central cathedral, Aisling finally called. She'd be in from the countryside the following night and they agreed to meet in the privacy of the hotel.

"Come after nine," said Ed. "The woman at the desk will be off duty and the lobby will be locked. We'll let you in."

"I'll take the bus in. I have things to buy for our project so nine will work. Getting back here might be iffy."

"Stay over with us," said Ed. What was the alternative?

"We'll see what works," she replied.

The following night, Ed and Bart heard a tapping on the hotel's heavy wooden door. They'd been sitting quietly in the darkened lobby, the only light coming from an electric candle in front of an altar to the Virgin of Guadalupe. Slightly out of breath and lugging a backpack, Aisling slipped in and they padded up the stairs to the Dekkers' room.

"We're spinning our wheels here," said Ed. "I mean, nice city, but we should be checking out what you've been telling us."

"We'll go early tomorrow," said Aisling. "You read my report?"

"Yes, this morning." Ed opened his computer and pulled up the file. "The figures look convincing, way beyond the standard deviation you'd expect with conventional crop damage. I have no idea what to make of your numbers on insect decline."

"You didn't get to the footnotes? The point is that the number of essential pollinators is crashing. Look at the figures on the *Agave macroacantha*. People use this plant to make mescal, tequila, and *charanda*. They've been doing it for centuries and recently they developed an export market. The plant's pollinators run the spectrum from butterflies and hummingbirds during the day to bats and moths at night. The bat, *Choeronycteris mexicana* in particular, is important. But there's far fewer compared with last year and this month they've been nonexistent." She ran a finger down columns on the screen. "This is serious."

"Before we get into the weeds, so to speak, can you clarify something for me first?" said Bart. "I can see why someone might want to know what this ace reporter was sending back from Austria," he pounded Ed on the shoulder, "but who would know we were headed up to Boston?"

Ed watched her face, expecting outrage. It wasn't there.

"Just wondering," Bart continued. "I know you scientists are all about correlations — for every A there's a B, and all that — so it had to occur to you that every time you're in the picture, there's trouble."

Aisling shook hair from her face and turned to Ed. "I should have explained this earlier but I didn't know where to start. I still don't. When we met in Austria, Ed, it wasn't entirely an accident." She held up both hands, open and defensive.

"Jesus, Mary and Joseph", muttered Bart. "A fucking imposter."

"Before you freak out, just listen. Remember, I said I was traveling on a grant from the Tropical Conservancy, which has been underwriting my work here in Mexico? A month before the conference, they called and wanted a favor. They thought something of interest might come up at Oetz about synthetic biology. Would I keep my eyes open? And that included what the press was picking up. More specifically, you, Ed." Her voice dropped. "These are the people signing my checks."

Bart threw up his hands. "I always knew coming here was crazy. First thing tomorrow, we're gone."

Ed gestured for him to settle down.

"They said of all the reporters, you were the one most interested in synthetic biology. I'd never heard of you."

"So, they profiled me." Ed's voice was matter-if-fact. "They also pay you to fuck me?"

She gasped. "No, no." Her face was pink. "It was nothing like that. "They wanted to know what was being reported about developments in gene splicing, specifically, where you might go with the it. TC didn't want another Frankenstein story."

"Why would they care?"

She brushed back her curls. "How this stuff gets regulated is as much political as scientific. You know that. Papers like the *Chronicle* shape public perception. TC, and whoever was behind them, wanted to know where you were taking this before it hit print."

"Why me?"

"You're a known trouble maker," said Bart. "But that isn't the question. It's why are we down here bailing out this imposter!"

Aisling turned on him. "I'm a scientist, you moron! So, I wasn't entirely forthcoming. What damage did it do? You have no idea how hard it is to pay for research."

"By all means, the career comes first," said Bart. "I'm trying to think of the politically correct term for what you were. 'Gentleman's escort'?"

"They wanted to know whether you were writing an exposé, something that would weaken support for recombinant DNA."

"Which I wasn't, until I talked with Hammersmith."

"They found out about that and it made them even more interested."

"So, you debriefed me on the sly, then told all to the Conservancy?"

She swallowed. "While I was at the conference, yeah."

"Let's talk about the shooter." Bart cut in. "Tell us about him."

"They booked me to arrive when you did, Ed, and I had your picture and a bio. They knew you were a skier and figured you wouldn't pass up a chance at the Alps. I was supposed to casually bump into you at a lift or something. With our common interest in environmental issues, they figured we'd get talking."

"It's all in the algorithm," said Bart.

"And you found me, how?"

"TC knew you were on the mountain, they didn't say how, and that you headed off-trail to the Solden glacier."

"I'd talked to the concierge while I was getting a map."

Still," said Bart, "mountains are big."

"Once I was on the slope, they sent me your coordinates."

"Your phone was a GPS, Ed," said his brother. "You were a rat in a glass maze."

"I couldn't catch you so I spent the afternoon doing normal runs, thinking I might intercept you on the way down. I was feeling more than a little put out by then so I almost didn't care. Then they called again with your projected line of descent. Almost immediately, they said forget about it. They'd lost contact with you.

"I really wanted to walk away. Then I thought, you're off the grid and it was getting dark. That's when bad things happen. So, I worked my way toward your fall line. Then my phone lost reception. Finding you was a matter of luck."

"But an effective introduction," said Bart.

Aisling shrugged that off. "I'll confess, I was about to turn around when I heard your voice."

"You were never sent to save my brother?"

"No, and I had no idea he'd blown out." She turned to Ed. "But I did get you down."

"Putting a wrinkle in their plans," said Bart.

"And saving my sorry ass."

"I had no inkling of a shooter. You have to believe that. I was being played as well."

"Sure, all the way to bed," scoffed Bart.

"What happened later, Ed, wasn't part of any plan."

"So much for my personal magnetism." There was no energy left in Ed's voice.

"You may as well know it all." She took a breath. "Later, I told them I was done. If they pulled the grant, so be it. They said that was never a consideration but coincidentally, my conference funding had been reduced and I was re-booked to fly out right after my presentation."

"A tap on the wrist." Ed scratched his head, thinking back. "I was dazed when you found me, but even at that point I had the impression you were pissed off."

"I was. At myself."

"So getting me down was penance?"

She shrugged.

Ed cracked open one of the beers they'd bought that afternoon. "When was your last contact with Tropical Conservancy?"

"The day I got back to Boston. I owed them a financial report for the previous six months down here. But I dealt with their administrative office, not the guy who'd gotten me into that mess."

"What was his name?," asked Bart.

"Loft. No, Lust, maybe Lustig."

"Clever when you think about it," said Bart. "An accidental death on the slope is normal at a resort. They were never trying to shoot you."

"I apologize, Ed. It just seemed like the cost of doing business. Seeing you crippled like that changed everything. When we had dinner in your room that night, I was hoping we were starting fresh."

"The spy comes in from the cold," muttered Bart.

"First I'm an imposter, now I'm a spy!" She rounded on him.

"Aren't you?"

"It's not like that." Now she was pacing.

"How is it then?" said Ed, watching her. "Come on, what did you say about me?"

"Before I left Austria, I said you were following a lead on genetic engineering but it wasn't working out. How was that relevant?"

"We could ask Dr. Hammersmith. Oh, wait, they killed him." Bart snapped the cap off the last beer and pointed the bottle at her. "For Christ's sake Aisling, sit down."

She sat.

"So they knew Ed was looking at genetic engineering, maybe trying for a scoop, no?"

"I guess."

"But they stayed in touch with you." This from Bart again.

"They did, or tried to. It was this guy, Lustig. He sent me a text which I ignored, wanting additional information on you, Ed. This was before that mess in Boston. I didn't want any more to do with them. Which was another reason for me to get down here."

"So, no more contact with the mother ship?" Bart's tone was studiously neutral.

"No. And I certainly wasn't going to say you'd hired me, Ed." She began to silently sob. No one moved toward her and she calmed down.

Bart gestured to Ed and the brothers left the room, settling into chairs on the deserted patio. "What's it going to be? I mean, she's straight as a snake, but this is your assignment."

Ed crossed his arms and stared into the night sky. "I believe there's something here we need to see."

When they returned to the room, Bart said, "I just have one question, Aisling. Why are we really here?"

"Freaky things are happening at that research station." She blew her nose into a handkerchief. "I'm convinced what's happening in those greenhouses is decimating the pollinator population. But to prove it, we need samples. We do an analysis, it will blow this thing wide open. You'll have what you need for the paper, I'll have a hell of a journal article. Mine will come out in a year, at best, so you'll break the story."

"You're thinking a smash and grab," said Bart. "Not likely to win over a judge."

"Let's face it, the rules of evidence are looser for a journalist. You had a source but promised confidentiality. I'll build my argument on what you find and document the insect loss. It will be speculative, but will warn them off."

Bart whistled. "Why not raid these greenhouses yourself?"

"If there is any blow back, TC will have me kicked out of the country. There goes all the work my team has done so far. And my graduate students would be high and dry. They've put in months of work here."

"I find your self-focus refreshing," said Bart. "No bullshit about saving the world."

"Let's stay civil," said, Ed. "If the company did come after you, Aisling, would Northeastern back you up?"

She snorted. "Their business plan is industry collaboration. The Conservancy would read them the riot act and I'd not only be out of Mexico, I'd be gone from Northeastern with my office stuff in a bankers box."

"It's still risky for you. Say we do get proof. I'm hearing you say getting something into print takes time, even if you're blowing the whistle. And people die in Mexico, including gringos.

"That's why I have to remain in the clear, for a while anyway."

"You may not like it, but things are going to stick to you," said Bart.

"I've already got an alarming collapse of pollinators. What I -- what we need is physical evidence. I'll risk it."

"I still say we should get the hell out of Dodge, Ed. Maybe visit an Aztec temple or something."

"Around here they're Zapotec, or Maya," said Aisling. Then, under her breath, "You cretin."

"But I can see where the *Chronicle* won't be happy with you coming up empty," Bart continued. "And how difficult is it to break into a greenhouse?"

Aisling claimed one of the two single beds and Bart won the toss for the other. Ed made do with the rug and Bart's pillow.

Chapter Forty-Four

THE NEXT MORNING THEY rotated through the shower and were ready to head out by seven. "Oh, how I appreciate the hot water," said Aisling, "even if I have to get back into last week's clothes." The clerk glared at them as they left the hotel.

They'd soon found an out-of-the-way restaurant and were sitting in a patio beside a dry fountain. Their eggs came with refried beans and tortillas. A brilliantly feathered but sharp-clawed guacamaya shredded a dry corn cob nearby. The door to its cage was open.

"Here are the things we need," said Bart. "Maglights, zip-lock plastic bags, box cutters, rubber gloves. And small bottles."

"Glass bottles. You'll also need pruning shears," said Aisling.

"Noted. And a second knapsack. We can't be rolling suitcases around in the woods."

"I can supply the plastic bags and the second backpack," said Aisling. "And you'll want a compass."

"Not to mention a detailed topo map. Then there's the plan, which we never discussed." Food and the morning sun made it easier to set aside their distrust.

"Let's start with extraction. Something Bush forgot when he sent you guys into Iraq." Ed was feeling playful despite a hard night on the floor.

"Yeah, that was an oversight," replied Bart. "If they come after us, it will be by car or truck. So we need to keep to the woods. But remember, we're carrying bulk and maybe weight. We need to get picked up fast and taken somewhere. But your camp, even the village, are too obvious." Bart ran a blunt finger over a hand-drawn map that Aisling had brought.

"Our project leased an old truck. It's noisy but if we park it a few kilometers away it should be out of earshot and you guys can walk in from there."

"Close is better. We're moving in strange woods at night, and Ed's an old man. We should assume they'll mount a huge search from the get-go."

"Old? Okay, you're stuck with the heavy stuff." Ed rubbed his knee. "But I take your point." He turned to Aisling. "Say we get clear, then what? You drive us to a bus station or the airport?"

"They'll have buses and cabs covered," said Bart.

"And Tuxtla is too obvious. The *cuota* — the toll road — has soldiers stationed at every booth. Be too easy for someone to raise the alarm."

"You've given this some thought, I see," said Bart. "Okay, captain, what's your plan?" He gave her a desultory salute.

"I'm making this up as I go along. A bus is out for another reason. We need to keep the samples wet and breathing, not tucked away with luggage. This kind of testing requires living tissue."

"You have a laboratory in mind for this?" said Bart. Things were looking more and more complicated.

"I do, but not in Chiapas. And a commercial place, even if we could find one here, would take six months."

"So we're talking out of state."

"A friend runs a maternity clinic in Oaxaca City. That should be far enough away. They have a lab to check genetic profiles. I've already talked with her. Depending on the number of samples we want to run and how busy they are, she's open to it. In Boston, with state-of-the-art sequencers, a single test takes three or four minutes, not counting setup. Here, with older equipment, figure eight. Let's say we get 60 samples. That's eight hours."

"Overnight, if they're on the machines during the day. Does she understand what's involved, this friend?" said Bart.

"The science, yeah. We might want to downplay the legalities. I've been sending her plant-based salves and tinctures for use in her work. She has a sweat bath up there, what they call a *temazcal*, and these things are great for pregnant women. The community here recommends the plants and I gather them and make the preparations. We met at a conference in Mexico City and hit it off. She's fierce on women's rights and natural plants but beyond that, I'm not sure how we align politically."

"That's our best bet?" said Bart.

"To test the plants before they die, yes."

"Which will give us answers?" asked Ed.

"Some. We'll need benchmark sequences from conventional varieties for comparison. That's something I can get at Northeastern. The matches can be done by computer, zeroing in on any genetic anomalies."

"So there's another step?" Ed's timetable was moving away from him.

"I'll need their genetics laboratory," continued Aisling. "But I can pitch it as student-related, another learning experience. But like I say, I'm stuck here until June, May at the earliest."

"And it's what, March 3rd now? I need something sooner."

She pondered that a moment. "You take a copy of the data you produce in Oaxaca and run your own comparisons. Pick a few common vegetables—say tomatoes and beans—that will be enough for your article. Commercial labs can give you the benchmark profiles. Later I'll complete the picture and you can do a more extensive comparison."

Ed grumbled. "Even that's stretching things." Mona expected something in a few weeks.

"Okay, we have escape and the lab," broke in Bart. "But aren't we counting our chickens? There's still the raid on the pharaoh's tomb. What's the set up at this greenhouse?" He let Aisling mull that over while he rolled up the last of his beans and eggs in a tortilla.

"And we have to get to Oaxaca City," said Ed.

"We're on the migration route up from Guatemala," said Aisling. "Obama was bad enough, but Trump has really put the squeeze on Mexico's police if they want their war-on-drugs money. Standard procedure is to search all northbound buses."

"That leaves traveling in our own vehicle. We stick to secondary roads, maybe dirt tracks." Bart didn't sound thrilled. He opened his smartphone. "I get 600 klicks or 375 miles point-to-point. But that assumes the fastest route. On backroads, double it."

"And we're talking heat-of-the-day, plants dying." Aisling shook her head.

"Here's an idea," said Bart. "We find a chicken truck. There must be shipments out of here to Oaxaca, right?"

"With a couple of gringos in the back. Forget it."

They ordered more coffee. "Okay," said Aisling. "We use the project truck, which is known and wouldn't attract attention. But just to clear the area. Then we transfer the samples to a rented car with a local driver."

"Who is this 'we'?" asked Bart. "I see Ed, me, and this driver. Can we count on you?"

"It wouldn't make sense. Naturtek guards will be all over my project and El Encanto. I need to be found innocently at work."

"Hard to argue with that," said Bart. "You had that in mind all along, didn't you?"

"If I disappear, it will look suspicious. But here's the thing. I have two local guys working for me, Manuel and Francisco. Francisco has a car he uses to drive people into San Cristóbal. He knows the roads and I think he'd go for this. People down here have been ducking the army for the last century."

"What will this cost? We're living off the ATM," said Bart. "Every time we dip our card we send a message."

"There's gas. And Francisco will want something. Leonor—that's my friend in Oaxaca, actually Dr. Leonor Zárete—I don't know what she'll want but you'll need a few hundred U.S. ready."

"Disappointed you'll be missing your Bonnie and Clyde moment?" said Bart, flashing her a smile.

She rolled her eyes.

Chapter Forty-Five

Aisling explained that El Encanto was having a fiesta tonight to honor San Rafael, their patron saint. Along with the whole village, the local officials will be there—the mayor, the volunteers whose job it was to lock up the drunks, the priest. It will run late into the night, so if she was noticeable, she'd have an alibi. As a bonus, employees from the mysterious research station would probably be there, if only for the women and beer. That means fewer guards back at the greenhouses.

"We need more on the guards," said the former soldier.

"I expected that," said Aisling, taking out another folded sheet. "There are night patrols. The guards walk in opposite directions, passing each other about every half hour. They walk about halfway between the greenhouses and a perimeter fence. There's one other guy at the gate, which is a swing bar. When he isn't sitting in a little hut there, he never moves more than ten feet from the barrier."

"CCTV? And who's watching?" asked Bart.

"Francisco and Manuel have studied the place for a while. They noticed one camera at the gate."

"If there's one, assume others," said Bart. "Be good to know where the monitors are located. Describe the buildings."

"The main one is fairly large, used for eating and sleeping. One end seems to be an office. Any monitors would be there. It's prefab metal. There are two large greenhouses, plastic fabric over hoops, maybe thirty meters long. Manuel and Francisco spent two days watching the operation from the edge of the forest. During that time, one plane landed and took off again."

"Carrying?"

"They had no idea. It looked like a rotation of the work force. A crew unloaded what looked like supplies along with duffel bags. Oh, and one other thing. There's sometimes dogs on a leash."

"Now she mentions it," said Bart. "Patrolling with the guards?"

"Yes. But Manuel thinks they're mostly to chase away the howler monkeys that might slip in to steal food or interfere with the plants."

"I don't like dogs," said Bart. "Even a stupid one is smarter than the average guard. They have better hearing and louder voices."

"So, we distract them," said Ed. "A car approaching the gate, someone tosses in a chicken and the dogs give chase?"

"Better a herd of cattle?" Bart scratched his chin. "Do cows wander around at night?"

"Say we had our own dog?" Ed was thinking out loud. "Theirs would chase ours. Unless they were very well-trained."

"El Encanto uses dogs to protect the cattle," said Aisling. "There are still jaguars around, though not many. The herders are usually boys. They use whistles and hand commands to get the dogs to move the cattle in the right direction."

"Say we send our dog under the fence, have him run around the compound. Theirs would feel threatened and take off after him. The guards would follow." Ed played with the idea.

Aisling tapped the map with a pencil. "What about a female dog, one in heat?"

Ed picked up the thread. "We get her through the perimeter fence, the watchdogs would go nuts, assuming they're male, of course. In the chaos, we slip into the greenhouses."

"Won't work," said Bart. "The distraction could be over in minutes.

And aren't the greenhouses transparent? We'd be stumbling around with flashlights in plain sight with the entire camp on their feet. Then there's the kicker."

"Which is?" said Ed.

"Are the patrols armed?"

Aisling nodded and all three returned to their coffee, now cold. "How's this," said Aisling. "We get a recording of jaguar vocalizations. I've heard them at night. When they grunt, it sounds like something very large, clearing its throat. You can't mistake it. At the same time, it's low and hard to locate. Same for when they scream. It seems to come from every direction at once. If we amplified this, the dogs would have a fit."

"And where dogs go, man is close behind. It could work, so long as the dogs don't sink their teeth into the DJ."

"We can experiment in the village, see how far away a dog can pick up the sound," said Ed. "But we'll need something like a boom box. People still have those?"

"They do," said Aisling. "I'll have to think about where we can get a tape."

"You could probably imitate a jaguar." Bart gave Aisling a slow smile. She ignored him.

The guacamaya was now screeching. Either its food was gone or it wanted the restaurant to itself. The three North Americans took the hint.

After visiting an ATM, they spent the rest of the morning at hardware and backpacker supply stores. They got shears, rain capes, knives, flashlights, a topo map of the area and one covering the countryside from the village to Oaxaca City. After striking out several times, they located a tourist shop that sold CDs of forest sounds — birds, chattering monkeys, peccaries. A jaguar was the featured vocalist.

By noon they were on a bus to Las Margaritas, a two-hour trip with dozens of stops where footpaths led down from the hills.

"There's a bus hierarchy," said Aisling. They were lucky to have found seats together in the back. "Mexico has some of the most comfortable buses on the planet for long distance travel. *Lujo*, they call 'em. For half the fare there are older express buses. They'll have a bathroom but it may not work. And unless you want to watch wrestling movies on tiny aisle screens, you'd better bring a book. Local transit is usually a retired school bus from California—the famous Bluebirds—or a *pasero*. That's a pickup with standing room only."

"And chickens, I remember," said Ed.

"What's interesting is that the cheap third-class buses are often so jammed the people have to pass their fare hand-over-hand to the conductor, usually the driver's ten-year-old son. Then the crowd hands back the change. It's all one big community."

"Can't see that working in New York," said Ed.

As they continued on, their bus swung out to pass people walking on the pavement, some ladened with firewood, others leading children. "You'd think the state would build sidewalks," said Bart.

"It's worse than you think," she said. "If a pedestrian is hit, the driver of the car usually leaves the scene."

"Disappears?" Bart scratched his head.

"And fast. The law allows jail pending trial. That sounds like justice, but the result is the opposite. No one waits to be arrested."

"The law of unintended consequences," said Ed.

"We saw unintended consequences all the time in Afghanistan," said his brother. "An NGO would rebuild a dilapidated school. There'd be a big dedication, with local notables and a photographer from the embassy. Then a week later, the Taliban blows it up as an American perversion. Now, instead of a decrepit school, the village has none at all."

As they bounced along, Aisling rolled with the jolts and fell asleep, her head resting on Ed's shoulder. "I was wondering," said Bart in a low voice, "Ever hear of Mata Hari?"

366

"Who?"

"World War One, a French dancer and foreign agent. Before the Frogs shot her as a spy, she walked both sides of the fence, changing her mind with each new lover."

"Your point?"

"No point. Just sayin'."

They bounced along for a while. At the occasional stop, a boy or woman would get on and hurry down the aisle selling soft drinks or cinnamon *churros*, then jump off as the bus revved into gear.

"Remember how we used to love Cracker Jacks?" said Ed. "You knew the prize inside was just a piece of plastic crap—a ring, a little figure— but you wanted it."

"Right now, I'd settle for a churro."

Just then a rooster on the lap of a boy sitting ahead of them began to screech. Aisling stirred.

"We there yet?" she asked.

"You tell me. I'm just along for the ride," answered Bart.

"I've been thinking about things," she said, rubbing her eyes. "We can expect the local police to more or less ignore what happens at the Naturtek facility. They're foreigners, after all. The real problem will be their own guards."

"Catch up," said Bart. "We covered that."

"Oh right." She yawned.

"But indifferent cops can still jail us", said Bart. "I picture something dank and dirty, times a few years."

"But we're still taking the plunge, are we?" Ed squinted at his brother.

"The bigger the windmill, the harder we charge!"

Chapter Forty-Six

EL ENCANTO WAS STILL a few stops beyond Las Margaritas, the area hub. The Americans sat while passengers came and went. Twenty minutes after setting off again, they finally reached the village.

El Encanto consisted of a barren plaza criss-crossed with walks and benches. Dust-dulled trees seemed ancient but provided little shelter from the sun; it was still the dry season. A mix of adobe and cement buildings surrounded the plaza facing pitted streets. One low structure was a primary school painted light blue with a yard of swings and slides fenced off in rusty chain link. Further along was a street market, its tables under tattered awnings, beyond that a white-washed municipal building. Brooding down from the high end of the plaza was a stone church. The double doors of weathered wood were closed. Here and there were small shops. Over one, a faded sign advertised 'Coke'.

"I haven't seen a red-button Coke sign for decades," said Bart. "Probably a collectible back in Washington."

"But not mint," said Ed.

"Down here time moves slowly," responded Aisling. "You can feel the weight of history. And wherever there's a school, there's a variety store."

"You're a sociologist of everyday life," said Bart, looking at Aisling. She shrugged.

"That building next to the church?" she continued, "used to house a clinic. Then, leading up to the election, the government built a maternity hospital outside of town. The streets may not be well-paved, but health care gets at least nominal attention from the government. Then it's up to the people to demonstrate how much they need adequate staffing."

"The old tug of war," said Ed.

Aisling led them around a corner to a garage where a group of men and boys were gathered around an old pickup. One was bent under the hood, the rest looking on. Aisling spoke briefly to one of the crowd who turned out to be a *taxista*. He pointed to his dusty Datsun parked nearby. A quarter hour of slow driving later, he dropped them off at a footpath by the roadside. Aisling guided them along the edge of a pasture, then turned in the direction of the forest.

"Another half mile." She quickened her stride. The field was baked hard by the sun and dry corn stalks rustled in a slight breeze. They'd been bent in the middle and left to dry. "The sun keeps the ears preserved until they can be gathered," she said. "Still, they're leaving this plot late. The rains could start any time."

Beyond the field, the cool of tree cover was welcome. Ed and Aisling walked side-by-side. "We're now on community-owned land. Last year loggers showed up and there was quite a confrontation. They waved what they claimed were permits from the state and were revving up saws to take down all these trees." She gestured. "Before they'd dropped their first one, the residents had them surrounded and were waving heavy hoes. This is where the community gathers firewood and hunts. The people weren't going to put up with any outside loggers. When it looked like a draw, the loggers withdrew. The pressure on natural resources here is unrelenting."

"So people are used to this kind of thing?"

"On municipal lands, yes. But I know what you're thinking. Why did they allow the Naturtek greenhouses? As I said, that was on a private parcel. There's a kind of checkerboard pattern here."

"Lots of boundary fights, I'd guess?"

"It's a shifting dynamic. But the forests are communal. If you belong to the community, you can take what you need for household use. And there's a carpentry cooperative that makes doors and windows. People here understand their dependence on mature trees. They also sustain the purity of springs and streams."

"I can imagine the standoff then," said Ed, now wondering if they would be challenged as well.

"The town cops—all two of them—barricaded the road and fifty people surrounded the logging truck, ready to burn it. The message was clear."

"No repercussions?"

"Nothing obvious. Here politics happens in the street. Say your school doesn't get assigned a teacher. Or the clinic needs an obstetrician. There'll be a period of petitioning, filing papers with the government, all of which they'll accept with a smile but ignore. Or they'll say wait, other places are worse off, which may be true. Public resources are scarce. But what the officials are doing is seeing how serious the people really are. If they turn out and block the most important road, or burn some buses in Las Margaritas, there'll be a solution. It's only in extreme cases that the state responds with force. Of course when that happens, the bullets and the tear gas fly."

"Would you say this town is pretty tight, pretty well-organized, I mean?" Bart had caught up. He was thinking, well-armed.

"Oh, yes. It's an *ejido*, a self-governing municipality. Its legal history goes back to the 1930s but it's been an indigenous settlement for centuries. When the Zapatista uprising took place in January '94, the town was initially neutral. It had important ties to the government's peasant association and to the ruling party. But a lot of people joined the uprising as individuals. You may not see any EZLN flags here but over the last twenty years, the residents have gotten quite assertive. To hold their loyalty, the state has had to come across with things like the new clinic. Only the really squeaky wheels get greased."

"So, are people pacified?"

"No. But they take what's offered and continue to demand what isn't."

"Why send in loggers?" Bart asked.

"A mix-up, maybe. The various agencies aren't always coordinated. Then again, it could have been a warning — play ball or lose your forests."

"Not exactly subtle," said Ed.

"Indeed. But a few hundred hectares of forest is small potatoes to a paper mill. And trucking it out would wreck what are already lousy roads. It likely wasn't worth a showdown on the government's part. Now if gold had been discovered, that would be entirely different."

"There's gold here?" asked Bart.

"Who knows? I'm not a geologist. But the area is volcanic and there's lots of up-thrust of crust. It's the kind of area where you might find gold, or copper, or silver. Say private prospectors snuck in. Maybe they'd heard stories of flakes of gold in the streams. If they found a seam, you'd see a completely different scenario."

"The army?" asked Bart.

"The federal police, at least. First, there'd be beatings and arrests, but if the people didn't cooperate well, you can guess."

"They'd kill people?" asked Bart.

"Better believe it. The state has a *mano dura.*"

"A hard hand," said Ed. "There's the term 'resource curse.' That's when ordinary people have the misfortune of finding themselves on top of a mineral deposit, or oil."

"Here it would be gold. You sound even more a market skeptic than in Austria", said Aisling."

"So do you."

"This place is getting into my blood." She gestured to the trees above them and the hills visible beyond. "I'm a vagabond, but if I had to identify with any place, it would be here. I don't want to see it destroyed."

"I take your point," said Ed. "In Oetz, the bankers were all about the global supply chain. Real places were just abstractions."

Aisling sensed his mood. "Except theirs, I hear you say. It's trite I know, but change requires people working both inside and outside the system. I hope my research raises critical issues. But I'll leave it to others to storm the barricades."

"Spare me," said Bart.

Ed turned to his brother. "We're past that or we're not going to get anywhere."

"Hey, I'm good." Bart gave him an innocent smile.

Aisling's camp consisted of half a dozen tents, some with beds, others used to store equipment. A thatch of palm leaves comprised the roof over work benches. Most held dead insects spread out on trays for sorting and counting. A tarpaulin sheltered a cooking fire and picnic tables. The staff, two Anglo women in shorts and tee shirts and two darker-skinned men wearing jeans and rubber boots—all apparently in their twenties—dropped what they were doing and walked over to greet the arrivals.

"Leslie, Audrey, Manuel, Francisco, this is Bart and Ed Dekker from the States. Dekker and Dekker. They're here for a few days."

"Sounds like a law firm, eh?" said Leslie in an accent that placed her in English Canada. "Good to meetcha." Her hand was strong and warm. The others murmured greetings and held out their hands in turn. New faces were a welcome distraction.

"We are brothers, but given the age difference, I've always thought of Ed as a father figure." Manuel and Francisco smiled though Manuel may not have understood the dig until Francisco murmured a few words in his ear.

"We expected you yesterday, Aisling, but we've kept busy," said Leslie. Taking the lead, she gestured for them to move to a bench where small jars held dead insects amid a pile of open manuals. "Wait. Let me get you something to drink." She trotted to the cook tent and Audrey took up the slack.

"Manuel made another trip over to 'poison central'. He's drawn a new map." The thin young man nodded and addressed Aisling in Spanish.

"He says there's no real change there," Audrey translated, "same number of workers, same vehicles. But they used a brush cutter yesterday to clear the north end of the field, including taking out some taller trees."

Leslie returned with glasses and a pitcher. "It's *jamaica*," she explained, "a tea made from hibiscus flowers." She handed out the cool, wine-colored drink and they touched glasses.

"The field serves as a runway," continued Audrey. "Looks like they're expecting a flight."

"Not unusual," said Francisco. Bart was glad at least one of the two spoke English.

"But maybe a larger plane this time," said Bart. "How long is the runway?"

"Three hundred, three hundred fifty meters."

"Enough for a Twin Otter. Getting back in the air would be tight but possible," said Bart.

"It's just a pasture, but there's no cows or anything now. The usual flights are in smaller planes," continued Francisco.

"Piper Cubs," chimed in Leslie. "They're common at home in Manitoba. I've seen a PA-28 down here, which can seat four. Did I say I have a pilot's license?" She grinned.

"How did they get here when they set this place up?" asked Aisling. "I wasn't paying much attention last spring."

"From what I heard, it was a Twin Otter then too, Canadian made!" she pumped her fist. Seats maybe 20, but if you removed most of them you could carry a good deal of cargo."

"So, we can expect a bigger plane coming in, either with more crew or freight," said Bart. "Whichever, something is happening. They even could be pulling up stakes."

"Oh, you mean leaving? No sign of that," said Francisco. We watched late last night and nobody is packing anything."

"You and Leslie together, I gather. I leave for a night and camp discipline goes to hell," said Aisling laughing. "Where's the beer?"

Ed admired the camp's laid-back style. That had to count in Aisling's favor.

"We need to know what surrounds the greenhouses." Bart had become all business. "You know what we're up to, getting in there and taking samples?" The women and the two local men nodded. Bart spread out Aisling's hand-drawn map and put his finger on a spot. "How thick are the woods here, and are we talking swamp? If so, that could be a problem."

"No, is passable," said Francisco. "The monsoon has yet to come. But the trees are thick. And there's these," he gestured to Aisling, moving his hands down in a rainfall pattern.

"Liana vines," she said. "They're parasitic and hang down from the branches of other trees. If these guys don't trip you up, the roots of the ceiba trees will. They're huge root structures that rise above the surface, bracing the trunks."

"So we go slow," said Bart. "This may take longer than we figured." At least the crew here had been thinking about this. "Now, the route from where we are now to there." He pointed. "What's your advice?"

Aisling rolled out the new topo map. "We need to get close, but still keep the vehicle out of sight. People could be coming and going from the compound."

"Can you work out those details with these guys?" Ed asked his brother. "I'd like Aisling to show me what she's doing here, what you've all found about the plants and insects." He gestured to the group. "Is that okay with you, Aisling?"

"Fine. But I need Leslie and Audrey. They know as much about this as I do and can fill us in on any progress they made over the last few days."

Aisling led Ed and her interns to the edge of the clearing and a mesh enclosure, looking like a covered tennis court. Inside, light filtered through the woven sides and canopy onto raised beds where plants grew in rich compost.

"There's not a lot in flower at the moment," said Audrey, "but everything you see growing was gathered from the wild. We open the side fabric for 24 hours at a stretch, then button things down and fumigate. That way we can count the insects. Then we start the cycle all over. We have to move fast before they decompose."

"Then there's the photography." Leslie took over, pointing to cameras placed near specific plants. "We try to catch the pollinators in flagrante delicto." She gave a brief grin. "That way we can associate specific flowers with particular insects. We couldn't do any of this without the enclosures. Anything dead, the ants dismember in minutes after it hits the forest floor. They're ferocious." She scratched her ankle. "It's not foolproof but over time, the errors wash out. What matters is the week-to-week change."

Ed noticed that Aisling was standing back, letting her students take the spotlight.

"Bottom line?" continued Leslie, "We've had three episodes over the last four months when insect numbers crashed. This was across the board, all species. Pollinators were hit especially hard. Ants, on the other hand, seemed impervious." She took up a specimen from a tray, holding it with tweezers; a bee. "There's a slight mortality difference among several species of solitary bees—we've identified nine—when compared with the hive-builders. Those visiting from hives have fared the worst."

Next, they walked a quarter of a mile to a hand-cultivated field. The women waved to several men hoeing in the distance, then they entered a second tent enclosure covering a section of the field. Even Ed could see that things here weren't right. Squash growing in rows seemed limp and anemic; tomato plants had set very few fruit, and their leaves were curled and yellow. "Early blight," said Audrey. This tent was apparently her particular responsibility. "But our interest has focused on the brassicas."

"Broccoli," filled in Aisling. "Along with cabbage, cauliflower, kale, collard, and turnips. These crops were introduced here for export but they've found a place in the local diet. Except turnips. No one here likes 'em."

"What's with them?" asked Ed.

"Brassicas tend to have self-incompatibility," said Audrey in lecture mode. "The flowers are small and the anther—the thing with the pollen—is close to the stamen. Oddly, the plants tend to reject fertilization with their own pollen. But since the pollen is sticky and heavy, it doesn't blow well in the wind either."

"Enter the bees," Ed wanted to show he was keeping up.

"Precisely." Audrey took up an invisible pointer. "The anther is situated so a bee has to brush against it when she goes for the nectar at the base of the flower. She captures it on hairs on her thorax and abdomen. Then, at the next flower, she brushes against the stamen. She can't help it. It's all determined by the morphology of the blossom." Audrey broke off a tiny flower and held it for Ed to look at. "The bee's a postman, picking up and depositing pollen over the entire population of, in this case, broccoli. Bee and flower have co-evolved."

"So the bee's just being a good citizen?" asked Ed.

"Not quite," broke in Aisling. "Sugars in the nectar provide her with essential carbohydrates while the pollen gives her protein, minerals, and fats to build body structure. What they don't eat immediately, they carry back to the colony to feed the larvae and the queen. As I explained in Austria," she continued. "It's co-evolution."

"But now the wheels are off the truck," said Ed.

The young women shrugged, seemingly at a loss.

"It's a disaster, actually," said Aisling. "Vegetable production for farmers here is off by half. Things looked good until October, then we got these periods of insect collapse. In December there was a small rebound but it didn't last. The community irrigates so rainfall's not the issue. February's over now and people have panicked. Ordinarily, they'd be shipping out a truckload a week of boxed vegetables to San Cristóbal."

Ed stepped carefully, avoiding the hoses.

"They have drip irrigation that runs by gravity," continued Aisling. "It was a big investment. But this year they'll be lucky to harvest enough to feed themselves."

As the light faded, the group walked back toward the center of the camp, Ed and Aisling side-by-side following the girls.

"Can you give me photographs—dead bees and moths, blighted plants? Are butterflies affected?"

"Yes on everything. As for the last, they're less important as pollinators but they still play a part."

"But they're charismatic. People love butterflies," said Ed. "If things don't rebound, what are these people going to do?"

"I don't know. Being on the edge of the rain forest gives them independence and a decent standard of living, so long as they have a market. Because corn is wind pollinated, I don't expect that will be a problem, but it doesn't bring in any cash. Up to now, people were better off here than in some squatter settlement in Mexico City or working the fields in Arizona."

"Your theory is that these bees visit the research station, get exposed to something toxic, and carry it to these plants?"

"My working hypothesis." She shook her head in disgust. "El Encanto also treats outsiders at their village clinic using natural cures. That all depends on things remaining uncontaminated. If it all goes, so will the people, young adults at the head of the line."

"Where did Francisco learn his English. Is it taught here?"

"Now it is, in the middle school. But Francisco learned in Los Angeles. He's a good plaster and tile man. He crossed over but got homesick. I was lucky to find him. He helps with research but can fix almost anything—an irrigation pump, a truck. Like a lot of people here, he speaks three languages."

"Three?"

"Tojolabal is the language of his family. Then Spanish, which you need out of the area, and as I said, English."

"So people here take education seriously?"

"More than you'd think. But there are problems. The primary school teacher lives in Las Margaritas and commutes. For whatever reason, he doesn't always show up. Then at contract time, teachers in the entire state usually go on strike. It's not just for wages but a way to pressure the government for better school funding. So the school year can be spotty. Add to that, there's no high school. You want to go beyond grade six, you have to leave."

"For San Cristóbal?"

"There's a technical high school in Las Margaritas, twenty miles away. That's too far to go by bus every day so kids board with relatives."

"Challenges, challenges."

"But there's a bright spot. Some go to La Universidad de la Tierra, Unitierra it's called. That's a vocational school outside of San Cristóbal run by a priest. As they're learning a trade—say shoemaking—they're exposed to literature and philosophy at the same time. When they finish, they return and give back to the community that paid for their room and board."

"So, old Bartolomé de las Casas is still around?"

"In spirit. Now they call it 'liberation theology'. The diocese here is unusually progressive."

Ed stumbled over a tree root and Aisling caught him by the elbow.

"And do these kids return?"

"Not all. There's a powerful pull north. That's what makes global agriculture such a tragedy. The system is pushing these people out."

"Now you're sounding like a Zapatista."

"Just a realist. What USAID is preaching—comparative advantage in a global market—isn't working. So people try new ways."

"Like exporting broccoli and honey?"

"There's a women's weaving cooperative. Communities at a higher altitude ship their coffee directly to Europe. If something works, it's usually communal. The impulse grows from common ownership of the land. If that were to go, so would most everything else. So they resist."

"So you said."

"They're not *guerrilleros*, not by any stretch. If you write that, I'll cut out your heart." She wasn't smiling.

Ed touched his chest. "Good to keep in mind. What if I write that they're communists?"

"I'm sure that's how it looks to the International Development Bank. I mean, owning land in common, how anti-capitalist is that? But 'communitarian' is better. Cooperative capitalists, if that makes sense. They're also individualists."

"So it's not a classless society?"

"No. Remittances are a big part of the economy, which puts some families ahead of others. Still, mutual aid is big. There's the *techios,* the collective work everyone has to do, like painting the school. It's a mixed bag."

"Meaning?"

"They were almost back to camp and she lowered her voice. "If you see a fancy house left half-constructed, it means someone living in Los Angeles. When you see a new Silverado pickup out front, he's back."

"Listen, I hate to be a wimp, but is there some place I can nap? I have the feeling I'm going to need it." She led Ed to her own tent but didn't go in with him.

Chapter Forty-Seven

AT NATURTEK HEADQUARTERS IN St. Louis, a dozen men and a few women sat around a highly-polished table, laptops and folders in front of them. A ceiling projector displayed a list of engineered plant types and their development stage. Through plate glass windows, the Gateway Arch, 630 feet of silvered steel, was visible. Constructed on the riverfront, it commemorated the city's role as the outfitter of pioneers headed west. In the present age, it seemed empty bravado. St. Louis had become a city of empty factories and idle freight yards. Like the Mississippi itself, industry had flowed south and ultimately across the ocean. But for those in the board room, the arch was affirmation, the sign of a renaissance. Their business was hitched to the new industrial revolution, the 'life sciences'. And Naturtek's sprawling research facilities eighty miles away held the key.

"Go ahead, John," said the chairman, Magnus Untermeyer, speaking from the head of the table. He gestured to an ascetic-looking Asian man. "What's the update on terminator development?"

John Kim was ill at ease, not used to attending meetings in the boardroom. Still, this was his moment. "As you know," he said, fixing his eyes exclusively on the chairman, "we undertook this project eight years ago. Our aim was to capture the entire market in winter vegetables shipped in from Mexico and Central America. With the guarantee of recurrent sales that GURTS offer—that is, genetic use restriction technology—plus the enhanced profit margin of premium seed, we are positioned to dominate vegetable production, not merely in the global South but in Europe and ultimately China."

"John, John. Can the sales pitch. Get to the point, if you would." The chairman drew back parchment-like lips in an indulgent smile.

"Yes, well, as director of research, I've guided this initiative. Sterility is the key, forcing growers to return to us year after year." John found it hard to deviate from the script he'd rehearsed at home in front of his wife, Muyung-Ok, his 'bright pearl'.

"Eight years ago, we acquired the rights to the associated technology—gene identification, splicing mechanisms, genetic markers, and clone replication." He cleared his throat. "Since then, our teams have enhanced most commercially-important vegetable varieties and we are ready to scale up production."

A silver-haired man of sixty with a florid face emitted a guffaw, startling the research head. "You mean suicide genes."

A blond woman in her forties with a golfer's sun-dried face waved her hand back and forth. "Words matter," Jill Stapleton said. "The State Department can't sell 'suicide genes' to Congress, let alone to the EU. How can we argue for trade liberalization if Europe thinks we're asking them to commit, well, suicide? You remember the dustup that 'death panels' raised? It nearly sank the Affordable Health Care Act?" To her left, Matthew McCord of the Office of Trade Representative drew back, separating himself from Stapleton's apparent politics.

"There, there Jill," said the chairman. "Marvin, would you please put this in a legal context?"

A rumpled man of sixty wearing tweed, his half-moon glasses perched precariously on a narrow nose, stood to bask in his moment of limelight. "This project, by whatever name, is less about technology than property rights," said Marvin Lustig. He cleared his throat. "What we have is a biological patent. However robust our no-replant contracts may be, growers in developing regions—I won't say backward—cheat. And these are the markets we're most interested in penetrating: Southern Africa, Latin America, South East Asia. Not only is intellectual property litigation expensive, in bush courts justice can't be guaranteed. You get judges that simply can't grasp the concept of intellectual property rights." Several around the table nodded while the State Department official rolled her eyes.

"Unlike hybrids, Ms. Stapleton, the seeds we're developing, simply won't reproduce a second season. End of story. Our customers will return to us if they want to keep enjoying a superior product." He narrowed his eyes. "Or avoid starvation." With evident satisfaction, he sat down.

"So I'm to pitch this in trade negotiations as patent protection?" broke in Matthew McCord. Along with Stapleton, he was part of the liaison team that linked the company with federal agencies.

"Precisely," said the legal counsel. "Isn't that the point of the WTO? Intellectual property protection has been the linchpin of trade policy for the last four administrations. All we're doing is adding a biological edge, you might say slamming down the lid on America's genetic cookie jar."

Stapleton jotted down a note and whispered to McCord, who nodded agreement. A moment later she signaled with her hand. "One small matter." She was looking at Lustig. "A little hitch called the Treaty on Biological Diversity. Since 2000, it has precluded the commercialization of terminator seeds. Every country has signed on."

Chairman Untermeyer rapped on the table, annoyed that the discussion was turning up obstacles. "Are you trying to blindside us here, Stapleton? And Marvin, I thought this was all worked out?" He looked around the room.

"Ah, yes. Well," said Lustig, "you'll note this so-called treaty doesn't forbid research on the topic. As for prohibiting commercialization, that's only advisory. Most important, there's no enforcement mechanism."

But Stapleton wasn't through. "The issue for State isn't merely legal.

It's public perception. Good God, people are worried enough about obesity from high fructose corn syrup. I don't think they'll ignore," she paused, "death seeds."

Lustig looked at her as if assessing her weight and gave a sly smile. "We are selling two things." He spoke the last words slowly and distinctly. "Modernization and national competitiveness. The first is self-explanatory. The second involves America's need to retain a economic edge. You're worried about perceptions? The Brazilian secretary of agriculture—whatever her name—publicly supports terminator." He barely flinched at having slipped on the label. "And they've got the research capacity to make it happen. I'm talking about a country in the top ten for GDP." He blew through his lips. "Look what they've done with the fuel potential of sugar cane!" He looked to Dr. Kim for support.

"Yes," Kim replied. "And Brazil has a robust genetics industry. We know they're working to bio-engineered coffee."

"Do you want this country to lose out?" continued Lustig, setting aside his own cup of coffee. "Bottom line, we're first or we're last. That's what you tell Congress and the president." He rubbed his thumb over his index finger, looking pointedly at the government team.

There was silence in the room. "Put that way," said Stapleton after a pause, "I don't foresee an insuperable publicity problem. But expect push-back." She shook a finger while looking to McCord for support. He seemed fascinated by a flock of pigeons circling the arch. They'd work it out later, she hoped.

"All right," said the chairman. "Let us continue. Dr. Kim? Can you put us in the picture about the field tests in Mexico?"

"Of course, sir. A year ago, we obtained a license to establish test plots in a semi-tropical region of Mexico. This replicates conditions in Central America and parts of Southeast Asia. We've tested the modified seed of twelve common vegetables. Because the seeds have stacked traits—protection against insects and fungus, herbicide resistance, and terminator characteristics—they require heavy support with inputs. That means fertilizer and herbicide. For each variety, say eggplant, we plan to market all three components as a package." He turned a page in his notes. "Because this array of enhancements is complex, we didn't expect immediate improvements in yield. But," and here he risked a smile, "we were pleasantly surprised. In eight of twelve varieties indicated here"— he clicked a remote to display a chart on the wall screen—"our enhanced varieties equaled or outperformed conventionals." The plants appeared lush.

"Using our fertilizer and herbicide," said Kotz, a small man with dark circles around his close-set eyes. He was in charge of marketing. "So, are we ready to scale up for commercial production?"

"I believe so," said Dr. Kim. "But there was one counter-indication. Plants fared best in a rich environment of pollinators, such as bees. In our Mexico project, nearby villages tend hives for honey production and inadvertently provide this benefit to us without cost. But we project the natural population of insects in some areas is insufficient to maximize plant potential."

"Because?" said Janice Woodruff, the redhead from public relations. With glasses hanging from a chain around her neck, she resembled a school librarian. Leaning forward toward Kim, she seemed a skeptical senator at a confirmation hearing.

"Because bee mortality increased. And this is a problem unless growers compensate by leasing commercial hives," the researcher continued.

"Yes, which is an added cost," said the redhead.

"The scope of this complication and its duration remain unknown. Ongoing research may clarify this. As of now, I'd say the problem is manageable."

"Manageable? Is that all?" said the chairman.

"Manageable-to-negligible," amended Kim.

"Negligible. Well, given your positive findings—thank you Dr.

Kim—and as we know it's a hotly competitive field" — he nodded to Marvin Lustig —"I see consensus among the stakeholders at this table. We will shift to volume production supported by an aggressive marketing strategy. That will mean submitting relevant applications to the DOA, FDA, and EPA." He glanced over at the government people. "Make it clear that we will be adding jobs here in Missouri. Check with Ms. Woodruff for specific numbers." He waved a hand dismissively. "Janet, you'll want to generate a press release, once we have a timetable. Saturation coverage, especially in the Southwest." He looked around with satisfaction. "Well done, gentlemen and ladies. We have, as they say in Hollywood, a wrap." He pushed away from the table.

People closed laptops and gathered papers before filing out. The chairman used a side door to get to his own office, adjacent to the conference room. Immediately his secretary entered, announcing a visitor.

"Edgar," he said, addressing a stalky man in a brown suit. The chairman spun his hand and his secretary left, closing the door behind her. Edgar Jagger was not strictly-speaking a Naturtek employee. He was an independent contractor, on loan from Guardian Services. While the company's own man, David Luff, secured their labs and offices, Jagger undertook special projects. "How are we doing with that reporter, Edward Dekker?"

"His column on the death of Hammersmith came out ten days ago in the *Business Chronicle*. Between the lines, it implied the murder had something to do with Hammersmith's work. You may have the basis for a libel complaint but his wording was cagey. Lead agency for the case is now the FBI, but we continue to monitor the situation through our contacts with the state police. While some of his lab colleagues in Jefferson remain concerned—we interviewed several as a formality—the case has gone stale. I predict your employees will treat it as a one-off and the authorities will put it on the shelf."

"A tragedy, but a closed case?"

"Cold case or dead end." Jagger allowed himself the pun "They have a suspect believed to be the perp. He's also deceased so there's nowhere for them to go. They know he's a Swedish national who arrived in the States by irregular means and is without papers —customs, prints, employment, driver's license. An Interpol search did reveal that he served in the Swedish armed forces. But that's all they've got."

"And the woman at MIT, Hammersmith's consort?"

"Cambridge police are provisionally treating it as an accident. The faculty raised a ruckus about building security and along with some dissenting members of the Cambridge police, they are not buying an accidental death verdict. For that reason, the inquiry continues, but it's poorly staffed. Unfortunately, your firm doesn't have the influence in Massachusetts you do in Missouri. But our sources tell us no evidence has turned up related to a perpetrator. And there's nothing to link the two cases together."

"Or to us?"

"Definitely not. Our only problem is two low-level detectives. Royco working the Hammersmith case and Ballancio up in Cambridge. Neither is on this full-time and the FBI's involvement gives their departments an excuse to back away."

"Royco and Ballancio, are they in communication?"

"Yes. And in occasional contact with this Ed Dekker. But there are no leads."

"Which you know how?"

"People on the inside talk to us. Furthermore—and this is Guardian's proprietary information—we have access to FBI servers. What they archive electronically, we read. We're trying to do the same with the two local departments. Problem is, Jefferson handwrites and then types its reports. And interestingly, the Cambridge cops have more robust security than the FBI. But we'll crack it."

"That figures, given their proximity to MIT," said the chairman.

"Well, despite the fire wall problem, we're reading what they share with Royco by phone."

"Is there political pressure to resolve this?"

"None. Ciobanu's colleagues have been interviewed along with everyone having access to the building. The police incident team turned up nothing by way of fingerprints or fibers. They're out of leads."

"Speaking of fibers, our Mister Dekker remains a loose thread."

"He'd like to make solving these killings a career move. We can't get into his communications at the *Chronicle* yet but," he shrugged, "we're working on it."

"That would be the royal road," said the chairman, tapping manicured fingers.

"There's something else. Airline records place Dekker in Mexico, along with his brother, one Bartholomew Dekker. They flew to Chiapas three days ago. We don't think for a vacation."

"Dekker has a brother?"

"Yes. Employed by a private security firm in Washington, small outfit called Executive Action. What could be relevant is that he's former military."

"Sounds like he's playing bodyguard," said the chairman. "The Dekkers in Mexico." He thought a moment. "You'd have no reason to know this but we have on-going research there. Does that suggest a connection?"

Jagger nodded.

"The good news is we also have an asset in place, one he knows and will surely contact."

"Oh?"

"The prof from Northeastern that we used to watch him in Austria. We're funding her research, if indirectly. A Dr. O'Keefe."

"Yes, O'Keefe. When he traveled to Boston with his brother, as we reported, he contacted her. But they slipped out of sight. When we reestablished contact, we only had eyes on Ed Dekker. We couldn't locate O'Keefe."

"Our oversight. We should have filled you in on the Mexico angle."

"Given their history, is she still your asset? People do go native."

"That's always a possibility," said the chairman. "We put her there long before any of this started. After Austria, we let our understanding with her lapse. Now we need to reestablish contact."

"What could the Dekkers do?"

"We need peace and quiet at our experimental station. Something tells me that's not in the Dekkers' plans."

"Without having the complete picture, it will be hard for us to react."

"Need to know, need to know," replied the chairman. "But good point. I want a team down there ASAP. Distract him, trip him up, whatever's necessary. If I can't get O'Keefe to cooperate, you'll have to treat her as collateral damage."

"Oetz was a stretch. Operating overseas requires planning. This could take a week."

"You'll have men there by tomorrow. Or is that more than you can handle? If you'd done the job in Boston, or New York, this would no longer be a problem."

"Knowing all the players would have helped." Jagger's posture was rigid.

"Let's move on. It's still possible we can use Dr. O'Keefe. I'll get the Conservancy on this. Fortunately, we have resources here at hand." The chairman hit a button on his desk. "Evelyne. Get David in here." Within minutes his security chief had joined them.

"I was telling Jagger, I need a half a dozen men en route to Mexico by tomorrow. But discreetly. You, David, will assist in all ways required. And Jagger, you know how sensitive the Mexicans can be, so tread carefully. We can get your team down there to our research station in a company plane. We'll see that the flight plans show a routine resupply. Your team will beef up security at the station and neutralize the Dekkers. I've heard Mexico can be a dangerous place."

"I understand," said Jagger.

"Work together, and contact me directly with any news." He called his secretary in again. "Evelyne will give you operational cash and make the flight arrangements for tomorrow. Make this work."

Jagger stifled an impulse to salute. Loping after Luff and the secretary, he went to the outer office where she handed him an envelope of cash. As he left, he wished he'd taped the conversation. 'Neutralize?' These guys always try for wiggle room.

Evelyne, a mature, striking woman in her early fifties, returned to the large office and placed a folder on the chairman's desk. It contained Dr. O'Keefe's vita, her grant application to the Tropical Conservancy, her report from Austria, and a transcript of her talk there. There was also a record of her on-going communication with Northeastern's office of sponsored research.

As his secretary stood by, Untermeyer leafed through the file, idly running his hand from her shoulder down her back. "We need to get this under control." Then he turned in his seat and looked out over St. Louis.

Chapter Forty-Eight

THE SAN RAFAEL CELEBRATIONS began with a parade of the saint's statue around the small village of El Encanto. Stern and imposing, he looked down on the crowd from a platform held aloft by the saint's *cofradia*, or brotherhood. The town band led the way with drums and trumpets, the players an enthusiastic mix of high-schoolers and grandfathers. Two boys at the head of the procession held paper mache globes on ten foot poles, dipping them up and down. Formally-dressed towns-peo   ple trailed behind, the women carrying flowers. When the procession reached the stone church in the plaza, the priest led the saint down the aisle to a place by the alter, followed by the women who placed their flowers in gleaming receptacles. Candlelight made the old stone walls glow. When the mass began, Ed and Manuel made their way outside, leaving Aisling, Leslie, and Audrey kneeling. Manuel led the way through empty streets to a small park. A half hour later Bart and Francisco joined them.

"We worked out a plan," said the former soldier. "With the music and commotion from the fiesta, no one will realize we're missing while Aisling and the girls will be surrounded by witnesses. First, Manuel and Francisco will locate themselves in the trees with their boom box and send out bursts of jaguar sounds."

Francisco huffed and panted dramatically.

"He tells me it doesn't have to be loud to still drive the dogs crazy.

They'll also treat some leaves with this stuff." He held up a couple of small bottles with sponge tops. "It's lion piss."

Ed looked confused.

"They tell me growers here use it to deter critters from ravaging their crops—deer, peccary, especially howler monkeys. Big game hunters also use it but they aren't supposed to. Francisco applies it around the camp here to protect the plant enclosures. It has a pheromone that attracts the female and sends a message to other males to back off. Smaller animals skedaddle." He gave one of the bottles to Manuel. "This isn't actually from jaguars though. Probably African lions."

"So, your big idea is to attract love-struck female lions?" said Ed.

"Francisco says there are very few around here, what with all the human activity. It's been over a year since he's seen any signs."

"Absence of evidence isn't evidence of absence. How'd you get this stuff?"

"Zoos collect it as a side venture and it's sold as a nontoxic predator control. In the States they use fox piss. Same idea. While you two do your thing in the woods, Ed and I will slip into the greenhouses and take what we can." Francisco was whispering in Manuel's ear, translating. Then they both nodded.

"It's in and out in fifteen minutes."

Fifteen means thirty, Ed thought. "And the lights and cameras?"

"We've got those ponchos in camo pattern we picked up in San Cristóbal. The dogs will pull the guards toward the woods and the fake jaguar, giving us our opening."

"But not to forget," said Francisco, "the greenhouses use grow lights, up until midnight."

"We can't wait for midnight if we're using the carnival for cover," said Ed.

"Yeah. It's a risk," said Bart, "but lights will let us see what we're doing."

"While we're totally exposed."

"Francisco says the walls are not really transparent," his brother went on, "more like translucent. Think waxed paper. Our silhouettes will be a problem, but if we keep below the tables, we should be okay. Plus, most of the guards will be at the fiesta." Bart rubbed his hands together. "So, any questions?"

"Yeah," said Ed. "How do we get out?"

"Got that covered," responded his brother. "We arrive in the camp truck and leave it at this fork in the road." He'd unfolded the map and now touched a spot half a mile from the experiment station. "From here we walk. Manuel and Francisco will head into the trees while you and I stick to the road so we don't get lost. When we see the gate, we cut into the trees as well, and circle around the landing field to the back side. We leave the same way. We regroup at the truck and hightail it. If we're lucky, it will be morning before the guards even know we were there."

"'If we're lucky' is the operative phrase. But hey, sounds ironclad to me." Ed sighed.

They walked to the truck where Francisco had left it and drove over to the campsite. It was too early to move out, so they sat around a large pot of beans, onions, and peppers that Aisling and the girls had left simmering on coals. They spooned it onto tortillas and ate. Beer would have gone down well and there was some in a cooler, but it seemed best to stay sharp. Towns in this part of Mexico, Aisling had explained, were split on the issue of alcohol. Communities that sympathized with the Zapatistas or had turned Pentecostal avoided even beer. Much to the relief of Aisling and her students, El Encanto was old-school and liquor, like fireworks, was integral to community celebrations. Which was another reason for the guards to be at the fiesta.

At 10 o'clock they rubbed soot on their faces and the backs of their hands. After loading their gear into the old pickup, they headed down a dirt track under a canopy of trees. Francisco and Manuel had repaired the muffler that afternoon, patching a rust hole and making it halfway quiet.

At a shoulder they pulled over into dense brush and got out. As it cooled, the engine ticked loudly. Then jungle sounds returned: cicadas and frogs low down, howler monkeys in the tree tops. Bats flitted past their heads, vacuuming up insects attracted to human body heat.

Time to set off. Ed and Bart tucked slack backpacks under their ponchos and set off down the rutted lane. Manuel and Francisco followed, then peeled off into the trees. Ten minutes later, the station's gatehouse came into view. Holding a pen light in his teeth, Bart confirmed their location on the map and they veered left to circle the pasture runway.

Lit by a quarter moon, the landing strip was light grey against the black wall of trees. Stepping carefully, the Dekkers slipped away from the gate. The guard had a radio on. "Another bit of luck," Bart whispered. With Ed stumbling on tree roots and once hitting his head on a limb, they eventually reached the top of the runway where they made the turn to the far side of the encampment.

Now they were back in dense woodland. Ed tried to mimic his brother's steps, slithering over downed tree trunks and trying not to shake branches. The huge root systems of the ceiba were leg traps. At one point, liana vines grabbed at Ed's face, feeling like serpents. It took a total of twenty minutes before they were finally in position. Some forty feet away, the greenhouses glowed under rows of full spectrum fluorescents. To the side was the sheet metal building Francisco had identified as the bunkhouse and office. Yard lights lit up much of the grounds but no one seemed to be on patrol. There was no smell of cigarettes, no voices. All that could be heard was the thrum and screech of the jungle, intermixed with the dull throb of a generator.

Bart gestured for them to crouch down. Then they heard it, a snuffling exhalation and guttural growl.

"Jesus," whispered Ed. "That better be *our* tiger!"

"Shush."

Barks exploded from the office and a man restraining two German shepherds on leads burst from the doorway, the dogs dragging him toward the front gate. Bending low, the brothers lipped under a low point in the fence and ran for the nearest greenhouse through pools of light, their capes flapping. They'd been prepared to slash the fabric to gain entry but the door, a flimsy affair, had no lock. Fortunately, it faced away from the gate. Raised platforms on either side of a central aisle held plants grouped and labeled by type. Others clung from trellises that reached nearly to the ceiling. Half the tables were empty while others had seedlings in various stages of growth. Bags of fertilizer and other soil amendments were piled at the far end while hoses stretched in the mud down the central aisle. The smell was pungent.

They split up, Ed taking the left and Bart the right, snipping cuttings from each plant variety and tucking them into ziplock baggies which they labeled according to lettering on sticks attached to the shelf edges. When this proved too slow, they began tucking the sticks in with the cuttings. One wall was lined with seed canisters labeled in English and Latin. They grabbed samples from each, shaking them into sandwich bags. They wanted to get everything but the variety seemed overwhelming. And having to crouch and duck walk was painful.. Ten minutes passed in what seemed five. They kept brushing away the humidity, or sweat, that ran into their eyes.

At the end of the structure were stacks of gallon containers. The Dekkers sloshed samples into small plastic bottles, spilling more than they took, and jotting down information from the labels. As a precaution, they photographed the canisters with their cell phones. They couldn't have done this in the dark. All the while, the guard dogs bayed and what seemed to be two guards shouted back and forth.

Already they were behind schedule when they moved on to the second greenhouse. It was also unlocked but by now, their packs were bulging.

"Don't crush the samples," hissed Ed as they worked their way between a second set of tables. Before they'd made it half-way, their packs could not be closed.

"Wait a minute," said Bart. He dropped his backpack and ran bent-backed to the first enclosure, returning with two black plastic bags. "Poor man's luggage," he said, handing one to Ed. By the end of the row they resembled hunchbacks carrying laundry. Now thirty-eight minutes had elapsed, all the while the sound of barking continued. The guards were slashing at foliage with machetes and firing occasional shots. They'd evidently left the compound and entered the woods.

Suddenly, the greenhouse lights went out. Ed glanced at the florescent dial on this watch; exactly midnight. Then the sound of dogs grew closer. Perhaps they'd given up or decided to prioritize defending the greenhouses? Barking gave way to whimpers and flashlight beams played across the outside of the hothouse fabric. The guards voices were very close. Bart couldn't remember if he'd closed the door. Then, very close to the flimsy plastic wall, a shot rang out.

"Go, go, go!" hissed Bart. "They're coming in." A flashlight beam fell on the door in front of them. "No, under the table!"

Rolling beneath the flats to the side of the enclosure, Bart flipped open his knife and slashed at the fabric, opening a three-foot tear. He pushed the two trash bags through and pulled Ed after him. Reaching into his jacket, Bart took out a roll of tape, ripped it with his teeth, and sealed up the cut in the tent. By now the guards were making their way down the interior corridor, pulled by the snarling dogs. Ed pointed to the gate. "Too far," said Bart. Instead he pushed his brother toward the bunk house. Its door was ajar. Just before he followed his brother inside, Bart emptied his jar of lion urine.

Inside, Ed took out his flashlight and began scanning the shelves. "These are the fucking grow manuals," He whispered, holding a stapled set of pages, then stuffing it inside his shirt.

Meanwhile the dogs had become hysterical and the men were

screaming at them. While the door faced the last greenhouse, there was an open window on the opposite side. They pushed their bags outside and wriggled through, landing on coarse grass. The question was, which way to run?

"Decision time," said Bart. "In thirty seconds they'll cut the dogs loose but there may be a guard still at the gate." The exit was sixty feet away, bleached in flood lights.

"It's men over dogs," said Ed. "Go!" Clutching the trash bags, they ran for the gate and the road beyond. As they passed through the fence line, automatic weapons opened up behind them, sounding like rocks tossed on a tin roof. The gatehouse window shattered.

"Why aren't we dead?" thought Ed. Then they were fifty feet down the road where it began to curve, giving them cover.

"The guard must have been drawn from his post by all the commotion. An amateur," said Bart.

"And we're not? Well, me, anyway. But Jesus Christ, we're ruining these plants." Ed loosened his grip on the black plastic. Bart was many steps ahead when more shots sounded and a tree limb exploded to Ed's right, showering him with leaves.

When the road turned more sharply, the gunfire became random shots into the darkness. If the dogs had been cut loose, they never left the property. A thousand yards and five minutes later, the Dekkers saw the truck backing toward them. Manuel was at the wheel, Francisco standing on the bed. He caught the bags and packs as they threw them up and pulled the brothers over the tailgate. When he pounded on the cab roof, Manuel ground the gears and the truck jolted forward.

"So much for not being noticed," said Ed.

With the headlights off, Manuel could only creep along. For the next fifteen minutes, the three in the truck bed faced backward and looked for signs of pursuit. The road behind was black. As they sprawled down, finally catching their breath, tree leaves suddenly glowed with light, then became brighter. Francisco pounded on the cab roof shouting *"Ellos están viniendo. Mas rapido!"* Instead of picking up speed, the truck swerved to a stop just short of a fork in the road.

"What are you doing?" yelled Ed in English. But Manuel was already out from behind the wheel, untying a spike-laden plank from the side of the truck. He lay it across the track and bounded back into the cab. Just as a vehicle came into sight behind them, their truck lurched off.

"Qué, mi hermano!" said Francisco, grinning. "This is risky because the community uses the road. We'll have to get someone to remove it later."

There were no more signs of the guards behind them. Daring to finally use their own headlights, they were quickly able to reach Aisling's camp. Rather than stop, the truck kept going. Soon they were on pavement and a half hour after that, they pulled into the yard of a truck repair operation on a back street of Las Margaritas.

Chapter Forty-Nine

ED AND BART HOPPED down, their legs aching. Francisco pointed them to an outside trough where they could clean their faces. Then, working together, they laid out the plants on the ground beside a worn Datsun. They'd brought the brothers' belongings with them on the assumption that they'd have to either leave the area or lay low far from Aisling's encampment. When they'd emptied the truck, Francisco put a crate with half a dozen chickens into the back. Then Manuel said a hasty goodbye, revved the engine, and lumbered off toward El Encanto.

"He has to return the truck. It wouldn't make it to Oaxaca anyway. These chickens are in case they stop him, but they won't. If anyone saw us tearing out of there, they'll keep quiet, at least to strangers." Francisco's grin lit the darkness.

"What happens next?" asked Ed.

"It's all been arranged while you were in Neverland this afternoon," answered Bart, socking his brother playfully on the shoulder. "There will be an argument at the fiesta. It's probably started already." He looked at his watch. "The village cops will lock up one of the workers from the agricultural station. His friends will protest, they'll be disarmed if that's necessary, and held. With the saint duly honored and returned to the church, the entire community will march to the greenhouses and rip them to shreds. The issue will be the death of their bees, something that never took place before outsiders came with their noxious plants and chemicals. The prisoners will be detained for at least a day until police arrive from Las Margaritas. Faced with the entire town, people shouting and holding up devastated bee hives, the municipal police will not be able to arrest anyone. This will be too small an incident to justify the army. But if the soldiers do come, that will take another day. By then, the research station will be destroyed and every plant uprooted."

"And Aisling and the girls?"

"They'll have gone back to their own camp before the ruckus. Foreigners can't participate in demonstrations in Mexico. There's no point in them risking arrest."

"And the town can give them an alibi for the break-in?" said Ed. "Clever, as long as people cooperate."

"It's all arranged." He patted Francisco on the shoulder. "The community decided it was time for direct action. They did us a favor by waiting until we had our evidence."

The cloud of diesel exhaust from the truck had dissipated. "So we have a day's grace, maybe two, until someone comes after us." Ed looked relieved.

"Not really," said Francisco. "We leave tonight. There's still the guards, and with our roads, the trip will be very long."

Bart picked up the regional map. "The Pan American Highway could get us to Oaxaca but it's partly a toll road. And remember what Aisling told us yesterday? There are soldiers at the booths. If the word went out to stop us, we'd be sunk."

"Not too surprising, the military presence, I mean. This is the cocaine highway up from Columbia after all," said Ed.

"Exactly. *El calle de cocaína,*" said Francisco. "So for much of this, we'll be on local roads, avoiding the towns. It will take fourteen hours to Ciudad Oaxaca, maybe more." He wiggled his hands palm-down in the more-or-less gesture.

"You've figured this all out, you two," said Ed.

"Not just us. Aisling, as well," replied Bart. "She called her contact at the Oaxaca clinic again about the DNA analysis. If we can keep our samples alive, this woman can run them through her system to make a chromosome record."

"Why not just spray them with Roundup and see what stays alive? Which would be the mutants," said Bart.

"Unfortunately, herbicide resistance isn't our focus here."

"So, we need to get moving, 'hell for leather' as we say in Texas."

Ed looked dubious. "Fourteen hours in a hot car? I'm not worried about us but the plants. And we're entirely in the hands of Aisling's friend as far as locating this terminator splice."

"She says it's possible to find the whatever by tracing the marker genes," said Bart. "You're the scientist, bro. I trust you to get this right. And look at the funny side. We're smuggling hot broccoli on the cocaine highway!"

Ed raised his eyebrows. "We're going to need Aisling eventually when we're comparing these killer tomatoes with the standard variety. I didn't like her saying she's stuck here."

"One bridge at a time. Once we record the mutations, it's going to be very attractive for her to stay involved."

"Can't argue with that," said Ed. Then he looked over at Francisco who was leaning into the hood of the Datsun wiping oil off the dip stick. Ed lowered his voice. "You're talking like you're on her team. I thought you had doubts."

"She's taking risks." Bart shrugged. "Just like we are."

Ed absorbed that. Apparently, she and his brother had come to terms.

"There's something else," said Bart. "She says there's cryptic notes on the margins of Hammersmith's papers, the ones you gave her. They may help her friend in Oaxaca spot the changes."

"Everything helps. Still, I wish she were along to smooth things out at that end." He looked at the plants. Some of the leaves had already wilted.

Francisco brought over a flat stack of cardboard. He'd clearly been listening. "They can't dry out. We must..." he clenched his fingers open and closed.

"Mist them," said Ed. "I figured that."

"I'll get food and extra gas," continued Francisco. After he stood there a moment, Ed handed him a pile of bills.

"With the peso worth about a nickel, this won't go far," Ed said. He was searching his wallet for more when Francisco said, "We're good!" and slipped away. The sun was a few hours from turning the sky pink.

Bart and Ed arranged the plants by type, setting those they'd uprooted back in wet potting soil from a bag they'd removed from the truck. They used a perforated tin can to wet everything down.

A half hour later they had a stack of plants layered in cardboard and covered with plastic. Fitting it all into the back seat and the Datsun's trunk was the challenge. "I'm worried about ventilation. And where are you going to sit?" said Ed.

"Hey, whose got the longer legs?" Bart stretched out. "I ride shotgun, bro. We'll get you in somehow. Think of all this as airbags."

Ed spread out the road map out on the car's hood. "It's cool here in the highlands, but that won't last when we get to Juchitán de Zaragoza on the coast. We'll have to stop and air things out from time to time."

"What I'm not clear about is why Aisling needed us," said Ed. "Sure, she might want me to write a credible article exposing what's going on here. But if the community was going to march on the research station anyway, couldn't she get her own samples in the confusion? And that would solve the community's problems with honey production."

"I asked her that," said Bart. "She said civil protests come and go all the time. Who's to say other test plots wouldn't open in the next munici-pality? According to her, ripping up plants and blocking a few roads isn't a permanent fix. And scientific papers can take years to get into print. She needs your exposé to kick over the garbage."

Ed gave Bart a baleful look. "But she'll still be facing Big Gen. Why hasn't she blown the whistle up the line to the Tropical Conservancy? It has to be that she doesn't trust them."

"You're the one that told me the Conservancy is hand in glove with Naturtek. Can you blame her?"

"I suppose not. And Northeastern?"

"What about it?"

"I wouldn't count on us having access to their labs. We're not the funders they care about."

"She admits it will be a challenge. But if you can make this into a scandal, it opens doors."

"We better find a smoking gun."

"Oh, and she mentioned contacts at UNAM, the National University in Mexico City," said Bart. "She's going to share data with them. That way she can reach Mexican environmental groups who are already worried about the integrity of the national symbol, maize. Given a stink, the Mexican government could start pulling permits that allow genetically engineered crops."

At that point Francisco returned, a five gallon can of gasoline in one hand and a large paper bag in the other. "Tamales," he said, grinning. They topped up the Datsun and tied the half-full can to the rear bumper. "No point in stopping until we have to." Then he threw water onto the outside of the Datsun and scattered dust over it, including the side windows. "The fewer people that see you gringos, the better."

Chapter Fifty

AISLING'S PHONE BUZZED IN her pocket. It was a wonder she heard it through the sound of the brass band, the fireworks, the children laughing and shrieking, but her level of anxiety made her especially alert. She and Audrey were at the corner of the stone church and had turned down half a dozen invitations to dance from shy men, young and old. Leslie, practicing cultural immersion, was moving her shoulders and hips as she swayed across the plaza trailing a gaggle of boys in their early teens. The local dancers were more decorous. Couples maintained contact only with their eyes as they circled one another. Paper shades on the public lamps cast a warm glow on faces and a light breeze ruffled stings of pennants and the women's hair.

"Dr. O'Keefe" said an unfamiliar voice. "I'm sorry to be calling so late but this matter is rather urgent." It was clear from the music that the call hadn't awoken her.

"To whom am I speaking?" There was a number but no name on the window of her phone.

"I'm Terry Hollister. I assist Dr. Arthur Mody of Tropical Conservancy. I'm calling because, along with your project, we are funding a parallel initiative not far from your location near Las Margaritas. Like you, they too are studying pollination dynamics."

"I see," said Aisling, turning away from Audrey. "How can I help you?"

"There are two matters, actually. The first involves information we received some hours ago about an incursion into that facility involving a theft of materials and damage to greenhouses. Are you at all familiar with what I'm talking about?"

"An incursion? I did know there was some sort of operation set up early last summer but I haven't had contact with them. I'm told by the community that these people keep to themselves. But I was told that large greenhouse structures were erected. Other than that, I can't tell you anything."

"And the robbery tonight? What have you heard?"

She lifted her phone toward the raised platform holding the band. "Can you hear that? The entire community is here for a celebration. It's been going on since the afternoon. There's been no talk about a robbery. I can see the two vigilance committee officers—what you'd call the police—and they're casually wandering around. There's no sign of any disturbance."

"I suspect there soon will be. But let me move on to another matter. You recall that while you attended the Global Sustainability Conference, you carried out a small task for Dr. Mody, specifically profiling the journalistic intentions of one Edward Dekker."

Aisling's tone was flat. "It was requested by someone named Lustig, I believe, but no matter. Yes, I recall."

"Likely Mody's deputy. And we remain grateful for your help, Dr. O'Keefe. It is unfortunate that in a highly politicized field like environmental innovations, it has become necessary to track the news media in ways that were once unnecessary. You do understand our concern?"

The past is never the past, she thought. "To be frank, this was well beyond my skill set. I never understood why you'd want me to monitor a newspaper writer whose work eventually goes public anyway. But not to belabor that, I certainly do recall the..." She paused, "the assignment."

"As you say, 'eventually' is the operative word. But we desired foreknowledge, especially if it turned out he was prejudiced against modern environmental initiatives."

He was smooth, Aisling had to grant him that.

"Well, it seems our Mr. Dekker has turned up again, and where he might be disruptive."

"Oh?"

"Yes, in Chiapas. In fact, we've traced him to San Cristóbal, your back yard. Has he contacted you?"

"Contacted me? Why would he do that? We were acquainted for a time in Austria, but then went in quite separate directions." Did he know about her contract with the *Business Chronicle*?

"You may have intended that, but we don't think Mr. Dekker shares your resolve. In fact, we have reason to believe he's searching for you, accompanied by his brother. You have met his brother?"

"Why would I know his brother? I'm confused."

"Well, long story short, we'd like to know if he's vacationing or on assignment. You could help us make that determination."

"Well, he's certainly not here in El Encanto, where I am. It's a very small community. I'd know."

"I'm sure you would." There was a lengthy pause. "Should he arrive there, we want you to call us at this number. We suspect that he was involved in the disruption at our research installation at the El Bravo ranch, the one I mentioned."

"You're saying he's involved in a criminal act? All I can tell you is that the man I met, at TC's request, was a respectable journalist working for a reputable newspaper. Could you be misinformed?"

"This surprises you? Don't be fooled. In my experience, the press will go to any length to get a story, by fair means or foul. He's a loose cannon, a sensationalist not above stirring up a scandal to make himself some sort of environmental hero. That, in fact, was why we'd marked him at Oetz as a person of interest. Believe me, Aisling—may I call you Aisling? — he's up to no good."

"As this is a business call, I prefer Dr. O'Keefe, if you don't mind Mr. Hollister."

"Well, of course. Nonetheless, we want you to call us immediately if Dekker contacts you. Is that clearly understood?"

"Indeed it is, Mr. Hollister." She broke the connection, almost throwing her phone to the ground.

"Who was that?" asked Audrey.

"Our funders. They've traced the Dekkers here. They want me to bird-dog them, turn them in."

"If you see them?" replied Audrey, smiling slyly.

"I'll certainly keep my eyes open."

Just then two pickup trucks filled with armed men roared to the edge of the square. Four figures in black uniforms jumped to the ground along with an equal number of men in overalls and tee shirts. They made a circle around the vehicles. The men in black held AK-47s at port arms, the others batons, and they stood immobile in a wide stance. The music from the band died like a dropped accordion and laughter faded away. Then Edgar Jagger stepped from the cab.

"Who is in charge here?" he shouted. The soldier to his left repeated the question in Spanish. The crowd stared at the men. After a minute of silence, Jagger took out his pistol and fired three shots into the air.

"I said, who is in charge?" Now his voice was softer. The band stiffly held their instruments, the crowd stood in shocked silence.

Then four community notables stepped off the podium where they had been sitting, men with white hair and mahogany skin, and approached. They wore ribbon-ringed hats and held elaborate walking sticks. The oldest, wearing a black wool vest even on this warm night, took the lead and stopped within a few feet of Jagger.

"Those with guns are not welcome here," he said in English. "Whoever you are, get in your trucks and leave."

Jagger sized him up and put his pistol back in its holster. "Well, now that we've established who's the big enchilada, let's do business. Who busted up our camp?"

406

"Your camp?" said the *cacique*. "Nothing here is yours." He gestured with open arms, encompassing the plaza, the fields, perhaps the entire valley.

"Your people broke into our establishment and stole important material. Valuable material. I am here to get it back." The crowd, meanwhile, started moving forward in small steps, pressing closer to the circle of armed men.

"When did this happen?" asked the be-ribboned elder.

"This evening, just before our plane touched down. And yours is the nearest village. You did it or you know who did."

"You may be unfamiliar with our way of life, *señor*, but today is when we honor our patron saint, San Rafael. We have been in celebration since mass this morning. We are not thieves and we have nothing of yours. It is you who are the—may I say—barbarians." He gestured to their weapons. "Those are not permitted here. Again, I tell you, leave." The crowd took a collective step closer.

Jagger hesitated. At least two hundred people now surrounded his men. No one seemed furtive or guilty. He'd clearly interrupted a festival. He turned to the driver of the truck and they held a brief conversation. Abruptly he backhanded the driver across the face.

Turning to the village leader, Jagger bowed his head briefly. "My apologies, *señor*. It seems we had erroneous information. Please continue with your—your party." He gave a forced smile. "But let us be clear. If you hear of these thieves you will detain them and send word to the research station. Is that clear?"

The cacique simply stared at him, silently. After a moment, Jagger drew a circle in the air with a pointed finger and his men returned to their trucks. Jagger himself was the last to board. The trucks revved their engines several times before the crowd gave way and made room for them to leave.

Rather than head back to the greenhouses, the force followed GPS coordinates to Aisling O'Keefe's encampment. With her as well as Audrey, Leslie, and Manuel in El Encanto, the site was deserted. After kicking over some tables and searching the tents, Jagger's men headed back toward the Naturtek installation.

"There was no sign of Dekker in the town or at O'Keefe's set up," said Jagger into his phone as they bounced down the jungle track. "We've spotted no material from the research plots in either place. Whatever happened doesn't seem to have involved the community, which was eating and dancing when we arrived."

"You questioned the head man?" said David Luff, speaking by satellite from St. Louis.

"The guy's a hundred years old," said Jagger. "I don't see him involved in any of this, not directly anyway."

"All right. Here's what you do. Work with the crew there and carry out an inventory. We need to know what was taken, every seed and seedling. I want that done starting now."

"I just learned from the workers here that six of your employees spent the evening at the party in that town. We didn't realize that when we got here or we'd have taken them back. As of now, they're unaccounted for."

"Send a vehicle back to the town and find them. If they're drunk, slap them sober. I want a full report by seven AM. No, wait. As for you, drive personally to the police station in Las Margaritas. It's maybe thirty kilometers away. Do not, I repeat, do not wave weapons. I'll send you the written agreement between us and the Mexican State Department. They're well informed about this in Las Margaritas. But remind the chief of police about that, with the proper degree of controlled outrage." There was a moment of yelling on Luff's end while his staff located the right document. "Talk to a Major José Maldonado. Tell him what happened and insist the Dekkers be put on whatever fugitive list they have down there. And have him notify the army. You have photos?"

"I have photos, a stack of them. Problem is, I don't speak the lingo."

"Take Luís Filipe with you, the site manager. He can translate. Remind Major Maldonado that certain gratuities changed hands. We want what we paid for."

"No guns?"

"No. Follow Luís Filipe's lead. There's a certain protocol down there. You don't embarrass officials in public or talk down to them. But in private, convey our serious concern about the attack and this Dekker business."

"Should I ask the police to investigate the break-in? Maybe there's evidence—fingerprints, something on the CCTV."

"Let's keep this in-house as much as we can. Check the videos yourself. My guess is Dekker and his brother did this themselves and wore gloves. I wouldn't be surprised if they wore Guy Fawkes masks."

It took Jagger a moment to remember that these were masks worn by demonstrators during the Occupy Wall Street protests. "And if they are detained by the police?"

"Have the Dekkers turned over to you. Suggest that's the simplest thing for all concerned, including the Major. Less paperwork. Imply another gratuity. Then bury them in the fucking jungle. Do I make myself clear?"

"Completely."

As soon as the trucks left the village, Aisling walked over to the *cacique* and they talked briefly. He thought of himself as the *alcalde*—the mayor—but Aisling had come to think of him as having more than electoral power. The band, having lost its audience, was packing up. With unsteady legs, the *alcalde* remounted the dignitaries' platform from which he'd watched the fiesta. He waited for the last few conversations to cease.

"Our dignity has been violated," he said in Spanish, his voice echoing as if in a great hall. "First, they poison our land. Then they release diseased plants. As if in a horror movie, our crops wither. The springs on which we depend for life have become acrid. The insects, the least among us, die. Our bees die. Even the bats drop from the sky. Are we not the keepers of the forest?" He slowly raised an arm toward the trees beyond the plaza. "What should we do?"

There was a long moment of silence. Then a girl of about eight raised her head. "March to this devil camp and destroy it!" If she continued to speak, no one heard it because there was a huge outcry of support. The *alcalde* banged on the wooden platform with his staff. "Let this be done."

Within minutes a dozen pickup trucks arrived from edges of the plaza and those who could fit climbed aboard. Even the community's rusted school bus was fired up. Slowly, the vehicles set off. Still, there wasn't enough transportation. With a roar, a hundred others set out on foot behind the vehicles carrying torches and chanting. Moving through the jungle, the caravan was a glowing line of army ants.

As they proceeded, young people jumped to the ground from the trucks, making places for those too tired or too old to continue walking. Or, in some cases, too drunk. The procession took more than an hour to reach the Naturtek site. By then Jagger and the mercenaries had left for Las Margaritas, leaving only a few laborers and two armed men. As the crowd pushed aside the lowered gate at the compound's entrance, the employees ran at them shouting and the soldiers fired into the air. The crowd did not pause. Within minutes two hundred people occupied the landing strip.

Standing at the rear of the crowd, Aisling and her research team watched as the *alcalde* climbed down from one of the trucks. Walking stiffly and leaning on his stick, he advanced on the Naturtek crew.

"We will leave you that plane," he pointed to the prop plane parked at the end of the landing strip, "so that you can depart for the sky. We are reclaiming everything else. You have ten minutes to gather your personal belongings. Then we will clean this camp."

Though armed with automatic weapons, the few mercenaries were leaderless and confused. They faced a sea of people, most with empty hands but some holding rocks, sticks, or machetes. A man in a lab coat was the first to turn away and head for the bunk house. The rest of the crew followed. Minutes later they reappeared with duffel bags and suitcases. The *alcalde* pointed to the Cessna 421 parked on the runway. "Go." The guards, rifles now slung on their backs and carrying their luggage, joined the research workers and walked to the plane.

As they gathered around it, unsure of their next move because the landing strip was choked with people, the elder pointed at the installations—the greenhouses, the office building, a storage shed, a truck parked next to a petroleum tank. In complete silence, the community fanned out and systematically dismantled the entire camp. Then running a hose from the fuel tank, they sprayed the rubble and ignited it. In a whoosh, flames shot up forty feet.

It took more than an hour for the fires to die down. All the while the crowd watched while the employees and mercenaries huddled around the plane in a defensive formation. It was their way out and they weren't going to give it up. With the camp reduced to glowing ashes, the *alcalde* got into his truck and the procession reversed direction.

Chapter Fifty-One

WORKING WITH A MAP and what Francisco knew of farm roads, the three criss-crossed down from the highlands. Four hours later they could see the lights of Tuxtla in the valley ahead. "This should be a one-hour trip," said Francisco.

"Better safe than sorry," replied Bart.

"I can't get over what those jaguar sounds did to the dogs." Francisco, behind the wheel, began to laugh. "Thanks to God they were on leads. Otherwise..." He grabbed his throat and pretended to choke.

"Yes, it was amazing," said Ed. "A stunt, but amazing. You gave us a clear field."

"Well, almost," said Bart. Now they were all laughing.

Skirting the city, they passed through a succession of small towns. Sometimes they made good time on paved roads, at other points they maneuvered along rutted tracks. All the while the gas gauge fell but they didn't dare to pull into any of the Pemex stations. They were too well-illuminated and had cameras. When they had to, they parked at a distance and sent Francisco in on foot with the gas can.

Despite its beat-up appearance, the Datsun ran smoothly. At one roadside piss stop, Ed noticed the tread on the tires were new. After seven hours, Francisco had had enough. They pulled off onto a dirt track running through a field of sugar cane. It was now late morning and in the distance they could see hundreds of wind turbines. Cattle grazed beneath them. "You can't drive," he said to the brothers. "That would make it complicated if we were stopped. More complicated. But I have to rest."

While Francisco stretched out amid the sugar cane, Ed and Bart took turns on-watch. At one point an ox cart passed within twenty feet, the huge animals clomping and wheezing, the driver staring ahead equally indifferent. That woke up Francisco and he indicated it was time to divide up the tamales and pass around the last bottle of water. Ed, watching the ox cart disappear in the distance, said, "If I ignore the windmills, this could be 1910."

"A time of revolution," said Francisco.

"Of one kind or another." Ed licked his fingers. "What's with the wind generators?"

"A Spanish company put 'em up. The Isthmus is a natural wind corridor where colder air from the sea meets a valley running between two sets of mountains. A natural chute for the wind. The company leases space from the farmers."

"Which suits everyone?" said Bart, bringing on a questioning look on Francisco's face.

"Which suits the company. They pay landowners a pittance but if you have land they want, you can't refuse. It's government policy."

"We'd call it eminent domain," said Ed.

"The electricity goes into the grid, then south to Guatemala City and north to the capital. Here, *nada*." He sighed. "And look, every third one is stopped."

"Why's that?" asked Ed. "I feel the breeze." Sugar cane was rustling in waves.

"When they first started, maybe ten years ago, they didn't figure on salt in the atmosphere. It rusts things out. They changed the technology but still haven't replaced all the original turbines."

"Still, they must be making money. There are hundreds." To Ed it looked like a postmodern forest.

Francisco rubbed his hands on his pants and took a swig from the water bottle. "We have to get going before that cart driver gets to town."

"He saw us?" asked Ed.

"People here see everything," replied Francisco. "Will he think we're people smugglers, *narco traficantes,* or just three stupid guys too poor to rent a room? That's the question."

Francisco topped up the oil from a bottle stored under the front seat and turned on the engine. They made their way slowly back onto the paved road, a straight and flat highway at this point. They were approaching Juchitán, a railroad junction with a heavy police presence because migrants from Central America rode through on the roofs of trains. To be safe, the three headed east into the hills.

"Because of the mountains, all the rail lines converge here," explained Francisco. "That means people smugglers and the gangs that prey on them are active." Staying on local roads, they wound their way past cattle operations, village centers with little more than one-room grocery stores, a cement-walled school, and fields of dry corn stubble. The sun moved lower in the sky.

"So, tell us something about Afghanistan, bro. It will keep us awake."

Bart remained silent for a while. "Over there, we talked about home. Or lied about it. Now we're on this continent and you want to hear about over there? Okay, I'll tell you about Skeeter. He won't mind, at this point."

"Skeeter?" asked Ed.

"Everyone had a nickname. Some were carried over from high school like this one fellow from Alabama. He was famous for having pulled down his pants and pressing his ass against the window of a car he was in as it drove past the school principal."

"My guess he was called Moon."

"And still is. With Skeeter, the problem was bugs. He always seemed to be itching or scratching. Whether it was bed bugs or actual mosquitoes, if there were bugs around, they always found Skeeter. For a while, some in the squad called him Itchy but just saying the word made us all start to scratch so we settled on Skeeter."

"Smart move," said his brother.

"Skeeter never got mail, never lined up to use the overseas phones they set up for us, or the Skype system. Skype was really popular because guys were always getting their wives or girlfriends to flash their boobs. If you were respectful, they'd give you a peek."

"Respectful?"

"Keeping down the hooting and hollering so the conversation seemed private, at least to the girls."

"Got it."

"Skeeter was never on the phone or in the audience when someone else was Skyping. But what he did do was talk in his sleep. Well, not so much talk as mutter one word, over and over. 'Donna'. But since he was from Boston, it came out 'Danna'. He'd look miserable when he was having these dreams and once in a while you could see he had a woody."

"Woody?" asked Francisco. "Ah, *erección.*"

"Right. We'd ask him about Donna but he'd never say anything. Was she his wife, his girl? His sister? No one knew. There were no letters coming for him and he had no pictures taped to his rack. Over time we figured that she existed entirely in his imagination. She'd come to him in dreams but never close enough to touch. But she was real enough to be the relationship he prized. Weird, huh? Still, when you live so close to other guys that you smell their stink, you have to give them some space. Probably what happens in prison too, I expect."

"Let's hope we don't find out," said Ed. Francisco crossed himself.

"When it was clear Skeeter wasn't sharing, we left it alone. I mean, weren't we all a little fucked up?"

"Live and let live," said Ed.

"Poor choice of words. Skeeter was our specialist in defusing roadside bombs. I say 'specialist'. That meant he'd had a week's training at some point and his hands didn't shake. Usually we'd just shoot the fuckers till they exploded or it was clear they would never explode. But occasionally the lieutenant wanted to know what they were made of. Were they using our own ordinance as components? That sort of thing. Course they were usually disguised—a knapsack, a trash bag, even one time inside a dead donkey. So that made 'em tricky to spot. To cut to the chase, this one day we were slogging down a road near a village and we see this kid's school bag. Light blue with the 'Hello, Kitty' picture. I'll never forget. Course we were suspicious and stayed well away but the lieutenant, he sent in Skeeter to check it out. The guy's trying to lift the flap very carefully using a stick when the thing explodes. We're instantly deaf and covered with dust but Skeeter is blown across the road. When we get to him, his eyes are closed and he's bleeding from all over. Even his mouth." Bart took a breath. "All he says is, 'Tell Donna', and he passes out."

"Fuck," said Francisco, tightening his grip the wheel.

"So what'd you do?" asked Ed.

"They airlifted us back to base. Two of us had concussions and one was bleeding from his ears but hadn't realized it. Skeeter, of course, they hospitalized. Last I heard he was in at Ramstein Air Base in Germany, supposedly for rehab. A week later we're back together, absent Skeeter of course, and we're sitting there looking at his empty bunk. One of us closes his eyes and says, 'Donna, are you listening?'"

"Holy, fuck," says Francisco.

"Then we all have our eyes closed and we're saying, 'Donna, Donna'."

"She answer?" whispered Francisco after a minute of silence.

"Couldn't tell. Not to me, anyway."

One gas stop later they were high in the mountains again. A wide but shallow river lay far below. In the river elbows, houses clustered on alluvial flats between steep inclines, bridges were one-lane. Higher up, they passed through a succession of villages. Though it was evening, children and dogs were in the streets, reluctant to give way and then watching from the side of the road.

At three in the morning they began a descent into a long, central valley thirty miles outside of Oaxaca. A waxing moon hung in the sky, making the Sierra Juarez mountains a black mass. "People have been growing corn here for five thousand years," said Francisco, nodding toward the fields to his left. "You walk there, you kick up pottery shards and tiny figurines. See that hill? Over there? It seems like rock ledge and trees but if you look carefully, you'll see straight lines. It's ruins. The base of a pyramid? A temple? Who knows?"

Well away from Chiapas, they were now risking the newer highway. Farms and night-shuttered mescal distilleries gave way to darkened stores and auto-repair shops as they approached the city. Billboards advertised blue jeans, the light-skinned models provocatively tilting their hips. After another half hour, they turned back onto a side road and a street of ramshackle houses. Here construction and industrial operations merged and yard lights were absent. "It's the center city we have to worry about," said Francisco, yawning and slapping his cheeks to stay awake. There's a military base just ahead and you never can tell when they decide to strut around and harass the people with a check-point."

"I marked the clinic on the map." Bart pointed. "If we go through this area into the hills, we can approach from the north without actually going through the downtown. We've got to lay up for a couple of hours anyway. No clinic will open before eight. On the other hand, we need to get there before the clients line up."

Francisco was drunk with fatigue. He turned onto a narrow road in a newly-built residential quarter and stopped the car. Houses here crouched behind cement block walls that deepened the shadows on the street. "I'm going to sleep. Wake me in an hour." With that he slumped forward on the steering wheel and began to snore.

"Better piss now while it's dark," said Bart, quietly getting out of the car. They relieved themselves, then opened the trunk and for the fifth time dampened the plants with the sprinkler can. As they leaned on the car hood, Bart lit a cheroot. A dog barked nearby, followed by a dozen others, each with his own individual voice. In reverse order, they fell silent. The engine block stopped ticking.

"Time to touch base," Ed took out his phone and dialed Mona. It was an hour later in New York, but it still took a minute for her to pick up.

"My God, I'm glad to hear your voice," she said, passing fully into consciousness. "Things are heating up here. A bunch of lawyers visited Hardy's office yesterday. They threatened a restraining order against the paper if we continue to report on anything having to do with Naturtek's research initiatives. According to them, even mentioning their discoveries compromises patent applications. Furthermore, if we know anything about the Hammersmith killing and are holding back, they said we are obstructing justice."

"These were company lawyers?"

"Some, but a guy with bulgy eyes flashed some kind of badge and claimed to be from the FBI."

"You were in the room?"

"Of course."

"And Hardy buckled?"

"Hardy doesn't buckle. He had me taking notes but I was really there as another witness. He was as smooth as ice, suggested they acquaint themselves with the Constitution, especially the Fourth Amendment. He told them that 'reportage'—his word—of what's newsworthy is only a violation in their dreams."

"So he ran them out?"

"More or less. The *Chronicle's* lawyers were on their way—I'd called them. I expect this crew was trying a quick run up the middle before the varsity team hit the field. When they saw intimidation wasn't working, they hit the showers."

"You've been talking to Manny too much."

"Surprised 'ya, huh? What they actually said was they were headed up to see the publisher. But as you know, he's rarely in his office. Anyhow, he never called to ask what was happening. And he would have."

Ed was quiet for a time, considering the latest.

"I do have a question, though," she said. "What progress can I report to Hardy?"

"We've got plant samples and we're about to get them tested for genetic rearrangement. We've been on the road for what seems like days and now we're near our destination, waiting for it to open. I don't want to be more specific."

"I get it."

"I'll call tomorrow with any results."

Chapter Fifty-Two

It was now after 6 AM and people were on the street walking toward the stores and schools on the main road. The sun was just cresting the eastern mountains. Time to move. They woke Francisco and within a half hour they'd located the clinic, a white stucco building with modern lines in a hillside neighborhood of apartments and offices. They drove up a narrow driveway along one side of the building and parked in the back, half hidden by a dumpster. Francisco ambled down to the road to look around while the brothers remained in the car, watching. There was no sign of activity at the clinic. If possible, they needed to catch the director before her staff and any clients arrived. When a women in her forties with black hair tied in a bun approached the front steps, key in hand, Francisco cleared his throat.

"*Holà, doctora. Tenemos las plantas.*"

She turned and looked at him, not surprised or fearful but appraising. "And you are?"

"Francisco. From Las Margaritas. From *la doctora O'Keefe*. We are parked in the back.

"Give me a minute. I'll open the back entry." She keyed the front door and then locked it behind her. Lights came on in succession as she made her way through the building. Francisco retreated up the alley to where Ed and Bart were now standing, the trunk and doors of the car wide open. A flood light scattered the remaining shadows and a basement service door opened. The clinic director was now wearing a white lab coat, unbuttoned and reaching to her knees.

"Bring everything inside and lay it on the corridor floor. We have to figure out a system. Oh," she said, catching herself. "My name is Leonora. Dr. Leonora Zárate."

They shook her hand—more a touching of fingers than a hard, North American grip—and the men identified themselves. It was clear that Aisling had prepared Dr. Zárate. As they carried in the cardboard flats, they tried to put them in some sort of order.

"Is everything labeled?" she asked.

"We wrote down what we could," said Bart, "But we grabbed all this in a hurry. And I'm not sure we got all we need." Beyond the corridor was a basement room lit with florescent tubes. Tables in the middle of the room held grey machinery—a centrifuge, a microscope, an autoclave. Flat digital screens hung on the wall beside glass pipettes and retorts.

"I brought a few things down here," she said, gesturing to racks of test tubes. "The staff has been told to ignore us and the clients stay a floor above, but we'll have to keep down the noise and work quickly. Are any of you chemists or biologists?" The men looked at her blankly. "Any of you with laboratory experience?" She looked from one to the other, dismay growing on her face.

After a moment Ed said, "I was an undergraduate biology major. I know my way around a lab." Twenty years after the fact, that was stretching it. "But I've never done DNA testing. You'll have to show me." Ed wondered if he could shake himself awake enough to look at a slide.

"And I've ridden in ambulances holding an IV bottle," said Bart.

She shook her head and thrust a pad of paper toward them. "Write down everything I say and watch everything I do. We have limited room to work here so you, Francisco, can sit over there till I need you." She saw he was rubbing his eyes. "Actually, there's space on the floor in the back. Why don't you lie down?" He didn't have to be asked twice.

Leonora snipped leaves from the first tiny sample. "*Mangifera indica,* or mango," she said, looking more at the leaf than the words Ed had written in grease pencil on its plastic bag. "As a tree crop, this wouldn't have the same terminator characteristic that apply to single-season vegetables but for some reason, they were testing it. We're going to do SNP sequencing," she said.

"Meaning?" asked Ed.

"Meaning we'll look at the most relevant portion of the full genome, about one percent. Aisling sent me some lab notes that will help to zero in on the problematic areas."

"Those would be from this Hammersmith guy?" asked Ed.

"So I gathered. She couldn't do this sort of research under a tent in Chiapas. But her suggestions will help."

This didn't sound like the 'no results' she'd told the *Chronicle*, thought Ed. Maybe other things occurred to her later.

"We need to work while things are still fresh," the doctor said, her eyes passing over the pile of samples. To Ed, they looked like last week's celery. "Aisling has been a big help to us, referring patients with problematic pregnancies and collecting certain traditional herbs, so I don't mind helping. I'm used to working with amniotic fluid, but I think I can make the adjustment. With your help." She smiled tightly at Ed. Bart, a foot taller than she was, had to lean forward to catch her eye. "We run about a hundred neonatal tests a month. People here are very concerned about fetal malformation and Down syndrome. Then there's chemical contamination. Our authorities don't test the water supply the poor rely on, those trucks that work the barrios. Others are just trying for a male baby and wanting to know in the first twenty weeks, uh..." She raised her eyebrows.

"What's in the oven?" filled in Bart.

"Yes. We discourage that. Abortion for gender choice simply isn't ethical. But when we say this, sometimes the woman goes to some other clinic. I can give advice but I'm not the guardian of anyone else's soul." She fingered the cross around her neck.

"When there is evidence of Down syndrome, then?" asked Ed.

"We are realistic. If a fetus isn't fully viable, we offer abortion. We don't advertise—there's public sentiment against the procedure—but it is an option in maternal healthcare. But I don't have time to give you a full orientation to our services."

Ed backed away.

"Anyway, with Aisling's mapping information, later you can focus on specific areas of the genomic sequence most likely to have been altered. Now watch closely. You'll be doing this yourselves when I'm called away upstairs. Don't worry. It's a fairly automated procedure once the samples are properly prepared. First step: take the newest leaves and separate and concentrate the nucleotides. All life is the same double helix, just in different patterns."

While the brothers watched and Ed took notes, Leonora prepared a sample for nanopore sequencing on a machine the size of a college dorm refrigerator. "The limiting factor is microprocessor capacity. But we've had help from a philanthropic foundation here in the city so we have better-than-average machinery." She ground up a leaf sample in a hand mortar and added a clear distillate. With a steady hand, she transferred the result to a test tube using a rubber-tipped pipette. "I've already mixed a buffer solution," she explained, "but keep the bottle on this warm-ing pad. Then let the tube incubate in this rack. While that's going on, you can prepare the next sample but label everything." She picked up a kitchen timer. "In ten minutes, go back to the first and add what we'll call 'solution B'. It contains a form of chloroform so use it carefully. Just cover the sample, shake, centrifuge, then add this much isopropanol." She held her thumb and index finger a half inch apart.

She repeated the procedure with a sample from a different plant, placing the second test tube on the opposite side of a centrifuge. "Always equalize the weight in the centrifuge. If you don't, things fly apart." She grinned. "Actually, it's like a clothes dryer. You want everything balanced." She closed the lid and set it spinning. "Not what you'd see today in New York, but we've got at least one foot in the modern age."

"What can we do wrong?" Ed was feeling uncertain.

"Fail to balance the centrifuge? Inhale the chloroform?" said Bart, answering for her.

"Good." She flipped a switch and turned on an exhaust fan. "But the worst would be to foul up the labeling. You do that, and you'll have less than nothing."

She checked her watch and waited for ninety seconds while the centrifuge coasted to a stop. "That should do it. Now, for your part, Edward. You'll transfer a droplet of solution onto this chip." Using surgical gloves and a capillary tube, she placed a tiny drop at the center of a silicone chip that was, in turn, placed on a copper plate attached by thin wires to an oscilloscope. "What we have here is a very small hole, three nanometers wide. Don't bother to look; you can't see it. The strands of DNA will be enzymatically drawn through the hole but the A,G,C and T nucleotides travel at slightly different speeds. The machine registers this and records the reading digitally. The thing to remember is to wash the chip and the plate in acetone after each reading and rinse with distilled water. Big labs would discard the used chips but we can't afford that. Dry the chip with this aerosol." She pantomimed a repetition of the operation several times. "The reader is fast but fast in this case means about ten minutes.

She powered up the machine and they all watched. After what seemed an interminable delay, the screen displayed a multicolored graph and Dr. Zárete hit print. "The image tells us the sequence was isolated. This symbol confirms that our digital copy is good. If you get an error code, you'll have to repeat the procedure. Slow and accurate is better than fast and sloppy. There's an automatic electronic copy recorded as well. Now, once more, on your own." She stood aside, arms folded.

Bart prepared two samples in little conical test tubes. Zárete watched in silence which Ed took to mean there were no mistakes. They each did the operation again, then continued until the centrifuge was full. At one point, Ed's hand shook when he placed a tiny drop onto the nanopore slide and she made him clean the chip and repeat the operation. At the last moment he remembered to type in the label on the keypad wired to the reader.

"Keep the labels straight or you're giving false information."

Ed resisted the impulse to point to Bart's poor penmanship.

Before long, Dr. Zárete's cell phone rang and she climbed the stairs to the procedure rooms. The brothers paused and looked at each other. "It's not like we have a human patient here," said Bart.

"Just the fate of mankind," responded Ed.

"Right, Captain America." They'd gotten the technique down, if not exactly a rhythm. Keeping everything moving was crucial if they were going to get through it. Before long, Ed's neck seized up, giving him a headache. "Stop," he said, giving himself a brief massage. "Better slow and accurate."

While they could measure their progress in the number of baggies processed, they had no idea what the results meant.

Bart looked around the basement and found scraps of wood, using them to raise the height of the table. "Four inches makes a difference," he said, rolling his own neck muscles. Working together, they approximated an assembly line. After two hours, Leonora returned. She sighed at their progress. The pile of samples to be analyzed looked almost untouched. She'd brought three samples of amniotic fluid in micro tubes and she waved Ed and Bart to one side while she took over.

"If women think this test is pleasant before they arrive, they don't leave with that illusion," she said. "And it can be dangerous, piercing the abdominal wall with a syringe, then entering the uterus and tapping into the amniotic sac."

Ed pictured a syringe needle as big a pencil and winced. Was she deliberately grossing them out? Maybe it was a female thing to keep them on edge? It was a relief to return to plant tissue after she left.

The morning passed quickly, the specimens moving from cardboard trays into black trash bags for discard. Toward noon they woke Francisco and sent him out to watch the alley from behind the wheel of the Datsun. Bart assumed he'd fall back asleep, but that was okay. He needed it.

"Out of the way. These tests take precedence." Dr. Zárate was back. "Why don't you two take a walk for half an hour, get something to eat?" Ed nodded assent. His shoulders were stiff and he badly needed a break. Other than visits to a toilet tucked into a corner of the lab, they'd barely moved.

Francisco was sprawled across both front seats as they made their way past the car and down the driveway. Now the street was pulsing with traffic, the air blue with diesel exhaust. It was still the Pan American Highway but its two lanes in San Cristóbal had become six. Trucks and buses roared past apartment towers and a hospital complex, then geared down to climb a hill. Here and there the roofs of estates from the colonial past poked above limestone walls.

Turning away from the main thoroughfare, they followed cobbled backstreets through the historic district. Having looked at a city map, they were sure they'd be able to find their way back. They passed stone and adobe buildings, some with stucco peeling away, bushes growing from the top of their decaying walls. Crossing a plaza built around a dry fountain, they passed portions of an ancient aqueduct. Ed longed for a decent camera, not his simple iPhone. Further along, walls on either side rose up fourteen feet shielding the domes and crosses of religious cloisters, repurposed as schools and a major museum. Thinking they'd gone too far, they noticed a small restaurant and entered. To save time, they ordered eggs and beans with corn tortillas along with a take-away pizza.

426

Francisco would be hungry. They were finished and on second cups of coffee then the waiter brought the boxed pizza, warm to the touch and fragrant with onions and tomatoes.

Careful to keep the pizza level on the way back, Ed didn't notice two men in work clothes standing across the street from the clinic. Here the sidewalks were again crowded. As they turned up the narrow driveway to the back of the clinic, they heard running footsteps from behind.

"Ed," Bart shouted. Whirling around, Ed saw a man holding a sap above his head and threw the pizza. Like a disk, it caught him full in the face. Startled, the stout figure reared back, his free hand defending his nose and eyes. Ed moved in with a left and a right to the man's stomach. He was back in the gym, pummeling a canvas bag. The guy crumpled and smashed his head on the pavement. Bart in the meantime, was using his forearms to fend off an attack from a second man. Instead of backing away, he then lunged at the assailant, hitting him squarely in the face. Blinking away blood, the man backed down the driveway and turned to run.

Ed's man was now doubled over, knees on the ground. Grabbing him by the back of the neck, Bart patted down his pockets and retrieved a revolver. Then he dragged him upright and pushed him after his partner. In seconds, both were gone. Ed shook out his hands. This was only the second time he'd hit a living opponent.

At that point Francisco opened the car door with a bang and ran toward them holding a tire iron. "Jesus, was there a fight?"

"All over now, but no problem. They're gone. I'm only sorry we didn't break a couple of arms." Bart, too, was flushed and breathing heavily. "Or clavicles. They're easier to snap and they put a guy out of commission for just as long."

"We call the cops?" asked Ed.

"No, never," said Francisco. "Even if we weren't fugitives, the police wouldn't do anything. They'd get in our business and want something for themselves."

"He's right," said Bart. "Besides, Leonora wouldn't want the attention."

"And we don't have the time," said Ed. "It's just as well they got away. I doubt they'll try to mug any more tourists."

"Muggers be damned," said his brother. You saw how they were dressed—overalls, but clean and new with good shoes, not boots. And jumping two good sized and reasonably sober males? No, they were looking for us."

"They followed us?" asked Ed. "From downtown?"

"From Chiapas," his brother answered.

The three looked at each other.

"How?" asked Francisco. "No one was behind us on the roads. We'd have seen them."

"Then they got into Dr. Zárate's phone and knew where we were headed," said Bart. He got the inflection in the doctor's name correct this time. "Why the hell don't people just write letters?"

"Let's get back to work," said Ed. "Now we have even less time. Oh, and Francisco, sorry about your pizza." The container, folded down the middle but still closed, lay on the cement.

"Maybe I can salvage something."

"Stay here and watch the street while you eat, Francisco," said Bart. They found the door unlocked.

"You handled yourself okay," said Bart as they stood side-by-side at the bench again, their arms moving in a coordinated sequence. He raised his fist and Ed gave it a knock. The doctor was somewhere upstairs.

"Yeah, well, we keep this up, I'll be a contender. We say anything to Dr. Zárate?"

"Your call, bro."

"Do you figure they have a tap on her phone?"

"No. The surveillance must have originated at Aisling's end. With the doctor's number, it wouldn't be hard to work back to her address. My guess is that Guardian Services, or whoever is strong-arming it for Naturtek, must have been in a rush and hired pickup talent locally.

"Still, a goon squad. You think they'll try again?"

"They have to know that now we're armed. They'll be cautious." Bart nodded toward the table where he'd put the revolver.

"I phoned Mona this morning. Could that be the leak?"

"It could have confirmed our general location," said Bart. "You say where we were headed?"

"Of course not. But we were already in the city and I said we had plant samples."

"Let it all hang out, eh?"

"The paper's bankrolling us. I wanted to show we were making progress. And to let them know where we are."

"And now they do," said Bart. "But don't beat yourself up. If they'd jacked Mona's phone, they'd have done the same with Aisling. Anything new there?"

"Naturtek's lawyers are crawling all over the paper. They want a cease-and-desist on anything related to their company's research. So far, Hardy is telling them to go fuck themselves." Just then Leonora clattered down the stairs.

"Jesus!" She pronounced it 'Hey-soos'. "We have five nurses working upstairs coaching these mothers on nutrition and hygiene, but they still expect me to be a fortune teller!" She blew out noisily through her lips. "Babies have come into the world since time began."

"You do deliveries?" Ed asked.

"Mostly we link up with midwives for home births. If we expect problems, we try and get them here. Then if there's something we can't handle, the municipal hospital is down the street. Enough about my problems, how far have you gotten?"

She began to check the paper readouts, muttering to herself, then looked over at Bart grinding a mortar and pestle. "Stop, don't make such large samples. You're not making guacamole."

"We had a problem while you were gone," said Ed, feeling the need to come clean. "Two muggers in the alley. We persuaded them to leave but they could come back."

"We don't have muggers here," said Leonora, turning to stare at him, "You saw the video cameras in the driveway, right? And even the worst *ladrones* don't go after pregnant women." Her eyebrows went up. "You were followed."

"Not from Chiapas," said Bart, "but they still locked onto us. We think that when you and Aisling talked, they traced your location." She should know that her communications could be monitored.

Leonora looked pensive. "We did talk, several times. And Aisling was clear about the possible risk in doing this." She gestured to the benches. "Still, I didn't think anything would happen." Then she rubbed her hands together and looked at the unprocessed plants on the floor, maybe half the initial pile. "What's in those bottles?"

"We think pesticides," said Bart. "There were gallon containers in their greenhouses. See, they have an acrid smell." He held one out.

"We're not set up to test chemicals. But I can send them somewhere else. Are they labeled?"

"I copied down what I could."

She drummed her fingers on the bench, then snapped them. "So, we continue."

"Even if they regroup, they'll need to assemble a bigger squad," said Bart, "We should have a few more hours."

At that point the alley door opened and they all wheeled around. It was Francisco. "Nothing out there so far."

"You mentioned CCTV cameras? Where are the monitors?" asked Bart.

"The cameras are fake," said Leonora, taking in a breath. "There's no monitors. They're for deterrence only."

"Most are," said Bart. "We have one pistol. Took it off one of the thugs."

The doctor held up open hands, shaking her head in disbelief.

"Francisco." Bart turned to the young man. "Watch from that window over there. You can see the alley. But first, give me a hand."

They dragged a heavy bench over to the basement door. "Just when we need something in steel, eh?" he said to Ed. "Leonora. It would be best if you stayed upstairs. Is the front entrance locked? And can you close early?"

"I'll have the receptionist turn away anyone new but we have several examinations in progress with an equal number of women in the waiting room. I can't send them home."

"No?" said Bart.

"No," she replied. "People come long distances for sonograms and fluid tests. Some need counseling for diabetes. I'm not stopping my work for yours." She shoved her hands deeply into the patch pockets of her lab coat.

"Okay," said Ed. "Do what you have to do. We'll get through as much as we can down here. And Francisco?" The young man looked over from where he was standing at a curtained cellar window. "*Cuidado.*"

Chapter Fifty-Three

THINGS PROGRESSED IN AN orderly way for the next several hours as the light outside faded. By unspoken agreement, they were forgoing dinner. Bit-by-bit, the foot traffic over their heads lessened. With Leonora returning to work the equipment from time-to-time, Ed was able to transfer the accumulated data to a flash drive and photograph each of the samples using his cell phone. As further insurance, he wrote the sample numbers in a school notebook he'd found on one of the shelves. Bart continued to dissolve leaves and take pipette specimens, never moving more than a few feet from the revolver. He'd broken it down and reassembled it, an old Colt with six cartridges. Big, certainly. Serviceable, maybe.

"What's the plan if they come at us?" asked Ed, now shifting specimens from centrifuge to spectrometer. Leonora had gone upstairs.

"Maybe I should start to pack up. Better we leave with something than try for it all and get cornered. I'm ahead of you anyway." He'd laid out a dozen samples in pipettes.

"Francisco! You awake?" Bart called over. The young man had pulled up a chair and propped himself against the wall. His eyes had been glued to a crack in the curtain.

"*Es cierto!*"

Another ten minutes passed. "Say we have to abandon the car or get separated," said Ed. "We need a fallback."

"The bus station," called out Francisco from across the room.

"Eventually we'll have to risk that but let's wait," responded Bart. "We passed a McDonald's on the way in. There was a parking area in the back with outside tables. If we get split up, I say we rally there once it gets dark."

"It already is," replied Ed.

"Darker, then. Which brings us to finances," said Bart. "How much money do we have?"

Ed emptied his pockets. "More than enough for a Big Mac. I have the pesos I got in San Cristóbal, minus food and gas. But to get far, we'll need to hit another ATM."

"So, in real money?" asked Bart.

"A little more than five hundred."

Adding to the piles, Bart laid out his own stacks of hundred peso bills and nodded toward Francisco. Then he crossed the room and handed a bundle to their driver. "You'll need gas going back, and this is for your time. It ain't generous, but that's all we have at the moment."

"That's cool." Francisco stuck the thick wad in his pocket, uncounted. "What you're doing, this is for us, too."

Just then there were footsteps on the wooden staircase and Dr. Zárate's legs came into view, then her yellow skirt and white coat. "We've had to do an abortion. With an aspirator, it's a simple procedure when everything goes well but the woman needs to recover for at least an hour. I've sent most of the other staff home but I can't close up until," she looked at her watch, "at least eight."

Ed looked at this watch as if expecting a different time.

"It's been five hours since we were assaulted," said his brother. "That's long enough for their plan B to go into operation. With a plane, they could even have gotten up here from El Encanto."

"I love Aisling and what she's doing, but I can't have our clinic firebombed." Leonora looked around at the equipment. "We are too important to the women here. And this kind of trouble, it wasn't what I expected."

As she stood with her hands jammed into her jacket pockets, her eyes were drawn to the shifting patterns of chromosome on two flat screens. "I hope this tells you what's clipped and cut."

"You've been incredibly generous and I know we've outworn our welcome. I don't know how to thank you." Ed looked at dozens of samples still waiting analysis and shrugged.

"All right. Finish a few more. It's past seven. Once it is fully dark, you must leave. I'm going back up to keep an eye on things."

As they hurried to finish up what they could, Ed asked Francisco if there was a FedEx in the city and would it still be open.

"Yes. The shopping center. Stores are open late there, maybe till nine."

"What are you thinking?" said Bart.

"We need to get this into different hands. I say we ask Francisco to find a copy shop, make up packets of what we have along with Aisling's printouts, and send it all to Mona and Manny. Maybe to your address in D.C."

"Not to my apartment. They'll have found that. But I have Elizabeth's work address, a law office on K Street. Sounds innocent, right? I can email her what to expect. I have to say, big brother, you're cottoning on to the tradecraft."

"That's a good idea," said the clinic director. She'd come down the stairs. "I should have suggested it." She was wearing slippers and they hadn't heard her. "Everyone is gone. I've dimmed the lights. I could copy things onto micro-drives but we don't have any. I suggest the Walmart in the shopping center."

Bart made a how-about-that expression.

"Yes, we have a Walmart," she said.

"And a McDonalds," said Bart. "We noticed. This work for you, Francisco?"

"I'll take the car," said the young man. "Shouldn't take long, traffic is light now," said the doctor.

"We're cleaning up here," said Bart, tucking the discarded plants into a plastic trash bag. Ed moved the bench blocking the door and Francisco slipped out. Then the Datsun roared to life.

"As I see it, we scatter. Francisco back to Chiapas while you and I catch a bus to Mexico City," said Bart. "There, we lose ourselves in the crowd, catch different flights. Then, in a week or so, you'll have your article in print and the heat will be off."

"Talk about deadline pressure." Ed trembled his hands. "Mona gave me a corporate card from the *Chronicle*. For emergencies. It's smarter to buy our tickets with that than my Mastercard." If it wasn't maxed out already, Ed thought. "Speaking of ATMs…" he handed Dr. Zárate a second pile of cash.

She paused, then accepted it. "I'm going to consider this a clinic donation. Half the procedures we do are gratis, what you people call pro bono. The rest are 'low bono', so keeping the lights on is always a struggle." She inclined her head, thanking him.

"No, the gratitude is all ours," said Bart. "You've run a risk and we've tied up your lab for a day. And probably given you an ulcer."

As they waited for Francisco to return, they ran a couple more samples, then bagged the refuse. "It would be better if there was a light on upstairs and maybe a radio," said Bart. "It would let people on the street think there's activity going on."

She nodded and mounted the wooden stairs.

Chapter Fifty-Four

THE CESSNA 421, OVERLOADED by half, barely cleared the trees at the end of the runway. Climbing above the mountains, it turned north. The fact that the tanks were two-thirds empty helped with liftoff. When Jagger returned from Las Margaritas, he'd found the research station reduced to charred rubble. Collecting the jailed workers from El Encanto was complicated but still reasonably fast. They'd had to shoot a village dog to emphasize their seriousness. But after having wrecked the greenhouse operation, the town's people expected much worse. In the end, two company employees were never found. Jagger had better luck locating a drum of aviation fuel. They'd had to send a truck back to Las Margaritas and bargain with a guy who clearly ran a smuggling route. It was a seller's market for fuel, but it wasn't Jagger's money.

As the plane leveled off, Edgar Jagger made a long-delayed call to the chairman. He explained that they'd had problems with some local authorities and that two of their employees couldn't be found. And that was the least of it. In evicting them, the townspeople had burned the installation. While they'd recovered a few plant specimens, nearly everything was lost. There were, however, some books of data that the lab head had managed to carry out in his luggage.

The chairman was initially less concerned than Jagger feared. "We have other test plots," he said. "We've been uploading data daily so the loss isn't irreversible." Then his voice deepened. "But this is still a disaster. Your disaster. I'm aware of the robbery at the facility, which, it seems, you were hesitant to mention." The Chairman waited for an excuse from Jagger that didn't come. "The Dekkers will have been behind this. Find them."

Jagger explained that the on-site crew wasn't sure. Two men did break in and cart away sacks of specimens. But that happened at night and the camera footage was hazy. The guards on duty knew Jagger's team was on its way and waited before they searched beyond the immediate area, which slowed down the response. Jagger didn't mentioned the jaguar.

"And you're telling me this a day later?"

"Secure ground communications there went up in the fire. I did call Luff but I didn't want to risk making a conventional cell call to you. It seemed wise to wait until we were airborne and could use the coms in the plane."

"Jesus, what a clusterfuck." The chairman was silent for a minute of static and dead air.

"At that point, I got back to Guardian," continued Jagger. "They've captured cell calls from O'Keefe to a clinic in Oaxaca City, including content. It's clear she and the Dekkers are working together and plan some sort of analysis of what they stole from you." Jagger hoped this news might placate his employer.

"The company assigned a local crew in Oaxaca to disrupt that process and snatch the Dekkers. Unfortunately, this effort was not successful. However, we're on the way now with a professional team and your employees from the research station. TOA Oaxaca City is 7:45, in twenty-two minutes." Assuming we have the av-fuel, he said to himself.

After telling Jagger to hold, the chairman broke contact, then came back on line. "We've made arrangements for you to land at Oaxaca City and refuel for Houston. Paperwork's waiting for you at the terminal. Explain you are on a thru flight from Guatemala and suspect an oil line problem—a pressure gauge, whatever. You need parts and you've located a supplier downtown. Then take four members of the security detail into town. There will be a van waiting. As an in-transit flight with temporary mechanical issues, you won't have to go through customs if most of you stay with the plane. I take it you have a location for the Dekkers?"

"I do."

"While the others fuss with the plane, you will retrieve our property. Worst case, destroy it, along with our miscreant friends. As far as anything official goes, you've never been in Mexico. But stay off the police radar. Understood?"

"Completely."

"Do you have eyes on the Dekkers?"

"They're in some kind of clinic. What we believe to be their vehicle is there, so chances are, they're inside."

"Chances are? Christ. I don't have much choice but to rely on you at this point, but you are on thin ice. Get the job done."

"And if Dr. O'Keefe is there?"

"If she's there, she's as much your target as the Dekkers."

"In that case, the fee will have to be renegotiated."

"Considering the loss of our research facility while you were on the ground there, I would say so. But you won't like the terms."

Chapter Fifty-Five

"What about O'Keefe?" asked Lustig, the head of legal and one of a small group at the table in Mangus Untermeyer's conference room. Outside, the last of the sun had set to the west.

"I had hopes for this woman, but it seems she's tainted," said the chairman. "She spent too much time with Dekker. When was the last we heard from her?" He was addressing Janet Woodruff from public relations but Marvin Lustig jumped in.

"We had Mody's office at Tropical Conservancy call her. The idea was to see if she'd continue to keep tabs on Dekker—we knew he was down there—or would she dummy up."

"A test?"

"She denied she'd seen him, which wasn't credible given her arrangement with the Oaxaca clinic. While feigning cooperation with us, she was deceptive."

"We did ask her to establish the relationship in the first place," said the chairman. "Perhaps the fault is partially ours."

"Her cell positioned her near Las Margaritas when Mody's man talked with her. For the Dekkers to be in Oaxaca City now, they must have been well on the road at that point." He doodled a time line on the pad in front of him. "While she's staying at arm's length, I suspect it's to salvage her reputation with us."

"Jagger will be on the ground soon." The chairman looked at his watch. "It's just as well that Dr. O'Keefe isn't caught in the crossfire. Let's hope the Guardian team pulls up its socks. They have their own reputation to repair."

"The mistake we made—and I share the blame—was to see her as our collaborator." Janet Woodruff sounded disappointed. "When the results she expected from her own study were disrupted, she blamed us and cracked."

"It was a calculated risk," said John Kim. "We knew from Hammersmith that pollination problems were possible. Though she didn't know it, she was actually our watchdog."

"A double-blind?" Woodruff couldn't suppress her surprise.

"It was a double-blind," said Kim. "To make her analysis more objective."

"Problem is, she was too objective and called in the Dekkers," said Lustig.

"No risk, no reward," said the chairman. "So, we course-correct."

John Kim looked alarmed.

"No, no Dr. Kim. I don't mean we cancel this initiative. But it may be necessary to arrange another field test."

"Our research site in Honduras could do that," responded Kim. "Similar tropical environment, equally remote."

"And the government is, if anything, even more pliable," said Lustig.

"Can you handle the details, John?" The chairman smiled.

"Absolutely, sir. We can use the manifest and design we created for Mexico."

"Still, this will cause some delay," said Mitch Kotz. "We in marketing will have to rethink the schedule, which could be a concern for investors."

"I agree with Mitch." Woodruff was piling on. "Marvin has been point man on this and, to speak bluntly, he dropped the ball." She tried to sound regretful.

"Now just a minute here..." Marvin Lustig was on his feet.

The chairman cut him off. "What's done is done. A salvage operation is underway. We can ramp up initial production even as we evaluate what we've learned from Mexico. If need be, we can bury the EPA in paper. I don't see a great deal of time lost. And we have two months until our next quarterly report."

"We can continue to say truthfully that we have tremendous innovations in the pipeline," said Kotz. "But these things take time."

"Sounds weak," shot Woodruff.

"We're working in the third world, here," continued the marketing man. "Not the tightest lines of communication. Investors will be patient."

"Assuming this is just a speed bump," muttered Woodruff just loud enough for everyone to hear."

"No matter. As my dad used to say, 'That's why they put erasers on pencils.'" Untermeyer chuckled. "Please help yourselves to refreshments."

Chapter Fifty-Six

"I'M FEELING ANXIOUS," SAID Leonora. Francisco had yet to return with the zip drives.

"What do you suggest?" responded Ed.

"That's just the thing, I don't know." She crossed over to a basement window and peeked out. "Okay, ten more minutes. Then you leave. Go to the McDonald's with your laptop. I'll send your companion along when he gets here. But for now we can load the data onto your computer." She connected Ed's laptop to the laboratory drive and completed the download. "You now have one digital copy. When Francisco gets here, I'll transfer everything to the zips and he can take you to the FedEx. I want you out in five minutes." She went back upstairs.

They packed their bags, including a selection of plant specimens and small jars of the chemicals from the greenhouses and the seeds they'd never gotten to. "Can't have too much insurance," said Ed. "Maybe something will survive the trip north."

Bart looked at his watch, then tucked the revolver in his belt.

"Let's have Leonora make one additional copy," said Ed. "I'll mail it to Janet Malcolm at Earth Defense."

Leonora was back, cradling a cup of tea. "I told Aisling that I'd give her whatever we found so take this." She handed over a manila envelope. "I'm donating our last zip drive. She deserves to be in the loop and she's got as much to lose as the rest of us."

Just then there was a rapping at the door. "It's me, Francisco." It was clear he'd been running. Bart removed the bench and cracked open the door letting their driver slip inside.

"There's a van illegally parked across the street." He handed a bag to Ed. "I noticed it when I returned so I parked two blocks over on a side street," he pointed to his left. "Then I cut back here through a couple of yards. Fuckin' dogs almost got me."

Dr. Zárete had taken the bag of drives and was plugging one at a time into her server. "We're ready," she said, a few minutes later, handing them to Ed.

"This is it," said Bart, edging open the door. They hugged Leonora. Unsure of how this was done in Mexico, Bart gave her a kiss on the ear. "All set?" He turned to go out.

At that moment, the half-open door burst in, knocking him to a sitting position on the floor. A figure in a black ski mask filled the doorway. Without a moment's thought, Bart pulled the pistol from his waistband and fired; the figure staggered backward into the alley, his hands on his throat. Bart kicked the door shut and jammed the bench under the latch.

Francisco stood gaping until Ed grabbed him and they rolled together toward the back wall, kicking over a table so that it faced the door. Bart dove to the side taking Leonora with him as a machine pistol stitched a constellation across the door at belly height. A computer terminal on the far wall exploded.

"Go!" screamed Bart, motioning all three toward the stairs. At that moment the glass in a side window shattered and the muzzle of a machine pistol poked inside. Bart fired again and there was a scream. The pistol clattered to the floor inside and Ed made a dive for it.

Before anyone could climb the stairs, there was an explosion and the door flew off its hinges. Deafened by the blast and still on his knees, Bart put two shots into the knees of a figure standing there, avoiding the chest area that might be armored. The man toppled backward, his weapon clattering to the ground. As he tottered, Bart leaped up and gripped him in a bear hug, moving out into the alley and shooting a third man in the shoulder. A fourth, backpedaling near the end of the driveway near the front door, opened up with a Mac 10. The spray of lead hit his human shield but one bullet caught Bart in the thigh. Spinning, he fell to the ground, half inside and half exposed to fire from the mouth of the alley. Ed grabbed his brother by the shoulders and dragged him fully into the room. Then he crouched low and opened up with the captured machine pistol, emptying the clip in seconds. By this time Francisco had darted out and collected Bart's pistol.

"Hold your fire!" rasped Bart. "Make them come to you!"

Figures were retreating down the alley, firing intermittently over their shoulders. One clutched his arm, two others were limp and being dragged. And being shields as well, thought Ed. Within seconds, the melee was over except for the smell of cordite filling the alley. Spent cartridges rolled toward the street.

Francisco lay prone in the doorway, peeking around the door jam and pointing a pistol. Ed now leaned over his brother. Taking off her lab coat, Leonora pushed him aside and pressed it against Bart's wound.

"Take off your belt! Tie it high on his leg, make a tourniquet. There!" She pointed to Bart's groin. "And Francisco, keep watching!" The young man gripped the weapon with two hands, aiming it down the alley.

Ed cinched his belt around his brother's leg, stemming what had been a steady flow of blood. "Not arterial, thank God," said Leonora. "But we have to get him to a hospital." He was lying in a crimson puddle. At that moment his eyes fluttered closed.

Ed found his voice. "I'll go for the car."

"No," said Francisco. "I know where it is." He handed the warm revolver to Ed to cover the alley while he darted around the back of the building and disappeared over a fence. Bart's head was now cradled in Leonora's lap. Her yellow skirt, the folded lab coat, the blood—it was a scene in lurid technicolor.

Leonora slapped Bart's face. "Wake up! Move your toes so I can see if there's nerve damage. And Ed, hold him steady. I've got to find something sterile." She got to her feet and ran upstairs. Her lacerated knees were visible beneath the skirt, smeared with her own blood.

What had he gotten his brother into? Gotten them all into?

In seconds she clattered back down holding bandages. "The police will be here any minute," she said. "Help wrap this wound." Using scissors, she cut away Bart's trouser leg. "We need to get him out of here. And your bags. We can't have done all this for nothing."

Just then the Datsun roared up the alley in reverse. The three of them got Bart onto the back seat without bending his knee and threw the bags into the trunk.

"Go right a few blocks to the general hospital. I'll go with you." Leonora glanced at the door, shattered and bullet-riddled. "We have to leave all this."

With Francisco leaning on the horn, they moved out of the alley and took a sharp right on the boulevard. In minutes they were at the emergency entrance to the city hospital and Bart was on a gurney being pushed inside by attendants. "I'll get him seen right away," said Leonora. "They know me here." She turned to face Ed and Francisco. "I want you out of the city, now. Once Bart is admitted, I'll return to the clinic and deal with the police." She took a deep breath, her jaw set.

"This was a robbery gone bad, *ladrones* after drugs. There's no reason for you two to be involved." She paused. "Bart is a friend, visiting. He disarmed one assailant, took their gun, sent them off, but not before wounding him and shooting up…" She waved her hand as if she were back in the alley. "My door."

Ed moved to follow the gurney but Leonora blocked him. "There's nothing you can do. I have some influence here. Give me a cell phone number. You must get this data back to the States. I'll phone you with, well, whatever happens."

Ed still hesitated.

"If you are involved with police, they'll hold you until they sort this out. Always someone must be blamed. You'll do your brother no good in jail." She'd pushed Ed toward the car. "I must go."

Taking her by the shoulders, Ed felt she was made of wood. Then he reluctantly let her go and watched her disappear into the hospital lobby.

The next he knew, he was sitting beside Francisco as they drove past the pedestrians and vendors who choked the emergency room driveway. On the main road, they continued north.

"What now?" asked Francisco. "The FedEx?" Surprisingly, with all that had happened, it was still only eight forty-five.

"Yes. We can make it. Then drop me at the bus station. After that, go to Chiapas. You'll have to be careful but after this debacle, the bad guys will be on the run as well. I can't see them sticking around. You should be okay on the road."

As they turned toward the shopping center, they saw a river of pulsing blue and red lights behind them; police cruisers closing off the Pan American Highway. "Go, go, go!" yelled Ed.

Francisco handled the mailing at the Fed Ex but once back at the car, refused to drive off. "You don't know your way around, *gringo*. You'll be spotted, sure." They both took in the blood on Ed's shirt from where he'd lain beside his brother.

"Can't be helped," said Ed. "But let's consolidate everything into one backpack. I'll carry it in my arms to sort of hide my shirt."

"That's crazy. Wait here." Francisco ran into the shopping center. Though on the verge of closing, lights were still on. In a few minutes he returned with a shirt and pants. "Always room for one more customer. I guessed your size. Me plus two." Francisco grinned. "You were looking a bit dirty anyway, no?" Ed leaned behind the open car door and wrestled into the new clothes while Francisco stuffed printouts and plastic-covered plants into a single knapsack. They left the bloody clothes in a waste bin. No one in the near-empty parking lot seemed to notice.

"Jesus, what have I done?" Now that the immediate tasks were done, Ed was paralyzed.

"¡Calmate!" said Francisco. "Think it through." He put his hand on Ed's shoulder. "Once the cops put things together, they'll come for you next. And you got no place to hide. And money? I saw what you have. You need to get on that bus and I have to head south. Now."

"There's an ATM," said Ed. They could see a lighted kiosk at the end of the parking lot. "I do need money, and this may be my last chance to get it." Francisco circled the car around and they stopped in front of the cash machine. Ed fished out his corporate card and sprinted to the terminal, well-lighted and with a conspicuous camera. A minute later he returned with 4,000 pesos.

"You've just given them your location."

"It's the newspaper's card. But they'll put two and two together, the bad guys at least." He handed the driver half his sheaf of bills. "We can't short you. Now, let me off at the square in the old part of town. I was here once before. There are grubby hostels. Someone with a backpack won't raise eyebrows. And here's a micro drive for Aisling."

They rumbled over stone paving blocks, skirting the Zócolo, a tree-lined park in the historic district, and headed for the industrial quarter. Shops were closed, the traffic light. Events up on the Pan American Highway had drawn in all the cops. Francisco slowed to the curb.

"If she wants to call me, have her use someone else's cell."

"Aisling has to know they're on to her. But staying here, it's a big risk, compañero." He shook his head. "But this is as far as I go. Unless you want to see Chiapas again." Now Ed was out the door, leaning into the window, his backpack beside him. "Love you, man! Stick to the back streets. Cuidado!" They bumped fists. Francisco pulled out and Ed stepped into the shadow of a street tree; sirens tore up the night.

Chapter Fifty-Seven

WITH EMERGENCY VEHICLES CONVERGING on the clinic, the team members still standing had barely made it to the van and then the airport. Fueled and pre-cleared for takeoff, they were in the air within ten minutes of the shootout. Their local contractors were told to torch the vehicle. It was probably too bloody to clean but he knew they'd try to salvage it. Jagger's mind went over the operation's checklist. At least he'd left no bodies, no dental work to trace, no personal identification. Guardian would see the wounded were patched up. Or disposed of. And the weapons they'd left behind? All anonymous, scrubbed of any identification numbers.

Okay. He'd failed. Nothing in Mexico had gone well. Still, Missouri, at least, had been a clean operation and the investigation at MIT was permanently stalled. Or so he was told. Could you call it a draw? That fucker, Bart Dekker! He'd anticipated body armor and shot around it. After Cambridge, they'd profiled him and knew he was an Afghanistan hand. But the bosses had focused on the middle-aged reporter, not the burnt-out vet.

I may as well change planes and just keep going, thought Jagger, now somewhere above the Gulf and headed for Texas. Maybe divert to Dulles.

"What a clusterfuck." Two of his men lay wounded on the floor of the Cessna. Another had died in flight. Beyond antiseptic powder and bandages, there wasn't much he could do for them. The other passengers, employees from the research station, crowded together at the back, too horrified to speak. Of course to divert this baby, he'd have to put a gun to the pilot's head. The plane rumbled on.

The plane made an altitude adjustment. What did he have to show for it? No computer drives, no records, no prisoner to question. And the problem players were still out there. His career was truly in the shit. All he could say in defense was he'd left no one to rot in a Mexican jail.

As Ed expected, there was a backpacker hostel on the next block. He'd remembered the location from the coffee trip years earlier. The lobby was deserted. He tapped a stationary bell on the counter and a girl who looked about twelve took his money, gave him a key. Then a second key to the hall bathroom. He climbed the stairs, found his door, and collapsed on a hard mattress with his bag for a pillow.

He had to think things through. He'd go to the clinic at first light, but watch it from across the street. It would still be closed as a crime scene, that's for sure, but Leonora would be there. Hell, the place was shot open. She'd tell him where Bart was, how he was doing. He closed his eyes on an image of his brother's wound. Thank God not a head wound or a gut shot. Bart was conscious, at least to start with. And no spray of arterial blood. Leonora had stabilized him. And the hospital on Avenida Chapultepec? They'd gotten him there fast. If he'd been attended to quickly, he'd survive. He had to.

Ed felt something hard beneath his head, his cellphone in a pocket of his bag. He could call Mona but what would he say? She'd have to make arrangements for the paper to cover the medical bills; line of duty and all that. Would Bart need a credit card to even be admitted? No. Leonora had that covered. Be best if his brother's name was kept out of it but that wouldn't be possible. Hospitals couldn't sit on a gunshot wound. But there was no point in panicking. He closed his eyes again. The mattress smelled dank, musty.

There was rapping on the door and a female voice. "Ten o'clock. You leave now or pay another day!" Ed stumbled to the door and handed the girl two hundred pesos. The sign had said less but that's what she'd demanded last night. Jesus, 10 a.m.! Time to move.

After he showered in a moldy stall, he left nothing in the room he cared about—just a thin wet towel. He spread a few papers on the bed to confirm that he'd be back, then walked north, keeping an eye out for a cheap restaurant. Eat when you can was Bart's motto. The memory of yesterday's meal was painful. They'd become a team. It was almost like they were kids again, shooting hoops and bouncing insults.

From across the busy roadway, he saw that the alley was blocked off with tape and a movable barrier. A black and white SUV was parked in the drive. Figures were passing in and out of the basement door, smoking, talking. A sign on the clinic's front door said *"Cerrado."* His appetite disappeared.

Downing one cup of take-out coffee after another, he passed by the clinic every half hour for the rest of the morning. By noon, the cruiser was gone but the barrier remained. By two in the afternoon, he was out of ideas on how to approach Leonora. Aisling would know the doctor's cell number. But then again, wasn't that connection suspect?

Just then someone tapped him on the shoulder, Dr. Zárete in an oversized sweater and dark glasses. "Follow me." They continued down the block, then down another toward the bus station. There was a cafeteria there and they found a table. Service was from a counter and no one bothered them.

"Your brother is in a private clinic. The care is better. The police will have to question him. If I just made him disappear, how could I account for the blood, the bullet holes?" She gave him a grim smile. "He's up the hill in Colonia Reforma."

"The police know where he is?"

"A private ambulance took him there this morning but they had an okay from the police. I rode along, made sure everything was processed."

"He's okay?"

"I'd say he's stable. He's had three units of blood and they had to sew up some large veins. He's got a drain and they're keeping an eye out for infection. They did a good job with the suturing, worked from the deep muscles out to the surface of the skin. There's internal damage and there'll be a serious scar. Two, actually."

Ed winced. "The bullet passed right through?"

She nodded.

"But he's awake?"

"In and out, yes. But that's a good thing. If the shot had hit bone, the trauma would be much worse and it's unlikely he'd be conscious."

"I need to see him."

"You need to go home." Then she sighed with resignation. "Perhaps this is best. As I said, it is a private clinic. You'll need to come up with a valid credit card or I'll have to move him out soon. We're off the public medical system."

"I have one," said Ed. He hoped the newspaper's card was still good. What would she have done if he hadn't shown up?

The hospital was on the mountainous edge of the city. It was small, more a boutique hotel. Corridors were carpeted and art hung on the walls. The head of surgery took them into Bart's private room overlooking the city below. They found Bart glancing at a wrestling magazine, the cover featuring chubby men in masks and tights. "Someday I want to see one of these matches live," he said, as if he'd expected them. "Just to watch good triumph over evil."

"How's it feel this afternoon?" asked the surgeon.

"Aches and itches."

"Itching is good. You want a lot of surface feeling. It shows good circulation and nerve connections." The doctor's complexion was brown but he had no Spanish accent. Probably educated in the States, thought Ed.

"In a few days, we start you with rehab, walking a treadmill. We can't have your tendons tightening up. And exercise will help drain the wound."

"Whatever you say, doc. You've met my comrade, Dr. Zárete. And this is my brother, Ed." Bart gestured with his hand.

"I did have the pleasure of meeting Dr. Zárete when you were admitted, though I don't believe you were awake. They gave you a sedative at the city hospital. It's good to see your mental faculties have returned." He faced Leonora. "My pleasure, again." Then he shook Ed's hand. "I'm Dr. Eduardo Castro."

"I don't know what arrangements you've made for billing, but I have a corporate credit card here that should cover things. I don't want Dr. Zárete to end up with any expenses."

"We'll take care of this at the desk," said Dr. Castro. He looked over Bart's dressing and checked his chart. "Now I must continue my rounds. Bartholomew, I'll check in with you later. And Mr. Ed Dekker, why don't we meet downstairs in half an hour to settle the paper work?"

"Fine," said Ed, checking his watch. Castro departed on silent, rubber-soled shoes.

"The *Chronicle* will stick by you on this," said Ed, gesturing to Bart's leg. "I confirmed things with Mona during the cab ride up. But they want you back in New York. Pardon me for saying this, Leonora, but our editor doesn't trust Mexican hospitals."

Dr. Zárete exhaled loudly.

Bart looked at his brother. "Wait till they find out how much cheaper it is here than, say, the Mayo Clinic. I'm saving them a fortune. And God keep me out of a VA facility! I'm good here, for a while at least." He looked over at Leonora.

"There's two times when you don't want to fly," said Dr. Zárete.

"When you're mending broken blood vessels and when you're eight months pregnant. He should stay here for at least a week, ten days minimum. But I warn you. Private care, even in 'backward' Mexico, isn't cheap." She made quote marks with her fingers.

Mona's plan was DOA, thought Ed. Who wants to risk high altitude blood clots? Leonora read his thoughts.

"But this doesn't apply to you, Ed. There's nothing you can do staying here. You're not a physician and you're not a politician. If the police become aggressive and we need an attorney, I'll let you know. But that's not my impression. Right now, they are angry that such an attack could take place near the historical district. They're focused on these *ladrones,* not the victim." She nodded toward Bart's bed.

"You've talked to them?"

"Last night. They were very polite. They came up here from the hospital downtown expecting to find—sorry to say—a cadaver. I had the impression they thought foreigners were involved. That makes solving this a matter of national pride."

"Of sovereignty, yes," said Ed.

"Another case of Americans bringing guns into peaceful Mexico. I can see how that claim will go over at the U.S. consulate," said Bart.

"I wonder if you noticed," said Leonora, "but this place is very secure. They treat politicians here, and rich foreign retirees. Safety and anonymity are foremost."

Now that she mentioned it, Ed remembered passing an armed man in the driveway. "What about Elizabeth? You want me to break the news, Bart? I can downplay it, say you had a little incident but you're on the way to recovery."

"Nah, let it go," replied his brother. He looked at his leg, suspended in a cradle hung from the bed frame. "Why worry her? Or Molly, for that matter. They'd want to come down, I suppose, and Molly's in the middle of the school year. I won't be here that long."

"Have you called her, Superman?"

Bart shook his head. "Hey, I'm just out of surgery, hardly *compos mentis.*" He looked at the wall clock, "It can wait."

"Don't put if off."

Bart's silence told Ed to let it drop. At that point a nurse entered, checked the drain and adjusted the IV drip. "We've got other things to worry about," Bart continued when she left.

"My deadline, you mean? I was more worried about losing my protector."

"Bullshit! The show must go on, and all that. Besides, the way you were throwing lead around, I felt it was me that was the wing man!"

Ed shrugged. "Well, you're right about one thing. I have to get Naturtek's little games into print if we're to lay all this down."

"Things are under control here," said Leonora, picking up a newspaper from the chair. "You see this?" She pointed to photos on the back page, her shattered clinic door riddled with bullet holes. A caption said the *pistoleros* had escaped. There was no additional text.

"They go for the graphic, don't they?" said Ed.

"Yes, And tomorrow, if it stays of interest, they'll be calling this drug-related. That's the universal explanation. But the coverage puts pressure on the police to arrest someone. Whoever's done this will be lucky to get away."

"Or they're gone already," said Ed.

"What do you mean, bro?"

"Think about it. We were dealing with real mercenaries in that alley, guys with body armor and automatic weapons. This wasn't some local gang. They had to be sent down from the States. And getting here so quickly after we left Chiapas? That means they flew in. And not commercial."

Leonora looked puzzled.

"If I'm right, they flew out as well. Which is good, as far as Bart's safety is concerned."

"There's still the police," said Leonora. "They'll be back."

"Should we involve the American embassy?" asked Ed.

"It's only a consulate here. But no."

"I agree," added Bart. "The fewer people involved, the better. With visa and passport information, they'll have your name as well, Ed. Why add complications? What do you think Naturtek will do?"

"They'll want to be at arm's length after this. That means they'll leave things alone, down here anyway, and with luck, you and I are now just a couple of tourists."

"Medical tourists, anyway. What does Aisling say?"

"We know her phone is compromised, said Ed. "I asked Francisco to have her call me on something anonymous. We need to keep her in the loop.".

"I can help," said Leonora. "There's a midwife service in San Cristóbal. I'll get a message to her that way. If the community isn't able to take care of Aisling, she has connections with several NGOs. Your Doctor O'Keefe is very resourceful."

"Let's hope," responded Ed. "One way or the other, I'll make sure your clinic is compensated for the damage." How? he wondered. Mortgage his loft?

Leonora turned the offer over in her mind. "A door? A computer? I think we'll survive. But you should leave."

"She's right," said Bart. "That B team of local guys could still be on someone's payroll."

Ed watched as Leonora ran her fingers over Bart's bandages and touched the hand that wasn't strapped to a drip IV.

"Sure? Send me an inventory of what's destroyed. I'll make good."

She nodded. "On letterhead."

Ed turned to his brother. "So the Doc wants you up in a few days?"

"The sooner I begin rehab, the sooner I'll be back in the game. But don't worry. Your job is to get the story out."

Ed nodded. What else? "You called your partner?"

"Him I did call. He thinks our company insurance will pick up what the *Chronicle* won't, but don't tell that to your boss." He grinned at his brother.

"You need to take care of those arrangements at the desk," said Leonora, shooing him toward the door. "The police could be here any time."

"Okay, guess we're done." He bent down to lightly touch his brother's cheek. Then he gave Leonora a gentle squeeze. She stiffened and then relaxed. "We're all family now, I guess," said Ed. "Get well, big guy. I want to hear from you, like every day." His vision blurred for a moment. "My bad for getting you into this."

"But if you hadn't and just told me the story, I'd never have believed you. Now g'wan."

Three hours later, Ed was on a United flight to New York via Houston, his backpack tucked under the seat in front, always in sight. He'd spoken with Mona again while waiting to board. In a quiet voice, she assured him she'd deal with both the hospital bill and the clinic damage. One more debt racked up, he thought. Taking out his laptop, he tried to work.

Chapter Fifty-Eight

It was early August, four months after Ed had arrived back in New York. His story on the corporate rush to exploit the world's food system using genetic technology had gone out in late June, and gone viral on alternative media. He'd followed it with a more pointed article about the dangers of induced sterility in agricultural crops. The industry hadn't gotten him fired, nor had Naturtek made new product announcements. He may have caused the company to hit the pause button. Thanks to a report from Janet Malcolm, he'd played up what he'd learned from Hammersmith and with Aisling's field notes, managed to put the death of pollinating insects on the front burner. A number of environmental organizations were now running with the issue. Still, he didn't think the industry's hiatus would last. Too much money was at stake.

Sitting at his desk, he sorted through a number of potential stories, wondering where to go next. Conservation activists were continuing to be murdered in Central America and the FDA had just reported that glyphosate-based weed killers couldn't really be shown to cause cancer. Some recent court decisions to the contrary, he said to himself. He needed something firm to take to Hardy or his checks would stop. But he wasn't complaining. Hardy had paid the bills — not an inconsiderable amount as the editor kept reminding him — and had extended his contract for another six months.

He closed his eyes. In a corner of his memory, he heard the sound of the huge rotary presses that once occupied the basement of the building. He liked to imagine they were the wheels of justice, grinding away. Even if that was an illusion, the paper had put Naturtek under scrutiny. And he could walk home in the dark.

He'd been bumped up to having his own cubicle in the newsroom. And if he needed inspiration, Mona was upstairs on the mezzanine.

After he'd gotten back, there'd been a flurry of meetings in the conference room. Mona as well as Hardy had attended, but the key person was Gerald Atkins. As the personal representative of the publisher, Atkins wanted to be sure Ed understood the rules. The story on recombinant DNA had gone back and forth with re-write several times, retaining its impact without bringing on a food disparagement law suit. New York didn't have such a law but states such as Missouri did. Naturtek had descended on the publisher with talk of writs and gag orders and the conversation became transactional, as Atkins phrased it. Ed had never met Gordon Samuelson, the publisher, or visited his top-floor office, but he'd heard that the guy was quirky. Atkins strengthened that impression. With self-confidence rooted four generations deep in Boston brahmin society, Samuelson was no pushover. Still, the paper was a business. Ed should understand where sanding off the sharp edges of his text was required. The whole room agreed that it was just as well that Naturtek had never advertised in the *Business Chronicle.*

Ed now actually had a beat, 'The Business of Science', and while not a weekly column, it carried his byline. Since his return from Mexico, he'd used the column to talk about civilian applications of drone technology—highly overrated outside of film production and real estate—and the potential for nano-based photovoltaics in roof shingles. More promise there. Nano-anything was hot news for investors. And just over the horizon, China would soon commercialize "steak" made in laboratories from cloned flesh. That would get folks' attention. So far, he'd never had to look at another gene-enhanced catfish.

And what to think about Mona? Relationships were like a hike in the mountains. You could move ahead toward the crest and the grand view, or go back to where you'd parked your car. He and Mona weren't yet looking at waterfalls, but the path seemed to be heading upward.

Twice a week they ate at the antique oak table in her dining room. Convinced he was the better chef, he usually did the cooking—pan-seared Kobi steak or scallops; sometimes just pasta with onions, mushrooms, and butter. She'd chop the vegetables and make the salad. By the time they carried the food to the table, their first bottle of merlot would be down by half and they'd sampled everything from each other's lips.

Still, she was hard to pin down. In New York, that meant that they each kept separate apartments. Not always as hands-on as she'd been with the Naturtek story, she'd continued being the best critic he knew.

Where had she come from? She gave very few clues. He knew the color of the dress she wore to her high school prom in Cleveland— 'pistachio' according to the saleslady, 'celery' her date had said. He knew she'd studied literature at Temple and worked for a spunky women's magazine he privately considered lesbian propaganda, but he never learned how she could afford her apartment. Hell, she could own the building. Some mysteries were best left alone.

He only found out she had a sister when he called her one time and he heard a stranger's voice. That was awkward. Yes, the woman knew who he was. Pity they hadn't met, she said, but she was only in the city for the day and had a plane to catch.

Give it time, he thought.

And what about Aisling? After giving him information in Mexico, they'd hardly communicated. She'd finished her work in Chiapas unscathed and she and her students returned to Boston with enough data to satisfy the Tropical Conservancy. Because his deadline was looming, he'd gone ahead and run a few DNA profiles through a commercial laboratory in Jersey City, comparing them with conventional varieties. It was enough, at least, to support his article. While there was definitely modification associated with plant fertility, the specific effects couldn't be pinned down without testing in the field, Earth Defense Fund had agreed. That would take several years and the skill of a post-doc, something the *Chronicle* couldn't support. Aisling, too, had moved on, ignoring his requests to delve more deeply into the material.

It was Manny who found that Aisling had left Northeastern. One afternoon as the sun floated the newsroom dust, the sports writer had casually mentioned that her name had come up on a search program. While they no longer worked together in any official way, Manny had continued to follow news about terminator crop development. Just yesterday, he said, he'd found O'Keefe's name on the program of a conference coming up in Ames, Iowa. Tomorrow, in fact. She was identified as senior researcher for—here Manny gave Ed a sharp poke—Naturtek.

"And I'll bet she's got a labeled parking spot for the Beemer," said Manny. "Can you blame her for cashing in? Still, it's a bit hard to swallow. Like 'the Babe' leaving the Red Sox for the Yankees back when."

Ed was stunned. Even though Manny had ferreted out a number for her in Jefferson, Missouri, he couldn't dial it. And say what?

The summer heat shimmered off of a gigantic parking lot as he pulled into the area designated for conference participants. He'd cranked up the AC on his rental for the drive from the airport and when he climbed out onto the sticky blacktop, it felt like stepping into a bread oven. Plus the whole area smelled of silage. Demonstration fields of corn and soy extended out from beyond Manchester Hall where the event was being held, each row posted with a numerical reference. Ed draped his sports jacket over his shoulder and trudged to the main door. His plane had been delayed in Chicago due to wind shear off the lake so he'd missed the introductory session on permaculture. As he mounted the steps, he thought he saw a blot of red at the far end of the glass-enclosed lobby, hair cascading over the back of a teal-green shirt, the sleeves billowing. Could it be her, thirty yards ahead of him? He pushed through revolving doors as staccato footsteps tapped a cadence on the stone floor and the figure disappeared.

His voice stuck in his throat. Around a corner, staircases flanked a bank of elevators and a greeter motioned him over to a reception table. Obviously a student—she was very young—she handed him a program and looked for his name on a clip board. No, he hadn't registered but he was press and very interested in the topics. Fine, she said, handing him a program and a name tag. Ed continued down the hall toward a large lecture room. There was nothing about GURTS on the program, as far as he could tell. He entered what was labeled Morrow Auditorium, slipping into a seat toward the back to scan the audience. The presentation was on lab-augmented alfalfa. Under the right conditions of moisture and sun, it would regrow after being harvested without the need for plowing or reseeding. Didn't all pasture grass, he wondered?

The room was hot. If he weren't so on edge, he might have fallen asleep. His vision wobbled for a moment and he pressed the bridge of his nose. Thinking he might run into her was one thing; actually seeing her after so long was something else.

While he listened, he tried to build a coherent picture of Aisling's motivation. She loved insects, he'd seen that, and not simply as miniature machines. She had genuine affection for people, at least her students and the farmers who'd supported her project. They'd introduced her to jungle plants she'd never known. But to work for Naturtek—had she been brainwashed? He imagined a cult-like group spiriting her away.

Like an automaton, he took down the requisite notes. He even stayed for a few minutes at the end to ask one of the speakers a question. Yes,

Japan at present wasn't importing GMO hay but they'd come around soon, he was told. They were a scientific people.

He circulated among the coffee and snack tables in the wide corridor, trying to decide which of the up-coming lectures would be tolerable. Maybe he should just head for the literature exhibit, check on the latest reports. Literature it would be. Being on his feet would keep him awake. The exhibit was in an attached gymnasium fitted out with portable booths. He grabbed a few interesting titles, exchanging his *Chronicle* business card for comps—here called 'examination copies'—and cruised the aisles as an act of will. No Aisling.

His bag was heavy by the time he settled down for a late afternoon session on rediscovered apples. He'd always liked apples. Surprisingly, this had nothing to do with genetic improvements. Just the opposite. It seemed that some amateur fruit enthusiasts got the idea that if they researched old county fair documents and cross checked them with property records, they could discover where apple orchards that once grew what are now lost varieties of apples were located. And might still be. These were usually small operations, long abandoned as markets and the scale of production shifted. But sometimes a few trees survived in the midst of second-growth forest, on the edge of tilled acreage, or beside a falling down farmhouse. In fact, this group had located and taken samples from over 400 trees and brought them to various land grant colleges for grafting. So far, many had proved both viable and unique. Ed was impressed. Maybe science was exhibiting some humility.

Then, there she was, sweeping up the far aisle, a leather briefcase on her shoulder. She was more composed than he remembered—her face, her clothing—but this was definitely her. He was in the middle of a row so it took him time to wedge his way to the end of the aisle and reach the lobby. She was standing at the far end, looking out through plate glass windows toward California or New York. The silver-grey haze in the sky gave no clue. As he approached, she turned and as if they'd had their last conversation yesterday and motioned him toward a cluster of arm chairs. This was as private as the room allowed.

"I saw you. In the parking lot I mean. Then again in the session." She nodded toward the auditorium they'd just left. "I've been debating if I should let you find me."

"I'm not here looking for you. I had no idea you'd be here." How convincing was that?

They settled down. "I'm doing more conventional research now, in the lab and greenhouse where I can control the variables."

"Not the jungle?"

"No. I've found that being in the field takes a lot out of a person."

"Why the change?" He appraised her softly-gleaming boots, her silk blouse. She was actually wearing a thin string of pearls. And what was that word, a 'skort?' "Don't you miss the adventure?"

"Adventure can be over-rated." She snorted softly.

"And teaching?"

"Well, I left Northeastern. I figured you knew. Actually, Northeastern left me. After what turned out to be Naturtek's research station was taken down and people started showing up with guns, the university concluded I was not to be trusted with the lives of their students. My students. Of course *they* never complained about the drama down there. It gave them great stories to tell. But that didn't matter once I'd lost the university's confidence."

"And you switched to—what?"

"I'd done what I could as a critic of biotech from the outside. You know that. You had my research report, my notes. After I closed things down in Chiapas and Northeastern cut me loose, I could have stayed on in Mexico. There's still plenty to learn about plant-based healing, for instance. Or I could have trained to work with Leonora as a midwife. But I needed an income. As for health work, I think my bedside manner leaves a lot to be desired." She tossed her head to emphasize the impossibility of that. "I do miss the community, especially Manuel and Francisco. But the wheel turns, things come to an end. And this will sound petty, I know, but I wanted regular baths." She laughed silently. "I wanted to lie in a warm tub at the end of the day and order Chinese takeout."

"People do burn out."

"Yeah. The shoot-up at Leonora's—once she told me about it— that was the last straw. My God, I could have gotten her killed. And you. Then learning Bart had been shot, at that point the world was looking pretty dark." She shook her head again. "How is your brother?"

"Recovering. Limping, but on his feet. He'd probably say he's lucky to be among the walking wounded. The guy spends hours on a treadmill. But he's back on the job, working from home. You could have called him, you know."

"Sure. And you as well."

"Why didn't you?"

"I needed distance. Then later, I didn't want to hear what you'd say." She looked at the polished toe of her boot. "You have to understand. I'd built my life around a career in biology—studied, sweated, borrowed. And then taught for almost nothing. That's all I have. I'd put in my time and instead of things opening up for me, they were closing down." She exhaled.

"I can understand that."

"Of course I protested to TC, and asked if they'd renew their sponsorship. They'd seemed happy with my progress that spring. But they declined. So there I was, back in Boston and told not only was the project dead, I was fired from teaching. It was, 'Turn in your office key and leave your grades on the way out the door.' Lots of bullshit about legal liability. I was lucky to have funding to bring my students back. The equipment, I turned over to the community. Maybe someone will continue with the project.

Her face flushed. "I was too depressed to even look around for Bio 101 jobs." She sniffled discretely into a handkerchief. "Then in mid-July as my apartment lease was running out—which was just as well because I couldn't pay for August—I got this thick registered letter."

"Thick is good, unless it's from a law firm."

"It was from the Conservancy. They said they'd studied my final report, regretted that things hadn't worked out as well as expected, but decided to renew my funding. Not for Mexico, though. For a project at the University of Nebraska. They had a position ready for me heading up a small team using CRISPR to fortify food crops with nutrients — vitamins and trace minerals."

"The CRISPR enzyme? Sounds like what Hammersmith was doing."

"The idea was to enhance vegetable crops for low-income farmers, develop varieties that were both nutritious and resistant to common pests and plant diseases. But without the use of chemical sprays. That way there'd be no need to wipe out the ambient insect population. It was a win-win. And that's what I've been doing."

Ed nodded, trying to seem sympathetic. She was looking into space.

"And I could bring Amber and Leslie along. They'd graduated but faced a difficult job market, impossible really unless they had more advanced degrees. I could get them into the doctoral program at Nebraska and on my team and the grant would pay for it all."

"Sounds too good to be true."

"Better than stocking shelves at Walmart."

"But you had to suspect all that was a front for Naturtek." Ed's tone was flat, matter-of-fact, like asking if she'd taken the 6.15 train and not the 5:45.

"They're involved, yeah, but at a distance. The university has its own rules. I get to use the Naturtek labs when necessary and they get a piece of any patents from our work."

"Who sets the research agenda?"

"That comes with the position, but we have a lot of latitude."

"You don't really believe that, do you?"

"You're fixated on terminator technology. What we're doing will actually make people better off. Do you really think I'd help crash the world's food systems?"

The haze in the sky outside had shaped itself into discernible clouds edged in purple; a thunderstorm was on the way. Below them, wind ruffled the tasseled corn. "Laudable. But Hammersmith and Ciobanu found out that some technologies can be dangerous."

"I've read your stuff. You don't know who killed them and neither do I." She looked exasperated. "Naturtek is at arm's length and I remain a university employee. Go ahead, say it. You think I'm compromised." Her lips seemed bloodless.

Ed stared at her without speaking.

"If they are still involved in terminator research, I have nothing to do with it. My job is to roll back the worst of chemical agriculture."

"Til they put you onto something else."

"At that point I'll make a decision. But science isn't self-funding."

"No, not since, I don't know, Fritz Haber gave the German's chlorine gas during World War One."

She seemed exasperated. "That's really uncalled for." She seemed to be trembling. "It's not as if your newspaper isn't a business rag."

"Sure, we're all on thin ice sometimes but…"

"But you make the best of it. How is that different?"

A wave of applause flowed from the auditorium. The event was breaking up.

"I want you to listen very carefully," She leaned toward Ed. "Do not contact me again."

She got to her feet.

"Naturtek won't stop, you know."

She looked at him intensely for a moment.

"Goodbye Edward."

Chapter Fifty-Nine

A WEEK LATER, DEKKER was in Washington. This was the third time he'd taken the train down to check on Bart. After surgery in Oaxaca and a week's recovery, his brother had spent the next month at Walter Reed. There'd been complications and they'd had to reconfigure major blood vessels and reestablish nerve connections to his lower leg. The numbness that had him dragging one leg was almost gone. One thing about Afghanistan, Bart told his brother. It had done great things for trauma surgery.

"But when you hear people say 'it's only a flesh wound,'" don't believe it. Not that I blame the cutters down there. They stabilized things. Without that, you'd be looking at Captain Ahab."

"As opposed to Captain Hook? I thought you had a hat fetish?"

"Enough. It still hurts when I laugh."

Bart was back living in Arlington with Elizabeth, who'd taken over support for his recuperation. "Not that I'm feeling sorry for you," she'd said. "Well, maybe a little. But I can't have Molly visiting you in some germy nursing home."

His wife left every day for the office but was usually home by evening. During the day, Consuela picked up the slack. The nanny remained formal and tight-lipped, but she brought him what he needed in the sunroom where he'd made his office. Surrounded by ferns and spider plants, he handled Executive Action's more irritating clients by phone and supervised billing.

"How's it going?" asked Ed.

"You won't have to help me to the bathroom, how's that? But really, I'm doing fine."

With the follow-up surgery, he and Elizabeth had lots of excuses to avoid intimacy. He slept downstairs in a rented hospital bed—the leg couldn't take the stairs—and the meds had taken away desire. When it did happen, awkwardly, it was more an act of determination than relief. Were they at a new beginning or still in free fall? With Ed at least, Liz had mellowed. Her distrust had thinned, which was odd given what she could blame him for. It was as though she accepted that Bart would do exactly what he wanted.

Molly had relaxed as well. She allowed herself to criticize one or the other parent, but only when both were present. Occasionally she lapsed into comfortable bitchiness, calling her math teacher 'stupid' and a short story they'd been reading 'naive'. Bart thought she enjoyed emoting, including stomping out of the room.

What gave Bart the feeling he wasn't dead weight were the research tasks Executive Action sent his way such as tracing convoluted money transfers. He'd also become fascinated with facial recognition software—transcribing data points on the human face from photos into an algorithm that allowed surveillance cameras to spot persons-of-interest at a distance. Even in crowds. ExAct thought this would be the next big thing in corporate security. After a few hours on the computer, he'd walk the static track or strap weights to his ankle and do sitting leg-lifts. Then he'd limp around the neighborhood on a cane. Wearing draw-string sweat pants and a baggy sweater, he was afraid he was becoming a local character.

Bart had just finished lifting arm weights and was thinking about a shower when Ed had came by. His brother usually arranged these meetings for the daytime when Liz was away. Having let him in, Consuela retreated to the kitchen.

"What, no flowers, no magazines?" Bart asked as his brother entered the sunroom.

"Next time I'll bring a balloon. How's it been?"

"Well, I'm not ready to play soccer yet, but that's coming."

"Well, bring it on! But just in case, I can teach you few tricks I picked up in Austria about using a walking stick. Like how to go down a flight of stairs."

"Got that mastered, at least the front steps. I'm moving every day. Muscles weaken when you don't use them. And the last MRI looked good." Bart's face was chalky, his tee shirt loose.

Ed eased into a folding metal chair, his elbows on his knees. "Did I tell you I feel like shit about this?"

"Only a thousand times. But hey. Isn't it what I do for a living, or did?" His grin forced color back into his cheeks. "Next week they're sending a van to take me to the office for some meetings. But I said, no lift gate. You see, I'm almost back in the groove."

Ed noticed new computer equipment spread out on the glass-topped table, including a double flatscreen. "Watching movies?"

"Just at night."

"And the pain?"

"Shit, if I could sell the meds I tossed down the toilet, I'd be rich. Not that I'm the suffer-in-silence type, but with a near-teen in the house, you don't want a medicine cabinet full of narcotics."

"How's the *Chronicle* keeping up with the bills?"

"They're covering what the VA won't, including the flight back from Mexico. I let your boss off the hook for pain and suffering." He took a sip of water. "You know, I don't have any recollection of that medevac flight. It must have cost a bundle."

"It's never come back to haunt me," said Ed. "But you'll be glad to know they still have their eye on the bottom line. I'm having to live without a body-guard. Did I tell you the city gave me a license to carry, just in case?"

469

"Which could be two-edged, from what I hear about cops these days. So don't wave it around. Anything from Missouri and Cambridge? I had hopes for Ballancio."

"They can't crack it at either end. They had an eye on Guardian Services, but turned up zilch. It will take a rat on the inside to open things up. And Ballancio says they don't have the evidence to manhandle the CEO."

"But we know that Oaxaca was them."

"Not to prove. So don't be getting ideas about settling scores. You're too valuable here."

"Your old girlfriend?" Ed had phoned his brother after bumping into Aisling and how she'd taken a job with the other team. Bart hadn't been surprised. "Never really trusted her, not that I wanted to rain on your parade," he'd said. "But Corn Corner, Nebraska?"

"Lincoln, actually. Corn Corner is further north. I wonder if at some level it's penance."

"Right!"

At that point Elizabeth came into the room, briefcase in hand. Without skipping a beat she greeted Ed with a raised hand and kissed Bart.

"I need to check on dinner." She disappeared.

Bart filled the silence. "You and Mona still at it?"

"At it? You think we're rabbits? Let's say we're at a good place. Until she gets bored correcting what I write. So far, that hasn't happened."

"Screw the false modesty. I hear you've become quite the hot journalist."

Ed shrugged, then nodded toward the kitchen where they could just hear laughter and occasional words in Spanish. "You two good?"

"She hasn't tossed me out. Course I kept the apartment. Which reminds me, if you're down here overnight, why don't you take the key? Keep it for whenever you need it."

"Naah. Keep your options open. And you don't want to be stumbling over me some night when you come in drunk." Bart had been on fruit juice for months. "And Lorena? I called her, trying to do something about the damage to her place. She has things up and running again. This was maybe two months ago."

"I know. She told me your paper sent a check after the clinic's insurance company laughed at her."

"So, it wasn't a total loss for her?"

"No, but the publicity wasn't welcome. She has more clients, but also an occasional picket line of Evangelicals yelling that she's a baby killer."

Ed lowered his voice. "How do you feel about her? I got the impression you two became close."

"She saved my life. I'll always owe her for that. But we're in two different worlds. I can't change that."

"No, guess not." Ed was silent for a while. Pans rattled in the kitchen.

Ed looked at his watch. "I can't stay. What I'd like, though, is for you to suggest to Molly that she take the train up to New York. I can show her around the newsroom. There's always the Rockettes at Rockefeller Center. And you said she likes art?"

"You'll have to ask her yourself. She's her own person. But I can tell you she loves touring around. She pretends she's an exchange student from Switzerland or something, learning about this very weird country we're in. So yes, I'm sure she'd love seeing the guts of a newsroom." Bart gave his brother a squint. "Not practicing for something, are you? I mean working on this uncle business?"

"The thought never crossed my mind." Ed laid his hand on his heart. "But she would be proof to Mona that I can actually talk with a child, well, young adult."

"Dinner for three in NYC." Bart smiled and his eyes crinkled up. "Molly has a school break coming. I'll bring Liz around to the idea. But twelve is too young to be taking a train alone. I can see the headline, 'Girl gets on the Acela in Union Station, never arrives in New York.'"

"Of course I'll come down and pick her up. But hey, I've got a meeting now. That's how I put my visits to you on the expense account."

"Take care," he continued, then ducked his head into the kitchen to say goodbye to Liz.

"Watch out for the school yard bullies," yelled Bart. "I'd get up but…"

"Not on my account. See you soon. Maybe in New York!"

About the Author

Charles Simpson is a professor of Sociology, and a political activist and writer. He has done sociological investigations in Guatemala and Mexico focusing on issues of development and food security. He lives in Burlington Vermont with his wife, Anita.

.

Fomite

More novels from Fomite...

Joshua Amses — *During This, Our Nadir*
Joshua Amses — *Ghatsr*
Joshua Amses — *Raven or Crow*
Joshua Amses — *The Moment Before an Injury*
Charles Bell — *The Married Land*
Charles Bell — *The Half Gods*
Jaysinh Birjepatel — *Nothing Beside Remains*
Jaysinh Birjepatel — *The Good Muslim of Jackson Heights*
David Brizer — *Victor Rand*
L. M Brown — *Hinterland*
Paula Closson Buck — *Summer on the Cold War Planet*
Dan Chodorkoff — *Loisaida*
Dan Chodorkoff — *Sugaring Down*
David Adams Cleveland — *Time's Betrayal*
Paul Cody — *Sphyxia*
Jaimee Wriston Colbert — *Vanishing Acts*
Roger Coleman — *Skywreck Afternoons*
Marc Estrin — *Hyde*
Marc Estrin — *Kafka's Roach*
Marc Estrin — *Speckled Vanities*
Marc Estrin — *The Annotated Nose*
Zdravka Evtimova — *In the Town of Joy and Peace*
Zdravka Evtimova — *Sinfonia Bulgarica*
Zdravka Evtimova — *You Can Smile on Wednesdays*
Daniel Forbes — *Derail This Train Wreck*
Peter Fortunato — *Carnevale*
Greg Guma — *Dons of Time*
Richard Hawley — *The Three Lives of Jonathan Force*
Lamar Herrin — *Father Figure*
Michael Horner — *Damage Control*
Ron Jacobs — *All the Sinners Saints*
Ron Jacobs — *Short Order Frame Up*
Ron Jacobs — *The Co-conspirator's Tale*
Scott Archer Jones — *And Throw Away the Skins*
Scott Archer Jones — *A Rising Tide of People Swept Away*
Julie Justicz — *Degrees of Difficulty*
Maggie Kast — *A Free Unsullied Land*
Darrell Kastin — *Shadowboxing with Bukowski*
Coleen Kearon — *#triggerwarning*
Coleen Kearon — *Feminist on Fire*
Jan English Leary — *Thicker Than Blood*
Diane Lefer — *Confessions of a Carnivore*
Diane Lefer — *Out of Place*

Fomite

Writing a review on Amazon, Good Reads, Shelfari, Library Thing or other social media sites for readers will help the progress of independent publishing. To submit a review, go to the book page on any of the sites and follow the links for reviews. Books from independent presses rely on reader-to-reader communications.

For more information or to order any of our books, visit:
http://www.fomitepress.com/our-books.html

Made in the USA
Middletown, DE
28 September 2022